THE WOLF'S LEGACY

WHAT UNSAVOURY ARISTOCRATS WILL ORLA UNCOVER IN HER SEARCH FOR HER FRENCH ANCESTRY?

MICHÈLE CALLARD

MILLEFEUILLE PRESS

ABOUT THE AUTHOR

Michèle Callard grew up in France. A country girl at heart, she swapped her Paris flat for a cottage in rural Bedfordshire where she lives with her Irish husband and one of her three sons. She writes novels set in France bursting with local colour, flavours and history. If you like to learn something new, this is the book for you.

For my Irish family in Dublin

CONTENTS

THE WOLF'S LEGACY

What unsavoury aristocrats will Orla uncover in her search for her French ancestry?

MICHÈLE CALLARD

CÉVENNES – 1765

THE STORY OF THE GÉVAUDAN WOLF

The rain had brought the May fair to an early end. The Marquis de Peirac kicked his charger through the labyrinth of pens. A stench of pigs, damp wool and wood smoke rose from the market square where stalls were being dismantled and debts hurriedly settled. Clusters of farmers were gathering in front of the town hall before heading home together. Thieves and wolves roamed the moors... No one wanted to cross the Cévennes Mountains alone.

De Peirac pulled down his hat over the scars that ran down the side of his face and glanced back at his valet. 'You were right, Martin, that rain has kept the populace away. The tithes from the fair won't even keep me in women and wine this year.'

A musketeer at fourteen, Aymeric de Peirac was a soldier. Killing for him had become an art form, but now the war was over, civilian life and marriage stifled him.

The two men trotted past the church where urchins sheltered under scaffolding. A new portal was being erected to remind the Protestant rebels –or Huguenots, as they were now called– that Rome ruled. The Marquis scattered a volley of coins that sent the children scrabbling in the mud. He had a reputation to keep. Last winter's famine had so distressed his wife, the devout Lady Fleur, that she had implored him to distribute wheat and chestnuts from their own granaries to the starving serfs.

'You will surely be remembered for your charity, Sire,' the old valet sniggered.

'One never knows how one will be remembered, Martin.' De Peirac lifted his mobile eyebrow. 'You would do well to remember that.'

As they reached the inn, he pointed to the dripping shield above them. 'Do you know why this inn is called the Golden Lion?'

'T'is a coat of arms, Sire, like your wolf passant.'

'No, dunce, innkeepers don't have coats of arms.' A grin distorted de Peirac's lips. 'It's a pun on the purpose of the place.' He lifted a gloved finger.

'Au lit, on dort, in bed we sleep,' sounds just like *'au lion d'or:* lion of gold.'

'Ha ha,' the valet brayed. 'In bed, we sleep. Ha! That is indeed clever.' He tilted his chin at a girl shivering at the end of the alleyway. 'I don't imagine you'll be doing much sleeping in that whore's bed, will you, Sire?'

'Ah, Martin, you know me too well.'

'Sire! Sire!' A ragged boy tugged at his cape. 'The priest sent me to you!'

De Peirac narrowed his eyes. 'The priest?'

The child stammered. 'The B-beast is back, Sire. They s-say the wolf has killed again.'

The Marquis swayed in the saddle. The whore would have to wait.

In the distance, a priest was brandishing a crucifix. 'The wolf has struck again!' His voice cracked. 'A body was found mauled at the edge of the forest. God protect us sinners from the Gévaudan Beast!'

Heart pounding against his leather jerkin, de Peirac strained his ears over the clatter of hoofs. A gravelly voice rose from a group of dark-clad Huguenot merchants. 'Three years this beast has been running amok! They say it's killed a hundred. When will it stop?'

Though hunted, hit and shot at, the fabled animal still attacked in broad daylight, leaving its victims mauled and headless. Last year, the wolf had jumped over the wall of a garden and grabbed a baby in its fangs. The mother had hurled herself at the animal with a stick and, together with her older children, beaten the wolf until it dropped its prey. Sadly, the child had died. So touched had King Louis been by the woman's bravery, that he had rewarded her with a hundred pounds.

'The Gévaudan Beast is a werewolf…' a woman screeched. 'T'was full moon last night...'

A sneer stretched de Peirac's scars.

The priest fell on his knees, his hands lifted towards Heaven. 'The Beast is a portent from God sent to punish us for our sins! Let us kneel. Let us repent.'

The mob wavered. Some knelt, others were turning away when there was a commotion. Pallbearers pushed through the throngs carrying a body on a stretcher of woven branches. They lowered it in front of the altar.

Ashen-faced, Martin croaked to his master, 'T'is Jehan the shepherd on that stretcher...'

'You knew him?' The marquis dismounted and handed his valet the reins.

'Who didn't?' Martin bit his chapped lips. 'He was the son of Jehanne the herbalist.'

'And?'

'She's a witch. She's got the gift, you know.' Martin crossed himself with a shiver. 'So did he.'

'That gift didn't help the fellow though, did it?' The marquis uncovered his head and strode to the victim. Grateful for the long curls of the wig concealing his face, he glanced down.

Tooth-shaped indentations punctured the boy's throat. The sleeves of the woollen tunic were ripped and the flesh of his arms hung in ribbons.

The power of the Beast was formidable. The Pope had declared it a portent from God. It had defied the King of France. The whole of Europe talked of nothing else. Terror rippled through the Cévennes Mountains and everywhere sinners cowered. While Catholics flocked to confess their pathetic misdeeds, Huguenot prophets heralded the end of the world. Whole battalions of Royal Dragoons sent in their thousands to hunt down the Beast wreaked havoc in the once tranquil region. And all this... for a wolf.

What was it about this particular wolf? After all, there were wolves everywhere, but this one was different. It was fearless. It struck in broad daylight. To date, it was purported to have attacked over two hundred people and killed ninety.

Aymeric fell to his knees. Hushed gasps met his humble gesture. Head bowed, he struggled to control his excitement. From Versailles –seven days' ride away– King Louis would despatch yet another regiment. From Rome, bishops and advisers would arrive in gilded coaches, reeking of incense and lucre. The local peasantry would comb the region and he, Marquis Aymeric-Amaury de Peirac would lead the hunt.

His blood pumping at twice the usual speed, he composed his features and cast a loving look at his work of art. This was his best yet. The iron jaw he had fashioned out of an old mantrap replicated the gashes of a wolf's teeth beautifully.

Whatever it really was, the Gévaudan Beast was his cover and as long as it ran free... he was safe.

After a long while, he pushed himself up, gave the dead boy a last glance and shuddered, irritated at the dread that seeped into his steely heart.

'Curse... you de Peirac. Curse you...' From the boy's dark eyes, thankfully pecked away by crows, an otherworldly fire had branded that curse into Aymeric's soul. 'Curse you to the seventh generation.'

PART I

ORLA - DUBLIN - PARIS - PRESENT TIME

1

DUBLIN – ORLA

PRESENT TIME

I was five when Mam, Mary Sullivan, married my step-dad, Mick Reilly. Although Mick had adopted me, his mother never forgave me for tainting the family name with an indelible whiff of sin.

When Grandma Reilly died six months ago, I walked from my parents' house in Clontarf to the grand Georgian terrace where Grandma and Judge Reilly had lived out their respectable lives.

My breath coming in small puffs, I stopped at the bottom of the steps. Triggered by years of rebuke, my shoulders tensed. I steeled myself for the worst and gazed up at the lugubrious black brick façade.

Touched with the bronze of a low winter sun, the house glowed. Chandeliers twinkled inside the once frigid parlour and the sound of laughter spilled out of the half-open door. I trudged up the steps and pushed it open. Mick's sister, Aunt Finnuala, greeted me with a hug. I gave her my coat and followed her in.

'Now, Orla, there's plenty of salmon sandwiches by the window if you're hungry.' She poured out a glass of Prosecco and handed it to me. 'But first, you'll be wantin' to pay your respects, won't ye?' She glanced at the coffin in a corner.

The double doors that separated the parlour from the dining room had been pushed open and stiff chairs lined against the walls. I followed Finnuala past a trio of nuns towards an elaborate coffin on a red velvet plinth... peered over the side and forgot to breathe.

Shrivelled inside swathes of white satin, my tormentor lay, waxen and pitiful, her toxic aura evaporated. I gripped the side of the coffin and let decades of pain soar away, borne on vapours of whiskey and peat.

Christ, how could I have let that creature affect me so much?

'Doesn't she look well?'

'Huh?'

Finnuala reached into the coffin and stroked the freshly curled hair.

'Haven't they done a grand job? I was in such a tizz this morning, I forgot to give them her teeth, but you couldn't tell, could ye?' She took the bloodless fingers in her own. 'So cold, poor thing. She'd always had bad circulation.'

I crossed myself and staggered to the kitchen in search of something stronger than Prosecco.

The kitchen was packed. Neighbours and relatives leaned against piles of crockery, casually swilling Jameson out of Grandma's priceless Waterford glasses. Though 'priceless' wasn't the right word, for never a meal went by when she didn't remind us how much the fecking things cost.

I searched out my two brothers and their wives, wondering whether they'd be bringing my little nieces along. Not finding anyone I knew, I returned to the parlour where a rotund man was praying over the cadaver. That would be the bishop, Grandma Reilly's brother Eamon.

'Makes you think, huh?' Finnuala nudged me. 'We're not

long for this world.'

Finnuala was my favourite aunt. I'd often wondered how Grandma Reilly had ever managed to raise two beings as sane as my stepdad and Finnuala. Perhaps the judge, bless him, had something to do with it. He was a good man.

'Are Mick and your mam on their way?' She handed me a bowl of cherry tomatoes.

Though wakes were supposed to put the 'fun' back into 'funerals,' watching my aunt eat near the coffin made me queasy. I pushed the tomatoes away and took a sip of whiskey.

'Dad should be here soon. Mam's putting the last touches to her trifle.'

'Ah, she makes a good trifle, does Mary.'

After a long silence, Finnuala placed a hand on my arm. 'Orla, I know Mammy wasn't always kind to you.' She lowered her tone. 'She wasn't a bad woman. God rest her soul. She had a hard life.'

A hard life... Really? The old owl had lorded it over us as if she'd been Red Hugh O'Donnell's daughter herself.

'She'd hate me to tell you...' Aunt Finnuala cast a side glance at the bishop and huddled closer. 'Their parents ran a shop in Connemara, a grocer's shop. Well, when Mammy was thirteen, her father lost all the money on the horses. They had to sell up and move to Dublin in disgrace with nothing but the clothes on their backs. It was brutal all right. Poor Mammy. She never recovered from the shame.'

Christ on a bike. I had no idea.

My aunt picked a bowl of crisps from the mantlepiece and held it out to me. I took one. We crunched respectfully through the silence.

'You can imagine how proud she was to have married a judge. Mind you, Daddy wasn't a judge back then, but they were a good family, the Reillys. Mammy loved the status, so she did.' Finnuala tilted her chin towards the bishop. 'Goes a long way to explain why Uncle Eamon became a bishop. Wantin' respect, I suppose.'

'I wish I'd known.' It would have softened the hurt. 'All I knew was that I wasn't a Reilly.' Bitterness crept into my voice. 'She never let me forget it.'

Finnuala's eyes crinkled into a smile. 'You've no idea how often I've thought how refreshing it must be *not* to be a Reilly.' Perhaps it was the Prosecco, there was no stopping her. 'Now, Orla, have you ever thought of looking for your father?'

I took a step back. 'My father?'

'You know, the Frenchman.'

I nearly dropped my glass. My head whipped around to the casket, expecting the old bat to spring up and give out. 'Oy! That Waterford glass cost me sixty Punts!'

My biological father, a Frenchman? I helped the information down with a glug of whiskey and had a coughing fit. Finnuala patted my back.

Around us the room was filling up. Visitors piled their plates with salmon and held conversations, leaning against the coffin.

Finnuala moved to the window. 'Sorry, Orla. Didn't you know he was French?'

'Of course, I didn't.' I cleared my throat. 'Mam's always acted like I'm the result of the Immaculate Conception.'

I had often wondered about my father, and since I had nothing to go on, modelled him on Archangel Gabriel. At some point, I'd even hung a painting of the Annunciation on my wall because the Pre-Raphaelite Archangel chatting to Mary had thick auburn hair like mine.

Whoever begat me must have been tall. In family gatherings like these, I stood above the Reillys like a giraffe in a herd of bullocks.

I had pestered Mam over the years, of course I had, but loyal to Dad she had kept her silence and I had no option but to respect that. I loved Dad. He had given me his name and, unlike his detestable mother, always treated me like one of his own.

I had just returned to the kitchen for another drink when a large paw landed on my shoulder.

'Dad!' I spun around. 'Is Mam not with you?'

He poured himself a Guinness. 'I brought the trifle, but she's messing with the cupcakes now. She'll be along later with your brothers.' He nodded to a few people and pursed his lips in appreciation. 'This is a grand turnout. Mam would have hated the mess, so she would.'

'Dad...' I ushered him into the hall. 'What will I say when I'm asked about Declan?'

Declan was my ex. We used to run a motorbike-parts business together. It had been going well until a couple of months ago, when Declan discovered the Holy Grail inside the cups of Sinead's push up bra. Sinead was our all too 'personal' assistant. When we separated, I had to sell the house, my share of the business and go home to my parents'. It broke my heart.

Dad drew me to him and ruffled my short hair. 'I'm sorry, love. I know it's hard on days like this.' He studied me over his glass. 'Perhaps if there was anything new you were planning to do... a holiday perhaps?'

I nodded. 'I could talk about the future.'

'It would diffuse the issue.'

That was my dad for you, always of good counsel.

'So, did you have anything in mind?'

'Actually,' I took his arm and headed back to the parlour. 'Aunt Finnuala's just had an idea, but first... I'd like to run it past you.'

2

PARIS – ORLA

Feeling satisfyingly French, I stood under a weeping willow at the tip of the Île de la Cité, the island at the heart of Paris. After three months, my investigations had brought results and I was very close to finding out why, in the great zoo of life, I'd always felt like I had been herded into the wrong pen.

I squinted towards the stairs set in the middle of the Pont Neuf and waved to a familiar figure in a dark business suit.

'Asha!'

'Orla? Oh my God, I didn't recognise you.' Asha hugged me and took a step back. 'You've grown your hair. You didn't tell me you'd gone blonde.' She giggled, a sparkle in her kohl-rimmed eyes. 'Gosh, is that really you wearing a skirt?'

'You look very smart yourself.' I appraised the sharp suit and expensive haircut.

'Wow, you look so... French.' She squeezed my hand. 'Remind me, what's his name again?'

'Jean-Loup.' I pronounced my fella's name *Jan-Loo,* as it should be. The French always leave out the last consonant. 'Loup means wolf.'

'Wolf, hey? Is he big and bad?'

'Nah, he's a lamb really. Just a wee bit intense. Do you fancy lunch on the beach?'

'Paris has a beach?'

'Sure.' I pointed to a row of palm trees along the bank. 'They barge up tons of sand every summer from the Seine estuary. There's music and dancing every night. It's great craìc.'

I linked arms with Asha and held on to her, the cobbles on the quay impossible to manage in heels. Morphing into a Parisienne was all very well, but after years as a biker's moll, changing my spots was a struggle.

'Paris really has done wonders for you.' Asha wouldn't be fooled for long. She knew me too well. 'So, have you found '*him*' yet?'

This was the hundred-euro question. Asha was not asking about Jean-Loup, the computer wizard I had met three months ago. She was hinting at the real reason I was here.

'I think so.' I stared hard at the cobbles. 'We found a de Peirac all right, but I don't know where to go from there.' I met her gaze. 'I can't go up to him and say '*bonjour Papa!* Can I?'

'Your mother never told him she was pregnant, right?'

I shrugged. 'She won't even talk about him. All I have to go on is a scribbled name on a piece of paper, that I… discovered.'

'Oh dear. So, what do you *actually* know?'

'I know that he's called de Peirac and he lived in Paris.' I nudged her elbow. 'Jean-Loup reckons he's an aristocrat, you know, because of the particle.'

'The particle of what?' Asha's eyes widened.

'The '*de*' in de Peirac, it's called a *particule*. It's posh.'

'Okay, so he's posh. What else?'

'Mam worked as an au pair in Paris during the student

protests.' Since this revelation, I had tried and failed to visualise Mam, plump, soft and pastel as she is, brandishing a duster atop a barricade. Back home in Dublin, the crowds on St Patrick's Day terrify her. 'I can think of one scenario that would explain her silence.' I cast a side-glance at Asha. 'The *pater familias* taking advantage of her.'

Asha squeezed my arm. 'Seduced by her employer... Gosh, that would be dreadful. Would you still want to meet him?'

'Not really.'

We pondered all the way to the 'beach,' a layer of white sand two foot deep banked up along the quay. The children building sandcastles and bikini-girls on loungers were so convincing, it was easy to forget that just a few feet above us, Paris was going about its business.

We took a table below the wall and ordered lemonade and a goat-cheese salad. Fanning ourselves with our menu, we watched the *flâneurs* strolling past, watching us.

'Oh Asha...' I grabbed her hand. 'I can't believe you're here. Now, tell me about life in London.' I pulled out my chair and lifted my face to the sun.

'Oh, you know, work...' She huddled closer to the parasol, lest the sun should darken her Darjeeling skin to Assam.

Asha and I had cut our teeth together in the City of London, working for an insurance company. Tired of London, I had moved back to Dublin and met Declan. Asha fell in love with a Canadian man and got married. Sadly, it wasn't 'Happy Ever After' for either of us. Fate dealt her a bad card. Five years ago, Asha's husband died of leukaemia.

Our thoughts hovered across the Seine and drifted back to the past, while swallows performed their aerobatics in the cloudless sky.

'Fancy you living in Paris...' Asha ran a hand through her

shoulder-length hair and rested her gaze on me. 'How did you find a flat? I hear they're like gold dust.'

I owed my luck to piranhas and a deaf cat but, unsure how to explain, I kept to the basics. 'A friend of a friend, Stéphanie, was looking for someone to look after her flat in Paris for four months while she worked in China.' I opened my hands. 'I wanted to make a fresh start, so…'

The summer air vibrated with heat, music, the clash of metal boules and the shrieks of children. Only the seagulls were missing to make the illusion complete. Yes, Paris was a powerful antidote to melancholy.

A roar rose from the *boulodrome*. Their game ended, old men wiped their *boules* with checked handkerchiefs and stood around, chatting in small groups. I watched them for a while and returned to my story.

'Mick said he was okay with me coming to France to look for my biological father. In fact, he was surprised I hadn't tried to do it sooner.'

'He's a good man your dad,' Asha said.

'Ah, he is that all right. If Declan hadn't behaved like an eejit, it would never have occurred to me to go searching for the Frenchman.' I left a pause. 'Anyway, we sold the business, Declan and Sinead bought a pub and… I came here.'

I made it sound easy. In truth it had been a terrifying mess. Losing Declan had not been the worst part of it. I had built up the business. Letting it go had torn me apart, but it wasn't just that. I had hoped at some point we'd have a family, though for Declan, it was never the right time.

Asha said to dispel the mood, 'I still don't get why you went from bike spare parts to vintage clothes.' She pointed to the large bag under my chair. 'Can I see?'

'It's a dress I bought from an old dear called Madame Debré. Her husband was a diplomat.'

'Very smart.' Asha shook out a fifties dress cinched at the waist.

'All I changed was the product, really. The formula's the same. After the wake, I helped Aunt Finnuala sort out Grandma's stuff. You'd be amazed at what we found in her presses!'

'Wardrobes.' Asha translated to herself.

'She had tea-dresses and evening gowns going all the way back to the fifties. I sold them on the Internet. Clothes, carburettors, it's what I do.'

Asha lifted her lemonade. 'Paris suits you. You look... different.'

'Jean-Loup's a great fan of Brigitte Bardot.' I mussed my newly coloured hair and added in a sultry French accent, 'my new French lover, he likes the stockings, the lace, the silk *négligés...*'

'Really? Do men like that still exist?'

I batted my eyelashes. '*Mais oui, ils existent à Paris.*'

'How did you meet him ?'

'There's a communal workspace below my flat...'

'What's he like in bed?'

As an Indian woman unhampered by a Catholic education, Asha could be disconcertingly blunt in matters of sex. In life-according-to-Asha, it was the husband's God-given *duty* to give his wife pleasure. For Declan, it had always been the other way around.

When things became stale with Declan, Asha cut out several 'love & sex tips' from Cosmopolitan and posted them to me, as one would recipes, with 'try this' and 'this is my favourite.'

When Declan and I broke up, she'd bought me a dildo.

'Use it,' she'd said at the time. 'It'll tide you over until you meet The One. Do yourself a favour, don't jump into the arms of the first idiot you come across.'

Expecting chocolates, I'd nearly died of shock when I opened the box. I had thrown it away, worried about Mam finding it or airport security scanning my suitcase. Predictably enough, I'd jumped straight into Jean-Loup's arms.

'Go on. What's he like?'

'Asha!' I focused on my salad.

'Scale of one to ten?'

'It's not like that. I mean...' What could I say? Sex was fine, though doing it every night was exhausting. Awarding Jean-Loup a couple of extra points for good measure, I winced. 'Eight?'

Asha lifted an appreciative eyebrow. 'Hmm. Eight isn't bad. Still got those Cosmo tips I gave you?'

'How about you?' I deflected her questions with one of my own. 'Does your I.Q. still frighten men off?'

Men liked dumb blondes. Fact. When Declan swapped me for the peroxided Sinead, I don't know what hurt more, the size of her pea brain or that of her huge boobs.

Asha blushed. 'I've joined a dating site. If it's meant to be, it will happen, inshallah.'

'Specifically looking for Muslims?'

She shrugged. 'Not really. I'm looking for an all-around nice guy. One that's open-minded and not too self-obsessed.'

'Aren't we all.'

Asha described herself as a 'culturally confused Indian.' Born in Kenya from Muslim converts, she had married a lovely Canadian man. She was exotic, fascinating and fun. A true one-off. Life, or God, took her husband away from her before they had time to have children and she had missed him ever since.

'You'll find someone, I'm sure. You're clever, you can cook and you've got curves in all the right places. Unlike me.' I ran a hand over my A-cups.

I had no breasts to speak off and hated my ridiculous backside. Whoever I took after had a lot to answer for. Bush People probably, with my Hottentot hindquarters.

'What do you mean? You're perfect as you are.' God love her, Asha meant it. 'Booty's back in fashion I hear, and yours is fantastic.'

'My boobs are too small and my derrière's too big. There'll be some reckoning when I finally meet my French family, I tell you. I'll recognise them straight away… from the back.'

I cast an envious look at the stick-thin bikini girls stretched out on deck-chairs. The cruel latex underwear I wore to limit the damage was killing me in the heat, and the gel 'chicken fillets' I'd slipped inside my bra had fused to my skin. How the true Parisiennes managed it day after day was a mystery. I did miss my old jeans and trainers combo but as the Parisian mantra went, *'il faut souffrir pour être belle'*. Not sure I was beautiful, but Lord knows I was suffering.

'Surely Jean-Loup loves you the way you are.'

I grinned. 'Soon he'll love me even more. He's buying me new breasts for Christmas.'

'What?' Asha dropped her fork. 'Orla. You did not say this. No. I simply did not hear this. God gave you this beautiful body. You should be grateful.' She poked angrily at a lettuce leaf. 'You're always trying to please somebody. It's ridiculous. Why can't you be yourself?'

I don't know who I am, do I? I wanted to shout, but it would have sounded pathetic, so I shrugged. 'I fancied a change.'

'Declan's betrayal has dented your self-esteem, I can understand that, but believe me,' Asha said with feeling, 'it doesn't mean there's anything *wrong* with you.' She harrumphed, 'Plenty wrong with him, that's for sure.'

'Thanks for this vote of confidence.' I let my gaze roam over the river, trying to compose my thoughts. 'When I came to Paris, I was hoping to shed my skin, shake off the smell of engine grease and Guinness… the whiff of depravity I've dragged around since my childhood. For Grandma Reilly, my living in sin with Declan only went to prove that I was one of Satan's minions. Being in Paris, looking French is… purifying.'

Asha made a face. 'The problem with Catholics is that original sin. Why you should feel guilty for being born inside this beautiful body makes no sense!'

'You're right. I can't help feeling there's something wrong with me, like there's a piece missing.'

'I know.' Asha tilted her head and said with a strange smile, 'I hope you like what you find. I really do.'

3

PARIS – ORLA

That night, the oompah of a Brassens song and the scent of *coq-au-vin* greeted me at the top of the stairs. I pushed the door, kicked off my shoes and joined Jean-Loup in the kitchen, glad that I had given him a key.

Soft tousled curls, grey-green eyes, pouty lips. How could I resist this man? I circled my arms around his neck and melted into him.

Stéphanie's deaf cat, a white creature wittily named Othello, wound himself around my legs and purred.

'Orla, you will be very pleased with me. I have done good work today.' Jean-Loup's eyes twinkled. 'I went to the main library and I found many references to the de Peirac family. They have a long pedigree.' He kissed the tip of my nose.

'Really? A pedigree?' After a lifetime as a mutt, 'pedigree' sounded grand.

A hand on my waist, Jean-Loup stirred the stew. 'The name de Peirac goes back to the Crusades.' He lifted the wooden spoon. 'Two hundred years ago in the Cévennes, a Marquis de Peirac was involved in the hunt for the

Gévaudan Beast.' Spoon aloft, eyebrow cocked, he awaited my reaction.

'The jeevo-dun beast?'

'What? You have not heard of the Gévaudan Beast!'

Parisians do that a lot, that look of incredulity followed by a roll of the eyes that engulfs you in contempt. 'What? You have not heard of pataphysics? Mimi Pinson? Boeuf mironton?'

I simply waited.

Jean-Loup switched to storyteller mode. 'A huge wolf that terrorised the heart of France in the seventeen hundreds.' He dropped the spoon and hunched over, elbows lifted. 'It was huge… and it devoured a hundred people.' His hands now danced as he warmed to his theme. 'It chomped off their heads, disembowelled them. It was fearless…'

I took an involuntary step back. 'Ergh. What was it?'

Jean-Loup's voice took on an edge of mystery. 'No one knows to this day... Was it a hyena, a hybrid between a dog and a wolf? A madman's pet? Is that why it wasn't scared of men?'

'Did anyone ever see it?'

'Oh yes, there were plenty of sightings.' He lowered his pitch. 'Once, it dragged a baby from its cot in a garden. The mother fought it off, but it was too late.'

I frowned. 'It's not a fairy tale?' We had plenty of those back in Ireland, women who turn to seals, changelings...

'Oh no, it really did exist. The king, I think it was Louis XV, sent an army of ten thousand men to catch it.'

I shivered. 'Ten thousand men, wow… Did they catch it?'

'They caught a first wolf, but the killings carried on. Two brothers caught a second one but, after having sent so many soldiers to the region, the king could not accept that simple peasants had beaten him to it. This is where de Peirac comes in I suppose. He was involved in the capture, but…' Jean-

Loup added in a funereal voice, 'some say he may have been involved in some of the killings...'

'You're joking, right?' I rubbed the goosebumps on my arms.

He turned down the heat, dropped a lid over the pan and placed both hands on my shoulders. 'I found a de Peirac in the 16th.'

'The sixteenth century?'

'No, the sixteenth *arrondissement*, the district that lies west of Paris near the Bois de Boulogne, you know, Passy.'

My heart did a little jig. Passy was auspicious. Passy was where Mam had worked as an au pair. The trail was hot. Tomorrow, I would check it out with Asha.

'Loulou...' I kissed his nose, 'a friend of mine is coming over from England tomorrow. Would you like to meet her? We could go to a restaurant in the evening, what do you think?' I would have been at pains to explain what was stopping me from telling Jean-Loup that I had already met Asha.

My new life was thrilling, but Jean-Loup and I had conflicting concepts of how close a relationship we expected from each other. For him, love had to be *'fusionnel.'* While he needed fusion, I needed space, and often found myself withholding information.

'M'amour?' I snuggled up to him

He wrapped his arms around me and muttered suggestively, 'That dress you bought today, can I see it?' He pulled me closer. 'Can you put it on?'

Jean-Loup's fascination for everything I did was something I had to get used to.

Declan, that waster, would only take notice when I was in the nip. Back in Dublin, life was simple: we worked hard during the week. At six on a Friday night, Declan would head for the pub, down a few jars, come home ossified and, one hand inside my bra and the other on the zip of his trousers, told me what a grand girl I was. It was what we did. It was probably what a lot of people did on a Friday.

It would never have occurred to Declan to request, as Jean-Loup now did, that I try on a white tea dress and push me against the steel kitchen counter to take his pleasure, aroused by the froth of starched petticoats and the scent of *coq-au-vin*. Yes, French men definitely did things differently.

Afterwards, we sat down to eat on the balcony, just big enough to squeeze in a folding table and two chairs.

'Madame désire un peu de vin ?' Jean-Loup produced a bottle of Chateauneuf-du-Pape.

I nodded with a sigh of pleasure. I could get used to this. I did not miss the days when Declan would pull a couple of pies from the oven and slid them onto our plates with 'fancy a glass of the black stuff, Doll?'

Feeling deliciously French, I tore a chunk from the baguette and held out my glass.

'Attention, chérie,' warned my guardian angel as the bread found its way to my lips. *'Tu choisis...'*

Flip. He was right. Bread or wine? I still had three kilos to lose, six stubborn pounds glued to my backside in spite of Jean-Loup's nightly massages with cellulite cream. *'Ma Vénus Callipyge'* he called me, affectionately I thought, until I saw a picture of the fat-arsed statuette.

Plump and bouncy, my rump attracted a whole cortège of unsuitable men. I chose the wine... and remembered Asha's lecture. Had I simply swapped one sin for another? Being born out of wedlock did not matter here, but three extra kilos certainly did.

I poured myself another glass and ate the bread.

After dinner, I had a shower, put on a robe and hung the tea-dress back onto the rail, a hint of panic rising as I looked around Stéphanie's bedroom. The clothes were piling up faster than engine parts ever had. Also, Paris was an expensive place to live. When Stéphanie returned home from China in a few weeks' time, I would have to move out. I was not only running out of money, I was running out of time.

Rekindled by food and sex, it did not take my computer wizard long to discover that *Arnaud* de Peirac, who lived rue Raynouard, was a very big wig and that he had two daughters. Aude, the daughter whose Facebook account Jean-Loup had infiltrated, worked in fashion.

Two daughters… I would have to tread carefully. I tightened my robe and stared into the fish tank. The de Peirac girls might think I was after their inheritance.

'I'm intrigued as to how Mam could have ended up in bed with that kind of aristocrat,' I said to the piranhas.

Glassy-eyed, toothy underbite at the ready, the six monsters glared back.

'Perhaps de Peirac deflowered Sweet Mary Sullivan as a dare?' I turned to Jean-Loup, trying to make light of it all.

'Hmmm.'

'Drove her around Paris in his sports car and got her drunk?'

'Could be.' Focused on the screen, Jean-Loup wasn't listening.

'Knocked her up behind a bale of hay in his country mansion?'

'Oh dear.' He looked up from the screen, a line across his brow.

'What? What have you found?'

'There is something here about a boy, a young de Peirac who died in a motorbike accident five years ago. He was eighteen.'

'Oh no. How horrid.' I closed my eyes, realising for the first time that I would be stepping into someone else's history, joining a family with its own tragedies and skeletons in cupboards... and that one of those skeletons was me.

Jean-Loup snapped the laptop shut. 'Who knows, your mother and this man, perhaps they loved each other.'

'Yes, perhaps they did.'

However hard I tried, I could not step away from the portrait I had manufactured over a lifetime, of Mam and Archangel Gabriel engaged in friendly chat.

4

PARIS – ORLA

The next morning, Asha and I emerged from the Passy metro. To our right, the Eiffel Tower rose. Majestic above lush greenery, it cast a benevolent gaze over the most elegant part of Paris.

I shielded my eyes from the sun and studied the classic façades of rue Raynouard where, according to Jean-Loup, the trail began. Built in grand Haussmann style where farms once had been, the street ran along a straight ridge overlooking the Seine. Behind wrought iron balconies, shutters remained half-closed to keep in the morning coolness.

Were we in the right place? I had somehow pictured Mam in a populous quarter, on a backdrop of peeling walls and twisty streets. My pink and plump mother just didn't fit in with all this classical stone.

'Do you know how your mum got the au pair job?'

'No. I asked her before I left, but all she said was that it was all so long ago, she'd forgotten everything.'

'Hmmm.' Asha pouted unconvinced. 'How did you find the address of where she lived?'

'It was on the letter I… borrowed.'

'Is it a love letter? What else does it tell you?'

'Not much. It's a sort of telegram. The fellow just tells her he can't go ice-skating.'

'Ice skating? That telegram must have meant something for her to keep it all these years.' Asha's brain was in full Sherlock mode.

'But Asha, why send a telegram for something so anodyne? The phone had been invented in France then, hadn't it?'

'Perhaps it's in code.'

I rolled my eyes. 'It was in nineteen sixty-eight, Asha, not forty-two.'

Puzzled, we trawled rue de la Tour to a five-storey building with a coach door. I stared at the blue door, urging it to release its secret. 'So, this is where Mam lived. It isn't too far from rue Raynouard, so yes, the two of them could have met. Now we have to find the mysterious Arnaud de Peirac who holds all the answers.'

'Why don't we work out a plan with your boyfriend when we meet him at the restaurant tonight? My school French doesn't extend beyond buying ice cream, I'm afraid. We need to bring in the pros.'

That night, we met up in a traditional Marseilles restaurant serving *bouillabaisse,* which we ate in a small vine-covered yard.

Jean-Loup, for whom dinner usually involved putting the world to rights by raising his voice and banging on the table, remained remarkably calm. His English was limited but Asha, ever the diplomat, chose safe topics, and since they both worked in I.T., there was plenty to talk about.

When we mentioned our excursion into Passy, Jean-Loup

said he had an idea of how we could engineer a meeting with our quarry but, however hard we tried, we couldn't convince him to say any more. He was 'working on it.'

Just before midnight, we left the restaurant, put Asha in a taxi and hand in hand, walked to Jean-Loup's flat in the Marais.

The old Jewish district was famous for its upholstery businesses. Jean-Loup's tiny flat had belonged to a demented representative of the trade who had padded everything in brown suede. Everything. Down to the window frame and handle. Jean-Loup slept on a Clic-Clac, a brown velour sofa-bed which, once opened, took up most of the room. It was like being trapped inside a giant chocolate truffle.

'She's nice Asha, isn't she?' I flopped onto the sofa with a happy grin.

'Hmmm.' Jean-Loup leaned out of the window and surveyed the street below.

I headed for the shower and slipped on the strawberry-coloured satin robe he kept for me.

When I came out, damp and refreshed, he was already in bed.

Sheet pulled up over half his face, he said in a quavering.

'Come here Little Red Riding hood.'

I giggled and replied in a fluty voice, *'Oh, Mère-Grand,* what big eyes you've got!'

'All the better to see you, my child...' Jean-Loup pushed down the sheet.

'Oh, Mère-grand, what big ears you've got!' I crept closer.

'All the better to hear–' Jean-Loup growled... and corrected his pitch. 'All the better to hear you, my child.'

'Oh Grandma–' I skipped the big teeth, yanked away the sheet and stood back, hands over my lips, a picture of awe. 'Oh Grandma, what a big zob you've got!' At this my wolf sprang out and gobbled me up.

I was happy that day, in my Paris fairy tale. My boyfriend loved me, a little too much perhaps and, after a life as an average Jackeen, I was about to find out that my real father was an aristocrat and lived in a chateau…

That night, as I fell asleep in Jean-Loup's arms to the patter of summer rain, the future looked rosy.

5
PARIS – ORLA

'You're not going to believe this. One of the de Peirac girls is making her debut in the world of fashion,' I said to Asha as we strolled along the Canal Saint Martin the following evening. 'And what is more... she's running her own show!'

'Wow. Exciting stuff.'

'Imagine…' I took in a long breath of canal-scented air and opened my arms, welcoming my future. 'A sister in fashion...'

My amateurish foray into the world of vintage clothes had been great craìc so far, but I was struggling. I don't know why I had imagined that buying clothes in Paris to resell on the Internet would be easy.

The proceeds from the house and business I had shared with Declan would keep me coasting for a while, but it would not last forever. Soon Stéphanie would be back and useful contacts in Paris would come in handy. I hesitated to impose myself on a ready-made family, but I needed a life buoy and I needed one fast.

'Her name is Aude de Peirac. She'll be presenting her–' I crooked my fingers, '–new and exciting range of jewellery' to the *Tout-Paris* at a posh venue near the Bois de Boulogne in a week's time.'

It would be a huge thing. I really needed an invite. Jean-Loup was still 'working' on his plan for me to meet Arnaud.

'Sounds interesting,' Asha replied as if I had told her that Aude would be running a stall at the Saint-Ouen flea market.

I faced her squarely. 'Ash, we are talking about the *Pavillon Dauphine*. It's where millionaires have their wedding receptions. I don't have an invite. They'll have bodyguards.' I lifted my hands. 'I can't just gate-crash.'

'Oh. Bummer. Don't worry, we'll think of something.'

Wishing I could share her confidence, I slumped onto a bench along the canal and took in the soft purr of Paris around us. I loved this district and could not bear to leave it.

'What a great place,' Asha exhaled a long sigh. 'So much more interesting than the concrete jungle where my hotel is.'

'Hmmm,' I said dreamily. 'I could live here forever. This quarter, the tenth *arrondissement,* used to be the industrial district. Barges coming from the north brought everything Paris needed out of the underground canal which comes out here.' I flopped a hand towards the tunnel to our right. 'Hay, coal, wheat, stone.'

We stared at the empty canal.

'This is such a far cry from la Défense.' Asha leaned forward, elbows on her knees and rested her chin on her fists. 'Soulless, sterile... It's like Gotham City.'

A long time later, as we headed home, I halted, a hand on the rail of the steps that led down to my crooked street. 'So, what did you think of Jean-Loup?'

'He seems crazy about you, that's for sure. Do you love him?'

I shrugged. 'I think so…'

'But?'

'Sometimes he can be a bit mercurial.' I hesitated. I didn't feel good criticising him, but I was keen to sort out my feelings and Asha was clear-headed. 'You know what the French word is for mercurial? *Lunatique.* Someone who changes with the moon, *la lune*. He's *lunatique* all right.' I brushed off my concerns with a confident grin. 'Bah, at our age, it's impossible to meet a man without a few flaws, isn't it?'

Inside a communal workspace, several people sat, huddled over computers. 'That's where we met. Fact is, I couldn't function without Jean-Loup.' I grinned. 'I really struck gold that day. He's my web designer. He's spent hours optimizing my site so that it would rank highly on Google. It helps drive a lot of traffic to my virtual store. He knows the insides of my computer better than I do. Without him, I'd be completely sunk.'

'How long have you known him?'

'We were friends for about a month and we've been together for two.' I lifted a hand. 'I know what you're thinking, and before you say 'rebound,' it was a whole eight months after Declan.'

'I didn't say anything.' Asha followed me up the stairs.

'No, but you were thinking it very loud.'

I left her to get acquainted with the cat and the piranhas, threw open the windows and poured our drinks, lemonade for her, cool Chablis for me. I set the tray on the coffee table and, glass in hand, snuggled opposite her at the end of the white leather sofa, my feet against hers. Othello curled up between us.

'Nice flat.' Stéphanie, like Asha, went for a minimalist organic style. 'Did you get a chance to meet the owner before she left?'

I nodded and pointed to a rough oak shelf. Framed between two pebbles, Stéphanie smiled at us. Boyish, she was a no-nonsense sort of woman.

Her lounge reflected her tastes, urban, pale oak and white linen, everything hidden in presses that sprang open with the tiniest push.

'Makes a changed from your previous place.' Asha grinned. 'Don't you miss the smell of grease?'

I kicked her foot. 'Don't get snarky. Come on, let me show you my new product.' I led Asha to my Aladdin's cave. In Stéphanie's large bedroom, the fifties frills took so much space, I hardly had any room to sleep. What I would do with the stock once she was back from China, I wasn't sure. Hopefully move in with Jean-Loup and hire a storage unit.

Giggling, we stripped down to our underwear and had a grand old time trying on everything.

'What do you think?' Asha posed, prim in Madame Debré's white dress, her hands fluttering over the broad corolla.

I chased away the memory of Jean-Loup and me against the kitchen worktop. 'You look like a flower fairy.'

Asha handed me her phone and stopped. Something caught her attention on the rail. Her eyes lit up. She pulled out a red wiggle dress I had paid far too much for. 'Gosh, where did you find this?'

'Oh that. I got it in a boutique, rue de Lancry, near the canal. The owner, Marguerite, is your ultimate sales woman. I originally bought it for myself, but I might sell it on. It isn't me at all, is it?'

Asha held it out. 'Try it on.'

I squeezed into the soft fabric, breathed in while she zipped it up and stepped back. 'Wow, you look amazing!' She brushed down the thick ribbed material, draped the shawl collar over my chest and asked me to twirl. She took a few photos.

I checked the effect in the mirror and cried out, 'Oh no, my bum sticks out a mile. No way. I'm too old for this plunging back thing. I'm putting it for sale tomorrow.'

Asha shook her head. 'You don't know what you've got, silly. With your flat stomach and thin waist… see? You don't even need a bra. It's perfect. I wouldn't wear anything so revealing myself, but I must admit, it looks fantastic on you.'

'You serious?' I twisted over and ran the back of a hand over the offending body part. 'I hate my butt.'

'Trust me. You look amazing.'

'Really?' I lifted up my new blonde hair, pouted and cast another look at the new sexy Orla. Hmmm, not bad. We took a few more snaps.

While Asha tried on a blue long-sleeved evening gown, I sank onto the bed, still in the wiggle dress and let out a sigh of pleasure. This was fun. The room looked fabulous. Messed up, perfumed, littered with silk, frilly gauze petticoats, satin and all manner of *fanfreluches, falbalas,* frills and flounces, it oozed oestrogens. I didn't miss motorbike spares one bit.

Back in Dublin, spares had a habit of creeping up everywhere… spark plugs on the kitchen table, brake pads on top of the telly, mudguards behind the sofa, we even had the fecking things under the bed. However hard I tried to decorate the house, we always ended up having tea on top of crates of oil filters and carburettors.

My phone rang. It was the third time Jean-Loup had called today. What was it with him? It was as if Asha's presence threatened him. I switched off the phone and glanced at Asha, gorgeous and brown in her knickers and bra. Why couldn't I just *be* more like Asha? She didn't need a man to validate her. While she was making her way in the world, I'd wasted ten years with Declan.

As she unzipped me, I plucked up the courage to ask a question which had been troubling me for a while. 'How have you managed to cope without a man for so long?'

She giggled. 'There are things with AA batteries designed to keep you sane while you wait for Mister Right.' She helped me out of the dress. 'Did you know that in Spain, they call it *consolador?*'

'Asha!'

'Don't tell me you didn't bring yours.'

I hung my head. 'I was worried about customs... you know.'

'Big mistake.' She tutted. 'You can't let hormones rule your life. Women get randy around ovulation. It's a dangerous time.'

'Ha! Too right. If the St Brigid's nuns had given my mother a *consolador* instead of rosary beads, I wouldn't be here now.'

'Yeah, well... I'm glad you're here.'

Back in the lounge, I lit a few candles and brought out a tray of snacks.

We snuggled down on the sofa and munched on cheese and bread, casting about desultory ideas of how to get me into the Pavillon Dauphine.

Beyond the rooftops, Paris dozed. The odd police siren pierced the warm night. Across the courtyard, televisions cast a blue glow and in the candle light, the six snapping monsters flickered silver and gold.

Questions popped up inside my mind like the bubbles of a lava lamp. Would my biological father be at the *Pavillon*? When I opened the door into that stranger's life, would I be able to shut it again? What if my biological papa didn't want to acknowledge me? How would I feel about the rejection? I searched for answers inside a second glass of Chablis, only to be hit with more doubts. What if de Peirac's daughters objected to me, thinking me a gold digger? After a third glass, the questions throbbed inside my head. I sank back into the cushions with a groan and closed my eyes.

'By Jove, I've got it!' Asha sat up.

'Huh?' I blinked.

Her dark eyes sparkled. 'That red dress. Where did you say you found it?'

'In a vintage shop rue de Lancry. I got chatting to the owner. She's called Marguerite. Why?'

'Could Marguerite not wrangle an invitation from the de Peirac girl?'

I was too tired and too tipsy to think. 'What do you mean?'

'Well, Marguerite works in fashion, doesn't she? She owns a clothes shop. Isn't Aude de Peirac running some sort of jewellery show?'

'Asha...' I manoeuvred myself into an upright position. 'You are not just a pretty face. I'll ask Marguerite tomorrow.' I rubbed my eyes. 'Do you want to stay here tonight? I'll make room...'

'Thanks. I'd love to, but I've a working breakfast in Gotham City. Flying back to London straight afterwards.'

'*Dommage*.' It really was a shame.

We finished our drinks. I called a taxi and promised to keep Asha posted. Once she had gone, I crawled into bed and fell into an uneasy sleep, '*what-ifs*' buzzing inside my mind like angry hornets.

A couple of days later, I received an e-mail from Asha. It was rather cryptic.

'Dear Orla,

It was wonderful to see you. Our time together is always so special. You showed me a side of Paris I could only dream of. Trying on the dresses was great fun. Good luck with the vintage business.

As for the New Orla, make sure it really is you... the new love, make sure it really is love... and above all, make sure Monsieur de Peirac really is your father.

With you always, Inshallah.

Ashawira.'

6
PARIS – ORLA

I rushed to Marguerite's shop that Monday morning, only to find it closed for the day. Jeepers, what was it with the French and closing on Mondays? Frustrated, I returned to the flat and spent most of the day ironing, folding, wrapping parcels and schlepping them to the post-office... after I'd found one that was open, that is.

That night, Jean-Loup bounced in, his eyes gleaming with excitement.

'*Chérie*, I have a surprise for you.'

'*Une surprise, Loulou ?*' I smiled and circled his neck with my arms.

'I've found the perfect flat. We're going to see it tonight.'

I carried on smiling in spite of the peal of warning bells ringing inside my head. What could I do? Stéphanie was coming home and, without a regular pay check and a guarantor, I had more chances of finding a place on Virgin Galactic than a flat in Paris. Jean-Loup had been struggling to find something he could afford for over a year.

He held me tight. 'It's in Montmartre, rue des Trois-Frères, an old artist's studio. You'll love it. My uncle knows the owner, so we're in with a chance at last.' He lifted my chin with a finger and kissed me deeply, his heart thumping against my chest. 'I'll meet you outside the metro Abbesses tomorrow at six, okay *M'amour?* We'll go and see it together.'

The following night, I paced under the trees around the Art Nouveau Abbesses metro station, mellowed by the music of a merry-go-round and a gorgeous smell of food. When Jean-Loup ran up to me from the tube, summer jacket over his shoulder, when he took me in his arms, there, for a moment, life too was a carousel.

He walked backwards up the slope and opened his arms wide, his curls a golden halo in the evening sun. 'Imagine how it was, *M'amour,* this hill covered with vines! There were once twenty-nine windmills in Montmartre. Twenty-nine! And people complain about wind farms.'

Hand in hand, we strolled up towards a patch of greenery hidden between tall peeling walls, shuttered windows and mansard roofs. Unlike elegant Passy, I could picture Mam here.

Behind the plane trees was a tall wall covered with 'I love you' written in every language and script in the world.

'Le mur des je t'aime.' Jean-Loup pointed to a speech bubble. *'Aimer c'est du désordre ... alors aimons.'* 'Love is messy ... so, let's love.'

I understood why he had brought me here. Love *is* messy. Our love was messier than most, though surely, once he became more secure in our relationship, he would relax, wouldn't he? Entwined under the wall, we kissed for a long time and slowly, like the *flâneurs* we were, strolled up Rue des Trois Frères and met the owner just outside the porch. Concealed like a turtle inside a worn gabardine coat, the old man held out a skeletal hand and, step by painful step, we followed him up five flights of stairs to the rooftop, pausing while he caught his breath, worrying it would be his last.

The question 'any plans to install a lift?' was met with a wheezy smirk.

His lungs whistling, the old man fumbled about with a key, opened a heavy door… and I floated into the dream. It was a true artist's studio. A whole side of the flat consisted of '*verrières*,' slanted panes of glass overlooking the whole of Paris. The spiral staircase to the mezzanine set my heart racing. In a corner was a butler sink, wooden kitchen units and a few feet away, a roll top bath, complete with pewter taps. It was all very 'Moulin Rouge.

'Wow!' Jean-Loup stroked the worktops, the bath, the walls. Designed for those French *fusionnel* couples, there was nowhere to hide. Apart from the toilet, there were no doors at all. No wonder he loved the place.

Unable to contain his excitement, he turned to me. *'C'est super, oui, M'amour? Le bain, c'est formidable !'*

The bath. He saw me soaking in that bath while he cooked, a few feet away.

All the air went out of me. The fantasy fizzled. This flat may be ten times the size of his padded pad, but it was just as much of a prison. My dresses would clutter up the space. It would be back to living in the shop as I did with Declan.

'*Alors?*' He held his breath.

'J'adore cet appartement,' I said disingenuously, aware that our chances of getting it were remote. Why upset the apple-cart? Someone was bound to snap up this gem, some *fusionnel* couple, complete with guarantors and tax returns. We did not stand a chance.

We circled the flat, checked that the *verrières* didn't leak, climbed to the mezzanine – it dominated every corner of the room below – giggled at the possibility of making love under the stars and discussed the rent. Because it was a fifth floor with no lift, the rent was reasonable. The lease was a standard three-year agreement. Three years... It felt like a life-sentence.

We shook the man's hand again, sauntered down the stairs, Jean-Loup humming *'c'est si bon,'* and emerged as Montmartre was coming to life. Radios blared, mouth-watering scents floated out of half-closed shutters and people hurried home, a folded copy of France Soir under their arm.

'Imagine living here… together.' Jean Loup's eyes caressed me. He put an arm around me, protective and reassuring. I glanced down at Paris and let its magic seep into my soul.

It was Paris I was in love with. Over the past three months, accordion music, scents of freshly baked bread and Gitane smoke had succeeded in deconstructing the Irish girl who, for nearly forty years, had been guilty of *not* being a Reilly. I was shedding my old skin at last, though the moulting process was by no means complete. Meeting my real father and connecting with my de Peirac roots would complete the transformation.

Who would I be when I came out of the chrysalis? I could not wait to find out.

7

PARIS – ORLA

As Stéphanie's return loomed and Jean-Loup spent more time at my place, dawn became my secret pleasure, the only time he didn't begrudge my being away from him. A coat over my pyjamas, I would tiptoe out of the flat and return with croissants warm from the oven, a litre of milk and a kiss.

As soon as I opened the *grille* out of my golden cage, my chest swelled, my body cried out *'Bonjour, Paris!'* I jumped over the water gushing along the *caniveau,* skipped up the five steps that linked my street to the quayside and, once I reached the canal, absorbed Paris with every one of my senses.

Sleepy and bustle free, there was a provincial feel to the tenth arrondissement. Housewives stood by their doors in dressing gowns, watching their dogs squat in the gutter; sleepy old men in pyjamas pushed open their shutters and threw their bedding over the sill. In the cafés, those who had been up all night ordered a *'petit blanc',* white wine to you and me.

This morning did not find me skipping. With only two

days to go until Aude de Peirac's jewellery party, I yet had to be invited.

Stéphanie's mission in China was over. She was on her way home. I had four days to find somewhere to live.

At ten o'clock, I headed for the shop where I had bought the red dress, hoping to find it open at last. The owner, Marguerite, was a typical '*baba cool*,' a bohemian, complete with kaftans, bangles and a mess of hennaed hair. Born in the wrong century, she jangled, smelled of patchouli, ate *macrobiotique* and watched endless reruns of *Woodstock*, *Blow Up* and *Zabriskie Point*.

'*Waou!*' She beamed when I mentioned the Pavillon Dauphine, and rubbed her thumb and forefinger, the sign for money. 'Me, I am always looking for more contacts with people full of *fric*. I see what I can do to get us an invite.'

Marguerite's English may be in need of subtitles, but her sales techniques were faultless. I knew she would pull it off.

'Marguerite, there is something else you could do for me. I need to move house and I've nowhere to keep my stock. I wonder if you could help out until I get myself sorted? I've got a rail full of dresses and...'

'*Oui oui. Pas de problème*. At the back here, I have a big storeroom. This is the shop of my grand-mother, she was a merchant of vegetables.'

'A greengrocer?'

'Maybe. This jewellery show, yes? Don't worry about it. We will get tickets. We'll make ourselves beautiful and drive there in my 2CV.'

'Thank you. That would be fantastic.'

'No, no, it's me. I thank you. I also want to go.'

Buzzing, I messaged Asha the good news. She texted straight back to say that she wanted to hear all about it.

That night, a very excited Jean-Loup galloped up the stairs, burst into the kitchen and squeezed the life out of me.

The owner of the flat had liked us. The rooftop studio was ours.

I squeezed him back so he would not read the hesitation on my face. The timing was astonishing. Surely, this serendipity was a sign from The Universe, a proof that Jean-Loup and I were meant for each other… wasn't it? I would have a Paris address, and the flat was big enough to hold all my dresses. There was enough floor space to fold and wrap my precious merchandise before taking it to the convenient post office located at the bottom of the street. More prosaically, the five flights of stairs would tone my glutes, redesign my bottom and afford me an extra glass of wine at weekends.

What was not to love?

My head against Jean-Loup's shoulder, I imagined myself in Montmartre, walking in the footsteps of the greatest artists the world had ever known. I would soak in the bath while Jean-Loup cooked under the stars. Photos of our *Moulin Rouge* life would do wonders for my Facebook profile. It might even make Declan jealous.

Truth was, I had no choice. However much of a struggle Paris proved to be, I simply could not face going home before I had made it. Dublin was grand, but who had ever gone to Dublin to fulfil their destiny –apart from Grandma Reilly that is? Dublin's pavements may be strewn with James Joyce plaques and quotes from Ulysses, but where did the great man live while he wrote '*He kissed the plump mellow yellow smellow melons of her rump*?' He lived right here, in Paris.

I lifted my face and beamed at Jean-Loup. 'It's wonderful Loulou. You're the best.'

A hand on my waist, Jean-Loup grappled about behind me and produced a magnificent bouquet of gerbera.

'*Oh! Mon Loulou* they're beautiful! But why?' I clutched the large pink and orange daisies to my chest.

'*Comme ça, parce que je t'aime.*'

To have a man offer me flowers 'just because' was a new and thrilling experience. Perhaps the hard times were over. Perhaps I should trust in life. Overcome with gratitude, I fetched a vase from the kitchen, placed it on the coffee table and shot Othello a stern 'don't you dare' look.

Othello was trouble. That cat had driven Stéphanie to minimalism. Anything out of place was instantly clawed to shreds by the deaf creature, deprived of the normal feline pleasures of chasing mice and birds.

I kissed Jean-Loup lightly. 'I'd say it's time to open that bottle of champagne. I bought some olives today. Shall I set everything on a tray and take it to the bedroom?' I pressed my body to his. He didn't have to answer. I could feel his acquiescence.

I was setting the champagne glasses on a tray when an almighty crash made me jump.

'What on earth was that?' I shot out into the lounge and gaped, faced with two pairs of guilty eyes. Othello stood amongst the wreckage, wet paws among broken glass, whiskers lowered in shame.

Over on the sofa, Jean-Loup was checking my phone. I took in a sharp breath but remained mouth open, too shocked to speak. When I did, I shouted at the cat. He was deaf, I know, but I just didn't have the gumption to shout at Jean-Loup.

'Othello!' I grabbed a towel from the bathroom and ranted as I mopped up the mess. 'You beast, look at what you've done! One more trick like that and I'll feed you to the piranhas.'

Jean-Loup dropped my phone. 'An SMS came up. I didn't

read it. I was just going to bring it to you.' His mouth was smiling, but guilt dulled his eyes.

'You were reading my texts.' He knew my password. I'd given it to him when he was setting up my business.

'I wasn't.'

'You don't trust me.'

His face fell, his tone became whiny. 'You say things to that friend of yours, Asha, that you don't tell me. You're following her advice when…'

I dropped the towel and stood to face him. '*What* are you talking about?'

His eyes narrowed. 'You went to Passy with her.'

'So what?'

'Orla, why are you friends with her? She must be short of a neurone if she believes all that Muslim claptrap.'

I raised a hand. 'Stop. Don't … even… go there. Ever.'

This was surreal. I was tired, I was hungry and I couldn't bear the thought of a confrontation, so I gently chided him. 'Come on, Loulou, what's really going on? You're better than that.'

Jean-Loup crumpled. 'We're a couple. We do things together.' A lopsided smile softened his face. 'I like to do things with you, just us, you and me. I want you to tell me everything. Who is Marguerite?'

Christ, what did Marguerite have to do with anything now? Too confused to deal with the situation, I nailed a mask of contrition to my face and looped my arms around him. '*Mon* Loulou,' I said. 'You know I love you.' I nuzzled his neck. 'Aren't you being a little silly?'

'Can't you see how insensitive you are? There I was, excited about finding your father for you and now you've arranged it all without me.'

'Have I?'

'You've arranged to go to this fashion show and you didn't even tell me.'

He had read my messages. Marguerite had got tickets!

'Orla, I hate it when you shut me out.'

'I didn't shut you out Loulou, I was just …'

This ridiculous conversation carried on for a while. All my emotions were on hold. Marguerite had got tickets to Aude de Peirac's party. Stéphanie was making her way home. Right now, falling out with Jean-Loup was not an option, so my heart just shut down. I would open it up and examine its contents later, after I had met my father.

I know it was a long shot, but somewhere inside me lurked the wild hope that Papa de Peirac would wave a magic wand and ask me to move in with him in his Passy mansion. Ridiculous I know, but that's how it was.

I kissed Jean-Loup on the lips, if only to stop the nonsense pouring out of his mouth. Exhausted, bewildered, I pushed him against the sofa, and to prove how sorry I was, knelt down and gave him a blowjob.

8

PARIS – ORLA

Tonight was the night of the jewellery show, the night I was to meet my potential father. I spent the day in a trance, my heart padded with ice to avoid a total meltdown. I locked myself inside Marguerite's back room and worked, photographing and wrapping the outfits I thought would sell the quickest, in a frantic bid to reduce my stock.

I blanked out last night from my memory… Jean-Loup's attempts at wooing me back, the mirthless drinking, the mindless sex... Concentrating on the moment, I checked the fabric, slipped each dress on the dummy, focused on the creases and folds and steamed out the scenarios of what could go wrong with Arnaud de Peirac, the painful 'what-if-he-doesn't-come', 'what-if-he-doesn't-like-me' loop digging a groove into my mind.

Hidden in my frothy limbo, I hunted down shadows and made sure the fabric fell properly. I caressed the garment and, eyes closed, composed enticing descriptions to wow my English-speaking customers.

At lunchtime, Marguerite came in, glanced at my notes and tutted.

'Orla, what are you writing here? 'Genuine fifties tea-dress. *Vraiment*?' She pulled out a yellow flowered dress and said, her mouth turned down. 'How much did you pay for this?'

I didn't like the way she laughed when I told her. 'What's funny?'

'Orla. They did not have polyester in the fifties.'

Christ, how I missed those carburettors. What the feck was I doing, competing with the French on their own turf? The yellow dress was not my only mistake. The embarrassment was excruciating, but it was not as painful as the mess inside my head.

A crunchy camembert-filled baguette went some way to dilute the pain. After a cup of strong coffee, Marguerite said she would pick me up from the flat at eight and left in a trail of cheese and patchouli.

The day crawled ahead. At six, I trudged back to my flat.

At seven, I managed to haul myself out of the bath and dried my fluffy blonde hair. I squeezed into my wiggle dress and checked the effect, relieved at how forgiving the thick ribbed fabric was over my body. From the front, I looked demure, the soft shawl collar hiding my inadequate breasts. The back was something else. The décolleté stopped just short of my bouncy derrière. A slit in the fabric allowed me to walk, revealing far too much leg.

I pouted at my reflection. Would this masquerade allow me to fit in with the Paris glitterati, or would the amount of flesh on display backfire?

'*Inshallah.*' I exhaled a long fatalistic breath. The trajectory was set. It was now in the hands of God.

I dropped a few things into a clutch bag, padded downstairs barefoot –now was not the time to twist an ankle– and only at the bottom of the stairs, did I slip on the red 'fuck-me-shoes' without which the dress was pointless.

Feeling too tall and too red, I crossed the cobbled courtyard with as much dignity as I could muster and folded myself into Marguerite's vintage vehicle.

'*Ouahou*,' she said, pulling out the shift stick into first gear, 'You look like a film star. The sugar daddy will be impressed.'

Marguerite had misunderstood the reason I wanted to attend the glitzy reception. I opened my mouth to put her right, but the woman driver in front of us ground to an abrupt halt.

'*Avance hey, pouffiasse*!' Marguerite honked and shook a fist.

The '*Knowledge*' every Parisian driver has to acquire in order to survive is no street map, but a remarkably complex lexicon of insults with added gestures for the hard of hearing.

As the old car lurched forward, I leaned back with a groan, so spaced out, I could have been an astronaut on the way to Mars.

As we drove by the Pavillon, the reception was in full swing. By the gates, burly doormen were checking out the guests. Apprehension turned to alarm as Marguerite swerved into a wooded alley of the Bois de Boulogne and parked between two white vans.

'*Marguerite, non !*' Jeepers! What was she thinking ? The place was crawling with seedy men looking for sex.

She yanked the handbrake and turned to me. '*Ben quoi?*'

A woman wearing even less than we were was leaning against her van. A man approached her, and after a brief exchange, followed her in.

'D– did you see that?'

'Yes. It very safe here. She will be here all night and look after my car.'

'But…'

'Ben alors, tu viens ?'

I unfurled from the seat, pulled down my dress and cast a worried look at the woods. The men trawling the pavements looked desperate and, in the dimness, nothing distinguished us from the pros.

Paris may be the city of love, but the flip side of it is a permanent free-for-all.

'Don't worry.' Marguerite hooked her arm in mine. 'They are not after you. They have money in their pocket and are happy to pay for what they need. Stop being so prude.'

Prudish or simply not used to this filth. There was a dark side to 'the city of love.' Venturing along its innards alone was a risky business. I'd got caught out several times by kerb crawlers asking for directions to some non-existent street, their flies brazenly open. At rush hour in the metro, being felt up was par for the course. I yet had to acquire the courage to carry out the true Parisienne's technique: extract the offending hand from my crotch, hold it up and ask whose it was.

Clutching Marguerite's arm, I walked as fast as our heels would allow towards the safety of the Pavillon's bright lights, my heart hammering under the red shawl collar.

We slowed down for selfies as we neared the Pavillon. It really was stunning. Time stopped and reeled backwards, taking us to a place Proust would have been familiar with. With its curved windows, painted ceilings, plaster swags and satin drapes, the Pavillon Dauphine was the epitome of French *fin de siècle* elegance. A pianist in coat tails played in a corner. While Marguerite once again produced our invitations, I scanned the high society, fighting the urge to turn back. How could my mother possibly have had anything to do with these people? Surely, the whole thing was a mistake, and even if Arnaud de Peirac *was* my father, I would never fit in his world. As soon as this was over, I would fly home to Mam and Dad, get a proper job and put the whole episode down to mid-life crisis.

I was about to call 'abort mission,' when Marguerite nudged me.

'Regarde! Aude de Peirac. Exactement comme sa photo de Facebook.'

A strange woosh filled my ears as I zoomed in on the girl. Could this fabulous girl really be my half-sister? Her aristocratic face, long thin nose and high arching eyebrows were enviable, but they were nothing like my high cheekbones and turned up nose. Nature had endowed her with thick fair hair, fantastic legs, a pert backside and generous breasts. The odds of her being my sister were as slim as she was.

Her black dress was genius. The LBD at its best. A structured V-shaped décolleté mirrored a scalloped opening above the knee. Cinched at the waist, the fabric hugged her like a clam, showing off the cobalt-blue jewellery which was about to make her fortune.

The ankle-high cobalt-blue suede boots were a strange choice for July, but looked a damned sight more comfortable than what I was wearing.

I searched for anyone likely to be de Peirac *père* amongst the titled and arty boho crowd. A waiter handed me a glass of champagne. Shivering with nerves, I drank it, grabbed a second one and followed Marguerite who had joined the well-wishers clustered around Aude.

When I heard her say *'Papa est en retard,'* I relaxed. Papa was late. Of Maman, there was no mention. Never mind Maman. Papa was the one I was after.

'Dis-donc, ça en jette.' Marguerite whistled, impressed by the chandeliers mirrored in the marble floors. 'Come, we go

and look at her jewellery before we eat the canapés. That's why we are here, no?'

'The jewellery or the canapés?' I croaked with a nervous grin.

Aude, whose little black dress showcased the translucent blue jewellery to perfection, was joined by her dark-haired sister who wore the clam dress in white and, around her neck, red iridescent circles. The contrast was spectacular. They posed for photos.

'Good luck to you, girls.' I lifted my glass. Cameras and phones flashed away and within seconds, the de Peirac sisters were tweeted into the stratosphere. Before I'd had time to say *'slaínte'* the pair had touched all corners of the world on Instagram, Tik Tok and Twitter.

Encased at the end of the room on a bed of black velvet, the jewellery collection was breath-taking. Fashioned from silver and resin, the ornaments were an artistic mix of primary shapes, leather and metal. Fun, aimed at the affluent young, priced at a mere fifty euros for a bracelet, Aude had targeted the urban arty uptown segment. To judge by the amounts of money changing hands, she had pitched it just right.

A necklace of sunny orange and yellow circles caught my eye. I had just picked it up when a voice behind me said, *'ah voilà Arnaud.'*

I dropped the necklace. My mouth went dry. I turned around slowly. My field of vision tunnelled to one man in an expensive suit and loafers. Balding, stocky, he looked… just… French.

I focused, trying to find something, anything that would link him to me. I pictured him younger and slimmer. Nothing. I couldn't say what it was… loyalty to Dad perhaps, or the grandeur of the surroundings, my mind simply refused to connect with the stranger.

I had expected him to be taller, though the de Peirac sisters were not much shorter than me. Confused emotions sent me tumbling down the rabbit hole. Coming here had been a bad idea. I should have written to Arnaud first and asked him in confidence whether he remembered a Mary Sullivan. But I hadn't. If he had refused to acknowledge me, the rejection would have been too painful. I wanted to remain in control.

I was not in control. Without Marguerite by my side, I would have self-combusted, leaving only a small puff of red.

I searched out her familiar silhouette and found her next to a potted palm chatting to a hunk, a famous French motorbike champion.

I knew a thing or two about motorbikes and fell into easy conversation with the champion. We were discussing the merits of the Italian Ducati when a photographer appeared. The biker drew me to him. I lifted my glass, gave my best Irish smile and said 'cheese.'

'How do you know Aude?' I asked after the shutterbug had snapped us to his heart's content.

'I was a friend of her brother's. He died in a bike crash.'

'Oh, I heard about that. So young. It's dreadful.'

'Yes, yes it was. The following year, his mother drowned off a yacht in the West Indies.'

'No! How awful. Is that family cursed?'

'You would wonder, wouldn't you. It hit the girls hard.'

I watched Aude and Papa in the distance, leaving Marguerite to make her way towards them with an agenda of her own. Thankfully, her interest was purely commercial. As soon as she had made contact with the target, as it were, I joined her.

Arnaud de Peirac lifted his eyes to me. They were green like mine.

'Are you in fashion too?' His gaze wandered over my shoulder for someone more interesting.

Words stuck in my throat. I said I was Irish. He said he loved Dublin.

'So, you like Dublin,' I blabbered, desperate to sneak in the question –the only question that mattered– and studied his green eyes, lest they should mist up at the memory of a girl called Mary. 'Have you met many Irish people here in Paris?'

'Sure, I meet people from every nationality. In my line of work…'

Had he told me what that was? I'd already forgotten.

'And your name is…?'

'Orla Reilly but my mother was…'

'O'Reilly, how very Irish.'

I would have corrected him, but he wasn't listening. 'De Peirac is an unusual name.' I stuck to my brief. 'I think my mother once met a de Peirac when she was working in Paris.'

'Did she work at the embassy?'

'Oh no, she was an au pair for a family in Passy.'

'Passy... Comme c'est intéressant...' Boredom was creeping into his voice.

I was fast losing him. Racking my brain for a fascinating snippet to hold his attention, I spun to place my empty glass on a nearby table. I had drunk enough. It was time to get serious.

When I turned back to him, something had changed. A spark danced in his eyes. Intrigued ? Predatory? I couldn't say. Perhaps it was that inexplicable bond between parent and child.

By the time his daughter dragged him away, I still hadn't managed to find out whether he had ever met Mam. Yet I noticed his gaze following me throughout the evening. An hour later, we found each other again and resumed our conversation. He had once stayed at the Shelbourne on St Stephen's Green, the poshest hotel in Dublin and as luck would have it, I had worked there a student. Withholding the fact that I had been a chambermaid, I impressed him by revealing that Hitler's half-brother Aloïs had worked there back in 1900. To pique his interest, I even added that Aloïs and his brother, so horrified by what their sibling had done, had made a pact never to marry, or have children.

Delighted at my interest in history, Arnaud called for more champagne and went on to talk about his roots, the roots of the de Peirac family... my family perhaps, I thought with a frisson.

While most women would have been bored rigid I, for obvious reasons, was riveted. The music and hubbub were such, I had to stand very close to him to catch what he was saying.

'We can trace our origins back to the Crusades.' He pointedly adjusted his gold cufflinks.

'The Crusades!' My blood tingled as it turned blue.

'Our family originates from the Cévennes. You might have heard of Les Gorges du Tarn.'

Surprisingly, I had. Declan's brother had once invited us to go kayaking down the Tarn River but, of course, we were too busy at the time, setting up the business.

'Two hundred years ago, an ancestor of ours, the Marquis de Peirac had a chateau near Mende. The Cévennes is a wild region. There were famines. Unlike his peers, my ancestor was generous to a fault. During harsh winters, he would open his cellars to the poor and distributed wheat and chestnuts.'

'Chestnuts? Isn't that a bit over the top? I mean, why not caviar?'

He laughed and placed a hand on my arm. 'Not at all, dear. Ground into flour, chestnuts were the staple food in the region. In fact, the chestnut is part of our coat of arms. A wolf passant topped by three chestnuts.' He held up a cufflink to the light. 'See here.'

A coat of arms. What were the chances? I pictured myself storming into Grandma Reilly's parlour, coat of arms emblazoned on my chest, hurling my pedigree at her, the Crusades, the wolf passant, the chateau, the chestnuts… and above all our *particule. 'I am of noble birth, Grandma, a* ***de*** *Peirac if you please.* ***DE*** *Peirac you hear? And you couldn't even manage an O'.'*

I tuned back in. Had he mentioned a chateau? I tilted my head to one side. 'Do you still have that chateau in the, huh…'

'In the Cévennes? Good Lord, no. I'm a Parisian through and through. Hiding in the Cévennes is not for me.'

'Oh. I thought the Gorges du Tarn were popular.'

'Yes yes of course, the region is charming in summer, but it's very remote. No one lives there unless they want to hide from the world.'

'I see.' *Ah well, no chateau then.*

'*Orla…*' crooned Arnaud, stepping towards an open door. '*Orla,* such a pretty name.'

'*Merci.*' I followed him outside.

'*Orla…*'

'Orla Reilly.' I raised my voice above the ambient noise and enunciated clearly, 'My mother's name was – Mary – Sullivan.'

'O'Reilly, how Irish.'

'Just Reilly, actually. Did you know a Mary Sullivan?'

He took in a deep breath of scented night air and lifted a hand towards the dark shapes of the trees around us. 'Look. To think we are in Paris…'

My mother's name had scored a complete blank. It was disappointing, but it might not be the end of the road. I was beginning to get the measure of the man. As an au pair girl, Mam may just have been a notch on the bedpost.

'Vous êtes mariée?' His eyes strayed to my empty ring finger.

'Non.'

'Orla...' He held my gaze. 'Golden girl *ou hors-la-loi ?'*

'Pardon?'

'Orla. *Or* means gold in French.' He stood so close to me, I could smell his cologne.

'Ah yes. Sorry, yes actually, it means gold in Celtic too. That would be the origin of my name. I see, golden girl, yes, thank you. Sorry, what was that other word you said?'

'Hors-la-loi. It means outlaw.' Arnaud sidled closer. 'I'm trying to find out if you are a good girl or a bad girl.'

'Monsieur de Peirac...'

'Arnaud. They call me Arnie.'

I did a double-take. Never had any man looked less like Schwarzenegger. 'Arnie, there is something I want to ask you...'

'Ask away dear girl, ask anything you want, I'm quite sure the answer will be yes.' He took my arm and led me further into the garden.

Sheltered, overhung with ancient oaks, the space was so dark, so quiet, we could have been anywhere, in the Cévennes perhaps, wherever that was, outside the chateau of that fabled Marquis.

'Ha!' I jumped. Was his arm really around my waist? I tottered backwards. My heels sank into the damp grass. I steadied myself against an Empire chair. His breath was on me. With a shudder, I realised where this was going. This was not fatherly interest. He had mistaken my fascination for his lineage for a blatant come on. I tried to escape his embrace, but it was too late. I was trapped. He leaned over, put his glass on the table behind me and let his hand travel down the back of my dress.

When he squeezed my bottom, I let out a squeal.

'J'adore ton cul.'

Holy Mary mother of God, had he said what I thought he said? I arched back and tried to push him away from me. Christ, now both his hands were clutching my bottom.

Eyes wide, I looked around for help and cried out with relief as the champion biker stepped onto the terrace, pulled a packet of cigarettes from his pocket and gazed into the night, about to light one.

'Oops, careful, here's my boy-friend.' I giggled, sliding under de Peirac's armpit.

He arranged his jacket over his erection and walked away, cool as a cucumber.

I ran towards the biker, grabbed his arm, mumbled that I urgently needed to find Marguerite and trailed behind him into the over-heated ballroom.

'Ben Orla, ça va pas ?' Marguerite asked with concern.

My breath coming in short-bursts, I waited until Xavier had gone and related my debacle in harsh whispers. 'De Peirac led me outside, groped me and told me he loved my arse!' I choked. 'He actually said he loved my arse! Can you believe it?'

Marguerite shrugged.

'What?' My voice went up an octave. 'Is this acceptable behaviour in Paris?'

'Sure. If you wriggle your bottom in front of rich old men.' She narrowed her eyes. 'It was what you wanted, no?'

'Huh?' I replied, dumbstruck.

'A rich lover is very useful. That man has good contacts and no wife. Yes, he is a good choice.'

It took my mouth a few moments to close.

On the other side of the room, a relaxed De Peirac was smiling charmingly, complimenting the ladies, joking with the men. My skin crawled.

'Right, we're out of here.' I growled. 'We're going home.'

'Going so soon Cinderella?' de Peirac said with a wolfish smile as we reached the door. 'If ever you fancy lunch, please do not hesitate to e-mail me. I have a table at the Meurice.' He handed me his card.

'Waouh!' Marguerite joined her hands. *'Punaise*! L'Hôtel Meurice, rue de Rivoli. He has invited you to the best hotel in Paris!'

I closed my eyes. This was *not* happening.

'Can we please go home?' I felt sick.

'Okay… okay. Wait a minute.' She removed her shoes. 'My toes are hurting too much.'

Mine were in a bad way too, though not as bruised as my feelings.

I removed my shoes and walked barefoot to the car. 'Jaysus, it's dark around here. I hope we won't step in dog turds.'

'Bof. It is a sign of good luck,' Marguerite countered brightly.

Bloody French. What was wrong with them?

The lady of the night greeted us with a tired smile.

'You had locked it, hadn't you, love?' She tilted her chin towards the 2CV.

'Yes. I think so, why?' Marguerite checked the door.

'Some chap was sniffing around it, so I told him to get lost.'

'Merci beaucoup, Madame,' Marguerite said. *'Bonne nuit.'*

'Bonne nuit.'

Good night? Feck. This was the worst night of my life.

9
PARIS – ORLA

I crawled back up the stairs wondering what I had done. Feeling dirty and stupid, I took a long shower, swallowed two sleeping pills and crashed out, my hair still damp.

The next morning, I staggered out of the bedroom, bleary eyed and pasty-mouthed, wondering why Othello hadn't scratched at my door at seven, as he usually did.

I trudged naked into the living room, pushed my tangled hair from my face and blinked. Was I seeing things? His back to me, Jean-Loup was bending over the fish tank. What was he doing here?

I retreated to the bedroom and grabbed a robe. Scratching my hair, I shuffled out and stopped in my tracks.

'Morning.' Jean-Loup gave me a critical once over. 'You look rough.' Freshly shaved, in jeans and white tee Jean-Loup was ready to roll. 'I came in to give those guys a treat. Always wanted to see piranhas in action.'

Up on a chair, stretched out to his full length, Othello was pawing at the glass, uttering strangled squeaks.

'Wh–at have you got in that bag?'

Jean-Loup dropped something into the tank. Two flashes of gold darted around, eyed by the hungry predators. The cat let out a blood-curling meow.

'Hey! Stop! You're not feeding live goldfish to the... Noooo!'

I sprang across the room and yanked the bag from his hand. It burst. A goldfish fell onto the wet floor. Before I had time to retrieve it, Othello had pounced, grabbed it in his teeth and scurried behind the sofa.

'Othello! Come here!' I yelled to the deaf cat.

Inside the tank, the piranhas went crazy. One fish was being torn to shreds. The other one darted away from snapping jaws.

'Jesus! Are you out of your mind?'

'Oh, you English are so squeamish.'

English? Me? Right. That did it.

I pointed to the door. 'Listen, I've got just *hours* before Stéphanie comes home from China. I've had the shittiest night of my entire life and the last thing I need is you hanging about doing... weird things. It would be best if you went.'

'Can I help you pack?'

I really didn't need this. I dug my nails into the palms of my hands and articulated calmly. 'If you really want to help, you can give me space. I really need to–'

'I love you, Orla, you know that.' Jean-Loup took a step towards me.

I was not listening. The torn bag was dripping on the floorboards. I rushed to the kitchen, grabbed a tea towel and threw it over the spill.

'It's not fair. You can't allow me to plan a life with you and then–'

I stiffened up. 'Sorry, I don't have time for this. I have to pack and clean out the whole flat.'

'You've met someone else, haven't you?'

I stared at him. 'What on earth are you talking about?'

'Last night…'

'Ah last night.' I ran my hand through the bird's nest on my head. 'Yes, I met Arnaud de Peirac, or Arnie as that Lothario calls himself. I don't care whether he's my father or not, I never want to have anything to do with that dirty old man again.' I halted, confused. 'What's de Peirac got to do with us?'

'I saw them, you know, the photos of you and that biker. You didn't waste much time, did you?'

What photos? What biker? I slumped on the sofa and buried my face in my hands. What was he talking about? Strange, he hadn't even been curious about Arnie. Jeepers, I'd lumbered myself with a madman. My head was throbbing. I needed a coffee. I pushed myself up and went to the kitchen.

Jean-Loup followed me. 'You looked quite cosy with the biker.'

The haze dissipated and I saw him for what he was. A pathetic loser. He had spent the night checking up on me through Aude de Peirac's tentacular social network, following us on Instagram and God knows what else. No wonder he wasn't curious. He knew everything I'd done.

I grabbed the coffee tin and banged it on the worktop to make my point. 'Listen. I posed for a photo, that's all. Remember why I went to that reception? I went to meet my *father*. Hah!' I gagged at the memory.

Penitent, Jean-Loup pulled me to him. I pushed him away and launched into a tirade, not caring if my French deserted me. 'Now you listen to me.' I waved a finger at him. 'You get yourself an analyst and when you've found one, tell her you have a *trust* problem. I know your mother betrayed you when you were young, dumped you with an aunt you hated, and didn't come back for you when she'd promised. I'm sorry about that, but you have to move on. You can't *own* people like… like you own a cat.'

I threw water into the percolator and noisily spooned coffee into the filter. Banging everything I touched, I gabbled on in halting French. 'Stéphanie's cat is confined to this flat because he's deaf.'

On cue, Othello came into the kitchen, reeking of fish, licking his chops.

'You can't keep me prisoner inside a studio, however charming it may be. I have to go out to... to work.' The word I was looking for was 'socialise.' I grappled about the lexicon in my fuzzy brain, came up blank and went for what had really been bothering me. I still had not forgiven him for suggesting that Asha was short of neurones.

'You know what? It's men like you who put women in burkas, not the Koran.' I put my hands on my hips. 'That's what you really want, isn't it, to have me under lock and key? Well, no one can live like that, not here, not anywhere and certainly not in twenty-first century Paris!' Enraged, I pressed the 'on' button of the percolator and faced Jean-Loup squarely. 'Unless you change your ways, you'll never have a relationship. With me or with anyone. Anywhere. Ever!'

I yanked out the jug and added in English, 'Get sorted.'

I poured the coffee into a cup. I don't normally take sugar, but I was so upset that I put in two spoonfuls and stirred them angrily. I took a sip and spat it into the sink.

Jean-Loup grabbed my hand. His lower lip quivered. Tears gathered at the edge of the thick lashes I'd once found so seductive.

I pushed past him and strode into the living room where,

stoic inside the tank, the last goldfish was facing the six piranhas.

'You're right.' Jean-Loup's voice wobbled. 'I'm sorry. I promise I'll make an effort. Orla, you've nowhere to go, so why don't you give me a few bags to take home?'

I glanced at the clock. What home? He still wasn't getting it.

I was treading on thin ice. If I pushed him too far, Stéphanie would return home to a war zone. I had to get him out of this flat quietly and fast. I softened my features and pleaded, 'Loulou I need time to think. I met Arnaud last night and I'm not sure what to make of him. Please let me digest all this… on my own.'

'But where will you sleep tonight?' His whiny tone grated on me.

'I've booked myself into a hotel.'

Before Jean-Loup could argue, I cut in with, '*Chéri*, if you're going to trust me, why not start now?' My whole body cringed at the blatant untruth.

He gave me a beseeching look, hugged me briefly, turned tail and closed the door.

I collapsed on a chair and dug my fingers into my hair. Oh God, what had I done? I couldn't stay in Paris. Wherever I went, Jean-Loup would hound me down. He was possessive to the point of madness. Where could I go? My head was spinning. Could I carry on with the sale of vintage clothes anywhere, with the occasional foray for supplies? As for tonight, I hadn't booked myself in a hotel. Marguerite had offered to put me up for a few days, at least until I sold my stock.

I tried calling her to arrange a time to meet but my phone battery was dead. I opened the laptop and sent her an e-mail to tell her that I accepted her offer of a room till the end of the week, stressing that she was to tell *no one* where I was. I checked my message and pressed 'send'.

I then made fresh coffee, stood by the fish tank and sipped it sadly as the remnants of an orange tail slowly floated this way and that, down… down… onto the gravel.

10
PARIS – ORLA

Buoyed by despair, I managed to return Stéphanie's flat to its minimalistic primness. Marguerite had despatched her boyfriend –Hector, a Senegalese psychology student who worked as a bouncer at weekends– to pick up my stock of dresses. It took him four trips in the 2CV.

Aude de Peirac knew what she was doing when she decided to set up a jewellery business. Unlike vintage clothing, or motorbike spare parts for that matter, jewellery is light, compact and lucrative.

I had just finished cleaning the lounge when Stéphanie buzzed the intercom. We'd briefly met before her trip to China, when she had introduced me to the Canal Saint Martin shops and explained her pets' feeding regimen.

She greeted me with me two resounding kisses. She really was stunning. Clad in Chinese raw silk, with ultra-short hair and a fit boyish body, she exuded that Parisian blend of class and impeccable taste.

She picked up Othello, who purred with delight, and dashed to the aquarium.

I winced, waiting for her to question me about the bright

orange tail still twitching on the gravel. Relieved to find her six monsters in good health, she didn't notice it.

'Would you like some coffee?' I asked, to entice her away from the crime scene, relieved when she agreed.

We carried our coffees to the balcony. An eerie light bounced around the yard, picking out the red of geraniums on sills and turning windowpanes to gold.

'Where will you be staying tonight?' Before I had time to reply, Stéphanie added, 'if you want, you can stay here.'

My heart warmed to her. 'Actually, I've had the most generous offer to spend a few –' the door buzzer stopped me in my tracks.

I ran to the intercom. Please God, not Jean-Loup again.

'Coucou ! C'est moi !' A familiar voice crackled.

Relieved, I pressed the button. 'It's Marguerite. She has a vintage shop Rue de Lancry.'

Puffed out from her climb, Marguerite burst in, sailed past me and wrapped Stéphanie into the folds of something out of the Age of Aquarius.

'Bonjour les filles !' She released Stéphanie and gave me two patchouli-scented kisses.

'You two know each other?' I gaped.

'Yes, Marguerite is a good customer,' Stéphanie said.

I gazed at each in turn. 'Marguerite is *your* customer? But, she's the one with the shop.'

'I love designer clothes.' Stéphanie encompassed her clutter-free zone with a move of the hand, 'and as you've noticed, I like it Zen. So, when I've finished with a garment, I give it to Marguerite and she sells it in her shop.'

Marguerite took over in franglish with much jangling of bracelets.

'Stéphanie, her clothes they are not old enough to be vintage. In England, you say pre-loved. She keep her clothes in very good condition and always, she keep the ticket. With the ticket, they sell very well.'

Jeepers, listen to those two. Who keeps clothes *labels*, for God's sake? The ones with the price and description… I realised that I would not last very long in this game. I should have stuck to valve springs and magnet coils. I was in the wrong trade. I needed to switch to something simpler.

They reverted to a French so peppered with slang, I completely lost track. Leaving them to their volleys of AK47 French, I went to the kitchen and returned with a tray.

Marguerite picked up her coffee, took a sip and put it down again, giving me a strange look.

'Is it too strong?'

'*Non, non, il est très bon.*' She shuffled on her seat, cleared her throat and twirled a finger to her temple. 'Tell me, Orla, your friend, Jean-Loup… is he not a little *fada*?'

Now there was a question. 'Why do you ask?'

She arranged her flouncy dress around her and told me in reasonably slow French, 'I had just closed my shop. Thank God, Hector was with me. We were sorting out stuff at the back when your boyfriend banged on the door and shouted, 'Open up! I know Orla's in there. I need to talk to her.' She leaned towards me, 'why did you tell that *pignouf* that you were staying with me, when it was supposed to be a secret?'

'I didn't.' I sat back on my chair and stared at her. 'I told him I'd booked a hotel.' It was as if Jean-Loup had second sight. 'Listen… I don't know what to say. I never mentioned you or your shop to him.' The two women were watching me. 'Honestly, I didn't. It's scary.'

How did Jean-Loup always know where I was? And then it hit me. My phone! I had texted Asha. I must have texted Marguerite too. Or had I? Had he checked my phone while I was asleep? A shiver ran through me.

Marguerite wriggled her nose. 'Urgh, what's that smell? Does anyone smell fish?'

At our feet, Othello was licking his paws.

I turned scarlet. The cat must have left the goldfish under the sofa.

Relaxed, Stéphanie stretched out with a happy smile. 'Ah, I am so glad you two are here. You know, I was dreading that first evening on my own. Why don't we order some food? Anything but Chinese! I don't want to eat rice for another six months. I'm dying for a real Italian pizza,' she giggled, 'without shrimp topping.'

Luckily, the phone number of the pizzeria was in the kitchen. While Stéphanie ordered our food, I put a finger to my lips, signalled to Marguerite to pull the sofa away from the wall, dived behind it, retrieved what was left of the fish, ran to the toilet to flush it away and washed my hands.

The pizzas arrived, Italian, huge and delicious. We opened a couple of bottles of wine, chilled out, and had a grand old time, counting our blessings instead of calories for a change.

Relaxed, comforted by the combination of wine and female camaraderie, I poured my heart out. Such was my new friends' empathy, I told them everything: Jean-Loup's possessiveness, the search for my real father, old de Peirac mistaking my interest for a come on, his roaming hands, Jean-Loup reading my texts, the broken vase, everything except the goldfish incident. Heck, did it feel good.

In the end, I fetched Mam's letter and laid it on the coffee table. Written on blue card, it rolled up of its own accord like a scroll.

Stéphanie took out a pair of round glasses. 'Oh, I know what this is. It's a *pneu*. A system people had in Paris till the eighties, a bit like a telegram.' She picked it up. 'This was pumped around Paris inside a tube.' She studied the message.

'Your guy's telling Mary he's sorry about not being able to go skating at Molitor.'

Though I did struggle with the vision of Mam on skates, I was warmed by the fact that anyone inviting her to such a healthy past time must have been a boy her own age, no depraved shark. Could he have been Arnaud? Damn, why didn't I ask him if he liked ice-skating?

'His signature is completely illegible.' Stéphanie adjusted her glasses and peered closer. 'Wait, the name is here again, at the front of the *pneu*. Look. Sender: Armand de Peirac.'

My heart missed a beat. 'What did you say?' I snatched the paper from her and took it to the light. It was no use. The name was indecipherable. However hard I tried, all I could see were waves.

Intrigued, Marguerite held out her hand. 'Show me.' She turned to me. 'That old man in the Pavillon Dauphine, he was called *Arnaud*, yes?'

I handed Marguerite the letter. She stared at it for a long time and returned her verdict.

'Stéphanie is right. It says *Armand*.'

I slumped down and groaned. Trust that eejit Jean-Loup to have got it wrong. Why did I listen to him?

Marguerite dropped the message on the coffee table and looked up, a grin spreading over her face. '*Formidable hein !* Arnaud is not your dad, so he can be your sugar daddy and take you to l'Hôtel Meurice!'

I silenced her with a murderous gaze.

She shrugged. '*Bof*, maybe not then. Listen, Arnaud, Armand, maybe they are the same family. I meet Aude tomorrow in my shop. She will know.'

Head spinning, I went out to the balcony and gazed out at the sea of roofs. In the distance, silent flashes of lightning shot through the inky sky. I felt soiled and dislocated, adrift in a city that clearly didn't want me. My boyfriend was a possessive predator and my potential father nothing but a pleasure seeker.

Paris wasn't safe anymore. If I stayed here, I'd be dragging Jean-Loup around like gum on my shoe. I had to leave, escape to a place where he wouldn't find me.

I wanted to run back to my parents, to the safety of my family, but going home wasn't an option until I'd made it. Overwhelmed by a sense of disappointment, I glanced down at the familiar courtyard for the last time. As the thunderstorm burst, Grandma Reilly's sharp voice clapped around my ears. *'What have you got to show for your life now, Orla, but two failed businesses and two failed love affairs?'*

She was right. I was a failure.

11

ORLA LEAVES PARIS

I left Paris at dawn. Mist rose from the canal along Quai de Valmy. Bathed in a pink haze, Paris was so beautiful it nearly broke my heart. I couldn't stay. The incident outside Marguerite's shop and the million pleading phone calls had proved that Jean-Loup was possessive to the point of madness. Wherever I was, he would pick up my scent and hunt me down. I had covered my tracks, pretended I was off to Dublin, purchased a new phone –one Jean-Loup could not hack– and told no one where I was going. No one except Asha, to whom I'd sent a mail before I left.

The bus to Gare de Lyon trundled through empty streets. Lifeless behind its shutters, Paris had turned its back on me. The bus stopped. A tramp manhandled his trolley into the standing area, a low trolley filched from a DIY store piled with everything he owned: clothes, mat, food, blankets, pillow, the lot topped with a folding chair. Heck, the fella owned more than I did. I pushed my case to make way for him. In the half-empty bus, he sidled up to me and held on to the bar, close enough for our arms to touch. I didn't move away. We remained like this, touching, all the way to Gare de Lyon. We were that lonely.

I was heading for Fleurac, a town in the remote Cévennes, a wild clump of mountains between the Massif Central and Provence, a place where one only ever went to if one wanted to hide.

I could have followed Marguerite's initial advice, done the Parisian thing, taken de Peirac as a lover and quizzed him, but the idea was beyond repulsive.

In the end his daughter, Aude, was the person we questioned to try and unravel the secrets of that aristocratic family.

'Leave it to me,' Marguerite suggested. 'I will pull the worms from her nose.'

What worms? My brain scrambled.

Thankfully, Aude volunteered information without the help of the strange torture. 'Yes, I have an uncle called Armand. His mother –she was called Arielle– had a chateau in some mountains and he has gone to live there.'

Arranging her jewellery in Marguerite's shop window, Aude de Peirac told us that her Uncle Armand had left Paris in the sixties and holed up in a *'bled'*, a God-forsaken backwater called Pétaouchnock.

Marguerite stopped me before I had time to search for it on a map and make a complete fool of myself. The equivalent of Much-Binding-in-the-Marsh, Pétaouchnock did not exist.

'Uncle Armand, yeah, he's, like…' Aude had spent time in New York, I could tell. 'I mean, the guy is, like… the bad sheep of the family?'

In a way, I was relieved. That Armand didn't live in Paris was good news. At this stage of my life, a *'bled'* in the middle of nowhere was exactly what I needed. Not only would my quarry be easier to track down, but in Pétaouchnock, Jean-Loup would never find me.

The stark portrait Aude had painted of Armand put the last damper on my fantasies of chateaux, infinity pools and the chance to gallop through my own forest. In my mind, 'Armand-the-black-sheep' became a Poldark character, an aristocrat who had lost everything but his noble heart.

Noble hearts and black sheep were all very well, but there were limits to what I was prepared to accept. What she said next worried me so much that I nearly gave up on my search, until I realised that her English was to blame.

'Armand lived in Paris near my father when they were young.' The girl's American twang grated on my ears. 'Then, in May 68, during a *manif,* he was knocked on the head with a cosh, you know, and he went, like kinda weird?'

Hmmm. It did not sound good.

'Ah, yeah, I remember now.' She threaded necklaces and coloured shapes through her long fingers. 'The place where he lives is called Fleurac. I stopped there once, like, on the way to Juan Les Pins? He works in a *librairie*.' She put the last touches to her display in the window, while Marguerite and I admired her perfect jean-clad derrière.

'Holy Mary mother of God.' I gripped Marguerite's arm the moment Aude left the shop, 'what will I do with a mentally deficient librarian in Petaouchnock?'

'*Mais non*, she did not mean that.' She patted my hand. '*Librairie* is a false-friend word. We learn it at school. It mean bookshop. Her uncle, he sell books. That's good, yes? This man, he is an old intellectual sixty-eighter. Me, I think he sounds very interesting. Yes, I would like to meet this man. And his mother too. She must be beautiful because Arielle is a beautiful name.'

Marguerite was right. Books were good. I could cope with books, and as for the thump to the head with a cosh, it was no big deal, Marguerite went on to explain. 'May sixty-eight was a mad time. Everyone was angry, so they were all hit on the head. There were *flics,* yes cops everywhere, coshing people down. It was normal.'

Distilling her Franglish, I understood that after a brief revolution, a cohort of youngsters gave up on the modern world and headed south to lead simpler lives in the sun away from capitalism and *la société de consommation*. They stuck to their ideology and became a consistent socio-economic group referred to as 'sixty-eighters,' *soixante-huitards.* They practiced free love, renovated cottages and ate everything *bio*, which is the French for organic.

From her description, I pictured those sixty-eighters like a breed of Forty-Niners who, instead of panning for gold, searched for the true meaning of life. Strange though, I couldn't see Mam falling for a hippie. I was intrigued.

Unsure as to how to proceed, I thought it might be best to head for the Cévennes, locate the bookshop, observe yer man from afar and if –and only *if* –I liked him, and had *absolute* proof that he was my biological father, would I make a move.

Marguerite agreed that it was a good plan and it could not go wrong.

PART II

JEANNE - FLEURAC - 1944

12

FLEURAC – MAY 1944

Jeanne held up the lantern and placed a careful clog on the steps leading down to the cellar. A chilly breath, redolent of the brews once held in Papé's casks rose from the vaulted space. She hooked the lantern on a nail, flicked back her plaits and began to fill a basket with eggs, padding the space between them with chestnut leaves. When this was done, she carefully lowered the basket into a donkey pannier slung over a trestle near the stairs.

'Jeanne? Be careful with the eggs, won't you? They're for Arielle,' Mamé called out from the top of the steps. 'Did you find the ham? It's right at the back, inside a cask.'

Jeanne's gaze went to the back of the cellar. The faint glow of the candle didn't reach the casks inside which Mamé had hidden the ham in case of a German raid. It really wasn't fair, in four years of war, the *boches* had plundered everything from the Cévennes. They had taken food, coal and men, forcing them to work in Germany. Those who had tried to avoid Hitler's *Service de Travail Obligatoire* had been shot or sent to camps. Lucien had escaped just in time, but if he was caught... Jeanne felt sick at the thought.

'Wretched *boches* have got their noses into everything these days,' Mamé grumbled, a foot on the first step. 'We thought they'd stop at Vichy, above the demarcation line, didn't we?' She carefully trod on the second step. 'But no, they found our mountains and made themselves right at home here.'

Now that Mamé was here, Jeanne went to the casks and felt about for the ham, unable to stop herself from checking over her shoulder. She was fourteen now and ought to be braver. She had always believed that a wolf hid in the cellar.

Tales of the famous Gévaudan Beast, told in Occitan while she sat on her grandfather's lap, still haunted her. That wolf was part of the local lore. It had fed her childhood nightmares.

'You silly goose, that beast has been dead for near two hundred years,' Lucien used to reason from his bed across the room. Nine years older than her, Lucien was afraid of nothing. Not even the Germans.

'I can't find it, Mamé.'

'There it is.' Mamé tilted an empty cask and pulled out the ham.

Jeanne spread a newspaper over the trestle. On the front page, an article caught her eye. Three German *Feldgendarmes* had been killed when their jeep blew up just before the Fleurac Bridge. She re-read the article. It had happened last Friday, four days ago. In the cellar, the temperature dropped several degrees. Mamé must have known. Why had she not mentioned it?

Mamé placed the ham on the trestle. 'You saw it huh?' She let out a sad breath. 'Resisting is all very well, and I'm all for making life difficult for the Germans, but we know exactly what's going to happen now.'

'Is that why there've been so many jeeps on the road?'

'There will be searches, reprisals. Makes you wonder if it's worth it for just three *boches.*' Mamé snorted, 'plenty more where they came from.'

'Did Lucien have anything to do with it?' Lucien and his gang of resistance fighters were hiding a few miles away in the old silk factory.

'He'd have more sense than that I hope.' From the face Mamé made as she folded the paper around the ham, Jeanne wasn't so sure.

'The silk factory isn't safe for them anymore. You'll tell them, won't you. They must leave soon.'

Her movements now heavy, Jeanne buried the ham under a layer of leaves deep inside the pannier, covered it with several pots of honey, and dragged the lot to the top of the steps. Mamé blew out the candle and pushed the lantern back into its niche.

Outside, solid heat filled the yard. Shielding her eyes from the sun, Jeanne searched out Boniface and found him dozing under the old mulberry tree on the second terrace. She whistled softly for him to join her in the shade of the stables.

Mamé pulled out a trowel from the rack above the water pump. 'Pick the dandelion on your way back. Don't skimp huh? Dig as much of the root as you can.'

'I thought dandelion was better dug out in November. You said it had more properties.' Jeanne took a broom and swept stray strands of hay back into the stable.

Mamé's round face wrinkled into a grin. 'You'll make a fine herbalist, Ninou, but I don't need it for remedies. We're nearly out of dandelion coffee. I'll dry the roots in the bread-oven tomorrow and make some more.'

'I saw some below the chateau. Mademoiselle d'Aubrac hasn't grazed her horse there yet.' Jeanne inhaled Boniface's comfortable smell as she tightened the girth under his stomach.

Mamé threw a short blanket over the donkey's back. 'Arielle sure won't need dandelion. I'd say they get real coffee over at the chateau… now that de Peirac's a regular.' She added, 'He's asked for her hand, you know.'

Jeanne dropped the strap she was adjusting. 'What? But… you said, you said he works for the Germans!' The whole thing did not make sense. 'Why would Mademoiselle marry a collaborator when she can have the pick of the bunch?'

'The pick of what bunch? All the young men are in hiding or sent to work in Germany.' Mamé fetched a jute sack from the stable and shook it. An aura of dust motes enveloped her. 'In spite of all her fancy titles, Arielle d'Aubrac is on the shelf. Turned twenty-five on St Catherine's day. Big silk merchants once, the d'Aubracs, but you know what they say, "from clogs to clogs in three generations..."The old Marquis was never any good with money.' She folded the bag and pushed it into a panier. 'From what I heard, Albin De Peirac may be full of himself, but he's also full of money, so if Arielle married him, it would be the end of all their problems. Well, their money problems.'

Mademoiselle Arielle was lovely. How could she marry for money? Jeanne stamped a clog. 'I'd rather *die* than marry a traitor.'

Though she was only fourteen, Jeanne had already received an offer of marriage. After licking her face like a slobbering ox, André, the carpenter's eldest son had told her he loved her. They would marry, he said, when she was old enough. Confident that she would pass her school leavers' *'certificat d'études'* –he had failed his– André had decided that she would help him with his carpentry business.

His presumption had left Jeanne speechless. She had set her hopes on becoming a schoolteacher but… what could she do? His parents were family friends and a great help to Mamé. Once she was at college, Jeanne hoped he would forget about her. In the meantime, she was polite and took great care not to encourage him. Mistaking her reticence for virtue, André waited with confidence.

Mamé handed Jeanne a second bag. 'Dig up the whole plant but do leave a tiny bit of root so it grows again next year. We can't leave gathering it any later. It'll only be trampled on by the sheep on their way up to the plateau.'

Jeanne's heart lifted. She loved the transhumance –thousands of sheep aiming for fresh grass on top of the plateau– great swathes of bleating sheep cascading down gullies, covering whole mountainsides with a living white froth… a wonderful harbinger of summer.

While Mamé chatted on, Jeanne lifted Boniface's hoofs one by one and checked that his shoes held firmly.

'We'll eat the leaves as salad. I'll dry some to make a diuretic tisane. I've a few customers with kidney problems. It's not called *pissenlit* for nothing.'

Jeanne giggled. 'They'll piss in their beds?'

Mamé came from a long line of healers who had inherited the gift. She could remove warts and heal burns, something Jeanne was learning to do.

The parlour, a cluttered room behind the kitchen, had been turned into an apothecary where Mamé stored the herbs and remedies she used to treat ailments that left doctors powerless.

She had cured Mademoiselle when she was a child. Shocked by the death of her mother –the Marquise d'Aubrac had died of consumption– three-year-old Arielle had stopped talking. Mamé had got the little girl to speak again and as a result, was taken on as a nanny. Though the d'Aubracs lived in a chateau, Mamé never had to stand on ceremony with Mademoiselle.

'Mamé...' Jeanne could not let the matter rest, 'how can Mademoiselle d'Aubrac even *consider* a collaborator?'

'I don't know, Ninou. These people aren't like us.' Mamé rubbed the donkey's head. He nudged her pockets, looking for titbits. Finding none, he turned towards the road. Mamé held on to his halter.

Jeanne insisted, 'He's French, so why would that man work for the enemy?'

'You were only a baby then, but in the thirties, there was a lot of unrest. Strikes. Businesses went under and rich people were terrified of another revolution, of Communism taking away what they had. People like de Peirac don't trust the Resistance to do the right thing.'

'Is Lucien a communist?'

Mamé uttered a tired sigh. 'Your brother is a hot head, that's all he is. Listen, make sure you tell him that Fleurac isn't safe anymore.'

'André said his brother is one of them.'

'One of what?'

'A communist.'

'Oh, for goodness' sake, Jeanne, André's brother is seventeen. What does he know about anything? These boys swallow half-baked ideas without a notion as to what they mean. We've all heard stories about Russia and what goes on there. Marcel is a very silly boy and he should keep his mouth shut. He's playing with fire.'

Jeanne thought of asking another question but, thinking better of it, she buried her face in the donkey's neck and rubbed his stiff mane. How on earth would they cope if Lucien left? What if a downpour took down a terrace? After Papa's death in the coal mine last year, Lucien and his comrades had left their hiding place every night to lend a hand around their little farm, but there was only so much anyone could do under cover of darkness.

A few months ago, Lucien's French Resistance fighters were joined by a cell of Germans pacifists, enemies of Hitler. Their leader was called Karl. Tall and charismatic, he looked like the hero he was. Over the past few months, Jeanne had watched Karl fell trees, catch rabbits, fix the heavy stone tiles of their roof, and listened wide-eyed to his talks of a world without poverty in which men and women would be equal.

Powerful, mysterious, Karl reigned over her heart like a Nordic god. There was something about him that made the world an exciting place. Lucien said that back in his country, Karl was an artist. This was no surprise, his drawings were the best she had ever seen.

Mamé straightened the panniers and checked their balance.

'Off you go. Not a word about that ham, huh? If you meet anyone, remember, you're just taking food to the chateau.'

'Mamé! As if I would betray my own brother!'

Jeanne kissed her grandmother's soft cheek, shortened the lead and led Boniface down the steep path. Once on the road, she looked up and waved. Tiny in front of the squat grey house, Mamé looked so frail, as if a gust of wind could take her. Jeanne felt a surge of love for her, for that patch of sloping soil where her roots ran as deep as those of the mulberry tree, for her home, solid, built from local schist, melting into the hill.

This life didn't suit everyone. After the death of Papa in the mine, Maman had gone up to Paris to work in service. Jeanne had insisted on remaining with Mamé, here in the Cévennes. She hated towns. People starved there and anyway, Paris was full of Germans.

Here, the manured terraces gave them all the vegetables they needed. Above their cottage, at the edge of the chestnut forest, ten grey slate-topped beehives Papé had once carved out of tree trunks allowed them to forget that sugar was rationed.

Boniface set off at a leisurely pace. At a cross road, he stopped, pricked his ears, and shivering with anticipation, brayed in response to the sound of hooves clip-clopping up the hill.

The graceful figure of Arielle d'Aubrac appeared through the trees. She lifted a hand in greeting and bowed her neck.

'*Bonjour* Jeannette!' the chatelaine called out in French when they were level. Mademoiselle understood Occitan – Mamé had taught her– but she spoke proper French.

'*Adiou* Mademoiselle.' Jeanne curtsied. Her cheeks burning under the green gaze, she asked permission to dig for dandelions.

'You'll soon be sitting your *certificat d'études* won't you, Jeannette?' Arielle added with a smile, 'I know you will do well.'

This was what made her so special. She was kind. But if she was kind, how could she even… perhaps the poor Mademoiselle had no choice.

Meanwhile, the donkey nudged the mare's elegant head with his nose, eliciting a soft whinny, nostrils flared in delight.

Boniface and Mademoiselle d'Aubrac's chestnut mare had become something of a legend when one spring day, the mare had escaped from her stable and, ignoring stallions of impeccable pedigree, met up with Boniface at the edge of the river for an illicit tryst. A year later, she had given birth to a mule, and in Fleurac, it was whispered that if Monsieur d'Aubrac did not marry off his daughter soon, he might find his lineage similarly tainted.

Arielle cantered away towards the turrets of her father's chateau, leaving Jeanne to pant up the hill behind her lovesick donkey.

Things had changed here in the past year. Around once abandoned houses, washing hung on lines, and terraces were freshly planted with vegetables. As the War progressed, the Cévennes became a haven for strange newcomers. Because they knew about persecution, the pastor had explained, Protestants would always protect refugees. Jeanne's school had taken in children who, though they gave their names as 'Jacques' or 'Maurice,' spoke hardly any French. Pastors preached tolerance, and Lucien had told her that farmers never refused food to anyone knocking on their shutters at night.

At the edge of the forest, Jeanne halted to wipe her forehead. Out of nowhere, a man slid from the bank.

She screamed.

Lucien grabbed the donkey's halter and laughed.

Jeanne's hand jumped to her heart. 'Idiot, you scared me! I was just on my way to you.'

Her brother lifted a corner of the bag covering a pannier. 'Ha ha! Eggs, just what we need. Let's see… what else have we got in here?'

Jeanne pushed his away hand. 'Sorry, the eggs aren't for you. But wait to see what I do have…'

A movement further up the bank drew her eye. Leaning against a trunk, hand in a pocket, Karl was watching her, a smile etched at the corner of his lips.

Her heart flipped. Aware that she was turning pink, she busied herself with the ham, Karl's gaze burning her neck.

He jumped down onto the road. His German accent so much nicer than that of soldiers heard barking orders around the square in Fleurac, Karl said, 'Little Channe, you look like a spirit of the forest.' Suddenly serious, his voice softened. He lowered his eyes and told her, 'I have a sister. She is called Klara. You remind me of her.'

Jeanne forced herself to meet his gaze. Karl was so strong,

so sure of himself, with so much to offer the world. When the war ended, Jeanne knew he would make it a better place, and she couldn't wait to be part of it.

'This is for all of you up there.' She pulled out the ham.

'*Formidable.*' Lucien rubbed his hands. 'A whole hock, what a treat! We were growing tired of chestnut bread and dandelion leaves, weren't we, Karl?' Lucien took the ham from her. 'I'd planned to kidnap a few sheep from the plateau when they arrive with the transhumance, but the others weren't keen.

'Are you in danger?' Jeanne searched Lucien's face for an admission of guilt, the murder of the three German soldiers heavy on her mind. She took his hand. 'Lucien, Mamé says you must leave.'

'We'll be leaving very soon. Don't worry. The locals are protecting us.' With a grimace, he added, 'It's not the *boches* we're worried about, it's the militia, that band of thugs.' He spat. 'To think they're French… But don't worry, Jeannette. The war is nearly over. The Allies are on their way. Right now, we're awaiting orders. We'll be out of here in a couple of days.'

Jeanne's heart sank. 'Mamé wants you to promise. She's heard things…'

Boniface's ears tilted.

An engine was labouring up the hill.

Jeanne turned around in alarm, but there was no one there, only the forest. Lucien and Karl had vanished. She took measured breaths and prodded Boniface, praying for the car to drive past without stopping.

A change of gear. A knot formed in her stomach. The car slowed down and pulled up beside her in a patch of sunlight, forcing the donkey against the bank. The window rolled down. A pale hand beckoned to her.

Jeanne approached reluctantly. Her throat constricted. Had she been seen speaking with the two men?

Impassive, a burly driver in German uniform stared ahead, hands on the steering wheel. A man in a black suit raised his gaze to her. Dark and cruel under hooded lids, his small eyes curdled her blood. His alabaster complexion and brushed back hair, shiny with Brillantine reminded her of a vampire.

'*Messieurs.*' She curtsied, clutching her skirt to hide her trembling hands.

'Where are you going?' The voice was metallic, the French educated.

Jeanne faltered. '*Au... au chateau, Monsieur.*' She pointed to her panniers and said in a hoarse breath, 'Mademoiselle d'Aubrac wanted some eggs.'

Pinning her under his steely gaze, the Frenchman said, 'did she now?' The next question hit her like the lash of a whip. 'Your name?'

Jeanne licked her dry lips. 'Jeanne Bessière.' Her heart was beating so hard, she was sure he could hear it.

'Any relation to Lucien Bessière?'

Jeanne's throat closed up. Tears pricked the back of her eyes. In the forest above them, the sharp crack of a branch rang out in the still heat. Desperate to stop her gaze from moving in the direction where the boys had vanished, Jeanne focused on the man's arm resting on the car door. A gold cufflink caught the sun, so close, she could make out the shape of a heraldic wolf.

The man tapped a finger on the side of the car. 'Well?'

Jeanne conjured up Karl's aura around her like a cloak, and met the cruel eyes. 'Yes. He's my brother. I – I haven't seen him in two years.' She held the reptilian stare and added, 'he's in Switzerland.'

'You know what happens to people who shelter deserters.'

Jeanne nodded slowly. This man knew something. She wished she could put a spell on him. But she was powerless. She was an apprentice herbalist and she was only fourteen.

Boniface lifted his big head and flared his nostrils. A joyous cacophony drifted up from the valley. Echoes of bleats and bells filled the forest, preceded by a strong smell of lanolin. A dog sprang from a path and made for Boniface's legs. The terrified donkey leapt forward and blocked the car. The caped figure of a shepherd briefly materialised, flanked by two pompomped rams and a malevolent billy goat. The shepherd cast the car an indifferent glance and strode towards a sunken lane a hundred yards ahead, followed by twenty thousand pregnant ewes, artistically sheared around the neck and shoulders, marked in various colours.

Jeanne's spirits soared. It was now or never. She grabbed the bridle and shot out in the shepherd's wake, putting a solid sea of sheep between her and her tormentor, thrust ahead by a groundswell of sheep pouring out of the forest towards the promise of lush grass. She glanced backwards with a sigh of relief. Only the top of the car was visible. The French militia-man and his German driver would be trapped for hours. Lucien and Karl were safe for another day.

13
FLEURAC – JUNE 11TH 1944

Inside the old Protestant chapel, the June air fizzed. Raucous hymns lifted the roof with an energy not felt for years. Jeanne sat on the hard pew, drinking in the pastor's words.

'Last Tuesday, the Allies landed in Normandy!' A loud cheer rose from the assembly. The pastor explained that the job at hand was now to obstruct the movement of German supplies heading north.

The old walls vibrated with relief and hope bursting from the hymns. At the end of the service, the flock spilled out onto the church forecourt in a babble of news.

'The *boches* weren't expecting them,' said one.

'They'll be in Fleurac by Christmas,' said another.

Jeanne pushed through the crowd and stopped by the plane tree to which she had tied Boniface. The rope was there, but the donkey had gone.

'Oh no!' She stamped her foot. Where had he gone this time?

Mamé was talking to Pujol, the carpenter. 'Boniface has run away again. I'll go and look for him.'

'I'll come with you.' Anticipation was written all over André's face.

'No thanks. I'll be fine. I'll ride him home through the woods.'

'It's dangerous in the woods, Jeannette.' The young carpenter took her hand, the scenario playing out in his mind all too obvious. His scent of cologne made Jeanne gag. She stepped away from him and hid her embarrassment with a giggly, 'I'm not afraid of the big bad wolf.'

This was not completely true. She was very much afraid of what André wanted, and anyway, she thought kissing was disgusting. Mamé had laughed at that and told her she'd soon change her mind.

She wouldn't.

Before André could insist, Jeanne darted down the road with a fair idea of where to find her lovesick animal.

It was a glorious day. She skipped down to the stream, buoyed with the sheer delight that soon the war would be over. She twirled, took deep drafts of moss-scented air and let her fingers run over rough bark. Yes, soon the war would end and Lucien would come home. She would go to college, train to be a teacher, and leave André Pujol far behind.

A splash downstream stopped her in her tracks. She crept forward and heard laughter... murmurs. Her steps muffled by soft leaves and the sound of flowing water, Jeanne tiptoed to a large oak and peered around it.

What she saw took her breath away. Entwined in a deep pool, Karl and Arielle looked like they were dancing, their naked bodies golden in a shaft of sunlight. Jeanne rested her cheek on the cool bark, entranced by their beauty. Oh... this is what love looks like...

Karl ran his fingers through Arielle's chestnut hair, caressed the small of her back, lifted her chin and gazed into her eyes as they twirled in a slow waltz, lost in each other.

Spellbound, Jeanne hugged the tree with a sigh of longing, beset with sensations she did not understand. She had seen Karl's muscles ripple as he felled trees, strong and powerful. Moulded around Arielle, his body was protective, loving, and strangely vulnerable.

The young German lifted Arielle out of the water, laid her on the grass and, lightly running a finger along the curve of her neck, her waist, her hip, he studied her, as if wanting to commit every fold of her alabaster skin to memory.

Time stopped. Bar the noise of the brook, everything was still. Even the magpies had ceased chattering.

A sigh escaped Jeanne's lips. Mamé was right after all. Love was beautiful. But her grandmother was wrong in thinking that Mademoiselle d'Aubrac had no better offer than de Peirac. The traitor may have asked for her hand, but she had not said yes.

Of course, Arielle would have to wait for the war to be over –Karl was German after all– but the Allies were on their way and soon, the two of them would be free to marry. Karl would stay at the chateau and from there, set about creating the beautiful new world he had promised. He would do so right here, in Fleurac and Jeanne knew she would be part of it.

She cast a last glance at the lovers entwined on the grass and quietly skipped away, her heart bursting with hope.

14
FLEURAC – JUNE 1944

Jeanne did pass her *'certificat d'études.'* Brand new calligraphed diploma in hand, plaits bouncing on her shoulders, she clomped up the path, shouting, 'I passed, Mamé, I passed!'

'Of course, you did, Ninou,' Mamé laughed from the yard. 'You're such a clever girl.' Eyes damp, she hugged Jeanne tightly against her. 'Your mother will be so proud of you, my Jeannette, so proud.'

'I'll write to Maman tonight. As for Papa...' they glanced over to the iron railing of the grave at edge of the forest. Jeanne would tell him later.

She considered her new status with mixed feelings. No more school, no more singing *'Maréchal nous voilà,'* hand on heart to the glory of Marshall Pétain at the start of each day. No more long icy treks in winter. Her stomach curdled. No more helping the teacher with the little ones.

It was the end of her childhood and soon, it would be the end of the war. Everyone said so. Maman and Lucien would come home to farm and life would return to normal.

'Mamé?' She asked moments later as they sat in the kitchen.

Mamé turned from the stone *souillarde* where she was scrubbing vegetables.

'Can I go and tell Lucien?'

'Yes, but hurry. They're leaving tonight.' Mamé nodded to herself. 'And not a moment too soon. They hung around much longer than was safe.' She sloshed out the water into the shallow sink, wiped her hands and took two warm chestnut loaves from the dresser. 'Here, put these in your backpack. Don't forget the goat cheeses Pujol sent for the journey.'

Her clogs ringing on the asphalt, Jeanne skipped up the road that snaked around hills planted with sparse chestnut trees. Half an hour later, she glimpsed the top of the silk factory above a clump of mulberry trees.

'Silk Factory' was too grand a name for the tall grey warehouse perched on a thin ledge. Even a century ago when the enterprising Marquis d'Aubrac had the foresight to import mulberries and bed them down in his Cévennes soil, the place had never employed more than ten people to gather, boil and spin silk cocoons.

The slope was steep and her backpack heavy. Jeanne stopped, took a few calming breaths and started again, trying to convince herself that Karl and Lucien were going to a safer place, that they would be all right. They had been here too long. France was a tinderbox. Swarms of angry Germans buzzed at every corner. Their backs against the wall, the French militia men behaved like rabid dogs.

A sound caught Jeanne's attention in the valley below. A car. Who could be driving up here at the end of the afternoon? The hairs bristled at the nape of her neck. Not one, but two engines were revving up the hill. She scanned the sheer banks for a place to hide but the trees were too sparse.

If anyone asked her where she was going, what would she say? Herbs, yes that was it. She was gathering herbs. No. She rubbed her sweaty palms against each other. One look at her and they would know. The militia would torture the truth out of her. The revving came closer. Jeanne spun around. Tears blurred her vision. There was nowhere to hide.

In the shallow ditch ahead, a glistening rock caught her eye, a trickle of water dripped from the hill into a large pipe that ran under the road. Jeanne hurried towards it, slipped on moss and landed in a freezing puddle, inches below the wheels of a black car followed by a jeep.

She peered through a clump of ferns and fell back with a whimper. It was *that* car again, heading towards Lucien's hideout. She caught a glimpse of khaki. Germans. *No, please God, no.*

She scrambled up, pushed her bag under a layer of leaves and hurled herself at the sheer slope, clutching at roots and undergrowth in a frantic attempt to reach the building before the cars. The *boches* still had to negotiate three bends in the road and their engines were struggling. Surely Lucien and Karl would hear them and escape to the woods. A mule path to the right of the building would be the only way for the enemy to reach the factory. Perhaps she would have time to scramble up from the left. Jeanne grunted with the effort. 'Please, God, please… Just give me time to warn them...'

The cars could only go so far, the noise would betray their approach.

On the last bend, gears screeched and engines laboured up. Thorns dug at Jeanne's legs, but she knew she could beat them. She made a last dash, wiped the sweat from her face and looked up. Twenty yards above her loomed the grey wall, perched above several impassable terraces. The schist crumbed under her feet. 'Climb… climb.' Relief… as a large rock held her weight. Her fingers slipped in the mud. She was so close, she was in with a chance.

Below the wall, she opened her mouth to shout a warning but the cars had stopped. Harsh voices reached her. Someone shouted something. Just above her, a window was open. The cars *must* have been heard inside…

She squeezed through a breach in the last retaining stonewall, hauled herself up to the next terrace, hid behind an ancient water butt and checked the layout for places to hide. Right at the top was a row of outbuildings. A deep irrigation gully ran along the edge of the forest, an open gutter a foot deep, lined with upright slates.

The soldiers were now sprinting up the path, keeping to the grass to deaden the noise of their boots.

Crying with fear, Jeanne flattened herself behind the rotten planks and made herself as small as she could. She bit her hand to muffle her sobs, waited until they had gone past and crawled up to the gully.

Just as she reached the shelter of the gully, the stillness was shattered by shouts, crashing glass and an explosion. Over screams of agony, a sharp metallic voice barked out an order. The words punched Jeanne in the chest. The order was in French.

Who were these men? If they wore German uniforms, why did they speak French? More shots erupted inside. She crouched on the cold stone and sobbed, 'No, no please God, not Lucien, please…'

She pressed her hands to her ears to blot out the screams.

A movement startled her. Not ten yards in front of her, a man darted out of an outbuilding. *Lucien!* Jeanne stopped herself from calling out his name.

'Aqui!' From the yard, someone yelled in Occitan, 'up there, there he is. *'Zo!'* He's escaping!'

Jeanne edged back, her insides coiling. *Run Lucien, run!*

Lucien didn't run. He stepped out of the cover of the *clède*, a sort of winter store, in full view of the soldiers.

No! What the... Her eyes bulging with horror, Jeanne stuffed her hand into her mouth.

Rock splintered inches from his face. Lucien ignored it and leapt out. With a single kick, he sent a hive flying down the hill and darted up into the forest... swallowed by shadows.

Two men scrambled up towards the gully, bellowing in patois. Jeanne heard their laboured breath a few feet away from her. She willed the ground to swallow her.

Driven mad by the smell of sweat and fear, clouds of bees burst forth from the hive and went for the soldiers. They buzzed around their heads, they clung to bare skin, they stung through thick cloth and they stung their eyes.

'Sting sting, sting!' Jeanne silently urged them on.

The men screamed in patois, scratched at their eyes and waved their guns in front of their faces. One of them tripped and fell, set upon by a furious battalion of bees. His friends dragged him away.

Inhuman howls from inside the house. Pain seared Jeanne's solar plexus. Karl! Karl was in there. Cowering in the mud, she prayed. 'Dear God, he's a good man, please spare him.'

From the house came one shot, and then another. The sharp French voice shouted an order. Jeanne knew that voice. Authoritative, educated, metallic, she had heard it before.

It was over. The buzzing receded. The German boots stomped away. A last order was given out in French. A moan, a last shot, a wooden door banging against its frame, unhurried steps. Engines revved and sped down towards Mende, leaving Jeanne alone in the leaden silence.

15
THE SILK FACTORY

Teeth chattering, Jeanne remained curled into a ball. Slowly, she unfurled and leaned against the cool stone, her breath coming out in ragged bursts.

A crow squawked above her. Around the upturned hive, the buzzing was now purposeful, the swarm rallying around its queen.

Confident that the bees would ignore her light-coloured dress and bland scent of mud, Jeanne crept out of her hiding place, Papé's voice protecting her like a veil. *'Bees hate dark colours Ninou. Bees fear black bears that steal their honey, so if you wear white, they won't notice you.'*

Papé... Jeanne blinked away her tears. How she wished he was here.

She took unsteady steps towards the outbuildings, her eyes drawn up to the edge of the woods, where Lucien had disappeared. He would be on the other side of the hill by now, slipping down the soft earth, hunted, a stag at bay.

She negotiated the narrow steps cut out of the terrace, her ears pricked for signs of life inside. All she could hear was her own heart. She halted by the door, pushed it open and froze. Amongst fragments of wood and broken glass, two bodies were sprawled out on the floor, horribly mauled. The space was already filled with the solid hum of flies attracted by the smell.

'Dagmar…' The young German's face was ripped, his eye dangled on his cheek, his curly brown mop soaked in blood. The other boy was a young apprentice from Lyon. Jeanne did not remember his name.

She heaved and pushed her plaits away from her face, wishing she could un-see the boys slaughtered like rabbits. Her body shook, unable to absorb the horror.

She ran out towards a patch of fresh grass. Leaning against a fence, she wiped the sweat from her face with the hem of her dress, smearing her cheek with mud. It could have been Lucien. Her head spun. Her legs went from under her.

She woke inside a cotton wool cloud, her ears ringing. Her fingers touched cool grass, real and comforting, but when the memory returned, the picture of what she had seen threatened to send her right back into nothingness.

A thought jolted her.

Karl. Where was Karl?

She had to go back. She waited for the blood to return to her head and sat up. It took everything she had to return to that kitchen. Sobbing, she staggered in, squeezed through the half-open door and skirted around what was left of the table, focusing on the lines on the stone floor and the crackling of a radio.

She reached the door of the large room, rested her forehead on the cool wall, inhaled a long draft of fetid air, and went in.

At the other end, Karl lay crumpled at the foot of a makeshift easel. Next to him was his harmonica. He had been drawing Arielle's fairy-tale chateau down in the valley. Had the window been pointing the other way, he would have seen the attackers, and run to safety.

Jeanne stepped over a makeshift mattress. Avoiding a spreading pool of blood, she knelt next to him and touched his face. His skin was warm. He was still breathing.

'Karl?'

His eyes flickered. The shadow of a smile ran across his face.

'Klara…'

Jeanne stroked his thick hair, gleaming in the sunshine.

A look of pure love softened his features. 'Klara.' He repeated his sister's name.

Her face wet with tears, Jeanne reached out for his hand and softly whispered the only German she knew, *'Ja Karl, ja.'*

With a last breath, he uttered a hoarse whisper. *'Mein Skizzenbuch – clède.'* His hand went slack.

She collapsed on top of him and howled.

Why? Why him? All Karl had ever wanted was peace.

'Man is a wolf for man,' Papé used to say.

This was what men did to each other. There would never be peace. She knew that now.

16

FLEURAC – JUNE 1944

They told no one. For three long days, Jeanne and Mamé lived with the terrible knowledge of those bodies festering on the hill, listening out for German cars, waiting for that knock on the door. But no one came. Only when she was sure that all danger had passed, had Mamé gone to the pastor and told him that 'while she was gathering herbs', she thought she had heard shots coming from the old silk farm.

They had just begun to relax when Mamé came come home from the market with the news that Marcel, André's brother, had been caught during a raid and was held in a cell. The circumstances of his arrest were not clear.

'A train with German soldiers was blown up north of Mende,' Mamé said. 'The militia was trawling the region, looking for culprits. They found Marcel with a communist pamphlet in his pocket.'

'What will happen to him?' Jeanne could not believe how stupid Marcel had been. How many times had André warned his brother that by acting recklessly, he was putting his whole family in danger?

'Nothing will happen to him.' Mamé unwrapped the small piece of lard that was supposed to last them the month, and placed it on a saucer. 'He's a child. He'll be released soon.'

The calm way Mamé folded her shopping bag went some way to reassure Jeanne. She returned to the job she had begun that morning: mucking out the stable. It had been Papé's responsibility until the effects of the mustard gas he had breathed in the trenches, back in 1915, finally killed him. After Papé's death, Papa had taken over. He'd managed to fit in the job when he wasn't digging coal to sustain the German war effort. When Papa died in a gas blast, Lucien was already in hiding, so Jeanne had inherited the chore.

'*Quala calor*,' Jeanne mumbled to herself. She brushed back tendrils of hair from her face and leaned on her fork. Her thoughts returning to her brother, her glance strayed to the back of the stable door where every year on their birthday, Mamé would measure how much Jeanne and her brother had grown. Lucien had stopped growing now. An old cap of his hung on a hook. He still had not given them sign of life. He never did. He was protecting them.

Three years ago, Jeanne was eleven at the time, Lucien had received his papers.

'No way am I going to work for Hitler!' He'd shouted and, before anyone had time to tell him it was folly, he had hurled the letter into the fire and that night, he was gone.

She could still hear the boots on the cobbled yard the next day, the fists thundering on their door. In spite of the heat, Jeanne shivered at the memory.

'*Raus!*' A soldier had grabbed her mother and shoved her against the stable wall with the end of his gun. Terrified, Mamé had shielded Jeanne against her while the house and outbuildings were searched for signs of Lucien. Jeanne could still feel the wool of her mother's skirt in her fingers, and Maman, shaking with sobs.

One of the soldiers had lifted his gun and aimed it at them. Mamé had placed a hand on Jeanne's head and said in a strong voice, 'Jeannette. It's time for us to commend our soul to God.'

The three of them had prayed. Trembling hands joined together, they had mouthed the words and waited to die, while inside the house German soldiers thrashed chests, emptied wardrobes, upturned casks and kicked the sides of the chicken coop, scattering the hens into the forest.

Just as Jeanne thought they were about to be shot, the soldiers left, taking with them the contents of the larder and the last of Papé's wine.

Several long weeks after that search, the pastor had finally come to them with news that Lucien had made contact. He was safe.

In the spring of that year –the first of May, the moment was etched in her memory– Jeanne was squatting by the range, watching her cat suckle a litter of kittens, when there was another knock, the knock that put an end to her childhood.

She leaned against her fork and saw it all again.

The mayor stands on the threshold, the tricolour sash slung across his chest. Her mother's hand flies to her lips. Mamé's chair scrapes on the stone floor.

'Lucien?' Maman cries out.

Jeanne's body turns to lead, the only life is pulsing from the warm ball of fluff mewing in her hand.

The mayor shakes his head a movement which seems to cost him a tremendous effort. The mayor went to school with Papa.

He sits down and tells them how Papa's body was pulled out of the mine after a gas blast. Four men were killed.

Mamé howls like an animal. Papa was her only son.

Jeanne is scared. Without Papa, the world becomes dark

and threatening. Her hand tightens around the kitten. She welcomes the pain of the angry claws and teeth digging into her fingers.

Jeanne wiped a tear and pushed her fork into the soiled leaves. The cruel irony of Papa's death was that, if Lucien had gone to work in Germany, he would have been recalled from the mine so he could carry on with the farm. By then it was too late. Lucien was wanted as a deserter.

17
FLEURAC – JUNE 1944

Jeanne threw a bucket of water over the stone floor. All she had to do now was fill the stall with clean litter. She spat into her hands, gripped the rungs of the vertical ladder and climbed into the hayloft. Built into the hill, hay could be carted into the stable from a path level with the back and dropped through a hatch into the manger below.

She squinted into the dim light, took a few steps towards the end of the loft and looked around. There were plenty of dried leaves, but the pile of hay had dwindled to nothing. Ah well, she would just have to learn to handle a scythe and cut the grass herself. There wasn't much a girl couldn't do if she put her mind to it, though muscles did come in handy.

Papé had always said that the Cévennes sustained and wore you down in equal measures. Chestnuts had to be dried and shelled by hand before being ground into flour. Terraces had a habit of collapsing and the old hills were steep.

Mamé did as much as she could, bless her, but she was getting old. Right now, she was shelling peas in the shade of the stable wall.

Up in the cool loft, Jeanne gathered dried chestnut leaves and stood at the edge of the hatch. She inhaled their earthy scent and dripped handfuls onto the stall floor. They floated and twirled, translucent in the sunlight.

In the distance, a clippety-clop caught her attention. Boniface's cacophonous welcome gave away the caller's identity.

'Adiou, ma petite Arielle !' Mamé's tin basin clanged on the cobbles. 'So lovely to see you! Come here, come here. Sit with me. Wait, you must be thirsty. Let me get you a glass of water.'

The squeak of the water pump reminded Jeanne of how thirsty she was. She headed for the ladder, but something in Mamé's tone stopped her, so she kneeled at the edge of the hatch, her ears pricked.

'Oh dear, what is the matter, child?'

'Oh Mamé...' Arielle sighed.

'Qu'es aquò, Ninou, qu'es aquò ?' Mamé repeated in Occitan.

Ninou? Why would Mamé call Arielle Darling? Ninou was Mamé's pet name for her. Then again, Jeanne reasoned, Mamé had raised Arielle long before she was born.

'I'm so lost,' the young woman said, 'I don't know who to turn to.'

Crouching in the hayloft, Jeanne held her breath.

The bench creaked. There were murmurs.

Jeanne kept very still, willing Mademoiselle d'Aubrac to speak loud enough for her to hear.

'Mamé, you knew Karl, one of the men hiding with Lucien, didn't you?'

Jeanne's heart leapt.

'Karl... Yes, wasn't he that lovely German young man who helped us when the terrace collapsed?' Mamé paused. 'The pastor told us what happened. Those poor boys. How dreadful.'

Amongst tears and murmurs, Jeanne managed to catch, 'Karl and I, we… we loved each other.'

'Oh dear, I had no idea. I thought you and that de Peirac…'

Arielle's voice faltered, 'Father wants me to marry de Peirac. But I don't want to. I'd hoped that…' she sobbed, 'that after the war, Karl and I could…'

'Oh, my dear child, I am so sorry.'

'Karl was German…' Arielle blew her nose, 'but he wanted no part in this madness. Oh, Mamé, we had such dreams.'

Jeanne crept closer.

'Do you know who's responsible for his murder?'

'Someone saw German soldiers driving up.'

Conflicting emotions crawled under Jeanne's skin, itching like scabies. She wanted to jump down and shout out the truth, tell Mademoiselle that Karl was killed by French bullies dressed as Germans, but these were dangerous times, and you could trust no one, especially with Lucien on the run. Small and powerless, Jeanne bit her fingers.

'Oh, Mamé, why did he have to die?' Arielle sobbed for a long time. 'Father wants me taken care of. He says at twenty-five, I must be married. You know Father, don't you. He is not of this world. Since Maman's death, he's buried himself in genealogy studies, poring over parchments and scrolls.' With a resigned sigh, she continued, 'Albin's ancestry has piqued Father's interest. You see, the de Peirac male line goes back to the Crusades.'

'Yes,' Mamé said. 'I can see how tracking that lot down would keep Monsieur d'Aubrac busy.'

'Father is convinced that Albin de Peirac is the perfect match for me, but I don't love him. He's cold. He scares me. There's something about him.' Arielle's voice broke. 'Karl… Karl was so warm. Oh Mamé, he loved me so much.'

'Of course, he did, Ninou, of course he did.'

A silence followed, so heavy, so pregnant with untold secrets, that Jeanne forgot to breathe, afraid to miss the denouement. Her nose tickled. She muffled a sneeze.

'Where is Jeannette today?'

Jeanne winced. She pictured the large green eyes scanning the terraces.

'I sent her to gather purslane,' Mamé replied coolly. 'Don't worry, dear. We're on our own.' The bench creaked again. 'And now, you will tell me why you are really here.'

Heart in her mouth, Jeanne watched a leaf spiral down in a flurry of dust motes.

Arielle began to speak in riddles. Frustrated, Jeanne tried to make sense of the snatches floating up to her.

'I just want to die... Father will be furious. I can't do this to him.'

There was a long silence. 'Oh dear, Ninou, what have you done? Two weeks late? Are you sure?'

Two weeks late for what? What were they talking about?

'Yes, I am sure.'

Arielle's final plea stabbed Jeanne right through the heart. 'I can't have Karl's child.'

Karl's child? Something inside Jeanne's mind unfurled, bloomed, and filled her with light.

'But Arielle, you're a Catholic. It would be a deadly sin!'

'Of course, I want to have Karl's child, but the shame would kill my father. Alone and without money, I would end up on the street. I have no choice. I can't keep it. Please, you know plants. Mamé, you will help me, won't you?'

18
FLEURAC – JULY 14TH 1944

Today was the fourteenth of July and although de Gaulle had declared himself in charge of a new government, Vichy clung on and, in deference to the Germans, Maréchal Pétain had cancelled France's national day.

Jeanne didn't care. She was alone at home, and she had work to do.

Mamé had gone to Mende with the Pujols to fetch their son, Marcel, due to be released from police custody. It would double as a shopping expedition and take them all day. Just what Jeanne needed.

She headed for the grave at the edge of the forest. Papé was the only one she could tell about the miracle, about Karl's child growing inside Arielle. She sank to her knees and put her hands together. In the hagiography of Jeanne's life, Karl had joined Papé in Heaven where he shone down on her like a latter-day Jesus. At Papé's right was her father, his face blackened with coal dust.

Jeanne probed her feelings for the German pacifist. Was it love, devotion, or hero worship? She would never have admitted to anyone alive what Karl really meant to her. Now that he was dead, he had acquired a spiritual dimension, and she had become his disciple.

As soon as the Pujol's cart had gone, she rushed to the hive where she had hidden her sacred relics. It was one of three modern hives Lucien had built. Unlike the old trunk hives topped with a slab of slate, the modern system allowed honey to be removed without killing the bees. She puffed smoke at the entrance to calm the workers, lifted the roof and retrieved a parcel wrapped in green canvas.

She clutched it to her chest. Scented with smoke and propolis, it held all that was left of Karl's essence. She carefully unwrapped it, ran her fingers over the marbled cover of the sketchbook, picked up his harmonica and brushed it with her lips. When she opened the sketchbook, the pain hit her like an arrow. She closed her eyes and waited for it to pass.

When she was able to breathe again, Karl was smiling at her, his hair brushed back, radiating energy, strong teeth ready to tear a great chunk out of life. Tears coursing down her face, Jeanne touched the cleft on his chin. Why? Why had he not been allowed to live?

She wiped her tears with her sleeve and gingerly turned the pages. Arielle was everywhere, languid but demure under a tree, elegant on her horse, lying on the grass. There she was again, in three-quarter profile, gazing into the future, confident that it would include Karl.

Jeanne snapped the book shut. No way could Mademoiselle be allowed to murder Karl's child.

'I'll see what I can do,' Mamé had said as the young woman took her leave. 'But I sincerely hope you will change your mind. I work to preserve life, not to destroy it.'

Jeanne knew that Mamé was sometimes called upon to save girls bleeding to death after trying to abort with a knitting needle, or to save the life of a mother who might die in childbirth. She understood these things.

'Alright,' Mamé had conceded after Arielle had threatened to hurl herself from a rock, 'if you really haven't changed your mind in a week's time, I will give you a bag of herbs.' In a tired voice, she had added, 'It will be a very bitter brew. It is a strong purgative and will have unpleasant side-effects.'

The week was over. If Arielle came to their house tomorrow, it would be for one reason and one reason only.

On her knees, Jeanne beseeched Karl and Papé to intervene, to make Arielle change her mind. She kissed the book, wrapped the relics back inside the canvas bag, picked up her smoker and replaced the bundle inside the hive. She knew what she had to do.

A few hours later, she had finished her task and the shadow of the mulberry tree stretched right to the edge of the terrace. Mamé should be home soon, but there was still no sign of the Pujol's cart. Feet dangling over the retaining wall, Jeanne listened out.

It was dark by the time they returned. She ran out of the kitchen and met Mamé trudging up the path, supporting Madame Pujol. Jeanne glanced down the road and saw a long box on the cart.

'No!' She scrambled down and screamed, 'No!'

Monsieur Pujol remained slumped on the bench, reins in hand. André jumped down, collapsed against Jeanne and sobbed.

'André, what happened?'

'Marcel was shot this morning,' André's big body shook in her arms.

'They can't have! He hadn't done anything!'

'He was due out today. We were told to fetch him. They said he would be freed.'

'Why?' Jeanne put her arms around him. 'Oh André, why?'

André shook his head and sobbed. After a while, he straightened up and wiped his eyes with his hands.

'The Gestapo asked the militia for twenty prisoners to shoot on the square… for reprisals, you know, because of the attack on the train. The bastard in charge –we don't know who he is– added Marcel's name to the list at the last minute. Even the Germans were shocked.'

Jeanne recoiled. Every day, news of raids, abductions and public shootings kept the population in a state of terror. But why kill a boy?

'That beast has made it his private mission to wipe out Communism single-handed.'

'But… who is he?'

'We don't know. He hides behind his minions,' André said bitterly. 'No one knows his name. He's known in the region as the Gévaudan Beast.'

Jeanne accompanied them home where the coffin was brought in and set upon the Pujols' kitchen table. That night, the pastor was called, candles were lit and a vigil was held around it.

The next day, Mademoiselle d'Aubrac rode up to the cottage as the church bells tolled for Marcel's funeral.

Jeanne had substituted the bag of herbs Mamé had promised, with her own concoction. What Arielle did not know was that instead of an abortive, she was taking home a muslin bag filled with dried celandine (a purgative Jeanne had included for effect), calming chamomile, convolvulus (a brain tonic) and the all-important bitter horehound (excellent against coughs.)

Karl's child was safe.

19
FLEURAC - AUGUST 1944

At the end of August 1944, the Allies finally liberated Paris from four years of German rule. They advanced towards the Rhine and still, there were no news from Lucien. It was on the last night of August that Jeanne heard the familiar ta-ta-tatata on her bedroom shutter.

She leapt out of bed, yanked her window open and whispered, 'Lucien! Thank God, you're alive!'

'Are you going to let me in?'

'Shall I wake up Mamé?'

'No, no, let her sleep. Wait! Actually, it's not safe for me to spend the night in the house. Bring a blanket over to the stables. I'll see Mamé in the morning.'

Jeanne grabbed a couple of blankets and threw them over the sill. She tiptoed to the kitchen and feverishly filled a basket with a half-bottle of wine and whatever food she could find. Holding up a lantern, she clambered to the hay loft where, wrapped in a blanket, she lit a candle and watched Lucien tuck into a slice of bread lathered with thick butter and some rabbit pâté found in the larder.

'How long are you staying?' Jeanne ran her fingers along her brother's arm, unable to believe he was really there.

'Only a couple of days. After that, I've to head South. We'll be intercepting the transfer of two captured British pilots on their way to Lyon. The Germans are taking them to be interrogated by Klaus Barbie.' He made a face. 'They call him 'the Butcher of Lyon,' so you can imagine the kind of man he is. We have to get to them before he does, or else...'

The 'Butcher of Lyon' meant nothing to Jeanne, but the moniker brought something to mind. She studied her brother. After years of hardship, he looked much older than his twenty-three years.

'Lucien, try and remember… the day you escaped from the silk factory, did you recognise the men who attacked you?'

Lucien creased his brow. '*Oh la la*, let me see. I was gathering firewood in the *clède*, I heard shots. I saw German soldiers –' He took a swig of wine and made a grimace of distaste. 'Pouah, what is this *piquette?*'

'I was there you know. I saw you.'

'What?' He spat out the wine. 'You were there?'

The words burned Jeanne's throat as she spoke. 'I saw them. I heard them too. They spoke Occitan, Lucien. They were French.'

'What?' Lucien's eyes burned in the dimness.

'I was hiding in the gully.'

'You were there? Oh my God, Jeannette, you could have been killed.'

'I tried to go up, but I didn't get there in time to warn you. I'm so sorry.' She burst into tears. Lucien drew her to him.

'Don't cry, Jeannette. What could you do against these animals? Are you sure they spoke French? They wore German uniforms.'

Jeanne sniffed and said with a lopsided grin, 'you didn't run into the woods, instead you…'

Lucien's eyes twinkled. 'My first instinct was to run, but they would have caught up with me. I remembered Papé's story of the Protestant preacher…'

Jeanne butted in, 'During the wars of religion…'

'About to be caught, he managed to dodge the king's dragoons by kicking a beehive.' Lucien licked the pâté from his fingers. 'Hmm, how I've dreamed of this pâté.' He crinkled his brow. 'French you say? You really saw them?'

Jeanne nodded sadly. 'Some of them spoke local.'

'And you've no idea who they were?'

She shook her head. Now that Lucien was here, she didn't want to talk about Karl's death, but about his life, she wanted to find out who he was, dying to ask about what he loved.

Lucien yawned and said, 'I haven't slept much these past two days.'

She watched him snuggle down on the dried leaves, covered him with the blanket and stroked his hair. As she said good night, her thoughts turned to a girl called Klara, over in Germany, a girl her age, whose brother would never come home.

'*Bonanuèch* Lucien.' She kissed his forehead. A tear dropped onto his face. A tear of happiness.

'*Bonanuèch.*'

She was halfway down the ladder when Lucien called back to her.

'Oh Jeannette, I forgot. Thought you'd be interested. Arielle d'Aubrac has gone to Paris.'

Jeanne rested her forehead on the dusty rung and processed the implications of Arielle going to Paris. She stepped onto the ground and counted on her fingers. Three months. The pregnancy would not be showing yet.

Boniface snuffled in his sleep. Above her, Lucien was still talking.

Jeanne lifted her face to the hatch. 'Sorry, what did you say?'

'I said, she married de Peirac last week.'

Jeanne climbed back up the rungs. 'She married de Peirac? But Mamé says he's a collaborator!'

Lucien yawned. 'Bah, birds of a feather those aristocrats. Can't blame him for running away. As soon as the *boches* are out of France, we'll shoot those traitors and his name is top of the list.'

Thoughtful, Jeanne patted Boniface and went to stand at the edge of the terrace. All around her, the grey schist glimmered in the moonlight. Arielle had married in a hurry and was leaving the region. It could only mean one thing…

Jeanne opened out her arms and addressed a prayer of thanks to the moon.

20
FLEURAC – FEBRUARY 1947

Gusts of February wind rattled the shutters and whistled through the wastepipe of the *souillarde*. A kettle was purring on the range. In the warm kitchen, under a petrol lamp hanging from a rafter, the atmosphere was convivial, the war now a distant nightmare. At Lucien's suggestion, Mamé had invited Pujol the carpenter and his family to help shell chestnuts, a ritual which brought the Cévenols together during the winter months.

Mamé sat by the range, flanked by the rotund Madame Pujol, her dark hair crimpled to an inch of its life. Monsieur Pujol presided from Papé's chair, his bald patch glimmering under the lamp. Over by the *souillarde,* Lucien and André chatted about engines, their Occitan peppered with French technical words.

Jeanne smiled at the efforts André had made to impress her tonight. Eighteen now, his acne was receding, but the amount of Brillantine he had slathered on his hair did him no favours. He would have looked better, had he allowed his mass of curls to soften his strong features. Sensing her eyes on him, the young carpenter enveloped her in a proprietary gaze. Cheeks on fire, Jeanne returned to her task.

A violent squall rattled the kitchen door.

'That rain's showing no sign of stopping,' Lucien said. 'I hope the first terrace holds out.'

'I'll help you fix it, son.' Monsieur Pujol lifted his glass of liqueur with a wink. 'Don't you worry about things like that now.'

The carpenter's comment drew Jeanne from her reverie. What did he mean by 'now?'

'Would you like some more *tilleul,* Madame Pujol?' Mamé turned to the range where a calming infusion of lime flowers was stewing in a pan.

'Oh no thank you. I don't fancy braving that rain to get to the privy in the dark.' Madame Pujol tightened her cardigan over her imposing bosom. She picked up a chestnut and sliced the hard skin with a knife.

'It was on nights like this that the *Bestia da Gavaudan* prowled around houses,' she narrowed her eyes, 'half-crazed and blood thirsty, it devoured a hundred souls.'

Jeanne wondered how people could bear to tell horror stories, when memories of the War were still fresh, even after two years. Did fairy tales make them feel safe?

'Madeleine,' tutted her husband, 'it might have *attacked* a hundred, but it actually killed seventy-six.'

'I thought it was eighty-eight,' André corrected.

Jeanne smiled. She knew how his mother's obsession with The Beast embarrassed him.

'They say it wasn't a wolf at all but a nobleman who had acquired a taste for blood in the wars.' Monsieur Pujol could not resist needling his wife.

'Not at all,' Madame Pujol fluffed herself up, 'there are plenty of people who saw the animal tear an infant from its sister's arms in broad daylight. It's a well-documented fact.'

'These are modern times.' Mamé brushed the chestnut peelings into a pot. 'Things like that don't happen anymore.'

'Don't they?' Madame Pujol's gaze hardened. 'That Gévaudan Beast over in Mende had our Marcel shot when he was only seventeen, calling him a communist. Well, they never found who he was, did they, that beast? Probably safe in Argentina by now, with all the other Nazis.'

The Gévaudan Beast… the memory of what she had seen at the silk factory would always haunt Jeanne. She knew who had shot Karl.

'Have they found who shot your comrades?' André asked her brother.

Lucien ran a hand through his hair and let out a long breath, 'Not really. I thought they were Germans at the time, but perhaps they were from the French militia. They've probably been executed during the clean-up. When the War ended, not many questions were asked. They're all either dead or have scarpered like the rats they were.'

'I'd recognise his voice.' Jeanne said. 'He spoke French.'

Lucien shrugged, 'Yeah well, who's going to believe a fourteen-year-old?'

'Jeannette's nearly sixteen.' André had been counting the days until the age of consent.

Jeanne tried to banish the last image of Karl from her mind. Her brother was alive. She had prayed every night for his life to be saved and her prayers were answered. Maman may still be in Paris, but a pig was getting fat in the pigsty and life had returned to normal. Boniface had enough hay to last him through the winter and they had ten rabbits. The terraced plots had been dug over, ready for spring. Lucien had found some sort of job in Lyon, which meant that someone had to stay and look after Mamé until he came home.

Jeanne's dreams of becoming a schoolteacher were on hold.

Over in the corner, Lucien gathered another pile of chestnuts and whispered to André, 'We won't be peeling these for much longer. There are machines to do this job. I've seen them.' The two young men exchanged a meaningful glance. '*Décortiqueuses* they're called.'

In the dim light, all faces turned to Lucien. He gave a self-conscious grin. 'Just saying.'

Mamé shrugged, 'I heard you. See, we've nearly finished, and what's more, we've enjoyed being together. So, what are you going to do with your evenings huh? Play *belote*? Read the Bible? Knit?'

An embarrassed silence followed. Jeanne searched out André's gaze, but he refused to meet hers. The atmosphere was tense. She had obviously missed something.

For a while, the hush was filled with the sound of chestnuts dropped into buckets, the wind shaking the shutters and the fire snoring in the range.

'Where did you see these machines?' Jeanne broke the silence.

'In my factory in Lyon.' After a beat, Lucien added, 'I've been asked to stay on. They're going to make me foreman.'

Mamé grumbled, 'You want to stay in town. Is that it?'

He simply opened his hands.

The ground shifted beneath Jeanne's feet. Through a thick fog, she heard Lucien mumble that no, it wasn't like that; he would come home on Sundays and help. He'd send money. 'Life on these slopes is just too hard.'

'It's suited the human race since the dawn of time.' Mamé's eyes were damp. 'I don't see what you'd gain by being at the beck and call of a boss. Money's all very well, but here, you're your own man.'

'I might be my own man, but I'd work like a slave, waking

before the hens and crawling into bed exhausted, day in, day out, just to eke out a miserable living. How will I ever find a wife? What woman will want to live here?'

I do! Jeanne screamed inwardly. I want to live here!

'I can do so much better where I am. I know how to operate the machines. When I'm foreman, I'll be able to buy a car.'

'But what about us?' Jeanne cried out, unable to believe her brother could just... abandon them... that without consulting them, he had already decided on a course of action. How could she keep this place going on her own?

She could tell from the glances darting around the room that the matter had already been decided.

'We're running out of storage for our building materials.' Monsieur Pujol's conciliatory tone made Jeanne want to claw his eyes out. 'We'll be glad to help out in return for the loan of some of your outbuildings.'

Here I go, thought Jeanne. Saved by the Pujols. There would be no escaping the love-struck André who'd have right of entry at any time of day. She would never make it to college. The dream was over.

Preening herself like a hen, Madeleine Pujol dropped her own bombshell, a juicy titbit of gossip to lighten up the mood. 'Times are a-changing indeed.' She lifted her nose in the air. 'Monsieur d'Aubrac has put his castle up for sale, and he's moving to town.'

'Qué?' Jeanne and Mamé cried out.

Delighted with the effect she had achieved, André's mother wriggled her pencilled eyebrows and added, 'oh yes, he's moving to the big house in Fleurac, behind the market square. The one that's been in his family since they were silk merchants.'

'But who's going to buy a chateau *here?*' Jeanne objected.

'Americans I presume.' Since they had liberated Paris, Americans could do no wrong in Madame Pujol's eyes.

'Papa and I are refurbishing the Fleurac townhouse for him,' André explained, quite the man now.

'You'll never get paid.' Mamé stabbed a chestnut, ripped off the skin and added with feeling, 'Old d'Aubrac won't pay you. He's useless with money. I should know.'

'Well, he seems to have found some. We've already been paid for the shutters we replaced.'

'His son in law is footing the bill... Monsieur de Peirac.' Madame Pujol said with a note of reverence. 'The Marquis de Peirac.'

Mamé gave a philosophical shrug. 'Ha. De Peirac. Of course.' She stood up to signify that the evening was at an end, poured out the tisane into the *souillarde* and unlaced her apron. 'Tell me, Madeleine, since you're in the know, how is that daughter of his doing in Paris?'

'Ooh, haven't you heard? They've left Paris. They're living in America now.' Madame Pujol giggled. 'They've a little boy.'

'Really?' Mamé pulled her chair and sat down heavily.

Jeanne caught the look on her grandmother's face. It was a slow smile, as if she had always known. She asked a little too casually. 'A boy, eh? And what did she call that *drollet*?'

'Now let me think... what did she call him?' Madame Pujol scrunched her brow. 'Something that begins with A... Ah yes, I remember. She called him Armand.' A wistful smile spread over her face. She repeated the child's name, as if tasting it. 'Armand... Aristocratic isn't it? Armand-Aymeric de Peirac... With a fancy name like that, he's got his life cut out, hasn't he?'

PART III

ARMAND - PARIS - MAY 1968

21
PARIS – APRIL 1968

'*Armand, tu es prêt ? Le Rallye commence à huit heures.*'

Armand shuffled to the record player and lifted the needle, suspending the flute solo of the Moody Blues' Nights in White Satin. He flung his Shetland jumper and flared trousers onto an Empire chair and opened the large oak wardrobe. From a poster stuck inside the door, Raquel Welch smiled from an exotic beach. Armand ran his gaze over her luscious figure, grabbed a white shirt and, holding it against his chest, took a long look at himself and the charade his life had become.

Thank God it was the last time he had to attend one of those ridiculous parties. What was the point of specifying 'suit and tie' on the invitation when anyone not fluent with the dress-code of '*rallyes dansants,*' anyone ignorant enough to imagine that a '*rallye*' involved something so mundane as cars or road maps, would never have made it to the guest list.

He was invited to all *rallyes*. He ticked all the boxes: old stock, Catholic, affluent, handsome and adept at four-beat jive. In these hardly disguised marriage markets, Armand de

Peirac, son and heir of the rich and titled Albin and Arielle de Peirac was a catch.

Tired of the pretence, he had let himself be caught… or so they thought.

He had been attending these social gatherings since he was fifteen, jived with hundreds of debutantes while their mothers played bridge in nearby drawing rooms, occasionally peeping in to weigh up the young males and assess their potential to further their bloodline.

'Armand!' His mother's voice rose a fraction. *'Anne-Ségolène est arrivée!'*

Fastening the heraldic cufflinks he had received two years ago for his twenty first birthday, Armand looked into the mirror and took stock. He looked like an idiot. The shirt and tie clashed with his long hair. He hated the cufflinks with their 'wolf passant' and ridiculous chestnuts, an allusion to some ancestor's fabled generosity during a famine.

He winked at his reflection. Freedom was so close he could taste it. He had found a loophole.

'Coucou Armand !' After a perfunctory knock, his fiancée rustled in. Slim and elegant, Anne-Ségolène carried herself like Audrey Hepburn. Today however, wrapped in blue silk, she looked like a boiled sweet.

She removed his clothes from the empire chair and sat down. 'Cheer up, it's our last one.' She patted her elaborate chignon, dropped her hand to her lap and smiled at the diamond engagement ring on her finger.

His eyes followed hers. The ring had belonged to his grandmother. An old dragon by all accounts. The engagement party had been a farce of the first order, but the pact they had made was working.

The tap tap of Arielle's shoes stopped by the door. Anne-Ségolène shot from the chair and flung herself into Armand's arms.

'Oh. Sorry.' Blushing, Arielle closed the door and admonished from the other side, 'Hurry up, you two. Joao has started the car. Don't keep us waiting.'

Armand peeled Anne-Ségolène from his neck.

'What did you do that for?'

Her eyes sparkled with mischief. 'Chill out, darling. That's what we're *supposed* to be doing. We're engaged, aren't we?'

To get his own back, Armand drew the girl to him and lightly ran a hand over her breast. 'You mean *that* sort of thing?'

'Stop it.' Anne-Ségolène pushed him away. 'No wonder I don't like men. Come on, let's go and show the world what a lovely couple we are.'

She threaded her arm into his and whispered, 'just think… two long years till I finish the Beaux Arts. Two long years before I'm free to play cattleya with my beloved – and you with yours – while our fathers are setting up lucrative deals in chestnut forests.'

'My father's tired of chestnut. He's branching out into oak,' Armand quipped.

She leaned into him. 'Ha ha, and while they are deforesting and reforesting France, you and I…'

Armand dug her in the ribs. They stood rock still. The door to his father's study opened. Balding, of average height, his father wore his usual attire of grey suit adorned with matching yellow silk cravat and kerchief.

Anne-Ségolène dropped Armand's arm and did a small curtsy.

'Monsieur.'

'Anne-Ségolène, quel plaisir !' His father took both hands in his. 'How elegant you look tonight, my dear. Where is this *rallye* again?'

'In Chantilly at the Bouvreuils.'

'Oh yes, of course, the banker. Plenty of money there. I'm

sure you two will have a wonderful time. By the way, I might catch sight of you tomorrow, dear girl. Your father has invited me to a shoot at his Fontainebleau property.'

'Really?' Anne-Ségolène lifted a plucked eyebrow. '… I did hear him complain about wild boar uprooting his saplings, but it's April. I didn't think the season was open for boar.'

'He's been given a dispensation for a beat.' Albin de Peirac rubbed his hands. 'I'm very much looking forward to it.' He turned to his son, 'the invitation extends to you, Armand.'

Armand's heart sank. As much as he loved rambling over the hills of his mother's native Cévennes with a camera, he could not stomach hunts.

His mother's voice from the landing saved him from answering.

'Children? I'll be in the car.'

The study door snapped shut. Somehow, in the corridor, the air became warmer.

'So? Are you coming to my parents' for the shoot? It'll make a man of you,' Anne-Ségolène teased as the ancient lift painfully cranked up the three floors.

The evening sun bathed the white stone landing with gold, reflected in the plaque stating *M. & Mme Albin de Peirac*, the brass rods on the stairs and the metal curls of the elevator cage.

'Trudge in mud behind a pack of starving dogs so that we can disembowel a boar?' Armand squeezed into the lift and pulled the concertina doors. 'Anyway,' he exhaled, 'we've planned to spend Sunday with Molière, remember?'

Armand de Peirac and his fiancée, Anne-Ségolène de la Bauderie, had planned to spend the afternoon at the theatre, enjoying a Molière play. Armand closed his eyes in despair. It was nineteen sixty-eight for God's sake, so why were they stuck in a time warp redolent of Balzac? The whole world was rocking around them in a groundswell of psychedelic self-expression and sex, and the two of them were brainwashed with 'values' which had been preserved in formaldehyde since Napoléon III.

Close to real life but unable to reach it, they knew the rules of the game. They had seen what happened to those who refused to play it. With their parents' money and contacts, the doors of the *Tout-Paris* stood wide open. Armand yearned to write. Anne-Ségolène had set her heart on becoming an interior designer. All she needed was a qualification… and an unsullied reputation. Therein lay the challenge.

'Le Malade Imaginaire.' Armand nudged her elbow. 'I reckon we've studied enough Molière to hold a conversation about it, don't you?'

She uttered a groan. 'Oh God, anything. I haven't seen Leila for two weeks. It's driving me insane and we've nowhere to go. Her parents just cancelled their outing. Mind you, I hate going to her place, it's so depressing.'

'Those horrid flats in Nanterre? Christ, is that where she lives?'

'Hmm. She can't wait to get out.' Anne-Ségolène shivered. 'Poor thing. They'd kill her if they knew.' The lift bounced to a halt. She placed a hand on the latch and turned to him. 'How about you and… what was her name again?'

'Mary.' They stepped out. The name echoed in the marble hall. Instinctively, Armand checked the concierge's window.

'Petite Anglaise, Mary Mary mon amour…' Anne-Ségolène hummed a song currently topping the charts.

'She's not English. She's Irish. Not at all the same thing, so she keeps telling me.' Irish Mary was virtuous, unlike English girls, who were easy. 'I'm just taking her to Molitor. We're going ice-skating.'

'Have you slept with her yet?'

'Oh, listen to yourself.' Armand held the glass door for her, 'you sound like that Marquise in Dangerous Liaisons.'

'La Marquise de Merteuil…' Anne-Ségolène glided past with a seductive smile. 'Totally me.'

In the chilly evening, a low April sunset gilded new leaves bursting from pollarded trees. The family Citroën DS was idling just outside the building, Arielle at the front, chatting to her Portuguese chauffeur. Joao said something. She laughed. How rare it was to hear his mother laugh.

Anne-Ségolène whispered, 'I say, handsome chap, your chauffeur.' She shuffled into the car in a rustle of silk and silently pointed to his mother and Joao in turn, a question in her eyes.

Armand shook his head in angry denial. Was she mad? No way was his mother having an affair with the chauffeur. Joao was a good man.

Annoyed, he turned away, his eyes drawn up to the third floor of the white stone façade. Framed by the window of his study, his father was glaring down at them.

22
PARIS – MAY 1ST 1968

Thank God it's over. Armand peeled off his shirt, slumped onto his bed and groaned. The whole stupid *rallye* had been an ordeal of pretence. Though four-point jive had replaced the waltz and crinolines, the rules had not changed since Empress Eugenie started the trend back in 1850.

While from Carnaby Street to Frisco, the Zeitgeist instructions for the young were to 'turn on, tune in and drop out,' tonight, Armand had to dance with all five fat Bouvreuil girls, acknowledge congratulations on his engagement and express his determination to further the de Peirac fortune... after he had completed his MA in literature in a few months' time.

While he danced with Anne-Ségolène, mothers peered over their card games and computed their combined fortune, seething at what their daughters had missed.

Armand picked up his copy of By-Line, a collection of Hemingway's articles and stroked the cover. In his heart, he wanted to write about real people, about conflict, passion and truth. Finding a position in a newspaper would be no problem; his father had contacts. An internship in a Catholic paper such as La Croix was within his grasp. All he had to do was ask.

Heck, La Croix… he ran his hands over his face. He didn't even believe in God. Getting his father's dispensation from Sunday mass was the only battle he had won. He was not alone in this. In the Sorbonne, most of his cohort still lived at home. How he envied American youths and the campus life he had read about.

Woozy from too much champagne, Armand threw on a pair of jeans and a T-shirt and went to the kitchen for a glass of water.

He was opening a bottle of Evian when his father came in… and pulled out a chair.

Here we go, Armand's shoulders tightened. *Lecture-time. What will it be this time? The pointlessness of studying literature, or a warning not to get my fiancée pregnant…*

'You know where she keeps the *tilleul*?' His father sounded tired. 'Make me a cup, will you?'

Armand opened a tin and breathed in Jeanne's garden, the scent of summer in Fleurac. Only one month to go and he would be back there, free from the straightjacket. His father was always too busy to accompany them.

At the end of June, Joao would pack the car and head down the *Nationale Sept,* the sunshine road. Six hours later, he would veer right just before Mende. Joao would spend a few days with them and help out André, Jeanne's husband, with DIY jobs around the house before taking the train to Lisbon, where his wife lived.

His back turned to his father, Armand poured water into a pan and struck a match under it.

'You passed your driving test last year, didn't you?'

'I did.'

'Thinking of getting rid of that damned chauffeur. You can drive your mother to Fleurac in June, can't you?'

'What brought that on?' Joao had been with them for years.

'Be cheaper for her to take taxis around Paris.'

Cheaper? The chauffeur was paid a pittance. 'He helps out in many ways, and back in Portugal, he's got a wife.'

'Sentimental claptrap. You're just like your mother.'

'But…'

'Can't be sentimental with staff. Lesson best learned early.'

'Still, there are laws, notice to be given, contracts. Just because he isn't declared and works *au noir* doesn't mean you can treat him like a…'

Armand crushed a handful of dried flowers into the teapot. Arguing with his father was futile. He took a cup from a shelf and instead, focused on the gold edging, the way it clanged on the saucer. He picked two small sugar cubes with silver pincers and watched them dissolve as he poured the golden liquid over them. He could not remember a time when Joao was not there.

'Save me the socialist spiel, Armand. This is what comes from attending a… *university*.'

'Father, really. The Sorbonne isn't exactly a hotbed of Marxism. It's not Nanterre.'

Nanterre's new university was making a big noise in the press with its demonstrations and political unrest. Hurriedly built in the middle of Arab shantytowns to mop up the surplus of Parisian students born after the war, Nanterre was the antithesis of the select *Hautes Ecoles* Albin had hoped his only son would attend.

'If I find you mixed up with communists, that's the end of your allowance, you hear? Any sign of trouble and you'll be building cars *à la chaîne* with those comrades of yours.'

Armand handed him the tisane and shot back to his room with a sigh of relief. Tomorrow was Mary's day off. Mary was a breath of fresh air. She was lovely, she was wholesome and she was fun. With her, the world made sense. With her, he did not have to pretend.

23
PARIS – MAY 2ND 1968

The morning of the wild boar shoot, Armand helped Joao carry his father's guns down to the car. He waved his parents off to Fontainebleau, an hour South of Paris, ran up the three flights of stairs and called Anne-Ségolène.

'The coast is clear!'

'Listen, I've an idea.' She sounded excited. 'Why don't we have a meat fondue? You can invite Mary, and I'll come with Leila.'

'What do you mean? Just the four of us?'

'Why don't we make it a party? How about that ginger friend of yours, the one I met once at the Sorbonne?'

'Virgile?'

'Is he the one from your philosophy class? Totally in the clouds that guy. Ask him to bring a girlfriend if he has one, and the best of his record collection. I'll buy the meat before the butcher closes. Mary can bring the baguettes.'

They would tidy up, she promised. His parents would be none the wiser.

'Are you sure we'll have time?' Armand hesitated. 'What if

they come home early? We're supposed to be at the theatre, remember.'

'Relax. They won't finish eating before midnight at the earliest. Mother's been talking about nothing but the grand dinner she has planned after the hunt. She's got the best caterers in. Trust me. The cats will be away in Fontainebleau until dawn. The mice will definitely have time to play.'

'Listen. No mention of our 'engagement' you hear? I don't want Mary to freak out.'

She laughed.

'*Oh merde,* I forgot. I can't phone her. Her employers have warned her. No boy-friend.'

'Really? How quaint.' Ségo tutted. 'Give me her number.' After a pause, she added, 'you really like that girl, don't you?'

'She's… refreshing.'

'Refreshing?'

Leaning on the console, Armand closed his eyes and conjured up Mary.

'She's like an ice cube in a drink. She's– she's totally devoid of the cynicism de rigueur in our circle, she's… normal.'

'Bah. Life will soon change that.' Anne-Ségolène laid on the cynicism as thickly as she could. 'It always does.'

Armand replaced the receiver and did a little dance, thrilled at the idea of gathering all the people his father despised under his roof: a lesbian, a hired-help (Mary was an au-pair), an Arab woman and a leftist student. How deliciously horrified would Monsieur his father be if he knew, the old bigot.

Humming *Let's Spend the Night Together,* Armand jived around the empty rooms, aroused at the thought of Mary on the couch, Mary in his bedroom, Mary in his bed… *merde!* Condoms. He needed condoms. The Pope had condemned them, de Gaulle had condemned them –France needed more children to replace the men lost during the wars– and *préservatifs* were kept behind the counter of pharmacies… that were closed on Sundays. If Mary was willing, self-control would be their only option. No problem for Armand for whom controlling his emotions had become second nature.

A few hours later, showered, chestnut curls blow-dried to perfection, up-to-the-minute in beige flares and roll-neck jumper, his heart bursting with love, Armand was ready for anything life would throw at him.

Mary was the first to arrive with an armful of baguettes, utterly desirable in mini-skirt, short jumper and dark bouncy ponytail, so desirable, Armand had to stop himself from ravishing her on the hall rug. Instead, he took the bread from her and lightly kissed the freckles on either side of her nose. He put the bread on the table and only then, lost himself in her lips.

She disentangled herself from his arms and went to the living room. Wedgewood-blue eyes open like saucers, Mary tip-toed through the flat, gaping at portraits, running her fingers along the silk-covered walls, trying out Arielle's empire chairs.

'*Très chic!* My employers' flat is modern, you know, sterile. *Ton appartement, c'est… comme un décor de film.*' She was here to learn French and was getting quite good at it.

'*Un film? Un musée oui.*' Armand shrugged. '*Mon père est fan de Napoléon III.*'

'*Magnifique. Très français.*'

'Oh Mary…' Armand hugged her, tipsy with the freshness of her, 'I'm so glad you're here. You're so…' He searched for a way to express how he felt. Compared to the calculating *rallye*-girls who vied with each other for the highest rungs of the marriage ladder, Mary was genuine. Lightheaded, Armand just repeated, 'I'm so glad you're here.'

There had been others before her of course. In the back

rooms of the grand houses where the *rallyes* took place, girls had been kissed, promises had been made, bodily fluids exchanged, together with 'be careful with my dress.' Their mothers' glares from the bridge salons haunted him at night.

Last year, he had dated a medical student with a room of her own. She was on the pill and it was great at first, but her forthright use of biology and Latin had put him off his stride. His father thought him a sissy. Armand saw himself as a romantic.

An hour later, the kitchen was buzzing. Anne-Ségolène, Leila and Mary were chopping up steak, Virgile heating oil in the fondue pan, while Armand uncorked a bottle of rather good Bourgogne hauled out of his father's cellar.

They sat around the kitchen table and, dipping diced beef into the hot oil, discussed the student unrest in Nanterre. Leila, who lived nearby, had witnessed clashes between right-wing law students and the '*gauchistes*,' their leftist counterparts. Virgile had been there too. The Literature faculty buzzed like a tinderbox.

Armand liked Virgile's energy. What had first drawn them together was the realisation that they were both a disappointment to their fathers. Unable to finish his studies because of the war, Virgile's father had bestowed on him the Roman poet's name in the hope that his son would one day teach French and Latin, as he had dreamt of doing. Virgile wanted to do his own thing, though he wasn't too sure what it was yet.

Tonight, Virgile was in great form, probably thanks to the Bourgogne. He lifted his glass and decreed that the government was full of dinosaurs and that it was time to get rid of de Gaulle. After the fifth glass, he declared it was time for the proletariat to rise and overthrow Capitalism. Leila clapped. Mary was lost in translation and Anne-Ségolène, who didn't care about politics, found the whole thing exhilarating.

'Why don't you just leave home?' Mary charmingly asked when Armand complained about his stifling life. 'My brother's just left Dublin for New York.'

'What good would that do?' Armand had given the matter plenty of thought. 'I'd be scrubbing dishes in some burger joint instead of being trapped here. I want to be a journalist, not a waiter. No, I've got to stick it out.' Armand wanted to add, 'With you around, I can just about manage.' But he was too shy.

'*Allez, on danse !*' Anne-Ségolène clapped her hands, closed the lounge drapes and together with Leila, rolled up the Aubusson carpet. The rest of the afternoon was spent in a stupor of hormones and alcohol, snogging to the languorous strains of 'Nights in White Satin' and 'Rain and Tears.' Feeling sorry for Virgile, who had come alone, Ségo and Leila took it in turns to dance with him.

The wine was good, Mary was warm and compliant in Armand's arms. Somehow, they danced into his room and found themselves on his bed, 'just kissing,' Armand whispered.

'Armand I…' dishevelled and flushed, Mary tried to pull away, 'I really shouldn't be doing this, I've never…'

'Ssshhh. It's okay.' Armand unbuttoned her top and nuzzled a breast. 'I love you Mary, you've no idea how much I love you. I won't do anything you don't want me to. I promise.'

Mary ran her fingers along his chest, kissed his taught skin, his face, and fell into the pillows with a sigh while he covered her body with tiny kisses. She didn't protest when moments later, Armand slithered down and kissed her thighs. At long last, she allowed him take her hand and place it where he needed it. Soon, they wanted more. Shivering with the need for him, Mary uttered a raucous groan and drew Armand to her.

He pushed damp hair from his face and looked into her eyes.

'I love you,' she said, her blue eyes liquid with emotion.

Her words trickled inside him like a blaze of light. It was the first time a girl loved him without any thought to his father's money, his parents' address or the hope of becoming a marchioness.

He kissed her cheeks, amazed at her softness, the smallness of her hands, the innocence in her large eyes, so unlike the calculating glares of the *rallye* brigade. Her fingers ran across his skin, driving him mad with desire. Hesitant at first, she explored his body, guided by his moans.

Armand gazed around his room, amazed to have Mary there at last, her milky body in his tangled sheets, her dark hair spilling over his pillow.

In her arms, he knew he would find redemption away from the pretence that plagued every moment of his life.

Mary was pure, she was kind, and most of all, she was real. As soon as the year was over, he would follow her to Ireland, shake off his father's affectations and work out what he had to offer the world.

She wrapped her arms around him like a child and kissed his cheek.

'Oh, Mary, you're everything to me,' he whispered into her hair. 'I'll be careful, I promise.'

She opened up to him, a little nervous at first. At one point, her fingers dug into his back.

'Am I hurting you?'

She shook her head and smiled through happy tears.

Armand took it slowly at first, amazed at how fragile, how surreal she was; the most beautiful thing that had ever happened to him. Lost in her, he finally touched the truth that had been eluding him for so long and soared to a place filled with love and ecstasy. For the longest of time, he hovered inside a vortex of pleasure such as he had never experienced before and much too soon, shuddered, crash-landing with a groan into a T-shirt hurriedly dragged over to spare the housekeeper's sensibilities.

Mary hugged him with all her heart.

They staggered back to the living room to find Virgile asleep on the sofa and the two girls whirling to Arab music in Bacchanalian abandon.

Armand sat down on the floor and, a hand on Mary's thigh, watched their suggestive dance. A contented breath rushed from his lungs.

A clock rang somewhere. Mary jumped. '*Oh zut !* I'm late.'

'Late to what? I thought it was your day off.'

'My French family are taking me some place early in the morning. Sorry. I've got to run.'

Armand drew her to him and whispered in a kiss, 'I loved what we did Mary. Please don't worry, I was careful.'

'Thank you.' She nuzzled his neck. 'Will I see you next Saturday at the skating rink?'

Proud of the love he saw in those blue eyes, Armand patted her bottom. 'Try and stop me. Get yourself some proper ice-skates this time, won't you?'

Out in the hall, the old lift clanked towards them. The doors squealed open and let out a dark-haired youth in a black velvet suit.

Mary turned to Armand in panic.

'Mary, this is Arnaud, my cousin.'

'You're Armand too?' Mary misunderstood his name.

'No, he's Arnaud, I'm Armand. I know, it' s confusing, but it's a family tradition that all boys' names begin with A. We call him Arnie, cos' he thinks he's Tarzan.'

The cousin rolled his eyes. '*Ha ha, très drôle.*'

Now, off you go. See you Saturday.'

Arnie's hungry eyes ran along Mary's legs. 'Wow, was that the English nanny?'

'She's Irish,' Armand grumbled, irked at the implication that he was shagging a servant. Arnie was a womaniser and a snob. Because this father was a cinema producer and did not belong to the Catholic *'rallye'* circuit, Arnie had no reputation to protect and was free to indulge.

'Do tell,' Arnie nudged his taller cousin in the ribs. 'What will you be doing with this *Irish* beauty on Saturday?' He followed Armand into the flat. 'Shagging her if you've got any sense. Those legs…'

'Ice-skating if you must know. Listen.' Armand placed a hand on his cousin's shoulder, 'I know it's going to be difficult, but promise you won't make any salacious comments to Anne-Ségolène about her… about Leila.'

'Wow!' Arnie rubbed his hands. 'Is SHE here? The Queen of Sheba? You mean, they're *both* here?'

'Her name's Leila.' Armand dug his fingers into Arnie's sleeve. 'Promise.'

'Sure,' Arnie said with a lascivious leer.

'Any untoward comment… and I tell your parents about the Swedish au pair and the abortion.'

'Hey man! A deal's a deal.' Arnie's leer intensified. 'Do you think they'll let me watch? Ouch!' He hopped away on one foot, rubbing the ankle Armand had just kicked. *'Putain...*the vestal virgins…' the young man murmured transfixed.

He studied Leila's large jade eyes, heavy black hair, perfect oval face and translucent skin... opened his mouth, thought better of it, helped himself to a drink and slumped on the sofa next to Virgile.

Much later, when Virgile had gone, Anne-Ségolène raised her head from the pile of cushions where she had been napping on Leila's lap and said, 'C'mon girl, let's tidy up.' She prodded Armand's leg with her toe. 'I don't think you're house-trained yet, are you dear? It's okay. Leave it to the experts.'

He thanked her with a grunt and went to the balcony to gaze at the sunset over the Eiffel Tower and the Seine.

'Where did you say Uncle Albin was today?' Arnie patted the pocket of his velvet trousers and held out a packet of Camel filters.

'He's gone shooting. My father loves to kill.' Armand let him light his cigarette. 'He's weird, my dad.'

Arnie leaned over the balustrade and slowly blew smoke out through his nose. 'Goes back to the war I suppose. Got a taste for it there.' He lifted his face to the evening sun and blew smoke circles, following them as they floated into the darkening sky.

Armand watched the smoke circles, processing his cousin's comments.

'What do you mean? He was in the Resistance... and it isn't as if they saw much action down in Mende anyway. The Cévennes weren't exactly a hotspot during the war.'

Arnie cast him a sideways glance.

'Uncle Albin in the Resistance?' He cocked an eyebrow. 'Is that what he told you?'

'Well, he certainly hinted at it, yes,' Armand replied candidly. 'I always fancied he was a spy,' he joked, surprised when his cousin didn't laugh with him. 'That was when I was very young.'

'Sure.'

The look he received, both smug and pitying, hit him in the solar plexus. What had they kept from him?

Silence stretched between them, taught as a steel cable.

Armand raked though his memories. His father was strict, his values depressingly conventional, but being strict and boring was the whole point of parents, wasn't it? How much did his cousin really know? Arnie was a show-off.

When he wasn't invited to Cannes by heiresses, he was dating starlets.

Armand wished he could wipe the smug 'I-know-something-you-don't' look from his cousin's face. He had drunk far too much and he felt sick. That was the trouble with fondues, you drank more than you realised. He shivered, the metal of the balustrade cold under his fingers. To their left, the Eiffel Tower stood at a strange angle and below him, the Seine had turned to lead.

Arnie flicked a speck of ash from his white shirt and spoke, his voice so low, Armand did not catch every word.

'Our de Peirac grandfather was an industrialist, as you know, and as such, he had a lot to protect in the thirties. Coal mines, factories... So, with all the strikes, and workers clamouring for holidays, Communism was a death threat.' Laughter rang out from the kitchen. He glanced back to the room and spoke even lower. 'We don't talk about it of course... but Grandpa backed Hitler.'

'Yeah, I'd kinda heard that.'

Their grandfather's dour portrait hung in the hall. What did this old story have to do with his own father, Armand was not sure.

'In the forties, Paris was crawling with Germans, so collaborating was unavoidable to a certain extent, but...' Arnie carried on in a whisper, 'down in the family seat in Mende, it was different. Uncle Albin didn't have to do what he did.'

'How come you know what he did and I don't?' Armand blurted out in exasperation.

'He doesn't want you to know what he was up to.' Arnie took a long drag of his cigarette. 'There have been allusions.'

'*Putain*, cut out the crap, will you?' Armand had to stop himself from shaking his cousin. 'What the fuck were these allusions?'

'I heard my parents say, *Albin était chef de la milice*.'

Armand's cigarette suddenly tasted foul. He crushed it underfoot and kicked it into the park below. Repressing a heave, he gripped the balustrade and watched the cigarette butt twirl down, together with the last of his illusions.

'Head of the militia. Are you sure? What, like rounding up Jews, dawn raids, kicking doors down, torture and reprisals? Ah come on,' Armand's head was spinning, 'tell me you're not serious.'

Arnie turned away and resumed his study of Paris. Inside Armand, the world crumbled.

24
PARIS – MAY 2ND 1968

A pale moon shone over Paris. The clock chimed nine. Virgile and Arnie had left. Only Ségo and Leila remained. After returning the flat to its original condition, the girls had disappeared into Armand's bedroom from which seeped giggles and moans.

He paced around the flat, confused and disgusted by his cousin's revelations. He was double-checking the kitchen when a noise on the landing turned him to stone. The lift whirred into action...

Inside the bedroom, the moaning intensified. Armand banged on the door and shouted a warning.

A loud clank. The lift doors squeaked open. His father's voice rolled across, stern and full of reproach. What was going on? His mother was sobbing.

The key turned in the lock.

Armand gripped the door handle, unable to move. After Arnie's revelations, his first reaction had been to confront his father, but with two girls in his bed, he was not exactly in a position of strength.

'Enfin, Arielle, ne soyez pas ridicule.'

Armand's fingers tightened on the handle of his bedroom door.

'What if he dies?' Arielle shouted in reproach. 'What will you say to me then? Don't worry, dear, we'll get you another chauffeur?'

Armand pushed down the handle.

'For God's sake, Albin, what am I going to tell his wife?'

'I'm gratified to hear that his wife is your concern.'

'What? What are you implying?' Arielle stepped into the lobby.

Armand squeezed into his bedroom, shook Anne-Ségolène's naked shoulder and said in a raw whisper, '*Merde*, my parents are back.'

Eyes opaque with pleasure, Ségo pushed the hair from her face. 'Huh?'

Leila emerged, brown and heavy breasted. 'What are you doing here?'

Hit full on with the flesh, the smell and the debauchery his parents were about to witness, Armand's brain stopped functioning. He stuttered, 'My – my parents are home. Something's happened.'

'*Mon Dieu, la chasse !* The hunt! An accident? Are my parents all right?' Anne-Ségolène sat up and pulled a sheet over her breasts. 'What are we...'

Her sentence hung in the air. His mother's heels tapped down the corridor and stopped outside his door.

He saw the scene his mother was about to walk into, and closed his eyes. That was it. He was finished.

'Armand? Can I come in?'

Anne-Ségolène grabbed his T-shirt and pulled down hard. Armand flailed and toppled into her arms while, with a strong swivel of the hips, she unceremoniously sent Leila rolling under the bed with a thump.

'*Ouille !*'

The door opened.

His mother's teary eyes took in the fripperies, Ségo naked in the bed and on top, her fully clothed son, a hand on her breast.

'No… Oh no…' Arielle's chest heaved. She checked the corridor, squeezed in and quickly closed the door.

Still in the hall, his father was bellowing down the phone.

Lost in some private nightmare, his mother kept repeating, 'no – not this.'

'I'm so sorry, Madame de Peirac,' Anne-Ségolène said in a small voice, 'we were only playing. We… we didn't. Oh God, is everything all right? Has something happened?'

Armand's mother held it together long enough to whisper, 'there's been an accident.'

'Are my parents…?'

'No no, they're fine.' Arielle's eyes pooled with tears. She rubbed her hands distractedly. 'Joao… Joao has been shot.' She crossed her arms over her stomach and crumpled in a sob. 'My… our chauffeur. Mistaken for a boar.'

'What? Who shot him?'

Armand pushed himself from the bed and walked to his mother.

'Maman…' He put an arm around her.

She lifted her face to him and recited like an automaton, 'We don't know who– who it could–' she hiccupped. 'It could have been anyone.' Her eyes lost their focus. 'We don't know who shot him. We really don't know. He was in the wrong place, that's all.'

25

PARIS – MAY 3RD 1968

Nothing was said after Joao's death. No blame apportioned, no explanations given, but then, when was anything ever spoken aloud? Albin de Peirac did not tolerate dissent.

Armand and his mother went through the motions. June was not so very far away, though without Joao or Mary, a summer in Fleurac would not be restorative.

Two months before the end of term, Armand awoke to the realisation that graduating was the key to freedom. He had not been very assiduous in his studies, but it wasn't too late. He vowed to make up for lost time.

That Friday, he would study in the Sorbonne library and meet Mary later. She wanted to watch 'The Graduate' in English at a local cinema. They would eat a quick *croque-monsieur* in a bar, and he would walk her home.

'No lectures today I see,' he said to Virgile, as their steps echoed along a deserted corridor. 'The strikes are handy. They'll probably defer our exams. I could do with a few weeks' reprieve.'

'Me too to tell the truth.'

They reached the colonnade and gazed down onto the university forecourt. 'Oh wow!'

The courtyard was teeming. Because Nanterre had been closed after the riots, its students had brought their grievances over to the Sorbonne.

Virgile shrugged. 'Bah, it'll be back to normal on Monday. Don't get your hopes up.'

Inside the classical concourse, several hundred students were waiting in suspended animation under the benevolent eye of Victor Hugo's statue.

'I'm not surprised there's trouble,' said Virgile. 'There's never enough room in lectures, the system's antiquated, and when we do graduate, we can't get jobs. Something's got to give.'

Armand was curious, but he didn't share his friend's concerns. A few weeks away from the end of his Master's degree in French Literature, he had no desire to rock the boat.

'Oh man.' He turned away. 'This looks dodgy. There's going to be hell to pay at home if I get caught participating in a demo. I'm out of here.'

'Wait!' Virgile scanned the crowd. 'Let's find out what's going on first.'

A girl in a sage green cape standing nearby, filled them in, 'Fascists from *Occident* are on their way here to make trouble. The chancellor's shut this place down too.'

The sound of chanting reached them from the main Boulevard. Armand did not like where this was going.

'What fascists? They're just thugs looking for trouble. Come on, Virgile, let's get out of here.'

Virgile was no longer listening. 'Shut the Sorbonne? Can he do that?'

Before the girl had time to answer, a microphone crackled. Someone spoke above the hum. All eyes turned to a baby-faced redheaded man standing in a corner, calm and confident. There was a smile in the boyish voice.

'The authorities have decided to close the Sorbonne. So, from now on we are occupying the Sorbonne. It has never happened before.'

The courtyard was silent.

The speaker's tone was mild, when Armand would have expected Robespierre-like rhetoric. The journalist inside him came alive with the realisation that he might just witness history in the making. 'Occupying the Sorbonne for the first time.' 'The enemy at the gate.' He could see the headlines.

The sound of crashes came from inside the building.

'Here. You'd better take this.' Someone handed Armand a chair leg. 'The fascists have coshes. This'll just have to do.'

'No thanks. Why would I need that?'

Sticks were passed around. Here and there strategies to fight off the fascists were discussed with calm resolve. Spirits were high. There was no sense of urgency.

Snatches of police sirens, shouts of protest, and the growling of the crowd seeped in from the Boulevard Saint Michel. To Armand's relief, all the action seemed to be outside. He had always imagined a rebellion to be a much more chaotic affair. As long as he and the others remained inside the courtyard, there was little to fear. The Sorbonne had the same status as a church. It was safe from any police intrusion. The whole thing would soon blow over.

What was really at stake here?

Armand's thoughts turned to his journalistic heroes. Camus would have dipped his brushes in pristine grammar to paint a sclerotic society bent on protecting privilege. Hemingway would have stood tall, feet firmly apart. A hand shading his eyes, he would have scanned the crowd, searching for the human element. Then he would have written the whole thing out in abrupt, diamond-sharp prose.

A ripple ran through the crowd. A hushed rumour.

Virgile tapped Armand on the arm. 'Did you hear that? Did you hear what they said? The chancellor has called in the police.'

'What? No way.'

'Shit. They're already here!'

Just above their heads, the chapel bell began to toll. With each strike, another wave of black clad CRS ran in, the clatter of their boots filling the eerie silence between each tocsin. The CRS stood in a corner of the courtyard, huddled behind their shields, tortoise fashion, in the manner of a Roman legion. And still, there was silence.

Out on the Boulevard Saint Michel, the din became louder.

'The police have entered the Sorbonne illegally.' Matter-of-fact, the redhead's words bounced around the walls, as if he was describing the opening of a fête. 'According to this university's charter, the police cannot enter the premises. The chancellor has acted illegally. This is a civil offence.'

A gravelly voice rose above the hubbub. 'We are not here illegally. We are here to guarantee your safety and that of the university. Please leave the premises now.'

'That wasn't much of a demo.' Armand joined the throngs filing out towards the gate.

'Come on, man. Don't you want to stay and see what happens?' Virgile hunched his shoulders and put his hands inside his pockets.

'Bof.' Armand gave him an apologetic smile. 'I'm meeting Mary in la Palette tonight. Tell me all about it tomorrow. *Salut!*'

Somewhere behind him, the gravelly police spokesman barked an order to his men. 'Take the rest into custody. Everyone down to the station. Check their identity.'

'Run!' Virgile shouted.

Armand pushed forward and tried to reach the gate. He was just feet away when the legionaries of the CRS advanced in tight formation and barred the exit. The top doors were locked. They were trapped inside the yard. There was nowhere to hide.

Extremists from the pro-China faction pulled motorcycle helmets out of their rucksacks. They plunged into the mêlée with animal screams.

Thoughts of his father's wrath urged Armand on. He just had to get out. Get out. Get to Mary. He clawed his way to the exit but found himself inexorably pushed back. He stumbled and fell on top of the girl with the cape. It was too late. The black shapes were upon him.

Cowering against a wall, he sank to the ground and covered his head with his hands. Faceless, oozing anger and testosterone, a CRS pushed him against the wall and hit. Armand's head exploded. The cosh caught him on the side of his face, ripping his ear. He screamed. Strong arms grabbed him. He tried to fight back. But he was hurled into the waiting arms of the police outside and thrown into a *panier à salade*.

The bus stank of piss and sweat. It was already full. Armand collapsed onto a bench, pulled a handkerchief from his pocket and tried to staunch the blood coursing down his neck. His ear throbbed. He pushed the hair back from his face and swore under his breath. There was blood on his fingers. They'd never stood a chance. The bastards had come prepared, police buses lined the whole boulevard.

Out on the pavement it was carnage. Armand watched through the wired-up windows as the CRS grabbed students by their hair, their clothing and by anything else they could lay their hands on. People of both sexes were pushed to the ground and beaten with unmitigated fury.

'Fascistes!' CRS... SS.'

In amongst all the different cries of hatred, the word 'Fascist' resonated the most. How his father would vilify him for falling foul of the authorities. How could Armand look up to him now, knowing that he'd been in the militia, the equivalent of the French SS. His stomach lurched. He began to shiver.

'Fascistes! Réactionnaires! CRS –SS!' Dishevelled and angry students were manhandled into the bus at gunpoint. Armand closed his eyes. Bile rose in his throat. The last shreds of respect he had ever had for authority dissolved.

Fighting back tears, he wondered if Mary had somehow been trying to reach him. Whether the riots had gone as far as Odeon.

Opposite him, someone was pissing on the floor, laughing. Armand turned his head away. Out on the Boulevard, the fighting had escalated.

At the foot of an advertising column publicising the Moulin Rouge, a boy was crouching under a frenzy of blows. The girl in the sage green cape was tearing at a CRS officer's sleeve, screaming. 'Stop it! Stop hitting him! He hasn't done anything!' Sickened, Armand closed his eyes.

At the front of the *panier à salade* a soldier raised his machine gun in warning, to the accompaniment of jeers and insults.

He caught sight of Virgile's mop of red hair. He was being carried screaming, by four policemen who hurled him into another bus. Shouts of *'communistes assassins'* came from the fascist factions, intermingled with 'Get out of Vietnam!'

The bus began to rock.

'Ah merde,' said the bus driver to the soldier with the machine gun. 'The bastards have punctured one of our tyres.' CRS surrounded the bus with a wall of machine guns while the tyre was changed.

Armand looked back at the girl. Hunched at the foot of

the advertising column, she was sobbing. Her cape was spattered with blood.

Armand found himself joining in the singing of the *Internationale,* surprised that he knew the words. *'Debout les damnés de la terre...* Stand up, all the damned of the earth...'

It was going to be a long night.

26

PARIS – MAY 10TH 1968

A week later, Armand's heart skipped a beat when Mary appeared on the steps of the Alliance Française building. Her face lit up when she saw him. Dark hair bouncing over her shoulders, bag thumping against her mini-skirt, she skipped down the stairs and melted into his arms with a cry of delight.

'You're here! Are you all right? I got your *pneu,*' Mary said. 'Thanks for sending it. I was worried sick when you didn't turn up.' She touched the bandage over his ear. 'Oh no! What happened?'

'It looks worse than it is, but at the time, it felt as if my head was bashed open.'

'That's terrible. Did you have to spend the night in a cell?'

Armand shrugged. 'Nah, I got out straight away. Father's pally with the *Commissaire de police*. Mind you, I'd rather have spent a night in a cell. I've never seen him so furious.'

Mary squeezed his hand, her small fingers fresh and reassuring.

'God... I can't take much more of his *'I'll throw you out of the house if I find you've been mixed up with communists...'* and his endless refrain of '*What will people say?*' It's driving me insane!

'Why do you think your da's like that?'

Mary's blue eyes brimmed with such pure goodness that Armand felt dirty, infectious. From now on, he would always carry his father's past as a shameful genetic defect.

He searched for words. Failing, he simply took her hand and made for the top of Boulevard Raspail, towards the Latin Quarter.

'Virgile's still in prison. Christ, he didn't even do anything. Loads of them are still locked up, can you believe it?' He clenched his fists. 'I don't give a shit what my dad says, it's so unfair. I am going on this *manif*. Come on, if we hurry, we'll be able to catch up with the demo in the Latin Quarter.'

As they reached Place Vendôme, Armand halted. 'Sorry. It's not your war really. I shouldn't be dragging you into this.'

The way Mary's eyes shone, she would have followed him anywhere. It was a good feeling.

'I reckon they're gonna be marching past the Ministry of Justice to demand that the people rounded up in the Sorbonne are let out.'

'Has Virgile really been in prison for a week?'

'Yeah. Bastards.'

'What's he done?'

'Nothing! They say he's an agitator. You know what?' Armand let go of her hand and faced her. 'Perhaps he is an agitator, and rightly so. Things do need agitating.' Gesticulating, he walked on, occasionally turning to her, bumping into passers-by. 'The Government are stuck in the past, old codgers in charge of the country, revelling in the vainglory of their wars. Look at de Gaulle. He's seventy-eight, for God's sake! What kind of life can we expect, ruled by eighty-year-olds who've known nothing but wars and won't let the world rest?'

Mary had to run to keep pace as he ranted, windmilling with his arms.

'We want peace. We want a clean future. We don't want the atomic bomb, thank you very much, and we don't want Vietnam either. We want to build something new, a better world.'

Armand took in a lungful of spring air and began to sketch a world where his father's sins could be forgotten, a clean world… a world fit for Mary.

'Come on, we'll cross the Luxembourg Park. It'll be quicker. We'll reach the Boulevard Saint Michel from the top.'

The light was fading as they hurried through the Italianate gardens. Armand stopped and lifted a hand. 'Listen.'

The boulevard was quiet. The usual drone of cars replaced by slogans and chants.

A guard blew a whistle and waved them along. 'Closing!'

'Run!'

Out of breath, they emerged from the gate and bumped into a hirsute brute, foaming at the mouth, barring their way. 'Get back, get back! They're here!'

Less than thirty yards away, a solid wall of CRS was advancing towards them, shields glinting under orange streetlight. Fifty truncheons swung in terrifying unison towards the human tide that surged up the boulevard on the other side.

Armand pulled Mary into a side street.

'Did you see this? This is provocation. This *manif* is legal.'

They crossed Rue Gay-Lussac and managed to double up and join the cortège. Linking arms, they scanned *'libérez – nos – camarades – libérez – nos – camarades.'*

The crowd had swelled to tens of thousands, an assortment of students in jeans, *'blousons noirs'* – thugs in black leather jackets – school kids and factory workers. The

Sorbonne was now within sight. A solid wall of CRS was waiting for them. They were trapped. Armand and Mary were swept with the mob into the medieval maze of the Latin Quarter. Immediately, they found themselves running along with a gang of blouson noirs.

There was a purpose to their flight, and intent. Their leader, a tall spotted youth, lifted a metal *grille* from the base of a tree and stood it across a couple of metal bins dragged over by his mate. A team of schoolboys ran in from a neighbouring street. They lifted paving stones, gathered car tyres, planks and crates. Atop the barricades, the newly formed resistance movement began to pelt the CRS with stones, while in the no-man's-land between the two factions, dark figures crouched against walls, occasionally shooting out to capture what they could on film before scurrying back to the shelter of doorways.

Cornered, Armand and Mary were handed planks and dustbin lids. A chilling tune rose from a side street. It was '*Ça ira,*' the bloodthirsty anthem of the first Revolution. Armand took in the rubble, the shouts, the air, yellow, thick with anger and dust, and did a quick calculation. 1871, the Paris Commune… now was 1968, a century later, and Paris was once again erupting like a geyser.

A strange smell reached his nose. The blouson noirs covered their faces. A man pushed past him, a black flag in his hand and climbed to the top of the precarious barricade. A stone rolled down. He stumbled against Armand, who mechanically steadied the fellow and, balancing on a car tyre, pushed the flag into a gap between the stones. From his vantage point, he scanned the street. Behind their dark shields, the CRS legion was waiting. He could feel their fear.

A shadow sprang out. There was a flash. Someone barked an order. A staccato pop. A canister whistled through the air.

'Down!' Mary grabbed Armand's belt and pulled him onto

the sand. A grenade exploded in front of them. Seconds later, a burning sensation hit his skin.

'I can't breathe!' Tears streamed down Mary's face.

Armand wiped his nose on his sleeve, blinded by the yellow cloud enveloping them.

'Putain, du gaz lacrymogène !' someone yelled. It was teargas.

The blousons noirs carried on hurling stones. Shouting, crying, people staggered to and fro through the noxious smoke, to be met with more teargas grenades around the corner, launched from another street.

There was no way out.

From a window, a bucket of water was thrown to help dispel the gas, followed by wet strands of cloth. Crying, coughing, they made a grab for them.

A CRS in a gas mask lurched forward and hurled another canister. Thick smoke-filled Armand's lungs and hatred filled his mind. Mary was choking.

'Over here, quick!' Inside an arch, a small door opened. Armand and Mary were tugged into an inner courtyard. The door snapped shut. Inside the yard, the air was clean. Lungs on fire, Armand bent over, unable to catch his breath.

'Blow your nose and spit it out, man, you don't want that stuff inside you.' Their saviour pointed to a door. 'Get up those stairs. You can reach the roof and from there, the next building. Come on, I'll show you.'

Armand followed the dark shape in front of him. Sobbing, Mary clung to him as they stumbled to the top of the winding staircase.

'That stuff takes half an hour to clear. You won't be able to run on the roof if you're blinded, but you'll be safe up here for a while.'

They collapsed onto a flat space and took great gulps of air. Below them, at the intersection between the road and the boulevard, the protesters had upturned cars in chicanes to slow the advance of the police. There was an explosion, the noise of broken glass.

'Putain, non...des cocktails Molotov.' Up to that moment, Armand had believed he was part of a spontaneous uprising. The thugs had come prepared. He reached for Mary's hand and slumped against the cool stone, glad he didn't have to hide his tears.

'I have to go home,' Mary whimpered, 'if they find out I was here, I'll lose my job.'

'They've blocked the whole quarter... bastards.' Armand wiped his face with a damp rag and squinted at the orange cloud rising in the streetlight. 'We have to wait for that guy to come back.'

'What time is it?' The sun had gone down a long time ago.

'No idea.' He patted her hand. 'Don't worry. We'll make it to the last metro.'

27
PARIS – MAY 10TH 1968

Clinging onto chimneypots and drainpipes, their mysterious saviour led them along rooftops to a stairwell, down to the main boulevard. They reached the metro and breathless, reached rue de la Tour, amazed to have made it back safely to Mary's flat.

Armand pushed Mary under a porch. Mouths too raw for kisses, they clung to each other, febrile hands searching for skin.

'Do you have a key to your cellar?' His senses on fire, Armand had never been so aroused.

Mary nodded. She unlocked the main door and led Armand down a small concrete stairway to the side of the lift. With only an orange pilot light for guidance, they scurried past large bins along a dark underground labyrinth that smelled of refuse and cat pee. A further part was lined with slatted doors. Mary stopped in front of one and unlocked it.

Armand scanned the space in the dim light of a tiny window. Wine bottles were stacked on one wall and on the other, shelves crammed with toys and beach equipment. A surfboard propped against the back wall brought a smile to his face. He covered a toolbox with a beach towel and lifted Mary onto it.

'Je t'aime, Mary.' He cradled her face in his hands.

'I love you so much too,' Mary whispered back.

Lightheaded, he gripped her shoulders and hugged her. He had never felt so alive.

Her response set him on fire, sensations hitting him directly through the skin. Searching fingers fluttered over his body. Panting, aching, Armand had to stop himself from tearing her panties and taking her there and then. With deep measured breaths, he ran a hand under her jumper, unhooked her bra and caressed her, holding back. When at last, he ventured between her thighs and dipped a finger there, what he found drove him wild.

Hair tangled over her face, Mary pulled off her clothes and wriggled out of the last cotton barrier. She lifted her face to him, eyes dark with desire, her lips plump and red. With a soft groan, Armand kissed her and sank inside her, moving as slowly as he could.

'Oh God, you feel so good.'

'Armand,' Mary panted, 'you will be careful now, won't you?'

'Don't worry.' Eyes wide open, Armand focused on the surfboard.

They found a rhythm, but it did not last long. The erotic combination of the night's dangers and glimpses of Mary's body in the orange dimness took him to the brink. He tried holding back, but when she started shaking, her pleasure hit Armand with the force of a hurricane. He gasped and pulled out just in time, coming in great shuddering spasms over the beach towel.

28
PARIS – MAY 1968

Armand had pulled the Stones' *Let's spend the night together* from its sleeve and was about to drop the needle on the record when an argument in the living room caught his attention. He crept to his door and listened.

'Arielle, enfin, lisez vous-même.' The ice in his father's voice made Armand shiver. 'It's stated here in black and white. "Death by misadventure." *Vous voyez bien.'*

The formal *'vous'* Armand had heard all his life, but today, his parents' affectation struck him as ludicrous. It was said – in the higher circles of Parisian society – that swapping the respectful *'vous'* for the familiar *'tu'* during intimacy heightened a couple's passion. Whatever passion there may have been in that marriage had long gone. His parents slept apart.

Arielle faltered. 'An accident, you say?' She hissed, 'Do you think I don't know what you did?'

Armand rested his forehead on the door, not daring to breathe.

'You killed Joao.'

Armand repressed a gasp, every nerve taught to breaking point.

'Joao... Joao...' His father twisted the driver's name like a knife. 'So many tears for a servant, my dear, and a foreign one at that. What am I to think?'

This was followed by a sob. Anne-Ségolène's insinuation in the car came back to Armand. The hairs on his arms bristled as he pictured Arielle's fingers on the chauffeur's sleeve, their friendly banter in Fleurac, stealthy steps and floor boards creaking at night and now, Arielle's swollen eyes blamed on a sudden onset of hay fever. Christ, could the two of them have been having an affair? No, it was too sordid.

'So,' Arielle sniffed, 'you suspected something, and so you shot him.'

His father slammed his fist on something and roared. 'It was an accident!' He drew out the word, 'ac-ci-dent.' There are over seventy hunting accidents every year in France. See what it says here? Accident. The *commissaire* wrote it in black and white.'

'And what did that earn him, that *commissaire* of yours? A year's hunting on your lands? Two weeks in your parents' flat in Antibes? An internship for his daughter?'

Armand let himself slide to the floor, sickened by the concept that his mother had been sleeping with– No, it was too gross. It was impossible. She was fifty for God's sake. She was old. Old people didn't need sex– did they?

Over in the study, Arielle was still fighting. 'How easily you convinced the *commissaire* of your innocence.'

'For God's sake woman, spare me the theatricals.'

'You're a monster, Albin de Peirac,' she growled, 'a cold-blooded monster.'

Steps echoed down the corridor. His mother's door slammed. Moments later, his father's study door clicked shut.

Armand buried his head in his hands and whimpered, hugging his knees, crushed with shame at what his parents had done, at the cesspit of lies he had been living with, under a thin veneer of respectability.

On the surface, they had it all. The flat in Passy, the staff, the summer residences, friends, businesses, the whole lot personally blessed by the bishop when he visited Notre Dame d'Auteuil twice a year. His parents never missed a church service, but what God did they really pray to, and what for?

Armand pressed his fists inside his eye sockets to dispel the image of his mother and Joao in bed, but when the tableau vanished, an even uglier one emerged, that of his father tracking his quarry in a forest, secure in the knowledge that he could, once again, murder with impunity.

Could his father knowingly have followed Joao and slaughtered him like an animal? Something inside Armand rebelled at the thought. But if it really was an accident, his father's lack of guilt was very disturbing. His cousin's words came back to him. *'Chef de la milice.'* He had killed before.

Armand leaned back against the door and gazed at his room through half-closed lids. The familiar bedroom – stylish empire furnishings livened up with books and psychedelic touches of his own– seemed as fake as the staging of a boulevard play.

He didn't want to be part of this farce anymore. It was time for the curtain to come down.

29

PARIS – JUNE 1ST 1968

As soon as Madame Leboeuf left for market, Armand crept to the kitchen, poured coffee and milk into a saucepan and set it on the gas ring. A newspaper on the table drew his attention, topped by an envelope bearing his name. He picked it up and shook it. There was something inside. His eyes were drawn to the paper. He dropped the envelope. His own face was staring back from the first page of France-Soir, under the title **ANARCHIE DANS LES RUES DE PARIS**.

He slumped onto a chair and pulled the paper towards him. 'Anarchy in the streets of Paris.' There he was, the anarchist, standing atop a pile of rubble, black flag in hand, an avenging angel storming a barricade, his stance the very replica of the revolutionary carvings at the base of the Arc de Triomphe.

How on earth... Of course! That bloody photographer. Armand hoped he gagged on tear gas.

There was no recovering from this. By now, the whole of the *rallye* circuit had sent their servants to buy France Soir and choked on their brioche. 'I say, young de Peirac an anarchist? Good Lord, who would have thought? He seemed such a nice boy.'

Armand crumpled, aghast at how fast his life was unravelling. Only a week ago, the best he could have hoped for was a kiss from Mary alongside the skating-rink, and at worst, flunking a test. Now not only did he suspect his father of being a murderer and his mother an adulteress, but in a split second, he had become an 'anarchist' and a pariah.

At this moment, he would have given anything to turn back the clock to the safety and innocence of April, before his life plummeted into a nightmare.

On the cooker, the *café au lait* threatened to boil over. Armand turned it off and took out a bowl.

The study door creaked open. His father's steps rang on the wooden floor. Armand hunched his shoulders and steeled himself for the onslaught.

'I supposed you're proud of yourself,' his father snarled.

Armand slowly filled his bowl and faced his father. Here was the man he had tried all his life to please, the man he had both loved and feared. Portly, balding, that man was a fraud. However distasteful it was, Armand held on to that thought and tried to stand his ground.

'My friend Virgile has been in police custody for a week now, held on inexistent charges.' Emboldened by the injustice of it all, Armand ploughed on. 'I wasn't alone at that demonstration, you know, there were twenty thousand of us.'

His father's hooded eyes filled with contempt. 'You heard what de Gaulle said. *C'est la chienlit,* a God-awful mess, orchestrated by leftists and…' he brushed away the envelope, picked up the paper and spat, 'anarchists.'

'I'm not an anarchist, Papa. You know that. This is just a snapshot.' For once, Armand held his father's gaze. 'It's not about me though, is it? It's about you. You're worried about your reputation.'

He crossed his arms, awaiting the usual litany. He hated it, but at least they would be on safe ground.

His father fiddled with his heraldic cufflinks, the unmistakable precursor to the 'if only' tirade.

Here we go, thought Armand, his insides shrivelling.

'All this would never have happened if only you'd buckled down and gone to a *Grande Ecole*. You're intelligent, we have money, you're part of an elite, but no, you had to go to a common university to study some woolly subject. You had the brains to go to *Normale Sup,* mix with future ministers, diplomats and captains of industry. But no, not you. No wonder you ended up *gauchiste.* Universities fill your head with political nonsense. It's as predictable as catching clap in a brothel.'

Still standing, Armand picked up his bowl and drank a mouthful to conceal a sneer as his father reached his predictable crescendo, *'le qu'en dira-t-on.'* What will people say.

'What will people say when they see a photo of my son on the cover page of this rag? How am I going to maintain any sort of credibility?'

Armand leaned back against the worktop, and for the first time, found himself strangely filled with compassion.

Deep inside the old man were fears, fear of losing face, fear of being exposed for the fraud that he was. Armand's grandfather had been a hard man. Perhaps young Albin had spent his life trying to impress the old Marquis. But Armand's empathy was short-lived. His father had killed innocent men and that knowledge would forever eat away at him.

'I don't know what *they* will say about you, Père. I don't know who you are. Who do you imagine *they* see when they look at you? A pillar of the church? An upstanding citizen? An ex-*résistant*?' Armand stressed the word.

His father flinched. He picked up the envelope and narrowed his eyes.

'I've no idea what you imagined all your marching and ripping up streets would change. Just look at what you've really achieved in your five seconds of fame.' He tore open the envelope and shook its contents onto the paper. 'The de la Bauderie family have returned your engagement ring. All my efforts ruined.'

Armand's bowl clanged as he banged it on the worktop. 'Right. Let me get this straight. I stood on a barricade for all of five seconds and *your* reputation is shot. Why? Was it that fragile?' He leaned back, now sure of his ground. 'You said it yourself, the Bauderie family. Not Anne-Ségo. She'll stand by me. You know exactly why Anne-Ségo's parents told her to break the engagement, because *you* murdered someone on their land, that's why. How convenient for you that you can blame me.'

His father's face turned from red to purple to deathly white. He clenched his jaw. 'Enough! Go to your room and pack your bags. You'll drive your mother to Fleurac in the morning, and since you are obviously intent on failing your course, I want you out of my house. I will not spend another centime on your education.'

Armand guffawed. 'My education? The Sorbonne charge you less than your subscription to La Vie Catholique, a magazine which by the way, you've never once opened!'

He stormed off to his room and threw jeans, shorts and jumpers into two suitcases, together with records and books.

Fleurac. Sadly, this time, it was for good. Although he had often wished himself away, Armand had never expected it to end so abruptly. Embryonic emotions bubbled, rose and burst without taking shape, clashing with each other.

Pensive, he slipped the Rolling Stones record back into its

sleeve. *Let's spend the night together'* How he would have loved to sing that to Mary.

Mary! Armand fretted about his room. He had to call her. No... there was no point. They wouldn't let her answer the phone. Ask Anne-Ségo to leave a message for him. No, he had blown that bridge too. Mary... he had to contact her somehow.

Angry sounds seeped through the wall.

A brain wave. *Un pneu!*

Leaving his parents to their quarrel, Armand ran to the post office.

Clouds had gathered overhead. A chilly wind lifted litter into the air. Inside the post office, he rubbed his arms to warm up, asked to send a *pneumatique* and took the blue card he was given to a quiet part of the counter. Pen in hand, he composed the words he wanted to send, a message at once clear to Mary, but cryptic enough to fool her employer. Pen poised over the card, Armand searched for a way to let Mary know how much he loved her. It was too dangerous. Frustrated, he settled for,

Dear Mary,

'No skating at Molitor on Saturday. I've been sent away for the summer. You will never know how sorry I am. Will write later.'
'Armand'

He lovingly traced 'Mary Sullivan,' wrote her address, and handed the form with a dispirited breath. The clerk insisted he add his own address. Worried lest Mary's employer should intercept the message, Armand scribbled as illegibly as he could.

A steel hand clamped around his heart. The desk shook as the attendant stamped the message with date and time, and unceremoniously stuffed it inside a cylinder. That was it. With a pneumatic pop, Armand's inadequate goodbye was pumped along the many arteries that pulsed and throbbed to the rhythm of Paris' two and half million hearts... a good bye that left a very bitter taste.

He trudged home, dragging his feet on the pavement. It began to rain. Around him, the spring colours leeched into monochrome melancholy.

Soon, he would be exiled in Fleurac, population one and a half thousand. "Sometimes, you miss just one person, and the world is empty," said Lamartine. Armand knew that for him, the world would be empty for a very long time.

It was still raining the next morning when he took Joao's place at the wheel of the DS. His parents were facing each other in the hall, the glass door propped open with a suitcase.

Armand turned the ignition key with a sense of relief. Fleurac was the only place where his father would never follow them. Growing up, he had wondered why Papa never came with them. Now he knew why. His victims might recognise him.

His father placed the case in the boot, held the car door open for his wife, put a hand on the nape of her neck and whispered something in her ear.

He waved them off, a wolfish sneer distorting his face.

Armand's mother slumped into the car like a broken puppet, all life sucked out of her.

They drove to Fleurac in silence. It was seven hours from Paris.

30

FLEURAC – JUNE 1968

The tall Fleurac house stood at the corner of a narrow street, above a florist's shop. The kitchen, lounge and Arielle's bedroom were on the first floor. Armand had taken over the large attic.

He had left Paris in a hurry and he missed his books. Scouring second hand bookshops gave him a sense of purpose while he tried to decide what to do with his life, and dreamt up schemes to contact Mary. She had never answered his letters.

Jeanne's voice rose from the kitchen below. He guessed from the smell of burning that his mother had once again tried her hand at cooking. Jeanne did her best to provide them with soups, stews and pies, but a task as simple as warming them up proved a challenge. They both missed Madame Leboeuf, their Paris cook. Though they missed Joao dreadfully, his name was never mentioned.

Armand came down and joined them.

'What's cooking?'

'Ah, here you are,' Jeanne lifted her face for him to kiss.

'Armand, you're a grown lad, why don't you take over so your mother can rest?'

Armand bent down to kiss her. Late thirties, Jeanne was pleasantly plump and a smile always rippled on her soft skin.

'And build my own bookshelves, *and* help André remodel your old house on the hill?'

'André's teaching you useful life-skills dear. Cooking and carpentry will be of more use to you than those books of yours. Anyway, you're quite gifted at manual labour, so he tells me.'

'I certainly don't get it from Dad.' Armand was glad to throw a dig, mild though it was, at his father.

Arielle and Jeanne exchanged a glance.

Jeanne slipped a quiche into the oven.

'Listen you two, gas mark four for twenty minutes.' She pointed to a charred mess on the worktop. 'I don't know how you managed to burn that apple pie.'

'But Jeanne, it's not me, it's the oven.'

'In that case, I'll get André to check it... Oh, hold on. Lucien said he'd be coming to see you later on. He'll have a look at it. Now I've got to rush, Catherine will be back from school.'

They kissed Jeanne goodbye and listened to her steps scurrying down the stone steps.

Armand walked to the window. It was drizzling. Across the road, a poster advertised a documentary film on Everest to be shown in the town hall in two weeks' time. Fleurac's idea of culture. Bored, he returned to his bedroom and opened his book, only to shut it again. Mary still filled his mind. Back in Paris, while they were together, she had made him promise never to call her at her place of work, but that was then. He had been holding out, waiting for a letter or a card. Anne-Ségolène swore that she had given her his address. Nothing. Unable to bear it, he had phoned several times, but there was no answer. Where was she?

He dropped his book. He simply had to know. Until he knew how she felt about him, he could never move on.

He was half-way down the stairs when the doorbell rang. He recognised the voice. Jeanne's brother Lucien had become a regular visitor since he was widowed a couple of years back. Armand liked him. When he wasn't managing a chestnut factory in Lyon, Lucien was a keen hunter. During the summer holidays, the two men went out together to look for game that Armand, ever the pacifist, was only willing to shoot on camera.

A second voice rose from the sitting room, a voice Armand had never heard before.

He went to the phone, lifted the receiver and, with trembling fingers, dialled the number he had scribbled on a piece of paper, praying with all his might that this time, Mary would pick up.

'Allo ?'

His heart sank. It was Madame Dumont.

He inhaled deeply and said with a tight throat,

'Bonjour, je voudrais parler avec Mary s'il vous plait.'

'Mary has left us.'

The news crushed Armand.

'Where is she?'

'She went home to Dublin.'

'Dublin?' He repeated dumbly. Words sticking inside his throat, he managed, 'could you give me her address? My name is Armand de Peirac and…'

'I know exactly who you are, young man, and no, I won't give you her address. You've done enough harm already, don't you think?' She hung up.

Shaking, Armand slowly replaced the receiver, wondering what she could have meant. And then it came to him. The photo in the paper. Christ, was Mary on it too? So worried had he been about his own fate, he hadn't even checked. That was it. Yes, that was surely it. The Dumonts had seen the photo and sacked her. Typical, they probably hadn't given her the chance to explain. Mary must have thought he had abandoned her. Oh God, what a mess he had made of it all.

Armand stared at the phone, broken-hearted and lost. Mary had planned to spend another year in Paris. Without her, or the hope of seeing her again, life made very little sense. He trudged down the stairs and was heading for the café, hoping Pastis would fill the void, and stopped. Words were exchanged in the sitting-room.

'No, no, Lucien, we were in Paris in May 44,' his mother declared in a tone that stood no controversy.

How often Armand had heard that refrain. *'We left for Paris and stayed with Albin's brother. We then went to Bordeaux and from there, sailed to America.'* Had they really gone to America? Only now did the insistence in his mother's voice make him wonder how exactly it had been possible for his parents to escape war-locked France.

Intrigued, he crept to the door.

Warm, the new voice said with the local accent, *'Albin de Peirac était chef de la milice à Mende, en 44.'* Was the militia story finally catching up with his father? A strange feeling hit him in the solar plexus and for the first time, Armand wondered how it would affect him.

'No. In 44,' Arielle repeated doggedly, 'he was in Paris. We were both in Paris at the time you're talking about.'

Strange that his mother should remain loyal to her beast of a husband. What was his hold on her?

Armand pushed thoughts of Mary to a corner of his mind and went in. What he saw made him flinch. Hunched inside a deep chair was a man straight out of a horror film, his features burned by something like the napalm the Americans were dropping over Vietnam.

Lucien stood by the window.

Armand went to shake Lucien's hand and, a polite grin glued to his face, shook the stranger's claw-like fingers.

'Monsieur.'

You could have cut the atmosphere with a knife. He had obviously interrupted something.

'Léon... Léon Blanqui.' Lucien introduced the man. *'Un compagnon de résistance.'* Lucien put a protective arm around Armand's shoulder. 'Armand is Arielle's son.' The way he said this broke whatever deadlock had been going on.

'I see,' the man shrunk, defeated. 'I see.'

Unsure of what he had disturbed, Armand beat a hasty retreat and headed for the bar where Lucien found him at midnight, drunk, slumped over the counter.

'Come on, son, you can't put yourself in such a state over a girl. Crying into your pastis has never solved anything.'

'I've met plenty of girls,' slobbered Armand, 'but she was the one I wanted.' He pushed himself away from Lucien's shoulder, wobbled about and straightened himself. 'What did Dad do to that man, Lucien?'

'Nothing. Don't fret over old stories. Instead, why don't you think about what you want to do with your life, eh? Your mother's so proud of you, Armand. We're all proud of you. You do know that, don't you?'

Armand staggered home, threw himself on his bed and cried over Mary, the mess he had made of his life and the realisation that he had absolutely no idea how he was going to get himself out of it.

31
OCTOBER 1971 – PARIS

It had been three years since Armand had last seen Anne-Ségolène. They had agreed to meet at the Orangerie end of the Tuileries Gardens.

It was a glorious October day. The leaves had only just begun to fall. He watched her hurrying down the central path, willowy and elegant in a casual outfit of white cropped trousers, long navy cardigan and sensible moccasins.

'Armand!' Slightly breathless, she offered him her cheeks. 'It's so good to see you! It's been too long.' She held him at arms' length and ran her eyes over his loose black jumper, flared jeans, beard and long hair. 'Look at you now!' She shook her head, setting her newly permed hair in motion, 'What happened to that *minet*, that preppy fiancé I used to have?'

'I'm afraid I've turned into a bit of a hippie. You on the other hand, look wonderful. The curly hair looks good.'

She ran slim fingers through her perm. 'Like it?'

'Very sophisticated. So, how's the job?'

'Bah,' Anne-Ségolène shrugged, 'I do up bars we call

'*drugstores*' and '*pubs*.' Tell me, you've travelled. What does a drugstore really look like?'

'No idea. I was in India, remember?'

'Ah, so I'll know who to call when I've to decorate an Indian restaurant. How about pubs? Didn't you work in one in Dublin before you went to India?'

Armand shrugged. 'Yeah, but it wasn't your style. Spit and sawdust.'

'You never found Mary huh?' She leaned into him.

Armand shook his head, grateful for the sympathy he read in her eyes. A dull pain throbbed inside his chest. Returning to Paris hurt more than he had anticipated. 'I went to look for her, you know, when I worked at that pub in Dublin, but it was hopeless. Every second Irishman is called Sullivan over there.' They circled Place de la Concorde and walked along the bank of the Seine.

'I don't know how you do it.' Armand broached a new subject, unsure of how much of his three-year descent into hell he was willing to divulge. 'You're so tolerant of Paris, of all that bourgeois keeping-up of appearances.' He took in a deep breath. 'God, how I struggled with it.'

Her eyes brimmed with affection. 'You haven't always felt that way though, have you?'

'I don't know. I've never really fitted in. The *rallyes*, the church, it was all about who you knew… who your parents were. It was never about who *you* were as a person. It has always irked me. Growing up, I was only ever at peace in Fleurac.'

They stopped to admire the sun streaming through the glass dome of the Grand Palais. Avenue de New York, plane tree leaves curled at the edges, mottled and dry, ready to fall. Armand found Paris beautiful, but its beauty was contrived, man-made. Something inside him, something he couldn't explain, always drew him back to the wild.

Anne-Ségolène ran a strand of his hair through her fingers, bleached as it was by the Indian sun. 'Poor little rich boy. Tell me, did they chop it off when you were conscripted?'

Head down, Armand increased his step. He stopped and leaned over the wall that ran along the river, the Eiffel Tower behind him.

'It's been three years.' Anne-Ségolène faced him. 'Do you think you've moved on? You feel so… angry still.'

He didn't answer, so she asked again, 'Did you return to Fleurac, after your military service?'

Armand turned his gaze to the Grand Palais in the distance and murmured. 'She never returned to Paris, you know, my mother.'

She leaned against his shoulder.

'It took her just over a year to die. Jeanne and I looked after her. It was horrible.'

'I heard. I'm so sorry.'

Armand spoke in a strangled whisper. 'My father didn't even come to her funeral.'

Anne-Ségolène placed both hands on his shoulders. 'Your father told us he couldn't face it. He isn't a bad man, Armand. Papa's still doing business with him. We were all desperately sorry about that hunting accident. It just happened'

'If it was an accident...'

'Ah come on, of course it was. Now, tell me about India.'

Armand lowered his gaze to the pavement. 'After Maman died, I… I got quite low. I didn't know what to do with myself, so I rented out the Fleurac house and headed for India.' He exhaled. 'I spent some time in an ashram in Pondicherry.' He met her gaze with a self-conscious smile. 'I had to find myself, I suppose. See what I was capable of. Back in the Cévennes, I was always the grandson of the Marquis d'Aubrac. It brought its own expectations…' Armand opened his hands. 'I've always been someone's son, someone's grandson.' He turned to her, full of rancour. 'I've never been just me.'

She patted his hand. 'For me, you are.'

'Thank you. Anyway, when I was away, the first thing I did was to drop the particle.'

'What do you mean?'

'My name is Peirac now, pure and simple. Armand Peirac. Believe me, it's liberating.'

She gasped. For Anne-Ségolène de la Bauderie, her name was a gift, her trademark. Her *'particule'* was a seal of quality, the master key that opened every door.

'Sorry, I've been talking about myself. Tell me, are you still with…'

'Leila? No.' Her face closed. 'Her parents took her to Algeria and forced her to marry. It was awful.'

'Have you heard from her?'

Anne-Ségolène closed her eyes and murmured with a defeated sigh, 'She's back in Nanterre, that dump of a place. She's just had a son. I can't imagine how she copes.'

'Poor girl,' whispered Armand. 'Have you found someone else?'

Ségo tilted her head to one side and grinned. 'I have. She's called Virginie. She works in TV. And before you ask, no.' She sighed. 'No. I haven't told my parents. I've a flat Rue du Bac in the fifth arrondissement. I can do what I want. Which reminds me, where are you staying tonight?'

'With Virgile in the eighteenth. You remember Virgile? Red haired chap. You met him at my place, the day we had the fondue.'

'You're not staying at your dad's?'

Armand's eyes popped. Was she for real?

'No! I haven't seen him since he threw me out. We've nothing to say to each other.'

They reached the Eiffel Tower. Aware of his change of mood, Anne-Ségolène pointed to the expanse of grass and said softly, 'I love this place… all those fields around the Eiffel Tower.' Pointing to the line of tourists snaking in the distance, she added, 'no one ever goes further than the east pillar, totally bypassing sixty acres of… well, countryside I suppose. Did you ever bring Mary here for a picnic?'

Mary… Armand winced. The old wound still smarted. 'Mary...' He thought aloud. 'She was open, generous. That's what I loved about her, her openness. She had no secrets, no hang-ups, nothing to hide. I envied her that.'

A strange noise echoed in the distance.

Ségo lifted a hand. 'Listen! What's that noise?'

Armand knew the noise well, but would never have expected it so far from Fleurac.

'Armand, look over there. Sheep!' Anne-Ségolène cried out.

A hundred yards from them, a flock of leggy sheep were advancing, chomping at grass, unfazed by the cameras aimed at them.

'They're probably shooting a comic film,' Armand hazarded.

'There's a placard. What the… Look! Something's written on the sheep!'

Armand screwed up his eyes and read out the placard. '*Contra l'armada e l'estat colonial. GARDAREM LO LARZAC.*'

'Do you know what it means?'

'Yes. It's in Occitan. It says '*against the army and the colonial state. The Larzac is ours.*' The Larzac is near where I live. It isn't all that far from Fleurac.' He looked around. 'It's a big cheese region. It's where Roquefort comes from.'

'Yum, my favourite blue cheese.'

'Do you know what's going on?'

Anne-Ségolène pushed a strand of permed hair from her

face. She chuckled. 'The army want to extend a firing range in that part of the Massif Central. They were convinced no one would notice. It's a desert. No one lives there but a handful of sheep farmers. They thought it would be a doddle to oust them, but I can see that if Roquefort is a solid product, the farmers would put up a fight.'

'And they've brought their sheep here to protest. Good on them.' Armand laughed. His face fell. He added with passion, 'I hate the army.'

Anne-Ségolène tapped a finger against her lips, trying to retrieve a memory. 'A year or so ago, my father was talking about that place. It was the first time I'd heard of it, before it was on the news.'

They joined a group around a shepherd making his point in a strongly accented voice.

'They won't get our land. It might look like the Gobi Desert to you Parisians, but it's our livelihood. There's a hundred of us farm there and we're not afraid of the army. We've signed a pledge and we will never sell. Ever. Let them try to evict us. Let them try! We've got guns and we'll use them if we have to.'

A cheer greeted his statement.

Anne-Ségolène jostled Armand. 'I remember now. Your father and mine were preparing some sort of deal. I overheard them discussing buying up land in that part of the world.'

'Are you sure?'

She half closed her eyes. 'Hmmm. I can still see them now, rubbing their hands at a particularly lucrative deal.'

'Just the sort of underhand operation my father relishes,' Armand growled. 'Buying up derelict farms for a song and reselling them to the Ministry of Defence. Totally up his street. Bastard.'

'Please don't let it fester, Armand. Go and see him. Go to

Passy and have a chat. He lives on his own, he'll be delighted to see you.'

Armand shrugged away her naive suggestion. A chat? The girl really had no idea.

'Fancy a coffee? There's a place over there. Come on, I'm buying.'

Armand looked longingly at the gathering crowd, the journalist in him suddenly titillated.

'You haven't told me how you make a living.' Anne-Ségolène dragged him towards the café.

'I wrote a few articles about India, about the ashram. The other day, I sold a piece about the Gévaudan Beast to a kids' magazine.'

'Oh yes, the famous wolf that terrorised– where was it again?'

Armand grinned. 'it's near the Larzac, not at all your area of choice. Too far from the beaches.' He smiled. 'Can you get me a *grand crème?* Sorry, I've got to call Virgile.'

'Sure.' She pulled out a metal chair and signalled to the waiter.

Armand went to get a token and called Virgile from the cabin downstairs.

Moments later, he returned to the terrace where they spent a pleasant half-hour catching up with gossip. His cousin Arnie was dating one of Anne-Ségolène's rich friends. To Armand, it all seemed like another life.

Anne-Ségolène checked her watch. 'Oh dear, five-thirty already. I promised Papa that I'd meet him at the Langham tonight. I have to go and make myself presentable.'

To think that only days ago, he was sitting on a dirt floor, eating chapattis and rice with his fingers.

They carried on along Avenue de New York, reached the Passy metro in companionable silence and halted by the railings, unsure of what to say. Overcome with a mix of emotions, Armand hugged Ségo very tight, his face buried in new her new curls. 'Thanks for sticking with me, Ségo. It really means a lot.'

'Don't ever lose touch, you hear?' She held on to his hand. 'Where are you off to now?'

'I thought I might follow your advice and knock on my old man's door.' Armand said to humour her. 'He's just around the corner.'

She said, 'Do that. I promise you won't regret it...' and sauntered back to her champagne world.

32

PARIS – OCTOBER 1971

As he passed Rue de la Tour, Armand's heart skipped a beat. Over the years, the pain had dulled, but since he was back in Paris, Mary rarely left his thoughts. He walked to the blue coach door where they used to kiss and tried to recapture the past.

Ségo was right in a way. It was time he sorted out his feelings. His father's noxious hold loomed over him like a shadow puppet, darkening his life, poisoning his dreams. So yes, it was time to let go of the hurt. After a year meditating in an Ashram, Armand felt man enough to confront his father in order to achieve some sort of closure.

His parents had never been close, but until Joao's death, they had respected each other. He had on occasions attempted to quiz Jeanne. As the Fleurac healer, she knew everyone's secrets, but she too had brushed his questions aside.

Armand pushed the heavy glass door into the hall and halted, hit by the familiar smell. A movement to the side drew his attention, the concierge peering through her tiny window.

He lifted a hand in greeting, squeezed into the elevator, his face lifted towards the third floor. The creaking, the clanking, the scent of the concierge's sorrel soup, the sweep of the oak staircase filing past reminded Armand of the time Joao was still alive, when his mother was happy. When he was happy. The last clang hurled him back to the day of the fondue, the day he had made love to Mary for the first time.

The lift juddered to a halt. His throat dry, Armand stepped onto the landing. Under the doorbell, the name was still there, carved in brass. *M. & Mme Albin de Peirac....* the pretence was baffling.

He pressed the bell and listened to it echo deep inside the flat. He took a ragged breath, pulled down the sleeves of his jumper and waited, rocking on the ball of his feet.

Something moved behind the peephole. The door opened slowly. His father had aged. What was left of his hair was completely white. Under the thick brow, the soft lids appeared fleshier though the dark eyes had lost none of their power. He held the door, his face devoid of emotion.

Armand cleared his voice and extended a hand. '*Papa je–*'

For the longest moment, his father considered the long hair, the beard and the shapeless jumper. Mouth puckered in contempt, he took a step back and slammed the door so hard, the old building shuddered all the way to its foundations.

33
PARIS – OCTOBER 1971

'*Tiens, mon vieux. Un pastis.* I've made it strong enough to take the edge of the pain away.' Virgile held out a glass of milky liquid.

Shell-shocked, Armand hovered near a worn club chair covered with what looked like a dead dog. Virgile whisked off the Afghan coat and gave Armand a light push.

Armand dropped into the chair, took the proffered glass and knocked back half of it, the alcohol instantly coursing through his veins. He couldn't remember the last time he'd eaten.

He ran his eyes over Virgile's den. A mattress covered with a Moroccan throw was laid on bare floorboards. An old wardrobe, a few crates and a guitar leaning in a corner completed the décor.

'I always knew your old man was dodgy.' Virgile put a hand on Armand's shoulder. 'But man, slamming the door...' he shook his ginger afro.

Virgile's hair had grown, but instead of growing downwards, it had spread outwards like a mushroom. He sported a short beard, corduroy flares and a flowery shirt.

Armand was about to say something, discuss the incident perhaps but, thinking better of it, he just drained his glass and held it out again with a heart-rending sigh. He had achieved closure. His father had ceased to exist.

'You're not very *vocacious* today, mate,' said Virgile.

'Loquacious.' Armand corrected.

'Huh?'

'The word is loquacious, not *vocacious*. I am not vivacious either. Sorry.'

'At least you're not salacious.'

'No, but I'm voracious. Haven't eaten in yonks.'

'Spaghetti okay?'

'With *Gruyère rape ?*'

'Just like the old days.' Virgile checked the level of the Pastis in the bottle and replenished Armand's glass with a more diluted version, adding, 'I'm skint. I've just quit my job.'

'I thought you were temping.'

'I was the last few months. Before that, I worked in some huge offices in Levallois, but I was too active in the union. They fired me at the end of my probationary period. Same story everywhere I go.'

'Did you get a record that time the police held you?'

'Yep. Doesn't help with finding a job.' Virgile slapped the table. 'Know what? I've had it with Paris, I need to find something else.'

'Me too.' Armand drained his second pastis. 'Let's bugger off to Australia.'

'Nah. Too hot. I'd burn.' Virgile pointed to his freckled skin.

'How about New York?'

'What?' Virgile spat out his drink. 'That hotbed of capitalism? Are you insane?'

'Sorry. How about New Caledonia?'

'Bah.' Virgile went to the gas ring, filled a pan with water and lit the gas. 'Why did you come back?'

'The war between India and Pakistan got to me in the end. Bloody Muslims and Sikhs and Hindus all used to live together relatively happily and then, it wasn't safe anywhere any more. Nixon and Mrs Gandhi's face plastered over every paper…'

'Bloody imperialist meddlers.' Virgile shook his ginger afro.

'My old man's a shit.' Armand stared into his empty glass, unable to let go.

'I got us some Préfontaine.' Virgile held out a bottle of cheap red. 'Open it while I'm doing the spaghetti, will ya?'

Ignoring him, Armand went to the mattress and slumped, staring blankly at the wall, hands behind his head. 'Leaving France altogether isn't a bad idea, you know.' He wriggled over and pulled his passport out of his jeans pocket. 'How about Greenland?'

Virgile tiptoed towards the bed, snatched the passport and thumbed through it till he found the photo page.

'Wow! Your hair's so short! What the fuck were you thinking?'

'Give it back, you moron. I was in the army remember? I didn't flunk off like some people.'

'Yeah well, if the CRS hadn't hit me so hard,' Virgile referred to the night of the riots, 'I might have been fit for service. Fuckers fractured my skull.'

Armand's blood boiled at the memory. The bastards had no right to whack people like that.

Virgile sniggered. 'Hey, I thought your name was Armand?'

'It is.' Armand lunged. 'Give me that!'

'Wait!' Virgile stepped out of reach, the passport clutched to his chest.

'It says here that your name is Aymeric Armand de Peirac. *Putain,* what a mouthful! I knew you were posh, but that is ridiculous.' Pursing his lips, Virgile over articulated in a mock aristocratic voice, '*Enchanté.* Yes, Aymeric Armand de Peirac, that's me. I live rue Raynouard, in the sixteenth…'

Virgile's jibe plunged to the core of Armand's open wound. With a roar, he hurled himself at his friend, knocked him onto the mattress and pounded him with blows.

'Ho ho! Armand! Stop!' Virgile screamed. He dropped the passport, huddled into a tight ball, rolled away and once out of reach, sprung up, haggard.

'Hey man, what's got into you? Can't you take a joke?'

Panting, hair plastered to his face, Armand scrambled up and grabbed his passport. 'No. I can't take that joke because it isn't funny. Listen–' His gaze bore into Virgile. 'If having me here upsets the purity of your socialist ideals, I won't force myself on you. I'm off. Bye.' Astonished at the depth of his anger, he lifted his backpack and reached out for the door. He was done with Paris.

'Come on, calm down, I'm sorry,' mumbled Virgile. 'Of course, you can stay.'

The spaghetti boiled over.

'Merde, les pâtes !' Virgile turned off the gas, strained the pasta and set two plates on a vegetable crate.

Chastened, Armand dropped the rucksack and uncorked the wine. He was checking the grated Gruyère for mould when Virgile spoke tentatively, holding the pan in front of himself as a shield.

'I'll just ask you one thing, and this time, promise you won't get mad, okay?' As a peace offering, he pulled out a baguette.

'Spit it out.' Armand placed the baguette on the crate.

'Right...' His eyes on him, Virgile hunkered down and

began to fork out pasta into their plates. 'Just one tiny question and the matter will never be mentioned again.'

'Get on with it. I'm hungry, so you're safe as long as I'm eating. I'll hit you afterwards if I don't like it.'

'How come you're called Aymeric? I mean, on your passport.' Virgile sat cross-legged opposite him.

'It's a tradition. All men in my family are called that. Goes back generations, back to the Crusades.'

'No shit!' Virgile's eyes widened as he slurped a generous forkful of pasta.

'We only use my middle name, Armand. My father, this…' Armand rifled through his private lexicon of insults and finding none strong enough, left a portentous blank. 'My father's full name is Aymeric-Albin de Peirac. I'm Aymeric *Armand* de Peirac. On paper, that is.'

'I see.' Virgile absorbed the information with an earnest frown.

'Virgile.' Armand put down his plate. 'I want you to remember one thing.' Fork poised forward, Armand fixed his gaze on his friend to make sure he had his full attention.

'If anyone asks…' he paused. 'My name is 'Armand Peirac.' 'No particle,' he stressed. 'Just Peirac.'

'Here is to you, Armand Peirac.' Virgile solemnly raised his glass of Préfontaine.

They carried on eating in relative silence, broken only by slurps and forks scraping on china. In the flats around them, radios were broadcasting the evening news.

'Guess what I saw under the Eiffel Tower today,' Armand ventured, pacified by food.

'What the fuck were you doing under the Eiffel Tower?' Virgile took one look at his friend and reined in his disapproval. 'Christ, I don't know, herds of dumb tourists, what else?'

'Close.'

'Search me. I've never been anywhere near the place.' He shook his afro in disgust but, keen to placate Armand, cupped his chin in his fingers and took a thoughtful pose. 'Hmmm, then again, that tower is quite handy when you think about it. Rather than have foreigners coming into our homes to see how French people live, why not simply channel them through a few strategic monuments so they don't interfere with our daily lives? Once they have trudged through the Louvre and floated down the Seine, why not pack them tight and send them upwards.' He lifted both hands. 'Takes less room. Easier on the infrastructure. Genius, when you think about it.' Virgile helped himself to a second dollop of pasta and poured the rest into Armand's plate. 'Tell you what… why don't we just build a replica of Paris in a field so they all flock there and leave us in peace?'

'Good idea.'

'Damn. We're out of Gruyère. Butter okay?'

'Butter's fine. Anyway, you were right about the herd.'

'Ah!' Virgile slapped his forehead, *'la manif* ! The demo with the Larzac sheep! Hang on. You were there? Oh God, sorry. And me thinking you'd turned into a tourist.'

'You really are paranoid, aren't you? Forget the Eiffel Tower. Under it is the *Champ de Mars*. Note, the word *'champ'* because that's what it is, a *field.* Sixty acres of *grass.* You're okay with grass, right?'

Virgile was fun to be with, but it was obvious that during the three years they had been apart, his political stance had toughened. For that, Armand blamed the truncheon blows received the day their life-trajectory had veered away from its predicted course. They had left deep scars, not all of them physical.

Virgile refilled their glasses, suddenly excited. 'Yes, the army want to take over the Larzac. Can you believe it?'

'You should have seen those shepherds. They rallied quite a crowd.'

'Armand, my man, you have just put your finger on it.' Virgile tore a piece of bread, enthusiastically wiped his plate and shoved it into his mouth, eyes sparkling with excitement.

'I have?' Fuzzy from the alcohol, Armand felt like Rip Van Winkle. After so long abroad, he struggled to tune into the Parisian subtext. France had moved on in leaps and bounds while he was away.

Virgile reached to the top of the wardrobe and pulled down a tent. 'I've had enough of Paris. You know, in sixty-eight, I really believed everything would change. For us, it was the year zero. I was convinced we had a chance of a fresh start, but we got nowhere. Well, I certainly got nowhere.' He stood in the middle of the room and scratched his head, contemplating his tent and his lost illusions. 'There's going to be a huge demo in the Larzac, right? Well, we're going there, you and me. I've to leave this dump of a place at the end of the month anyway.' Hands in his pockets, he surveyed his meagre belongings. 'How much stuff have you got?'

Armand indicated his rucksack with a jerk of the chin.

'That's it?'

Armand nodded.

Virgile hefted the rucksack and made a face. '*Putain*, it weighs a ton. What have you got in there?' He lifted a hand. 'Don't tell me... books.'

Armand took the bag from him, undid the straps and with a self-satisfied grin, pulled out a bottle of Chateau Margaux.

'*Putain de bordel de merde*, you sneaky bastard! You let us drink Préfontaine and all the time, you had this treasure in your bag. Where did you get it from?' Virgile squatted next to Armand and reverently stroked the bottle.

'Chateau Margaux 1945. A particularly good vintage.'

Armand grinned. 'I still have the keys to my flat. So, after I was so rudely dismissed by that… man, my thoughts turned to revenge. I couldn't fit more than five bottles in this bag, but some are worth about a million old Francs each, so I reckon we'll drink one and sell the other two to kick-start our new life. What do you say, Partner?'

Virgile fell back, his mouth open. 'You mean, with just *one* bottle, we could buy a car?'

'Absolument.'

'Can't… can't we… I mean, wow, Chateau Margaux! Have you got anything cheaper in there? I'm not sure I could drink that. I might choke on it.'

Armand unwrapped a bottle from bunched up underwear. 'Here you are… Pommard. Pure nectar. Only three hundred francs. That won't choke you.'

Virgile burst out laughing. 'Hey, things are looking up.' He settled on his haunches. 'OK, this is what we'll do. We'll get ourselves some sheep…'

While his friend rambled on, Armand carefully poured the wine. He would have preferred to drink it out of something better than Duralex glasses, but Virgile's dream was making him feel better than he had in a very long time, so he closed his mind to the fact that neither of them knew anything about sheep, and that winters were punishing on the Larzac plateau.

'Yeah, a few sheep and a kitchen garden…' Virgile dreamt on. 'With the money from the articles you write, we'll be able to buy the basics and take it from there.'

Armand settled against the wall and let Virgile's description of their new life cleanse away his anger. Yes… starting from scratch appealed to him.

'It really will be year zero for us.' Armand handed a half-filled kitchen glass of the precious nectar to Virgile, who sat next to him on the mattress. 'Tell me what you think of that.'

Virgile took a sip, closed his eyes in raptures and misquoting Wilde, said, 'Aaahh, we are in the gutter, but we are drinking Heaven.' He smacked his lips and asked, an edge of concern in his voice, 'there will be women won't there? In the Larzac?'

'You said there was going to be a huge demo,' Armand answered, 'so why wouldn't there be women?'

'I haven't had a shag in six months,' Virgile confessed bluntly. 'I mean, when we live in the Larzac, you know, what with it being the French equivalent of the Gobi Desert…'

'Hmm.' For Armand too, it had been a long time. His mind took him back to the ashram where an American girl with flowers in her hair had seduced him after a couple of joints. Her attentions had been welcomed at the time, even if her patchouli made him gag.

Inspired by the wine, they sketched out their new life, away from unreasonable parents, noisy neighbours and difficult bosses. They would take on the French army and show the world the stuff they were made of.

'So do you think we'll find women, then?' Virgile could not let it drop.

'Bah, who needs women...' Grinning, Armand twirled his glass, admiring the deep ruby of his wine. 'Just think of all those ewes.'

PART IV

ARMAND - VIRGILE - LARZAC - 1975

34
LARZAC - SPRING 1975

'Armand, Armand, wake up!' Virgile's insistent voice permeated Armand's dream. He opened an eye, registered suffused light and let go of Mireille's warm body. Groggy with sleep he sat up and shivered at the cold of the stone on his naked back.

He squinted at the alarm clock. *Merde, four o'clock? What's going on? Was six not the time they fed the ewes?*

'You're needed.' Virgile stood by the bedroom door, fully dressed. 'It's serious.'

Since he had arrived in the Larzac four years ago, Armand had often been awakened in the middle of the night. The first time was when the French army bombarded the Girauds' farm. He'd evacuated their seven children and helped put out the fire. It was a miracle the family survived.

This year, the conflict had escalated. More acrimonious than anyone had anticipated, it now was the symbol of the struggle of every dispossessed ethnicity on the planet.

Watching him dress through half-closed lids, Mireille yawned. 'Betcha the army's been up to their tricks again.'

'Bastards are sitting on an arsenal big enough to sustain World War Three, itching to take pot shots at us, a handful of shepherds.'

Mireille sat up, her breasts spilling over the warm sheets. Like a stray cat, she had wandered over from a nearby commune led by a disciple of Gandhi where she wasn't fed enough. She was insatiable. Technically, she was Virgile's girlfriend but sheep farming was hard work and Armand thought it only fair, once a week, to allow his friend a night off. Eager to prove how broad-minded he was, Virgile had agreed, but it was obvious that this arrangement was coming to an end. Those two were getting serious about each other.

Armand hugged Mireille and peeled her warm arms from his neck.

'I'd better go and see what's going on. Do you mind feeding the sheep this morning?'

'Really? I do most of the milking.'

'Come on, Mimi, what milking? They've just lambed. Listen, I've got to go. Sounds as if there's a war council out there.' He pushed his feet into clogs, and shuffled into the kitchen, enticed by the smell of coffee.

Under a petrol lamp dangling from the ceiling, Pierrot Delpech and an older man Armand had seen at meetings sat at the table in work blues and checked shirts.

'Salut Peirac. You know my uncle Delpech.'

'Salut Pierrot. Monsieur Delpech.' They shook hands.

Virgile was slicing large slices of bread, holding the loaf against his chest.

'What brings you here so early?' Armand cleared away his typewriter and took a seat on the bench opposite the men. Virgile pointed to the pot of coffee and plate of butter and invited them to tuck in.

'Dogs woke me up,' Pierrot said. 'Wouldn't stop barking.

It was full moon, so I took my field glasses, climbed on the bluff at the back of my farm and saw a platoon running into the Mazures.' He filled his bowl with coffee.

'Les Mazures? *Merde*... That's bad news.' Armand's chest tightened. It was the land adjoined theirs, just across the valley. The army had been acquiring farms, edging forward, acre by acre.

'We came to warn you.' The uncle's voice rumbled, gravelly as the hills that had fashioned him. 'That farm is all that stands between you and the firing range. If the army get their hands on it, you're next.' He dipped his buttered bread into his coffee.

Pierrot nodded. 'Been empty for ages. Had some squatters in there after the big demo, but they didn't stay long.'

The big demo. Armand remembered it well. A festival more than a demo, it had drawn a hundred thousand people and gone down in history as the French Woodstock.

Delpech took a long draft of *café au lait* and wiped his thick moustache with sausage-like fingers. 'You're squatting, right?'

Armand hesitated. 'The house belongs to my father,' he stated in the local patois. If his father sold it to the army – the old man was quite capable of it – the bucolic dream was over. The three of them would be joining the dole queue.

The uncle was about to pop his soggy bread into his mouth when Mireille came out of Armand's bedroom barefoot, T-shirt taut across her breasts. With a cheery *'bonjour !'* she sashayed through the kitchen, took the pan of water and, as she stretched to activate the pump, it was obvious that she wasn't wearing knickers.

The uncle's bread plopped into his bowl.

Pierrot cleared his throat and pointed in turn to Mireille and Virgile and stammered, 'but I – I thought–'

'Wednesday's Armand's day.' Mireille gave Virgile a peck on the lips and lit the gas under the pan. 'This boy needs a rest.'

Pierrot swallowed hard.

Armand felt for the guy. Since Pierrot had taken over from his father three years ago, the boundaries of his world had exploded. His desert had been invaded by hippies, American Indians, Indian Indians, Palestinians, peacemakers and warmongers.

Whatever happened now, the lives of the hundred and three Larzac farmers would never be the same. It was as if their land stood on some mysterious ley lines that drew all the dispossessed of the earth.

'Peirac...' Pierrot's eyes trailed away from Mireille's body. 'We thought you might have an idea.'

The uncle's boots scraped the stone floor. 'They've got a platoon sleeping in that cottage. Tomorrow, they'll stake their claim. We want to strike before those soldiers wake up. We reckoned you'd know what to do.'

A platoon? Christ. Armand ran his fingers through his long hair, amazed at the men's trust. That he wrote articles and talked to journalists didn't make him a strategist.

'We don't have much time.' The uncle spooned out the bread out of his coffee.

Pierrot explained. 'We're drilling at the moment.' He added, 'we need to get back to work.'

The uncle drummed his fingers on the table, *'eh oui, on plante, on plante.'*

Armand rubbed the sleep from his face. 'Thanks for taking the trouble. We really appreciate it.' He took a long draft of coffee.

The farmers now standing in his kitchen were expecting him to know what to do. He thought of the lambs in the barn, Mireille and Virgile planning for the future. He had to come up with a plan and he had to think fast. Those men's livelihood depended on planting what they could while the weather held.

And then, he had it. Planting! He grinned. This time, French law would be on their side.

'How many tractors can you get hold of at a moment's notice?'

'Oh la la, non...' Pierrot lifted a hand, misunderstanding his intent. 'No way. We are not driving our tractors up to Millau again. The gendarmes are wise to our tricks. They'll have roadblocks and we need the tractors for –'

'Listen…' Armand leaned forward. For his plan to work, he needed just one piece of information. 'The old boy who owned les Mazures… did he just graze sheep on his land?'

'Now, let me think.' The uncle pushed back his beret. 'I remember him planting barley just before he died. I had to harvest it for his bloody heirs who didn't even–'

'Arable yeah?' Armand remained focused. If the old man had planted barley, the fields could be ploughed again. He slapped the table. 'We have a plan. Let's go.'

Virgile chuckled. The Delpechs exchanged a puzzled look, but when the penny finally dropped, the uncle laughed so hard, they thought he was having an attack.

Armand swallowed the last of his coffee. 'How long d'you think it'll take?'

Old Delpech pursed his lips. 'That small field tilled and drilled? Let's see… five… six tractors? Under an hour I'd say. It'll be done by the time they wake up.'

They headed for the door. Each man knew his role.

'Can we use your phone?' Pierrot asked from the threshold.

'Sorry.' Virgile winced. 'Still relying on smoke signals

here. The Apache woman who was here the other day showed us how to do it.' He chortled. 'We don't have electricity either.'

There was a pause as the two farmers took in the information.

'You milk by hand?'

'You've met the milk maid.'

Virgile and Armand read new respect on the farmers' faces. This being said, with over three hundred ewes each, for them milking by hand wasn't really an option.

'Hurry. It won't be dark for long.' Armand grabbed his Aran jumper and followed the farmers out of the door.

From the top of a rock, like Caesar before a battle, Armand surveyed his army assembled in the misty dawn, a squad of old tractors tut-tutting up the plateau towards les Mazures. They spread out and took up their positions at the edge of the field, waiting for his signal.

Inside the old cottage, nothing stirred. The young recruits were still asleep.

Armand raised his right arm. The five ploughs were lowered, advanced in formation and, in a cloud of dust, churned the abandoned acres.

The whole valley throbbed with the noise. His eyes glued to the house, Armand urged them on.

When the sun finally topped the hill, a soldier in pyjamas ran out, waving his arms about.

It was over. The last of the tractors tut-tutted down the hill. A huge grin crept over Armand's face. Pregnant with wheat, that land could not legally be touched… until harvest time. By which time the courts would have taken over.

Jubilant, Virgile ran up to him with the press photographer and together, the three of them watched the dust settle over their battle field.

Virgile slapped Armand on the back. 'We did it! All they can do now is watch it grow.'

'Come on, mate,' Armand helped the sleepy photographer gather his tripod. 'Virgile will make you some coffee. You can have breakfast with us while I type out my article. You'll take it back to the paper with you.'

35
LARZAC – SPRING 1978

'The seventies are coming to an end and still, after an eight-year battle, the Larzac is under threat. At the eve of the 80s, we must ask the question: is France at war? If so, who with? Who is our enemy? Why is it so important for France to extend the Larzac firing range five-fold?'

No. Too confrontational. Armand pulled the sheet of paper from the typewriter and aimed it at the log basket. How about – *Larzac – the fight against globalisation*? Bah, after eight years, it had been done to death. He was tired, tired of writing the same thing, tired of fighting and getting nowhere.

He slipped in a new sheet and typing with two fingers, started afresh.

'Our fight is financed with the three per cent reserved for army spending, the three per cent that every citizen is entitled to withhold from taxes.' A crescendo of barks and bleats rose from the dale, Virgile bringing the flock home. Armand carried on. *Over the past eight years, six thousand plots have been sold to three thousand sympathisers in an attempt to slow down compulsory purchase orders...'*

How Virgile and Armand had managed to hold on to their land was anyone's guess and every year, the return of spring put the fear of eviction in their hearts. They had survived eight springs. How many more would there be?

Armand was ready to move on. His eyes wandered up to the mantle shelf. The depressingly tall pile of yellowing envelopes was topped with a couple of new ones: an invitation to his cousin Arnie's wedding, and one from the lawyers working for The Cause.

He pulled on a jumper and stepped into the evening sun. The dog –called Plato as a nod to Virgile's aborted Classics career– ran up and accompanied him to the barn.

'How's the article going?' Virgile closed the barn door behind the last ewe.

'*Bof,* after all this time, I'm struggling to find something new to say.' The smell of lanolin filled the warm space.

'It's important to keep The Cause alive,' Virgile said with a passion Armand envied. 'Think of what we have achieved. It's been eight years. The whole world supports us. Sartre calls it the most beautiful fight of the twentieth century.'

'I know, I know, we're famous. Maori, Hopi, Solomon Islanders, we've managed to represent all the damned of the earth, but we never know if we'll still be here next week. If my father sells this place to the army, we've had it.'

'Handy you being called Albin though.' Virgile grinned. 'We fooled the bailiff last time.' He pushed a stray ewe inside a pen.

'Not this time.' Armand grabbed a bag and shook pellets into the troughs. 'We're fighting a ten-headed hydra. We don't even know who owns what.' He kicked a milk churn in frustration.

'But not for long...' Virgile loosened bundles of hay and pushed handfuls down into the racks. 'Not for long.'

'What do you mean?'

'At the meeting last night, it was decided that we'd investigate the situation ourselves.'

'Investigate? What are you talking about?'

'Tomorrow night with Mireille and a few others, we're breaking into the army barracks to see what deeds they have. We'll find out exactly who owns what.' Virgile's eyes shone in the half-light.

Armand hit his forehead. 'Are you insane?'

He could not believe it. Virgile and Mireille had been exclusive for several years now. How could Virgile be so unconcerned about his girlfriend's safety? Christ, did they *want* to be caught?

'It's the only way. We'll sneak in, take photos of documents and sneak out again.'

'Sneak out again? Really?' Armand shook his head. '*Putain,* breaking and entering army premises with intent to steal secret documents will get you a minimum of six months. *Minimum.* Maximum could be six years. How am I going to cope with lambing on my own, *hein* ? Have you thought of that?'

'Listen, it's carefully planned. We got inside information. We'll be in and out in fifteen minutes. No risk involved.'

'Yeah well, count me out. Someone's got to run this farm while you two *hurluberlus* are playing at being James Bond. I'm staying here. You'll need someone to bail you out.' Armand turned to the dog and headed for the door. 'Come, Plato, it's dinner time.'

Two days later, against his better judgement, Armand found himself a few miles away, clutching the base of a folding ladder thrown over the wire perimeter of the firing range, unable to believe he was taking part in the mad caper.

Though their targets were only temporary huts, the whole idea of breaking into barracks was suicidal.

The French equivalent of Siberia, the Larzac had started life as a base for the Knights Templars. Because of its spectacular isolation, the fortress at La Cavalerie had housed prisoners during WWII and refugees after the war of Algeria.

Virgile and Mireille weren't alone in this foolish venture. Holding the ladder, Armand counted twenty 'freedom fighters' who scuttled over and ran towards the prefab hut, Virgile's mushroom head easily recognisable under the stars.

Alone by the fence, Armand scanned the darkness, conjuring up a band of knights galloping over the moor, a prisoner tied atop a mule. The scream of a vixen made him jump. He checked his watch. Flashlights were moving inside the hut. He cursed under his breath. How were they expecting to find anything of value in so short a time? The whole thing was absurd. In eight years of legal wrangles, both sides had amassed enough paperwork to fill a barn. What the hell did they hope to achieve in half an hour?

Mireille had gone in with one specific aim: to find the documents related to their farm.

A shout. Armand's head snapped to the right. Floodlights… the wail of a siren. *Merde* ! They'd been rumbled. Holding his breath, he held on to the ladder, willing them to run.

Inside the huts, all the lights were blazing. It was over. Shapes filed out of a door, hands over their heads.

Armand swore and went to pull the ladder from the fence.

'Wait!' Virgile sprang out of the shadows and vaulted over the ladder. 'Scarper!' he rasped. 'Leave the ladder. Run!'

'But – what about Mireille?' Armand couldn't detach his eyes from the line led into a truck at gunpoint.

'Nothing we can do till morning.' The white of Virgile's

eyes sparkled in the dimness. 'I was keeping watch under a window.' He sprinted towards their Renault concealed a hundred yards below. Dogs were let loose inside the compound.

Armand darted after Virgile and, panting, threw himself into the car. He disengaged the hand brake and, Virgile twisted on his seat to check they were not followed, the car bounced silently down the medieval street of La Cavalerie.

Jaws clamped, Armand peered into the darkness, struggling to keep his irritation under control. Ahead of him, the walls of the Templar's citadel rose, ghostly in the moonlight.

The whole bloody exercise had been a fiasco, a bomb of the first order. What had they been thinking? Mireille risked months in prison.

Only when they reached the bottom of the hill did he turn the engine on. Next to him, Virgile was grinning.

Armand shot him a glance. 'Beats me what you're so smug about, blockhead. The whole thing was fucking pointless. What was it about, really? A publicity stunt? Christ, I don't get why you're so pleased with yourself, unless Mireille went in there to get herself arrested.' He swerved around a tight corner, cursed and switched on his lights. 'Was that it? Make sure she gets onto the front page of *Gardarem Lo Larzac,* or even some national rag like France-Soir?' Armand imagined the headline. *'Mireille, la passionaria du Larzac.'*

Virgile placed a hand over his heart and with a gleeful smile, crinkled something in his inside pocket.

'Do not fret my not-so-valiant friend, for we have found what we were searching for.'

'How can you be so flippant at a time like this?' Armand skidded to a halt in front of the cottage and slammed the car door.

'When you see what I've got, you'll want to open that last expensive bottle you've still got stashed under your bed.'

Armand stormed in, let Plato out, hung his coat and growled, 'Out with it then. I'll only open the champagne when your Dulcinea comes out of prison.'

Virgile rustled inside his jacket and, with great flourish, slapped crumpled documents onto the table and, like a conjuror, pulled several instamatic cameras out of his pockets.

'They had time to drop them through the window.' He pushed the cameras away and ran a hand over the paper to flatten it. 'Look… here. This proves that Aymeric-Albin de Peirac *père* still owns this cottage, though not for long from what I can see. The army's agreed to buy it, but on the condition *that it's free of squatters*. Squatters…' he tapped the words. 'That would be us.'

Armand sank his head into his hands with a groan. 'Oh, how can this man be my father? Heck, even wolves protect their own.'

'He won't throw you out.'

'Why not?'

'Because the pen is mightier than the sword, that's why. You once told me that his greatest fear is *le qu'en-dira-t-on,* what will people say.'

'So?'

'You're a journalist. You'll meet him at your cousin's wedding and tell him that if he evicts us, you'll write an article entitled... *Greedy aristocrat evicts son from sheep hut...* See where I'm going with this?'

Armand gave a moody shrug. 'Except I'm not going to Arnie's wedding.'

Something in Virgile's expression told him that his decision might not be final.

36
LARZAC – SPRING 1978

Ears pricked, Plato stood on alert, tail wagging. Virgile's car was chugging up the hill, back from Millau where Mireille had stood trial.

From the bench, leaning on the warm stones of the house, Armand watched his friend greet his dog playfully.

'So? What's the verdict?'

'Three weeks behind bars and a three-months suspended sentence. The judge was lenient with those who actually had farms to run. Mireille will be out before lambing starts.'

Armand grunted with relief. As an operation, breaking into the barracks had been a flop, but he had to hand it to Mireille. *La passionaria du Larzac* had raised their profile. France may have forgotten the Larzac, but together, Virgile, Mireille, and their reckless comrades had pushed The Cause right back to the front page.

Armand was exhausted. Fighting the relentless Goliath had been exhilarating but, he would never have admitted it to Virgile, he'd had enough of sheep. All he wanted to do was write. He was itching to move on.

'How's Mireille bearing up?'

'She's in good spirits.'

Shadows of rocks lengthened on the cropped grass. Under the setting sun, the grey stone of the cottage was burnished to copper. Virgile joined Armand on the bench and between them, Plato buried his head in his front paws with a contented sigh.

'Just look at this valley.' Virgile locked hands behind his head and surveyed his kingdom with pride. Pushed by the wind, clouds made changing patterns, alternately hiding and highlighting the brush and bald patches of soil across the valley.

'How lucky are we, hey? Man, you've got to feel sorry for the poor buggers stuck back in Paris.'

'Yeah.'

Soft bleats and the sound of hooves shuffling about in the straw rose from the barn.

Virgile cleared his throat. 'I wanted to talk to you. Mireille and I...'

Armand had been expecting this. Wednesdays with Mireille were a thing of the past. The house had shrunk and he often felt *de trop*. Virgile was going to ask him to move to the hut he had built on a separate plot. Now might be the time to tell them that he needed more from life, that what he really wanted was to run a bookshop, though how he was going to go about it was anyone's guess.

He simply didn't possess the funds to set up his dream –a dream he had secretly cherished since India– nor did he have the right contacts to make a name for himself as a journalist for anything much bigger than *Gardarem lo Larzac.*

Virgile tried again. 'Mireille and I…'

Armand lifted an amused eyebrow.

Virgile took in a deep breath, held it and exhaled the words, 'Mireille wants a baby.'

This wasn't what Armand had expected. It took him a

moment to adjust. He stuttered, 'Not exactly going about it the right way, you two, are you? What with her in the nick and you…'

'What's got into you, man? I can't understand why you're so *réac* about the break in.'

'I was worried you'd get shot, okay? Those guys were armed, they…''Relax! It's over now and we got what we wanted. Delpech was on the nine o'clock news last week, and that's got to be good, hasn't it?' Virgile fidgeted on the bench and eventually returned to what was troubling him. 'Listen, about the… hum, baby. I…' He brushed a strand of straw from his jeans and muttered, 'we've only been talking about it but… *if* and *when* she conceives…' He met Armand's gaze. 'I'd like to be sure it's mine.'

'Of course! What do you–'

'I'm serious.'

The intensity on his friend's face surprised Armand.

'If you want me to move out, just say.'

'No.' Virgile grabbed Armand's arm. 'That's not what I'm saying. It's just that… some women sort of… select the best genes for their kids and I'm not sure that if she had to choose between a ginger top like me and someone whose family goes back to the Crusades…'

'Hold it right there.' Armand faced him squarely. 'Get this straight.' He lifted both hands and punctuated his point. 'I do not… want…children… ever.'

'Ah, you say that, but you'll change your mind one day.'

His face set, Armand repeated, 'I won't change my mind, Virgile. Not now, not ever.'

'Why?'

Armand ran a hand over his face. 'The things my father did aren't the sort of legacy you hand down to any kid. It's too heavy.'

'But it was the War. I'm sure anyone–'

'It's not just that. It goes back further. It wouldn't be fair.'

Virgile shifted on the bench. 'Perhaps your old man had a tough childhood. But when you have your own, you'll find–'

'I hear what you're saying and you're right in a way. The old marquis, my grandfather, was a violent sod who used to horsewhip his sons. But he beat my uncle too. Arnie's father never joined the militia, sent Jews to their death, nor tortured people. No. I'm from rotten stock. It goes way back. I've made up my mind. The line ends with me.' He ruffled Virgile's hair. 'Go forth and multiply my friend. The ginger race will live on.'

37
ARMAND – PARIS – 1980

'But you must go to that wedding,' Mireille had pleaded when Armand first received the wedding invitation, 'Sacha Distel will be there!'

'For God's sake, Mireille, my *mother* used to like Sacha Distel's songs. He's boring. I've no idea where to find a suit and anyway, what am I going to say to those Parisians? Talk about my sheep?'

For a committed left-wing activist, Mireille was far too easily impressed by glitterati and titled gentry. When the pictures of Arnie's engagement to a society heiress had appeared in Paris Match magazine, Mireille spoke of nothing else for weeks and showed the photos to everyone.

Armand had been surprised to see his camera-shy father amongst the beautiful people. At functions and official dinners, his old man always had a knack of hiding in the back row. Now he knew why, Armand was surprised that he had relaxed his guard enough to appear in a national paper.

In the end, it was a letter from Anne-Ségolène that convinced him to go.

"Dear Armand,

By now, even you must have heard that your cousin Arnaud is marrying my friend, Anne-Clarisse de Lombasle. It was in all the magazines. You will be invited of course and I can't wait to see you.

I still cannot believe that Albin shut the door in your face. Relations between him and my father have cooled down somewhat since I mentioned it to him. I understand that you don't want to speak with your father, but let me reassure you. The Lombasle have booked the Pavillon Dauphine for their reception. The venue is so huge, you will easily be able to avoid him. You will find him aged. He hasn't been well lately. Dodgy heart I'm told. He probably won't come to the party.

I'm very much looking forward to catching up with you. Armand, it's been too long. I read all your articles of course, and cheer you guys on. So glad you pulled off the last stint. That the judge was lenient to your friends proves what a farce the whole thing has become. I'm convinced the cause will win, though I'm not so sure you were ever cut out to be a sheep farmer. Perhaps you will tell me.

Virginie and I have been living together for five years now. She works for a famous television producer. The glamour of the job has helped get us accepted as a couple. She is looking forward to meeting you. Her producer would like to do a piece on the Larzac. If it is something which you feel would further your cause..."

How could he refuse? The two women had even offered to host him. Now all he needed was a suit.

Notre Dame d'Auteuil Church was packed. Armand stood hunched between Virginie, a thin vivacious blonde, and Anne-Ségolène in a Laura Ashley rustic dress. He loosened his tie, uncomfortable in the rented suit. His hair was gathered in a ponytail and he had even shaved off his beard for the occasion. His skin itched. Gazes burned a hole in his back. There were far too many familiar faces. Anne-Clarisse, Arnie's rich fiancée belonged to his old *rallye* circle.

Why his free-thinking, free-bonking cousin would want to marry into the staunch Catholic de Lombasle family became clear after the first notes of the bridal chorus. Anne-Clarisse entered the church on her father's arm with the poise of a catwalk model. The Paris-Match photos had not done her justice. She was stunning. Now cousin Arnie was a diplomat, it was not so much the union of two souls as of that of two dynasties.

Armand turned around and found himself under fire of the combined glare of the five Bouvreuil sisters, all in various stages of pregnancy and motherhood, bulked out of all proportions by the current fashion for shoulder pads and big hair. The eldest elbowed a sister, her lips puckered in distaste.

Christ, what had he been *thinking* in coming here? Resisting the sudden urge to run, Armand closed his eyes and rifled through his mind for a mantra once learned in the Indian ashram.

'Arnaud,' said the priest while a game of *who's who* went on sotto voce behind the prayer books, 'you are about to promise to be faithful. Is it for your life time?'

Armand cringed at the ridiculous phrasing, probably chosen by Anne-Clarisse, aware of her fiancé's proclivities.

Wishing himself back in his farm, Armand could already hear the gossip, *le qu'en-dira-t-on,* awaiting him at the end of the service. *Why, Armand! Is that really you?* And, *still not married, Armand?* The side glances at Anne-Ségolène, the whispers. *Those two were engaged once –a smokescreen, they're both, you know– He's still single... lives with another man.*

'I pronounce you man and wife.'

Arnie slowly lifted his bride's veil, cradled her face and

made a great show of kissing her. To the left, Armand's father stood, half-hidden behind a pillar.

The couple waved and followed the priest though a small door.

The service was over.

'Where have they gone?' Armand whispered to Virginie.

'They're in the vestry with the witnesses, the priest and the photographer, signing the Register.'

'Right.' He faced Ségo. 'I'm out of here. Where can I get a Pastis?'

'Oh, Armand.' Ségo laughed, her thick helmet of hair shaking prettily, 'Pastis? Don't be so plebeian. In only a moment they'll be serving champagne to all those who attended the service. It's just around the corner, in a 'pub' I refurbished last year. Tell you what, let's beat the crowds and try to get there first.'

'Sounds like a plan.'

A gasp rose from the front. Armand froze. In front of the altar, a ruin of a man gripped the side of the lectern with claw-like hands.

The chatter stopped. All eyes turned to the pitiful patchwork of skin grafts, the snout and lipless beak displaying yellow teeth. The poor wretch had neither ears nor eyebrows. Rare tufts of hair sprouted between the scars that criss-crossed his skull.

Armand had seen him before.

'A wedding should be a happy occasion.' The mixture of pathos and southern sunshine in the man's accent jarred with the horrific face.

'My name is Léon Blanqui. I too was about to get married when…' He pointed to Armand's father, who had slithered behind the pillar, casting frantic glances at the vestry door.

Armand's stomach lurched. Léon's face was not easily forgotten.

The man's warm voice rose again through the silent church. 'It was thirty-three years ago. I was handsome then. I had hair and fingers then. I was engaged to be married.' He lifted a hand and wriggled his claws. A gasp of revulsion rose from the pews. 'I've spent thirty-three years searching for the man who did this to me, hoping to bring him to justice. But however hard I tried, doors closed one after the other. *The War is forgotten. We must move on*, I was told.' He beat his chest and shouted, 'How can I move on?'

He pointed an accusing talon towards the pillar. 'Albin de Peirac, you stole my life and for what? I was guilty of nothing. Nothing!'

A couple of men rushed out of the pews to silence the troublemaker, but the authority in Léon 's voice made them halt.

'When you invite this man into your home, you are inviting the monster who strung me up and dipped me into a vat of boiling tar...' This was met with a gasp. 'I was nineteen. My only sin was to believe in a better world.'

The two men hesitated.

Repressing sobs, Léon Blanqui carried on, 'he allowed my friend Marcel Pujol to be shot by the Gestapo. Marcel was seventeen.'

In the pews, women pressed gloved hands over their lips, eyes filled with naked pity. Anne-Ségolène's hand searched Armand's. His head spinning, he held on to it. The people surrounding his father had moved away. Albin de Peirac stood alone. Ashen, he clutched his chest, leaned against the pillar and slowly slipped down to the ground, mouth open, eyes rolling like those of an animal before the kill.

Something in Armand's heart stirred, what, he wasn't

sure, remnants of filial piety perhaps. He gripped the back of the pew to stop himself from running to his father. At the front, in the shadows, a thin man with an eye-patch fixed his one eye on Léon and encouraged him to go on.

Blanqui wept as he reached his conclusion. 'When that monster caught my comrade…' The other man stepped forward. 'He… he took a… and he...' Incoherent with grief, Léon slumped on the lectern. With a supreme effort, he pointed down to Albin whose lips were turning blue, and shouted in a broken voice, 'When you were head of the militia, Albin de Peirac, we didn't know your name. We only knew you as the Gévaudan Beast! So, curse you, de Peirac, curse you and all those who come after you!'

There was an almighty crash as Armand's father clutched at his heart and collapsed with a groan, taking the front pew with him in his fall.

Léon stepped down. Tears coursing down his ravaged face, he limped out of the church, supported by his friend.

Armand found himself pushing past Virginie to reach his father. He knelt down on the cold stones and cried out, 'Papa!'

His father opened his eyes. The terror and the shame Armand read in them somehow broke the spell. Overcome with a strange sense of calm, Armand held his father's hand and waited until it went slack. After what seemed forever, he closed his father's eyes and raised his head above the pews.

In the solid silence, all eyes were turned to him, an infernal helix of eyes, accusing, opaque with disgust, burning and self-righteous. Armand swayed as the kaleidoscopic nightmare shifted to lips. Painted lips, prim and pursed, open in shock, pinched in disapproval, thinned in contempt or clammed shut because deep down, they had always known.

Inside Armand's throbbing mind, the leitmotif to his father's life rang like the devil's jig. '*What will they say?*' What *they* would say, Armand did not want to know. Ségo called out, 'This man needs an ambulance. There is a phone in the vestry. Armand, come with me, you too Virginie.'

In the vestry, Arnie and Anne-Clarisse were holding a pen, smiling to the camera, oblivious to the drama played out in the church.

'Someone has had a turn.' Ségo said calmly. 'Is there a phone in here?' The priest pointed to an alcove. She added, 'Is there a way out?'

The priest hesitated and pointed to a side door.

Anne-Ségolène gave Armand a quick kiss and pressed her keys into his hand. 'Go to my flat. Stay as long as you want. Drop the keys with the concierge if you leave before I get back.'

She opened the small door and propelled him shell-shocked into the street. Blinking in the sun, Armand stood on the pavement, unsure of where he was.

She called out, 'Armand?'

He turned around wearily.

'Don't worry, we'll sort everything out.' She lifted a finger. 'No guilt trip please. You are *not* responsible for your father, and there are no such things as curses.'

38
LARZAC – 1978

Armand threw himself into physical work to help process his father's death. He had just finished clearing out the barn when Plato's barks drew him out. He turned off the –newly installed– water pipe, wiped his hands on a rag and shading his eyes from the sun, watched an elegant white Citroen creep up the hill.

An elderly man stepped out. His neat white hair and smart beige jacket hinted at someone who had reached a comfortable stage in life.

'Armand! Ça fait un bail !' The man extended a hand.

'Lucien? *Ça alors !* You're right, it has been ages. I wasn't expecting you. To what do I owe this honour?'

A small woman stepped out of the car. Her hair too closely permed, in a strict dark blue dress, Jeanne looked older than the late forties Armand assumed her to be. He bent down to kiss her.

'Look at you.' Jeanne kneaded the muscles on his arms. 'You've become so strong.' The smile she gave him took years off her. 'What's happened to your beard? Ah, getting thin on top. It runs in the d'Aubrac family. You always took after your mother's side.'

'None of us are getting any younger, Jeanne. Let's go in. Tell me what brings you here. How is André?'

'André sends his love. He's remodelling a kitchen in Fleurac today.'

'We drove all the way here, son,' Lucien put a hand on Armand's shoulder, 'because you still live in the eighteenth century and you don't have a phone.'

The phone rang inside the house. Virgile must have answered it, for it stopped after the third ring.

Contrite, Armand turned to them. 'Sorry. Had it installed last week. Don't even know my own number yet.' He grinned, 'we also have electricity.' He encompassed the house and rocky fields with a sweep of the hand. 'It's taken its time, but we've just about joined the human race.'

He followed them into the kitchen. 'The house is mine now Dad's gone, but we still haven't won the fight.'

Jeanne was about to reply when Virgile came out of his room, jangling his car keys. He halted in surprise. '*Tiens, des visiteurs !*'

'This is Virgile. I told you about him. The third musketeer is away at the moment.'

'But not for long,' Virgile said with glee. 'She's coming out today. I'm off to Millau to fetch her.'

'Oh?' Jeanne knitted her brow. 'Mireille, isn't it? Is she in hospital?'

Virgile cast Armand a side-glance. Armand nodded.

'Mireille, ahem, had to do time. You might have heard about it. The judge was lenient. She only got three weeks.'

Lucien's voice filled the room. 'You lot have guts, I have to say. Whose idea was it to take sheep into the court room?'

'Mine I'm afraid,' Virgile said with a bashful grin. 'Me and

Aristotle, a ram I bottle fed from birth. He'll follow me anywhere.'

'It was good publicity. Jeanne never misses your articles, Armand. We're on your side one hundred per cent.'

'Thank you for your support, Lucien. The staff of your factory…'

Jeanne's brother dismissed it with a shrug. 'Bah, that was nothing *Petit*, just a whip round. The Union members were keen to contribute. So, Virgile, what did she discover during the raid, that friend of yours?'

'We found plenty of evidence of foul play. Contrary to what had been agreed,' Virgile's voice rose, as it did whenever The Cause was mentioned, 'the army had been buying up land during the official 'consultation' period, when they should have remained neutral.'

Armand took over. 'Friends of some minister –mention no names– got wind of the extension plan for the firing range and purchased several hectares with a view to–'

'–speculate and accumulate.' Virgile opened his hands.

'I imagine one of those was my father.' Armand indicated the benches on either side of the table. 'Take a seat, Jeanne, take a seat.'

'Petit,' began Lucien who still thought of Armand as a child, 'your father is why we're here.'

Jeanne cast Virgile a nervous glance.

'Right.' Virgile headed for the door. 'I'm off. I've got to be in Millau in an hour.' He held Jeanne's hand in both his. 'It was a pleasure to meet you at last. Armand thinks the world of you. I was thinking of asking if you could adopt me too.' He turned to Lucien and held out a hand. 'Monsieur.' Just before he closed the door, Virgile pushed his head through the gap. 'We'll be back for milking.'

'No no, don't worry. Take her out, I'll be fine.' Armand

was glad the days when milking required three people were over.

Virgile loped off, sunshine suffusing his red hair with halo-like radiance.

Lucien cleared his throat.

Jeanne spoke first.

'We heard what happened at your cousin's wedding.'

Armand's gaze went from one to the other, wondering what had brought them here.

Lucien rubbed his chin and glanced over at his sister. Jeanne picked up a crumb from the table and pushed it nervously along the grooves in the wood.

Lucien started, 'We've tried to spare you the worst–'

'Spare me? Spare me what?' Armand had always wondered how much Jeanne knew about his father's role in the militia. 'That man, Léon Blanqui, you knew him didn't you, Lucien?'

Lucien and Jeanne gave a small nod.

'But you let him flounder all these years, looking for his torturer.'

'It wasn't like that.' Lucien adjusted his bulk on the bench.

'Perhaps we should start at the beginning.' The glance Jeanne gave her brother was heavy with meaning.

'Out with it. Whatever you have to say can't be worse than what I've been through.'

Jeanne reached out and patted Armand's hand. 'It's difficult, Armand. There's no right and wrong.'

He waited, his throat tight, wondering what horrors Jeanne was about to reveal. For most of his life, she had been there for him, true north on his compass. What had she kept from him?

His senses on alert, Plato padded across the room and rested his head on Armand's lap. For a while nothing broke the silence, bar the soft thud of his tail against the foot of the table.

Jeanne said in a thin voice, 'Albin is not your father.'

Armand closed his eyes. Fog filled his brain. Relief, confusion and anger rose and fell inside him until out of the miasma, one question popped out. 'Why now? Why are you telling me this only now? I mean, you knew what a monster he was and you… you …you let me…' He shot up and paced the kitchen. 'All my life, I've felt like a failure. I've never fitted in anywhere. Even here, I don't fit in. For years I bent over backwards to try and please a man who turned out to be Vlad the Impaler. Is it any wonder that I've left the human race and live surrounded by sheep?' He rested both hands on the table and faced the both of them. 'Why on earth did you not tell me that before? Why did you let me go to India, unable to look at myself in a mirror? I never married, I never wanted children because I was afraid I would contaminate them with de Peirac blood and now I find out that he isn't even my father!'

'Armand,' Jeanne pleaded, 'it isn't that simple, you have to understand that.'

'So, explain. Who is it? Who is he then, my real father, that makes everything so complicated?'

'He was a German pacifist. He was in hiding near Fleurac during the war. He was called Karl Müller.'

'Oh God.' Armand slumped onto a chair.

'Arielle fell in love with Karl at the end of the War and became pregnant. Karl was… wonderful.' Jeanne beamed as touched by the Holy Ghost. Her brow darkened. 'But he died. When Karl was shot, Arielle married Albin in a hurry. The rest you know.'

'Hang on. When did you say that was?'

'Right at the end of the War.'

'Why wait until now?' Armand's voice rose. 'It's 1978! Why did you wait till now to tell me?'

Jeanne began to cry. Lucien took over.

'I didn't know the full story. Jeanne only told me recently, but I think she did the right thing. De Peirac had money. He owned half the forests around Fleurac. It's all yours now, son.'

'But I don't want forests! I don't want his – his ill-gotten gains!' Armand shouted. '*Bon Dieu*, when you think how he's acquired that money!' He broke into a higher pitch. 'What on earth makes you think I'd want any of it?'

'Ah come on Armand,' objected Lucien, 'is sheep farming really your calling? Don't you want to write? We read your articles. We know how good you are.'

'Don't you see? I want to get there by myself.'

'We thought you would say that.' Jeanne blew her nose. 'You can do what you want now.'

'He's probably disinherited me anyway,' Armand said in a throaty growl.

Patient, Lucien corrected him, 'no one can disinherit their children Armand. Legally, it simply is not possible. However, we knew how impetuous you are... and we knew what that monster was capable of. He would have destroyed you. Crushed you into the ground… inflicted maximum damage. We never had the heart to risk it.'

'Our relationship ended the day he closed the door in my face.'

'That's what you think, but in spite of everything, he never did evict you from this place, did he?'

'No.'

'I've given all this a lot of thought.' Lucien's eyes misted over. 'André's brother Marcel was shot simply to get back at me, to make me pay for running away. What other reason could he have to shoot a seventeen-year-old?' He dabbed his tears with a large handkerchief. 'I'm proud to have been a Resistance fighter, but deep down, I know that if I'd gone to work in Germany, I'd have been called home when Dad died, and none of this would have happened.'

Armand's heart softened. 'Come on Lucien, you can't–'

Jeanne took over. 'Our priority –and Arielle's priority– was to protect *you*. She hid the truth because of you. You're our future, Armand. You shouldn't have to pay for our mistakes.'

Unable to absorb anymore, Armand went to the cupboard, took down a bottle of Calistou and held it against him, trying to make sense of what he had just heard. He jolted himself out of his trance and proffered the bottle of chestnut liqueur.

'That's all I have to offer you. Calistou made by Mireille. It's a bit sweet but it's good. Would you like to try it?' He set three glasses on the table and filled them.

No one spoke. Cold air rose from nowhere, the kitchen haunted by the souls of the Beast's victims.

'So...' Armand could not let it rest. 'You kept the truth from Léon Blanqui his whole life, just to protect me?'

'It isn't that simple,' Lucien said. 'Karl and I were in hiding together. Those who attacked us were not just after Karl. They were after me too. The soldiers on that hill wore German uniforms, so I assumed they were German. It was months later, when I returned home and Jeanne told me they were French, and locals at that. By then, de Peirac had married Arielle and gone to America. You've probably noticed that in Fleurac, Arielle never kept a single photo of Albin.'

'She knew?' Armand couldn't bear to hear the answer.

Jeanne and Lucien exchanged a glance.

Jeanne added kindly, 'We don't think so.'

'Oh God, so Papa killed Karl, my real father.' Armand's

head was throbbing. When would the nightmare end? Jeanne was right. No way could he have coped with this when he was younger. It would have driven him over the edge.

Lucien placed a hand on Armand's shoulder. 'Jeanne wanted to protect you and Arielle. You can see that, can't you? It was all so long ago. When the War was over, we just wanted to live, move forward and forget. What good would it have done to expose him? You and your mother would have had to carry his shame and he still would have got away with it. You know how it was.'

Armand raised weary eyes to Jeanne, 'you will tell me about him, won't you Jeanne? About Karl?'

'Come to Fleurac soon my dear, and I'll show you his portraits.' Jeanne's face lit up. She looked like a young girl. 'He was an artist. He loved nature, just as you do. Oh, he was a wonderful man.'

There were still some details that didn't add up, but for the first time in his life, Armand felt… unchained. He felt complete. His spirits soared. He wasn't the son of a monster after all, but that of an artist, the son of a nature lover. At last, everything, or nearly everything, made sense. He was a pacifist, son of a pacifist. It was a good feeling.

PART V

ORLA - FLEURAC - PRESENT TIME

39
PARIS – FLEURAC

The train left Gare de Lyon. I let go of Paris, said goodbye to skipping over cobblestones for my morning baguette, walking by the Canal Saint Martin and being a *flâneuse* on the boulevards. A vision of Jean-Loup's wolfish grin jolted me back to reality.

As the train hurtled south, I took stock. Why had I wasted ten years with a chancer like Declan who'd thrown away everything we'd built together on a whim, why? As France rolled by at speed, I realised that what had kept Declan and me together was The Business. It was our baby. Declan had taken me for granted and I had not noticed, focused on The Business, the one thing that made me feel fulfilled and valued.

While he was at the pub, staring at Sinead's tits over a jar, I used to love nothing better than to sit under the Anglepoise lamp, adding up our profits and carving out new markets. I was good at it.

For Declan, it obviously wasn't enough, so he gave it up to live his dream: beer on tap and big boobs. You had to hand it to him though. Unlike me, sitting here in a train on the road to nowhere, yer man knew what he wanted and went out to get it.

Could I have carried on running The Business without Declan? No. Motorbikes were a man's thing. He provided the testosterone, shone in business lunches with his repertoire of jokes, and he had a talent for knocking back the jars. But I did all the work. *Good luck to you fella,* I let go of Declan as we coasted into Lyon.

A few hours later we reached Valence and France turned into Italy. As the first Roman roofs appeared, I autopsied my second failure: my inability to see Jean-Loup for what he was: a possessive maniac.

Jean-Loup may have sworn he would find me, but how could he find me when even the French didn't know where the Cévennes were? Sure, everyone had *heard* of the region, most knew that it was in a *département* called the Lozère, famous for its thick chestnut forests and thinly spread population, but where it was on a map? No one had a clue.

The mysterious Cévennes were France's best kept secret. I would be safe there.

I began to relax, apprehension turning to excitement. I was on the way to finding my ancestors and in the process, finding myself.

Just before we reached Nîmes, I wondered whether the aristocratic Orla I was about to discover would dovetail into the Dublin Jackeen I so wanted to shake off.

The script I had grown up with was that of an obedient girl, tidy and good at maths. A good retentive memory had allowed me to absorb French, I was skilled with my hands and blessed with an easy nature, but then so were many people. I had no particular talents or outstanding physical features, apart from my butt, of course, my green eyes and my thick chestnut hair. (Okay, 'chestnut' is what it said on the bottle. The fight against grey had already begun.) I wore it short again. Gone was the flaky Bardot-bimbo Jean-Loup had tried to create.

I'd had plenty of chances to prove what I could do, but Dad was right, I did need to know where I came from. Mick, God love him, had been a better father to me than most, and though I had his blessing, I couldn't help but feel disloyal in searching for my roots. I knew I wasn't a Reilly, but who was I? *Primo I radici, poi I ali* the Italians say. Roots first, then wings. I couldn't wait to fly.

In Mende, I left the train station and followed stumpy housewives and men with caps into a green bus for the last leg of the journey into Fleurac and into my roots.

'Now, Orla,' I muttered to myself as the bus climbed the first hill towards Fleurac, 'let's find out what species you really belong to.'

But what of the bookseller who had left the world behind for Pétaouchnock, I wondered as we climbed the second hill. Where did he fit in my story?

40
FLEURAC

The roads twisted up and down between the old mountains. Worn, ribbed with the memory of ancient terraces, the slopes had turned to grassy undulations.

Forests which, I knew from my conversation with creepy old Arnaud were chestnut, covered the hills.

A chateau appeared around a bend as we approached Fleurac, its turrets peeping above trees. Built from local grey stone, it was both elegant and solid.

I stepped down from the bus, surprised to find the sleepy Cévennes town wide-awake and fighting to be invited into the twenty first century.

I dragged my suitcase through throngs of protesters, tickled pink to have arrived bang in the middle of one of those fabled French demonstration.

'Please, come and live with us!' A woman noticed my luggage and pointed to a banner which said, *'Come and live in our QUIET village. Nothing will disturb the calm, not even the phone. Just don't try calling the doctor.'*

Flip, if there was no signal, how would I tell Mam and Dad I had arrived? And how the heck would I find a hotel?

I'd been so terrified that Jean-Loup would discover where I was, I had not even booked anything for the night.

I hung around for a while, reading pamphlets, talking to people. Eventually I sat at the terrace of a café overlooking the main square and ordered a *grand crème.* I sipped my coffee watching a handful of local mayors mingling with the crowd, thin tricolour sash looped over checked shirts.

The good citizens of Fleurac had been patient, a sympathetic *gendarme* explained to me. This had been going on for years. But what could they do? Taking to the streets was a last resort. They had tried every other avenue, but lost in Lozère limbo, they had been forgotten by the government and the phone company.

I knew from French Wikipedia that the Cévennes (rebaptised Lozère department) were first connected by road to the rest of France in the 1700s just so Louis XIV could send his dragoons to massacre Protestant insurgents.

That's right. *Protestant* insurgents. I know it sounds odd but there you are. Ireland might be suffering from the opposite evils, but it looked like the new French Orla would have to feel sorry for Protestants for a change.

While the Irish Catholics once hid in caves and celebrated mass over a rock, the Cévenol Protestants hid in caves and held their services over rocks in secret places called *Désert*. I had been told that these mountains were a good place to hide away from the world. Well, from the barren landscapes I'd seen from the bus, they weren't exactly short of deserts.

Anyway, here I was. Although the town was much more picturesque and friendlier than I had imagined, I could already see that my plan to set up an Internet business was dead in the water.

Never mind, I didn't need to linger. All I had to do was check out this *biologique* father of mine –see if I liked the look of him– and presto, return to Dublin, complete with roots.

I waved to the waiter. '*Excusez-moi,* is there a *librairie* in Fleurac?' Charming as Fleurac may be, if I couldn't find an Armand de Peirac running a bookshop, I'd be scooting off on the next bus.

The waiter slung his towel over a shoulder and pointed across the street. 'If you want to buy a paper, there's a newsagent just opposite, but if you want books…'

'I want books.'

'The bookshop is up there to the left, a tall stone house with green shutters on the next street corner.'

'*Merci*. Would you mind looking after my suitcase for half an hour?'

'*Pas de problème*.'

He tucked my case behind the bar. Now wasn't that grand? People still trusted each other in the Cévennes.

Clustered in front of the Mairie, demonstrators were listening to tale after tale of businesses floundering because an unreliable Internet service restricted contact to between five and six in the morning. My heart went out to them.

I followed the waiter's directions along ancient streets lined with grey stone houses that spoke of a prosperous past based on the sale of "mules, cloth, salt, silk and of course, chestnuts." Now, wasn't the internet a wonderful thing… when it worked.

I turned left, reached the crooked street indicated by the waiter and there it was, a tall dour building and above the door, *Peirac livres*. My mouth went dry. Topped by curly balustrades and dusty green woodwork was the bookshop where my potential father had gone to ground. I did a double check. 'Peirac,' the *particule* was missing. Flip, Aude had seemed so sure of herself. What if he was the wrong man? I took in several breaths and tried to think of an opening line.

What would I say? All the scenarios conceived on the train had evaporated. My mind was a blank.

Bah, it was down to the luck of the Irish. I crossed the street.

Here we go. I thought as I pushed the door. *Here we go.* I pushed the door again, and tried pulling. It wouldn't budge.

It was closed.

41
ORLA – FLEURAC

Back on the square, a few small groups of protesters lingered. I returned to the bar, ordered a large glass of white wine and considered my options.

The café terrace had filled up with demonstrators and a peppering of oddballs. In a haze of patchouli and marijuana, the convivial group of oddballs expanded as the afternoon wore on, their dogs and children playing and peeing undisturbed against the plane trees that shaded the square.

As evening fell, I sank into a pleasant torpor and listened to the hubbub until I remembered that I had nowhere to sleep.

'Excuse me,' I asked the barman, 'Do you know where I could find a room?'

'Oh la la, c'est pas la saison.' He put down the glass he was wiping and turned to a man nursing a Pastis next to me, 'Régis, any ideas? The lady is looking for a room.'

He shot a hard glare at two derelicts who came up with suggestions of their own.

'Jeanne Pujol rents out rooms,' suggested the man called Régis, 'but it's the low season. She might be closed.' His eyes widened at the size of my suitcase. 'How long are you staying?'

What I wanted to say was, 'my stay is open-ended,' but my French deserted me, so with my best attempt at a Gallic shrug I mumbled *'Bof, chais pas,'* which is Parisian for 'dunno.'

Régis cocked an eyebrow, pointed to my glass and twirled a finger. I nodded.

Perched on a bar stool with a refill, I studied my new friend. Mid-forties, he had greying temples, dark hair gathered in a ponytail and the traditional garb of a man who never has to go to the office: jeans, jumper and interesting shoes.

'So,' I began with a confident smile, 'was today's *manif* successful d'you think? A demo's all very well, but how are the Internet providers going to know that the people of Fleurac took to the street at all?'

'Oh, they'll know all right.' His brown eyes twinkled. 'Giving our regions more power is all the rage now. Everyone is deserting Paris and rushing to the sun. But if we can't get linked, what's the point?' Now serious he added, 'The Internet providers are well aware of our existence. We've used every possible means to contact them over the years, but nothing–'

I butted in, 'perhaps the mountains…'

'We pay our bills.'

There was no answer to that. The wine making me garrulous, I told him that I ran an Internet business, which made him laugh, and he told me he was a beekeeper and lived alone with his dog somewhere up a hill.

'Come on,' he grabbed my case, 'let's go and see if old Jeanne has a room. If she hasn't, don't worry, there are other places.'

Following a man I had only just met was reckless, but Fleurac seemed like a nice place and I felt safe with Régis so, nose in the air I abandoned myself to the adventure in Fleurac's medieval streets.

'Oops.' I stumbled into my suitcase. My companion had stopped and was knocking on the door of a house set in a long wall. A window opened.

'Régis?' said an old voice. 'Is that you? Sorry. I don't normally have visitors at this time of night.' An aroma of vegetable soup and the hum of a television enveloped a thin woman with tiny dark eyes and white hair.

I stood in the shadows and listened, disappointed to hear that yes, she did have a garden room, but it was only available in summer.

'Never mind.' Régis stepped away. The streetlight fell on me. I smiled and went to turn away, when the woman cried out, '*Attendez !*'

Her face softened. She looked at me strangely and murmured, 'Arielle?'

'*Bonsoir Madame.*' I stepped closer so she could see me. 'My name is Orla and I'm looking for a room.'

'Yes, yes, of course, dear. Come in. I'll just go and open the door for you.'

Hugely relieved, I followed her into the yard to the loveliest little workshop you could imagine, and thanked the beekeeper for his help.

'*Dear Asha,*

I've reached my destination. Neither outpost of the Gobi Desert, nor picture postcard, my new place is wholesome and I already find myself at home. Someone has already recognised me, which only goes to prove that I look French.

I've found a cheap and comfortable room at the back of a cobbled yard with beams on the ceiling and lovely old furniture.

My landlady is a dear. She thinks that I look like someone she knew before, a woman called Arielle. I am hopeful.

I have found the bookshop. It looks surprisingly well-kept and bears no sign of being run by a madman, but frustratingly, it was closed in support of a demonstration. Christ! I knew the French liked to take to the streets, but had not expected to find them marching around those old streets.

Internet reception here is not great (hence the marching.) There is no guarantee that you will get this e-mail today. If you need to contact me urgently, call me on the landlady's land-line. I will send you her number by snail mail to make sure you get it. Phones are not 100% reliable either, sorry. Tomorrow I'll go and investigate all the good places to impress you when you come over. I'm so glad you managed to get some time off. I can't wait to see you.

Lots of love

Orla.'

I pressed send and was rewarded with a satisfying ping. What now, I wondered. It was six am and I was too excited to go back to sleep.

I filled the percolator and while I waited for the coffee to drip into the glass jug, I planned my day. The plan was simple: walk the hundred yards to the bookshop and hope for the best.

I set my cup on the bathroom shelf and studied my face in the mirror. Who was Arielle? Who else had my oval face, green eyes and chestnut hair?

It was chilly outside. Wrapped in a thick Aran cardigan my Kerry grandma had knitted – my Sullivan grandma, the nice one – I stepped into the empty streets. Snug inside its blanket of clouds, Fleurac was still asleep. A few cars swooshed down the main road on the other side of the river. My breath rising in small puffs, I headed for the cemetery where I hoped I would find a few de Peiracs.

What I found there were disturbing glass offerings of

flying doves and pictures of cattle. I checked the names on the most prominent graves, and found that the big wigs in this town were the d'Aubrac family. Jeepers. Their grand mausoleum would have made Tutankhamen proud. I examined the stone edifice and to my surprise, noticed the name. 'Arielle'. I peered closer.

Arielle d'Aubrac 1920- 1970.

'Lord above,' I took a step back, 'the poor woman was only fifty when she died.'

Goose spots rose all over my body. If Arielle d'Aubrac was linked to the de Peirac family and I looked like her, I had reached my goal. The chateau and swimming pool of my dreams flashed one last time and disappeared. I would not find it here.

With a new purpose, I looked around me and tried to connect with the stony hills, the chestnut forests and the gushing river, so far removed from the urban cityscape that had shaped me. There were now so many questions I wanted to ask the elusive Armand, I couldn't wait to return to the shop and meet him.

I checked my watch. Flip, it was only eight. Time had never crept so slowly. The bookshop, if it opened at all today, wouldn't open before ten. At a brisk pace, I headed for the hills, taking care to inhale and exhale calmly.

The road snaked up and thinned to a rocky path. Halfway up the hill, a black and white spaniel ran out of a cottage and barked at me. I stopped. It looked friendly enough. I held out my hand for him to sniff and noticed a sign, '*Miel à vendre*.' Painted on a grey slab, the 'honey for sale' sign rested against a short tree trunk topped with a slate. 'This,' I whispered, my heart beating slightly faster, 'is the home of a beekeeper.'

Set on an earth terrace dug out of the hill was a low stone cottage and, on the second terrace above it, a row of beehives in faded grey and orange wood.

I patted the dog and smiled to myself. 'So… this is where Régis is holed up.'

The smile fell off my face when I noticed bees flying in and out of the trunk. Bees! I shot back. I hated the feckin' things. What a way to welcome visitors. Was your man insane?

From a safe distance, there was quite a nice feel to the cottage. It looked organic, it looked– what was the word again? *'Bio'* yes, that was it, a *'biologique'* wholeness oozed from Régis' place.

Anyway, between the jigs and the reels, by the time I'd made it back to town, I found it in full swing. The shops were open and I was spoiled for bars in which to have breakfast. With an hour to go until ten, I calmly ate a croissant and shopped for the week. I studied the ingredients on packets, weighed my fruit, walked home at a steady pace, put away the shopping and deliberately – concentrating on my breath – ambled to the bookshop, pretending I didn't really care. I stopped by the green door, pushed – and stepped in. Pfew.

'Bonjour, Orla.'

I jumped out of my skin. 'Janey Mac! Who knows my name here?'

A head appeared above a shelf.

'Régis? What are you doing here?'

'I work here. Or at least I do this week. I'm looking after the shop while Armand is away. What can I do for you?'

42
ORLA – FLEURAC

I had been in Fleurac five days and still not met Armand. I couldn't sleep with the frustration of it all. I had imagined that tied to his shop Armand would be a sitting duck, yet he was more elusive than a snow leopard in Tibet.

It was all very well Régis running the shop, but I had run out of excuses to visit the damn place. To be fair, it was a great bookshop. I'd never seen the like of it. There was everything there, from blockbusters to philosophy to comics, novels set in the Cévennes of course, cookery books and even second-hand paperbacks in English.

I was dying to ask Régis about Armand, but couldn't give the game away too soon. It was exasperating.

'What are you doing tomorrow?' I casually asked the next day at the café, trying to establish my chances of meeting my snow leopard.

Régis and I had progressed to a table by then.

'Why, what have you got in mind?' Régis grinned.

'Will you be working at the shop?' I asked, hoping he

would tell me how long it would be until the rightful owner returned.

'No, Armand's back now. I've got to check up on my hives. Would you like to come along?'

'Yes!' I answered blithely. It took all I had not to punch the air.

'What time?'

'Huh?'

'What time do you want to come to my apiary?'

We spoke French. Because I was focusing on my chances of finally meeting Armand, and the French for apiary was *rucher*, a word easily mumbled, I hadn't really understood the question.

'Now Orla,' I was thinking to myself, *'consider this carefully. Today's Monday. The bookshop, like all French shops, is closed. Tomorrow Tuesday, it will open at ten. How about strolling in around ten thirty, spend fifteen minutes there at the most... just to get the measure of yer man–'*

'Eleven OK?' Régis said. 'Let me explain where I live...'

'Oh, I know where you live.'

He gave me a long look and tilted his head. 'You're not afraid of bees, are you?'

Huh? What did bees have to do with anything? I reran our conversation in my mind and found no mention of *'abeilles.'* Jeepers! What had I done? When he confirmed his offer, I suddenly realised that he had invited me to look at his bees and what was worse... I had agreed.

I swallowed hard and answered with a sweet smile. 'Me? Of course, I amn't.' Ouch. No turning back now.

That night, I tried to call Asha to share my news, but I could not get through. I didn't sleep a wink, too excited at the thought of meeting the snow leopard. I tossed about in bed. Jesus, the state I was in. Having gone through this with Arnaud had not vaccinated me at all, quite the opposite.

'*What if you've got it wrong, Orla? What if he isn't your father?'* I thrashed about in bed. *'And what if he is your father and you dislike him, then what?'*

I tried to knock myself out with some Cointreau liqueur I'd bought. At dawn, I got up and made myself a strong coffee, soon followed with a second one topped with another dose of Cointreau. Around nine, ten in London, I tried calling Asha again, but there still was no signal.

Cursing the telephone company, I paced around my room in a state of heightened anticipation, my mind stuck in the old groove of *what if he is and what if he isn't.*

I flopped in the bath, watched morning television, dried my hair and bunched it in a ponytail. I put on make-up and removed it. There were bags under my eyes and my skin was blotchy. I decided to go incognito, which shouldn't be difficult since Armand didn't know of my existence. I found a baseball cap at the back of a press, rummaged in my case for sunglasses and checked my disguise. I looked ridiculous.

By the time I reached the bookshop, I was hyperventilating. When I pushed the green door and staggered in, I was that close to passing out.

I don't know who I was expecting, an aging Archangel Gabriel perhaps, but no way had I ever pictured my father like the man sitting behind the till, reading a newspaper. I strolled to a corner, pulled down a large comic, and peered over it.

My phone rang. I checked the caller ID. Asha? At last!

'Wow,' I shouted, unable to contain myself, 'you got through! I tried calling you all morning.'

'Where are you?'

'Asha, you are not going to believe this,' I whispered loudly. 'I am in the bookshop. He's sitting right opposite me. I mean, it might not be him. Christ, I don't know what to say.'

'What does he look like?'

'Well, hmmm, he looks like Santa.'

Behind the till, Santa's eyes cast daggers at me over his half-moon glasses, obviously disapproving of the use of mobile phones in his grotto.

I gave him an idiotic grin and whispered to Asha. 'I can't talk long. Just tell me when you're arriving.'

'I got your message. I'll hire a car in Nîmes airport. We'll meet half- way, at that *Festival du Désert* you suggested, in Mialet. One o'clock, Saturday afternoon, okay? Meet you at the entrance of the museum.'

'Saturday at one in Mialet Museum in front of the ticket booth. Fantastic. Bye.' I slipped the phone back in my pocket, made my way to the English section, picked up a second-hand Chandler and pulled down my baseball cap, a huge lump in my throat.

As we stood face to face, I searched for something, anything that would link us, but behind the half-moon glasses, his eyes were hidden under bushy white brows and his face was covered in hair. My hand shook as I handed the money.

He scrutinised me over his glasses, and said in a sigh, '*Vous êtes américaine?*'

Ouch. The way he said it was more of an insult than a question.

That grumpy old man had mistaken my Dublinese for an American accent. Perhaps Americans had a habit of shouting down their phones, who knows. I was so put out by the whole encounter that I lost my nerve and missed my clue to say, '*non, je suis irlandaise.*'

Instead, I grabbed my book and ran home, furious and confused. Damn. What an eeejit I had been. I'd made a total hash of it and would have to start all over again.

43

ORLA – FLEURAC

I threw myself on the bed and pounded the pillow to vent my frustration, berating myself for being stupid-stupid-stupid, but then again, what sin had I committed? I'd answered my mobile in his shop. Was it my fault if in this place, the phone –and bookshop owners for that matter– only worked when they felt like it? Of course, if I'd stayed off the Cointreau, I might have had the wits to reply *'I'm not American, you cantankerous old hippie, I'm Irish and for all we know, I might be your long-lost daughter.'* Yes, that Cointreau early in the morning had been a bad idea.

I was over reacting. Perhaps it was not him at all. I scrambled up and ran a hand through my hair. It could be that Armand, whom I had yet to meet, had asked one of his hippie friends to look after his shop. All I had to do was watch the shop from afar, track down Armand, establish whether or not he was my biological father and if, and only if I liked him, would I reveal my identity. My encounter with Arnaud de Peirac had taught me a lesson I was not likely to forget.

Something buzzed at the back of my mind and distracted me from my misfortune… *bees.* I had actually said yes to

Régis. I must have been mad. Or not, I realised as I headed for the hills. It was a grand idea. Those bees could not have come at a better time to distract me from my woes.

Régis's dog greeted me at the bottom of the path.

'*Saxo ! Ici !*' In white cosmonaut garb, Régis strode towards us, his face hidden inside a dark netted hood. After a gloved handshake, he handed me a similar outfit. Close up, Régis smelled of wood smoke and resin, a *bio* combination that set my hormones racing.

If my heart rate had doubled after the three coffees I'd had that morning, trebled when I met Armand for the first time, and quadrupled when Régis helped me into the bee suit, it all but stopped when he removed the roof of the first hive. Was I really 'protected' by the thin cloth? I didn't think so. We were relying – my mentor assured me – on the fact that bees 'don't see white.' I was not convinced. They see daisies, don't they?

'Bees fear fire. Watch. When I blow smoke into the hive, they don't attack me, instead, they scurry back inside to fill their bellies with honey, ready to escape. Once they are full of honey, it's so much harder for them to sting.'

Oh, but they could, if they put their mind to it. The buzz was terrifying. Jeepers, did they sound angry. 'Buzz off, Orla,' they were saying to me, 'Leave us alone.'

From a distance, I watched Régis pull out frames one by one, inspecting them, he explained, for damage, disease, and to check on the queen. I took a timid step forward.

'There she is.' He pointed to a slightly longer bee dragging her abdomen across the frame.

I peered over his shoulder. This was the queen? 'Why does she have a red dot on her back?'

'I marked her with red because she's last year's queen. This year's queens are marked in white. That's how I know how old my queens are.'

I crept closer, sweating buckets inside my suit, somewhat reassured by Régis' calm sense of purpose.

'And what are these little plump white things?'

'These are the larvae, the baby bees. When they're ready, the workers seal them in. Once they've turned into bees, they munch their way out, all cute and fluffy.'

Bees, cute and fluffy?

Régis closed the hive and moved on to the next one. By the fifth hive, my ears had tuned out the threat and registered a purpose in the buzz.

'How about those fat bees here?' I pointed to a macho variety milling about the entrance. 'Are they workers?'

'These are the males, the drones.'

'What do they do?'

Régis straightened up and smiled. The dark veil did nothing to filter the pheromones oozing in my direction. There was something strangely attractive in a man with a dangerous occupation.

'They don't do anything. They just hover above the hive, waiting for a queen to appear so they can mate with her.'

I swatted away the image of an inflatable Declan hovering over Clontarf, waiting for someone to impregnate.

My stomach clenched. I took in a calming breath of wood smoke and focused back to the narrow Cévenol terrace.

'Come on, let's take a break,' Régis said. 'I've got some fresh apple juice.'

I followed him into the cottage and carefully closed the door. Only once I was sure that no bee had followed me in, did I remove my suit.

The place was spacious and well worn, with an old velvet armchair covered in dog hair, a leather sofa and a coffee table littered with sheet music and CDs. A saxophone leaned in a corner. The kitchen worktop took up the side facing the terraces that rose behind the house. Across the room a large picture window framed a snaking river and a panorama of chestnut covered slopes.

Régis filled two glasses, handed me one and took a seat at one end of the sofa. I hesitated by the velvet chair.

'That's Saxo's chair.' He patted the space next to him.

'*Slainte.*' I knocked his glass. We sipped our juice in silence.

'Tell me,' I pointed to the music partitions, 'which is the day job, beekeeper or saxophonist?'

'Hmm. Actually, the day job used to be advertising.' He gave a self-deprecating laugh. 'Up to two years ago,' he put his glass down. 'I had everything, the gorgeous wife, the big house, the BMW.' His eyes lost their sparkle.

I was surprised. He looked nothing like an advertising executive.

He gave a small shrug. 'Now I keep bees during the day and play *saxo* at night.' The corner of his eyes crinkled. I loved his eyes. They changed colour according to his mood. Right now, they fizzed with life. Suddenly serious, his pupils narrowed and focused like lasers into my soul. 'Orla, why are you really here?'

His directness gave me a jolt. Why was I here? He had been kind to me. I owed him an answer, a partial answer at least, but before I opened my heart, I wanted to know more about him.

'You?'

'Bah, it's the old story.' He leaned away from me with a long sad sigh. 'It's the same old, old story.'

'Oh dear.'

'My wife and my best friend. I never saw it coming.'

'I'm so sorry.' My empathy was real. It really was the same old story.

'Me, my partner and our assistant,' I said with a deprecatory laugh. 'Why Fleurac?'

'This cottage was in my family. My wife hated it.' He snorted, 'She preferred Cannes. I used to come here on my own, while she… while they…' he shrugged. 'I was in shock when it happened. I dropped everything, packed up the job and moved in here with Saxo.' Upon hearing his name, the dog wagged his tail. The smile on the dog's face went some way to dispel the gloom.

Régis lifted an eyebrow in question. My solar plexus throbbed as I poured out my story, so predictable, so pathetic, so similar to his.

'What upset me the most,' I blurted out, 'was that Declan never wanted – children – and –' lulled by Régis' warmth, I relaxed my guard. Buried emotions rose to the surface, bubbled up and spilled out of the cracks. When Régis covered my hand with his, the dam burst. It had been building up for years. My mouth twisted. My chest began to heave. Christ, I really hadn't seen that coming.

'We were together for ten years but–' I stuttered, 'it was never the right time and now … now I've just found out that Sinead…' I hiccupped, 'That's the girl he's with… is… pregnant.' My body wracked with great big spasms, I sobbed.

Régis patted my back.

Embarrassed, I pulled myself together, wiped my eyes with my sleeves and sniffed an apology.

Régis handed me a pack of tissues. 'Listen, I made some soup. Do you want some? It's chestnut.'

I nodded and said in a small voice. 'Thank you. I'm so sorry.'

'Don't be. Come on, we'll have some of this soup and then Saxo and I will walk you home.'

While he prepared our meal, I pulled my cardigan around me, walked to the picture window and stared down at the valley below and ran a mental check around my heart. Perhaps the abscess had been lanced.

I cast surreptitious glances at Régis, working his magic in the kitchen with an elegant economy of movement. I liked everything about the man, but after the last episode with Jean-Loup, I didn't trust my instincts.

The soup was hot, sweet and delicious. There wasn't much he couldn't turn his hand to. Though he was sexy as hell, I reminded myself that the real reason I had followed him was to find out more about Armand. Was he the man I'd glimpsed at the shop? I couldn't really ask without betraying myself so instead, I frustratingly confined my questions to the Cévennes region and prattled on about Dublin.

After a pleasant hour or so, Régis and Saxo walked me home. Just before we reached Jeanne's house, I took the plunge.

'You remember, when I first arrived, Jeanne thought I looked like someone else?'

'Did she? I don't remember.'

'Yes, she thought I looked like someone called Arielle.'

'Really?' Régis gave it some thought. 'Arielle… yes, that would be Armand's mother. Her name was Arielle. Arielle d'Aubrac.'

A warm honey feeling spread around my chest. Arielle was Armand's mother, and I looked like her.

'Did you ever meet her?'

'No, she died before my time.'

Not wanting to give the game away, I pursed my mouth and giggled. 'Ah well, they say we've all got a doppelganger somewhere.'

He wasn't fooled, I could tell. We both knew that I still hadn't answered his question as to why I was really here, but he didn't push me, and for this, I was grateful.

'Allez, au revoir, Orla.' By the door, he drew me to him and hugged me. I relaxed against his chest, his body strong and comforting.

He studied my face and smiled.

That smile tingled around my body, pinged in several places, hovered in the middle and coursed down all the way to my toes, which curled up in pleasure. A page of the Great Book of Orla was about to turn, I could tell.

44
ORLA – FLEURAC

My landlady, Jeanne Pujol, was a widow. Her only daughter, Catherine, was a primary school teacher in Lyon. Catherine came home in the summer to help out with an old cottage on a hill, which they rented out as a holiday *gîte* during the high season.

From the sturdily built kitchen presses, I had picked up that Jeanne's husband, André, had been a carpenter. *'Menuisier,'* she'd said with pride. From what I understood, Jeanne had wanted to be a teacher, but the war had put paid to that. She was a Protestant and taught Sunday school, which in France was on a Wednesday, when schools were closed and children were free to pursue the religious education of their choice. A grand idea, if you ask me.

A few days before Asha arrived, I knocked on the glass of Jeanne's kitchen door but there was no answer.

'Madame Pujol?' I pushed the door and found myself transported by the smell to my Kerry grandma's kitchen.

At one end of a long table, Methuselah was dozing, hands crossed over his stomach, a paper open in front of him. His hair was thick and white and his body bulky.

I cleared my throat. *'Excusez-moi, Monsieur, je cherche Jeanne.'*

The rheumy eyes blinked behind large glasses and slowly focused on me. I stepped closer. A huge smile spread across his face. 'Arielle?'

I held out my hand for him to shake. He drew me to him and wrapped his arthritic fingers around mine, his smile so beatific, I could have been the Blessed Virgin Mary of Knock herself. We remained like this for a long time.

'Ah hello, Orla.' Jeanne hauled in a basket of potatoes she had just fetched from the cellar. 'I see you've met my brother, Lucien.' She turned to the old man and raised her voice, 'Mademoiselle is my Irish tenant.'

Lost in some private dream, Lucien was not listening.

'Madame Pujol,' I began.

'Everyone calls me Jeanne.'

'Jeanne, a friend of mine is coming to stay for a few days. Would it be okay for her to share my room?'

'Oh oui ! Pas de problème.' She bustled past the table and dropped the potatoes into the sink.

'Jeanne,' I halted by the door. 'This Arielle I look like… who is she?' I wanted to know more about my mysterious doppelgänger.

'Ah.' Jeanne beamed. Her hands jumped to her chest. 'She was an angel.'

Oh, this was good. I switched to the past tense. 'Did she live here in Fleurac?'

'Oh yes. She grew up in the chateau, a few kilometres from here, the one with the turrets you can see from the road. You might have seen it.'

That chateau with turrets… I let go of the door handle, a very strange feeling wooshing around my body, as if I was made of air. Clontarf… the bare breeze-block wall around our garden, the box-room where I grew up… suddenly seemed like some sort of joke.

'Asseyez-vous, asseyez vous.' Jeanne indicated a chair, settled herself opposite me and leaned forward, jet eyes twinkling. 'You see, my grandmother was hired as her nanny after the poor girl's mother died… she was only three, poor little mite. We saw a lot of Arielle when we lived over on the hill.' Jeanne pointed east, somewhere beyond the butler sink and the half-glazed door, I guessed towards the cottage she rented out in summer.

'What happened to her?'

Jeanne sifted through her memories, not all happy, I could tell from her expression. 'She got married at the end of the War and went off to America. Then she came back and lived in Paris.'

I was aching to ask where in Paris, but I held my peace. If any disclosures were to be made, they would have to involve Armand first. I bit my lower lip to stop me from blurting everything out.

The smile returned to Jeanne's face. 'Arielle spent every summer here. She was happy in Fleurac.'

Not so happy in Paris then.

'Did she have children?'

'She had a son, Armand.' The name magically smoothed away the years on her face. Eyes half-closed in rapture, Jeanne stated with fervour, 'he runs the bookshop.' Crikey, had yer man been a bishop, she couldn't have been more proud.

'Long white hair and beard?'

'Yes, that's him. Such a lovely man.'

So, this *was* Armand. I drew a long breath.

'Armand is a good boy!' Methuselah shouted from the end of the table.

'Oh yes, he is that.' Jeanne cast her brother a benevolent

smile. 'Armand used to follow Lucien everywhere when he was little. The two of them helped André build this kitchen.' She rocked gently, lost in her nostalgia.

Mr Grumpy a good boy? This was reassuring. I might give him a second chance.

Lucien stirred. 'So, you're back with us then. Not scooting off to Paris again, I hope?'

Jeanne reached over and patted my hand. 'He thinks you're Arielle.'

I turned to him and, moved by the emotion I read in his rheumy eyes, assured him that I'd be staying here for a while.

It suddenly occurred to me that if Armand was my father, it was crucial to find out whether he had any other children. Back in Paris, Aude had assured me he didn't, but she was an airhead.

'Armand never got married.' Jeanne murmured, reading my thoughts. 'Never had children.' Filled with something like wonder, her old eyes rested on me.

45
ORLA – FLEURAC

Régis and I slowly became closer, but both bitten badly enough to be twice shy, we circled each other with caution. We met at the café and I stopped by his house whenever my walks took me that way. The last few days, Régis had been away, busy moving hives to a high moor in search of heather, a change from the chestnut honey his bees produced in the spring.

I'd got to a standstill with Armand. The man who ran the shop was so far removed from the picture I'd held in my mind all my life, that I was stumped for how to proceed.

While I waited for Asha's visit to clear the mist, I walked, watched French television and tried to communicate with Marguerite in Paris, to whom I had sold all my stock. I'd had no choice. Running an Internet business from Fleurac was not an option and anyway, from what I could see, vintage clothes were standard wear around here. Men wore their father's checked shirts, collars and cuffs lovingly unstitched and turned over by their women. Older women had an inexhaustible supply of easy-care apron-dresses. As for the marijuana-scented hippies that filled our café at night, they snaffled sixties garb from Emmaus for a couple of euros and wore it until it fell apart. Armand did anyway, shuffling about in worn cord trousers and tweed jacket from the ark.

It was a strange world. Communications with Paris had to go by snail mail of course. Marguerite and I considered ourselves lucky not to have to rely on the Pony Express.

Since my infamous conversation with Asha in Armand's bookshop, I had not dared set foot there again. I was going stir crazy. Asha couldn't come soon enough.

The day she was due to arrive, Régis had a gig in Alès and agreed to drop me on the way. He picked me up outside Jeanne's house. Though today the boot was filled with amplifiers, his old Renault estate had that smell of wood smoke and honey I found so erotic.

'Remind me why you're going to Mialet?' Régis asked as we reached the main road.

I took in a long breath, giddy with the scent of him, and tried to explain that Asha and I were about to attend a gathering of Protestants in some remote woods. I opened my mouth to speak, but my French deserted me, stunted by his closeness. 'I'm meeting a friend from London,' I croaked. He knew that, I'd already told him.

Frustrated, I wanted to explain that the gathering was something that, as an Irish Catholic, I simply had to see. As for Asha, she was a culture vulture at the best of times. Prayer meetings are not my cup of tea, but I was fascinated to hear the other side of the story. In Northern Ireland, over the border, Protestants and Catholics still didn't trust each other. My interest was piqued from a purely social point of view. It goes without saying that Grandma Reilly's bigotry had gone some way to dispel my illusions about the goodness of the Church.

'You're going to *l'Assemblée du Désert?*' Régis wasn't a fan of organised religion, I could tell.

'Oui.' I struggled to stay cool. *C'est local, c'est intéressant et c'est historique.'* There, he couldn't argue with that.

He rewarded me with an approving smile.

'L'histoire des Cévennes m'intéresse.' I added to impress him. How could I tell him that it was my history too without giving the game away? Luckily, the history of the Cévennes is brief. After Louis XIV abolished religious freedom in 1685 – the famous 'edict revocation' that sent thousands of Huguenots fleeing to England – the Cévenol Protestants were hounded, burned, tortured and hanged, their pastors flung into galley ships, and whole villages slaughtered in the name of The Lord. That's religion for you.

'History is taught with battles and dates,' Régis said, 'but the Cévenols' fight against nature, their daily struggle to grow food on their crumbling shale hills never made the headlines.' With a side glance, he asked, 'So, what do you know about our history?'

'Stevenson and his donkey stopped in Mialet in 1879.'

'Have you read it, his book?'

'Sure. It's a grand little book.'

Of course, if Stevenson had headed for the Provence instead of flogging his poor animal around these ancient hills, no one would have heard of the Cévennes at all. You have to hand it to him. In just twelve days, yer man put the region on the map singlehanded.

What I intended to do in the Mas Soubeyran was offer Asha a quick potted history of the Cévennes so that we could, with a clear conscience, spend the rest of her holiday eating, chatting, shopping and chilling out. But I didn't tell Régis that.

'How about you? What's the gig?'

'A two-hour set in a working men's club in Alès. Blues mostly.'

As we drove along, I studied his profile, trying to keep the butterflies in check. The glasses he wore for driving gave him an intellectual touch. I sat on my hands to stop myself from stroking the leather of his bomber jacket and caressing the elegant fingers resting on the gear stick, so close to my knee. What was it about this man? It wasn't just the high cheekbones, the silvery temples and the wiry body, or perhaps it was all of that. I hardly knew anything about him, but he felt right. Then again, so had Jean-Loup when I'd first met him. I held back. My manometer wasn't something I could trust.

'How are you getting back?'

'Asha's hired a car. She's meeting me there.'

'I presume Asha is coming over to Fleurac for the Soup Festival?'

'Sorry?'

'The Soup Festival.'

He had said soup. He was dead serious too.

'People come from far and wide for this event. Make sure you don't miss it.' Before my mouth had time to close, he drove up a narrow lane and pulled the handbrake.

'Here we are, Le Mas Soubeyran. I might see you tomorrow at the Café de la Place, unless you've got other plans?'

'I'll be there.'

A hand over the wheel, Régis leaned over with the intention of kissing my cheek. Unsure of which cheek he was aiming for, I turned my face the wrong way. His lips brushed mine. The world stopped turning. I floated up into the stratosphere inside a flurry of angels. A horn behind us brought me back to reality. I fumbled for the handle and staggered out.

I shielded my eyes and turned to wave but he had gone.

Once my molecules had settled, I looked around me. What a strange place. I wasn't sure what I had expected. The *Désert* was a large glade in a chestnut forest where a pastor in prim Puritan collar was preaching from a pulpit to crowds of believers sitting on camping chairs.

Our Irish saying goes, *'the believer is happy, the doubter is wise.'* I'm more of a doubter myself, though they *were* happy, bless them, those Protestants under the chestnut trees, and unlike the disturbing displays of Protestant fervour in Northern Ireland, there was not a drum or an orange flag in sight. It was all very spiritual really.

The Mas Soubeyran –more of a Roman villa than a farm– lacked the dourness of Cévenol constructions. We were south of the Lozère and there was a Provençal feel to the place. In 1700, the Mas had been the farm of Pierre Laporte, a figurehead of the Camisard movement, as they call the local rebellion. Something to do with the shirts the rebels wore.

I walked around the museum, baulking at depictions of atrocities committed in the name of God, and with half an hour to spare until Asha arrived, went out to clear my head from all the violence in a plant-filled courtyard. I sat on a low wall and offered my face to the October sun.

A familiar voice made me jump. A voice I hoped I would never hear again. *'Orla ? Quelle bonne surprise.'*

I opened my eyes and repressed a scream. Jesus Mary and Joseph, what was *he* doing here? I'd travelled four hundred miles to get away from him and here was my worst nightmare, grinning like we were best buddies.

'Bonjour, Jean-Loup,' I stuttered, chilled to the core.

'Orla, it's so wonderful to see you.' He sat next to me. His negative aura spilled out like miasma. I shuffled away from him. 'How have you been?' He reached out for my hand. My skin crawled.

'Oh, you know, sorting things out.'

'Same here.' He shifted closer. 'I had a lot of sorting out to do too. I've thought about what you said. I've changed, you know. I'm much more cool.'

'That's grand.' I got up and went into the building. How had he found my trail? He had stalked me to this place. How did he know?

He followed me in. His breath on my neck, I stared unseeingly at a display of floggings and tortures. He came closer. I stepped away.

'What brought you here?' I snapped. This was no coincidence. It couldn't be. I'd changed my phone, I'd told no one where I was. How on earth could he have known?

'I thought it would be interesting. I remember us talking about it back in Paris. We had such great conversations. We're soulmates, you and I. Just think, the synchronicity. Something led me to this place and…' He placed a hand on my sleeve. 'Here you are.'

I edged away, checking his face for signs of madness and sure enough, within the handsome features that had once attracted me, I noticed the obstinate brow, suspicious eyes and thin lips that betrayed his abject neediness.

'I've brought a picnic. Would you like to share it with me? I've got it in the car.'

This was just too weird. He was acting as if nothing had happened. He'd hacked into my phone, he'd threatened Marguerite and had to be manhandled out of her shop. How did he do it? I knew he was lying. How could we have discussed this Assemblée du Désert, when I had never even heard of the Cévennes at the time. Or had I mentioned the region? Had I? I was confused.

I glanced at my watch and saw with huge relief that it was one o'clock, the time I'd arranged to meet Asha. I hurried towards the ticket booth and of course, Jean-Loup came with me.

My heart sank. Asha wasn't there.

'Listen, you have to go now. I'm meeting Asha. She'll be here in a minute.'

'Oh really? I'd love to say hello. Come on, let's see if she's arrived.' Jean-Loup pulled me towards the car park. In the clearing beyond, clutching the lectern, a very thin woman was recounting the three years she had spent as a hostage in Africa. People discreetly wiped their eyes. I couldn't start giving out here, it would be disrespectful, so I followed Jean-Loup, determined to put an end to his delusions once and for all.

'I brought smoked chicken, your favourite,' Jean-Loup said with a creepy smile. I backed away from him and stumbled against a car.

'Come home to me, Orla.' He caught my arm and faced me, his face shining with a strange fervour. 'Things will be different, I promise.' He took a step forward and pinned me against the door.

I checked the car park. Where on earth was Asha?

I ducked under his arm, but he caught me and rammed me against the warm metal, somehow banging my nose as he tried to kiss me. Gagging, I gripped his jumper and fought him away, but he was much stronger than me. His fingers closed around my neck. I struggled to breathe.

'I found us a flat. You'll love it. It has a lift,' he rasped with a demonic grin. I struggled for air while caught up in his fantasy he ranted on, 'Orla *ma chérie* – we were good together – you know we were. You told me I was the best time you'd ever had.'

I felt sick. He let go of my throat. I coughed and gasped for air while he dug his fingers into my short hair. 'You've changed your hair. I don't like it.'

'Get off me, brute. How did you know where I was? You've been stalking me, haven't you? God, you're sick.' I scanned the car park again, urging Asha to come. He pressed himself against me and tried again to kiss me.

'I love you, Orla.'

'No, you don't. You don't know how to love. You want to own people!' I writhed inside his grip. 'You're mad!'

'Don't say that!' He slapped a hand over my mouth. I kneed him and sank my teeth into his hand. He hunched over with a groan. I felt faint.

Behind us, a car screeched to a halt. Asha jumped out.

'What's going on? Oh my God! What's he doing here?' She sprang onto Jean-Loup's back with an otherworldly yell and dug her fingers into his eyes. I bit him again. He roared with pain.

Retching, damp hair plastered over my face, I stumbled away. Jean-Loup elbowed Asha and grabbed me around the waist.

A pastor who had heard the ruckus strode in our direction, robes flowing. Jean-Loup caught sight of him, realised he was trapped, dropped me to the ground like a rag doll and jumped into his car. Just in time, Asha pulled me away. The lunatic reversed, narrowly missed the preacher and screeched down the road.

'Pfew! I sure know how to choose them,' I joked, spitting out Jean-Loup's blood.

'Orla, are you OK? You're shaking.' Asha was shaking too, but she turned to the pastor and indicated that we were fine.

I fell into her arms. 'Thank you. You saved my life.'

'What happened? How did that lunatic find you?'

Dazed, I checked my nose and rubbed the back of my head.

'I don't know. I changed my phone, I've blocked him from my Facebook, I've not been in contact with Marguerite. Honest, apart from you, only my parents know where I am. It doesn't make any sense!'

'Perhaps he's conned that man's daughter into sharing information.'

'Whose daughter?'

'The de Peirac girl, the one who sells jewellery. He could have chatted her up to find out where you live.'

Chilled at the thought, I rubbed my arms. 'Aude? Really?' I wouldn't put it past him. *Christ, if he knows where I live, he'll turn up in Fleurac.*

'You're shivering. He's gone now. Come on. Let's walk, it'll warm you up.'

We left the *Mas* and followed a path into the forest. I clung to Asha's arm, looking over my shoulder, making sure we kept close to other walkers. Eventually, bird song and the smell of resin soothed my soul. It really was beautiful here. Pine and wild thyme released the tantalising scents of Provence.

The encounter had shaken me to the core. I was safe while Asha was with me, but once she was gone, what would I do? I gave myself one week to find out whether Armand was my biological father and if he was, whether we wanted to be part of each other's life. At the end of the week, I'd fly back to London with Asha and that, I would tell no one, not even my shadow.

46
ORLA – FLEURAC

The following evening, Asha and I enjoyed the warmth and atmosphere on the terrace of the Bar de la Place. We ordered *sirop d'orgeat* – a sweet almond syrup I thought Asha would like – and watched children and dogs play on the square.

'Orla, Bonsoir.'

'Régis!'

He greeted me with the usual two chaste kisses.

'This is my friend Asha, from London.'

Régis was about to kiss Asha, when Armand walked out of the bar, lighting up.

'Ah! Les Américaines.' He looked away.

'Monsieur.' I nodded to him.

Asha graced him with a smile. She even held out her hand and said, *'Enchantée.'*

Enchanted, where had she picked that up?

Régis pulled out a chair, so Armand had no choice but to join us. The conversation, hesitant at first, progressed to English or in Armand's case, a brand of Franglish similar to Marguerite's.

We exchanged pleasantries while the waiter wound up his conversation with the hippies. When he finally came to our table, Armand said, 'I'm going to order a *croque-monsieur*, anyone else wants one?'

I was ravenous. I had planned to take Asha out to dinner, but this was too good an opportunity to get to know the old bookseller.

'Sure, I'll have one too.'

'What's in it?' Asha asked.

'You might want something else,' I whispered, 'it's a ham and cheese toasted sandwich.'

'I'd be okay with pizza. Do they have pizza?'

'Yes, I'll have a pizza as well.' Régis said.

'Without saucisson or ham, yeah?' I said to the waiter.

Armand checked out Asha's drink. 'You don't drink alcohol?'

'No, I'm a Muslim,' she answered with a sweet smile.

Asha was a saint. However many times we'd been through this when we worked in London, she never seemed to mind. I cringed, aware of what was coming.

'Where's your… veil?' Armand twirled a finger around his face, hinting at a hijab.

'My family are from India. We are Muslim converts. We don't…'

'And you are comfortable converting to a religion that oppress the woman?' Armand said in garbled English.

That's the French for you. Find out whether you're friend or foe before they even give you the time of day.

Armand didn't let up. 'You look like an intelligent woman. I am surprised.'

The waiter brought our drinks.

'Sorry, but you're a fine one to talk.' I butted in.

A hand around his glass, Armand turned to me in surprise.

'We are in the Cévennes, aren't we? All I saw in that bookshop of yours, apart from tales of the grand twelve days Stevenson spent here with his donkey, is how this place was obliterated by wars of religion, how the Catholics accused the Protestants of eating children and copulating with the Devil. Now Asha's not been here five minutes and already, you're having a go at her because she won't eat a *croque-monsieur.*'

Armand's eyebrows shot up. He lowered his drink, surprised at such high-mindedness coming from an… American.

As the conversation progressed, his gaze would slide to me. He would frown and look away again.

Asha explained calmly, 'Islam is a religion of hospitality and respect for the family. It advocates humility and charity. I'm a single woman and I work. I see no conflict there. If people from backward countries promote ignorance and misinterpret the Koran to their own ends, it's a cultural problem, not one of religion.' She shrugged. 'Sometimes people mistake religion with identity, squabble about details and forget the bigger picture, which is always one of love and understanding, really.'

Armand opened his mouth to reply and, thinking better of it, dipped his moustache into his beer.

Our food arrived surprisingly quickly.

'Tell me, Monsieur de Peirac…' Asha began.

'Peirac.' Armand grumbled.

I tensed up, expecting a reaction. Armand attacked his croque-monsieur instead.

Asha put a hand on his sleeve. 'Tell me, Monsieur Peirac, how do *you* see the world?'

God love her, she kept her cool.

Piqued, Armand stopped stabbing at his toast, sat back and stroked his beard while he considered the question.

'Me, I like the Gaia *théorie*. The world is a living, *euh*, a living *entité* yes? All the things they are…' he wove his fingers together 'linked, yes, all the things, the animals, the trees, the seas, the peoples.'

'Then we agree you and I,' Asha conceded. 'We say that Allah is in everything.'

Armand refused to mellow. 'Maybe, but why do you have to go on your knees five times a day?'

'When I pray,' Asha took a small bite of her pizza and chewed it calmly before continuing, 'I don't ask the old man in the sky to grant my every wish. That would be silly. I look inside myself and I pray for others. Most of the time, I offer prayers of gratitude for the gifts life sends my way, like new friends for instance.' Her dark eyes twinkled.

New friends… didn't you just have to love her?

While they chatted, I studied Armand, wondering whether I felt any connection to him. Though I found his Gaia theory reassuring, I could not help comparing his gruffness to Dad's easy humour and comforting presence. Dad. How I missed him.

Asha carried on undeterred. 'Religion is also a discipline. We all need discipline in our life.'

'Umpf.' Unconvinced, Armand munched on his toasted cheese sandwich, and concentrated on untangling the threads of Gruyère from his beard.

To dispel the tension, Régis mentioned *la Fête de la Soupe.* The way he enthused about it coloured the Fleurac soup fest with the mystique of the Rio Carnival.

'Is this true?' Asha clasped her hands to her chest. 'Soup at every street corner? How wonderfully original! Will you be making soup too?' She asked Régis.

'No, we're playing. I'm a saxophonist in a blues band.'

The atmosphere relaxed as the conversation veered to non-confrontational topics. It transpired that, before he switched to the saxophone, Régis had played the trumpet. He told us how, living with his mother near a military band's barracks, he had paid for trumpet lessons out of his own pocket money to ensure he would stay home during his military service.

'And? Did it work?' Asha laughed.

'Yes and no. In order to be accepted, they told me I had to become a career soldier.' He laughed. 'That for me, was not an option but they did take me in, and I spent eighteen months sweeping the grounds. And yeah, I was allowed to join them during the rehearsals'

Though the rest of the story was a little lost in translation, I found it endearing that Régis should learn the trumpet in order to go home to his mother's. I was beginning to like him. A lot.

Armand mellowed enough to share that his mother's family, originally from Fleurac, had made their fortune in silk. The climate – topic he was more comfortable with than his father's genealogy– was propitious to the cultivation of mulberries. I tried several times to divert the subject to Ireland, but there never seemed to be the right moment and, when we left, Armand still believed I was American. I hoped Régis would put him right.

'Armand is very guarded, Asha remarked as we ambled home.

'Yes, he's a bit of a closed book.' I pushed my key into the lock.

We made our way across the yard, dimly lit by the glow from Jeanne's kitchen. I closed our shutters and followed Asha in.

'Relax, Orla. I really think you should give him a chance. Perhaps he's had a hard life.'

'Oh, you always see the best in everyone. I don't know how you do it. I'm beginning to regret coming here. I've a perfectly good dad in Dublin and I'm not sure I need another one. Of course, I'm curious, I'm desperate to know about my origins, but...'

'You're doing the right thing, but you're not going about it the right way. Most people don't spend time finding out whether they *like* their biological parents, Orla. They meet them and take it from there.' Asha rummaged in the kitchen presses for two sachets of chamomile. 'You might not have an affinity with him, but at least, you'll solve the puzzle that prevents you from moving forward. You'll discover your roots.' She lit the gas under a pot of water and grumbled, 'what is it with the French and kettles?'

'What is it with the French and a lot of things. Jeez, the way he went for you! Lumping you with the Ayatollahs.'

'I'm used to it.' She sighed. 'Especially from boho intellectuals who imagine they're free of prejudice. They imagine they're the only ones to see the world as it really is, but so do the Inuits and the Tonga Islanders. We all think we know better, don't we?'

The water began to simmer. Asha lifted the pan, but as she poured, the water overshot the cup and spilled on her foot.

'Ouch! Aaargh!' The poor girl hopped around the kitchen in agony. 'Ooh my foot! Oooh blast, I burned myself!'

I filled a basin with cold water and told her to dip her foot in it. Her skin was red raw and I had absolutely nothing to soothe her. I frantically searched the bathroom for a first aid kit. Finding none, I ran over to Jeanne's. Thank God her light was still on.

I apologised and explained. 'We don't have any ointment. I wonder if you–'

'Ah bon? Alors j'arrive.' Jeanne stepped out into the yard.

'Would you by any chance have ointment or bandages?' I'd expected her to rush indoors and rummage for a soothing balm. Instead, she simply tottered towards our rooms.

Asha sat, her face twisted with pain.

'Jeanne? I insisted, '*Vous avez une crème pour...*'

'Oh, there's no need for that. *Bonsoir Madame.*' She pulled out a chair opposite Asha, picked up the towel I'd tossed near the basin, placed it on her lap and indicated that Asha should rest her foot on it.

'There's going to be a huge blister.' Asha sniffed.

I didn't know the French for blister, so I didn't translate, and mouth open, watched Jeanne cradle Asha's foot and gently place both hands over the burn. A few minutes later, Jeanne rubbed her fingers together and shook them, as if flicking away the heat she had absorbed.

'*Je coupe le feu,*' she explained. She 'stopped the fire?' What did that mean?

Once again, she placed her hands over the burn and once again, flicked off the heat as one would drops of water. After the third time, the redness had gone and Asha's skin returned to its lovely amber shade.

What were the chances? This miracle had taken place without the help of a single Pater Noster.

When it was over, Jeanne simply wished us good night and trotted home.

'Asha?' I asked much later as we were in bed. 'How is your foot?'

'Fine, Alhamdullilah. That was unbelievable.'

'I think she is a healer.'

'Definitely.' Asha mumbled sleepily.

Slivers of moonlight seeped through the shutters. Unable to sleep, I relived my encounter with Jean-Loup.

'Asha?'

'Hmmm?'

'D'you think Jean-Loup knows where I live?'

'Not yet no.' After a moment she mumbled, 'he'll try again.'

'Thanks for the reassurance.'

'Don't worry. I'll look after you.'

I promised myself that I would stay for the *Fête de la Soupe*, but the moment the soup festival was over, I would return to London with Asha. Everyone was very nice here, but with that wolf on my trail, I didn't feel safe.

47
ORLA – FLEURAC

Asha loved the Cévennes. She loved its unmanicured harshness, the mix of forests, barren plateaux and picturesque villages but above all, she loved the sound of cowbells. I put it down to the Indian connection… which made no sense really, her parents had fled Kenya before she was born, and she had never known anything other than London.

How much of our origins did we carry inside us? So far, there wasn't much of the Cévennes I had connected with, but I'd been so busy protecting myself against disappointment that I hadn't really given the place a chance.

Asha found the *Fête de la Soupe* 'terribly exotic.' Attending it was to be the highlight of her Facebook year.

'C'est pas compliqué la soupe,' Jeanne assured us, when she enrolled our help. 'We'll prepare it together.'

Now, as festivals go, I'd say that St Patrick's Day is the easiest to organise. All you have to do is wear green, put on a silly hat, add a twig of Shamrock if you want to go the extra mile, and get drunk. No wonder it's catching on the world over.

La *Fête de la Soupe* is a wee bit trickier to set up, but only just. As the weekend approached, Fleurac's old streets and squares filled with bunting, trestle tables and vintage gas cookers.

It was 'not just about the soup,' we were told, it was 'about taking part,' about being together in the Cévennes doing wholesome Cévenol things. There would be local jugglers, local raconteurs, local bands and stalls of local foods. For a local soup festival, its fame had spread surprisingly far and wide. We were assured it would be well attended, though when we looked at the weather forecast, we weren't so sure.

That Friday morning was a grand day for the ducks. The rain fell in sheets. My pyjamas were soaked as I pushed open the shutters. Asha and I had planned to go for a walk but were sitting disconsolate, nursing out third cup of tea when Jeanne sloshed through the yard under an umbrella and proposed a plan B.

'What soup are you wanting to make?' I tied an apron around my waist, peeler at the ready.

'La soupe au poireau.'

'Leek soup? Oh dear, no chestnuts?' I was surprised.

'They take too long to peel.' Jeanne shrugged. 'In the olden days, we'd sit together around the fire in winter and peel tons of them, but machines took over. My brother, Lucien…'

I nodded to reminder that I had met him.

'…Lucien used to run a chestnut canning factory. No. I'm too old to be making chestnut soup for a hundred people.'

'A hundred people?'

'Oh yes.' Jeanne met our startled stares. 'My chestnut soup was famous. It was always the first to go.'

This was worrying. If the soup festival was that renowned, Jean-Loup was sure to hear about it.

My unease ebbed slightly as we sat around Jeanne's table, chopping up mountains of potatoes and leeks, snug in the old kitchen, rain battering the windowpanes.

Asha's French was patchy and Jeanne's English non-existent. I acted as translator.

'I hope it won't flood like last year,' Jeanne said. 'A month's rain fell in three days. Roads collapsed.'

'The ground around here is brittle, I noticed,' Asha said.

'It's schist, you see. When we lived out on the hill, we had to repair our terraces after every bad spate of rain. In the end, it just got too much. My husband André and I moved here in the seventies to be with his parents.' She tilted her chin towards a photo of a sturdy curly-haired man.

Asha nodded to him, said he looked kind and pointed to a smaller frame on the wall. 'Who's that young man up there?'

A cheeky-faced youth stood grinning in front of a barn door, a beret rakishly pushed to one side.

'That's Marcel, my husband's younger brother.' Jeanne's face filled with sadness.

'What happened to him?'

'He died during the war.'

Since the burn incident, Jeanne fascinated Asha. For her, old people were living treasures. She would have changed her mind if she'd met Grandma Reilly, that racist old owl.

Jeanne put down her knife, wiped her hands and pulled an old photo album from a drawer. She cleared away the peels and placed it on the table.

'This is André, my husband, with his brother Marcel when they were young.'

The two were chalk and cheese. André was gauche with a bad case of acne and plastered down hair, while Marcel's graceful mischievousness jumped out of the page.

Gently, Asha persisted. 'What happened to Marcel?'

We had spotted the boy's name on the town's war monument.

'He was shot by the Gestapo.' Jeanne stared at the photo, nodding slowly, working her lips. Her voice wavered. 'He was seventeen.'

Asha and I both gasped with horror. 'Why?

'We don't know. His name was given to the Gestapo by the head of the French Militia.'

'The Militia?' Asha asked.

'French Nazi sympathisers working for the Germans – traitors – they put France to shame.' She shook her head. 'Now they tell us that there weren't many, only a few thousands they say, but for us, one was enough.'

Her shoulders slumped. Poor Jeanne was still attempting to come to terms with something so intolerably wrong that it could never be forgiven.

Crimes fester in the collective memory and make us who we are, like Bloody Sunday for us Irish, Protestant persecutions for the Cévenols, the Cathar slaughters for Carcassonne. The Holocaust and other horrors, too many to mention, live on and on.

Jeanne exhaled a long painful breath. 'They held Marcel in a cell for a couple of days. He was due out. We went to fetch him, but they – they just handed us his body.'

She lifted a corner of her apron and wiped away a tear. Asha reached out for her hand and repeated, 'why?'

Jeanne shuffled on her chair. 'Revenge I suppose. To get back at my brother Lucien who was a Resistance fighter. They could never catch him, you see.'

Lucien. Yes, that was the name of the old man I had met. Things were falling into place.

'Was the man in charge of the crime ever tried after the War?'

'No. They called him The Gévaudan Beast.'

'Who was he?'

Jeanne hesitated. She slowly shut the album and returned it to the drawer. 'Bah, these are old stories, best forgotten.'

48
ORLA – FLEURAC

The rain carried on all night, but the Gods –and there are quite a few of them up there, waiting for us to tune in to them as we do radio stations– decided in concert to beam down over Fleurac's *Fête de la Soupe* and allowed the sun to soak up the last of the rain from the cobbles.

While Asha was in the shower, I sent Mam and Dad a quick e-mail to tell them about the soup festival. It would reassure them that I wasn't doing anything daft like white-water rafting or skydiving. God love them, worrying about me had become their new hobby.

The uneasy feeling returned to my stomach. What if Jean-Loup really was stalking me? I vowed never to wander off on my own.

By lunchtime, the town was teeming. We ambled past comedians and raconteurs, their French too convoluted for me to understand. In front of the church, a mock 'seventies' band had drawn a happy crowd settled on the ground with blankets, sandwiches and flasks. Under the porch supported by columns, the four of them looked so funny with their long hair, garish sleeveless tank tops and flares, I took out my camera and snapped them.

'Asha, just look at them. How do you think they managed to fancy each other back in the seventies, with long hair, dressed like that?'

Asha giggled in agreement. 'What are they singing? It's French, but it sounds like Funky Town.'

She was right. In an ode to the Cévennes, the lead singer reeled off local landmarks, swapping the words *Funky Town* for a falsetto *'Gorges du Tarn.'* It really was comical. We stepped over blankets and baskets, found a space, sat down and joined in the fun. I was having a grand old time, clapping and screaming *'Gorges du Tarn'* at the top of my voice, when out of the corner of my eye, I spotted a familiar figure.

'Look, over there behind that pillar, in the bomber jacket.'

'Who? Where?'

'Oh God, Asha. He's here.'

'Are you sure?'

The square throbbing in a delirium of *'Gorges du Tarn,'* we scanned the area.

'How the feck does he know where I am?' I panicked. How dare this lunatic hound me like this? And where were the fecking gendarmes when you needed them? Not here obviously, not in Fleurac. For once, the French police had not deemed it necessary to guard the soup vats with machine guns and dogs, as they guarded everything else these days. Soup was obviously a low priority on the *plan vigi-pirate*.

How did Jean-Loup know where I was? Had I imagined him? I checked my camera.

'Asha, look, there he is on the photo, half-hidden behind that pillar.'

'I can't tell.'

'I can. I remember the jacket. I bet he schmoozed Aude de Peirac as she came out of Marguerite's shop. It's the only way

I can explain it.' I scanned the square again. 'Come on, let's find Jeanne and see how our soup is doing.' I was sick with worry, but I didn't want to spoil Asha's day.

We found Jeanne in what was usually a large car park just above Armand's bookshop… which was closed for the day. The space had been decorated with flowers and bunting, and filled with trestle tables covered in paper gingham. Régis and his blues band were playing on a small podium. My heart leapt at the sight of my love-interest, dead cool in jeans and cotton shirt. He noticed me and winked. His sax-appeal sent my hormones in a spin.

'He really is dishy.' Asha approved. It felt good. 'You're sure he's single?'

'He's recovering from a bad divorce. I think I'm in with a chance, his dog likes me.' I lowered myself at the edge of a bench and watched Régis play, longing for those nimble fingers to play something on me. 'I really fancy him, but I'll have to tread carefully. I don't want to start something and then leave.'

'You're not thinking of staying?'

'I'm not sure. I don't like Armand much.'

'But you've hardly had the time to–'

'*Orla, Asha, Coucou !*' From behind her camping gas, Jeanne waved us over with her wooden spoon.

'Quick, it's nearly gone!' She ladled what was left of the soup into two polystyrene bowls and handed them to us with a chunk of bread. We carried our bowls to a long table.

Moments later, Régis and his band received their standing ovation, packed their instruments and joined us. I sank into him for the regulatory two kisses, but didn't have time to linger, pushed away by his fans.

Dressed in black, long white locks under a wide brimmed hat, Armand joined us, a combination of Gandalf and the Lone Ranger.

'The hat suits him,' Asha whispered as we slid onto the bench. 'No sign of your stalker?'

'Nah, we've got bodyguards now. We'll be fine.' The three burly members of Régis' blues band were uncorking bottles of red wine. They had ordered enough cheese, salami and salad for everyone to share. It was a feast.

Asha slid next to Armand. She had an agenda. Good luck to her, I thought. I found him intimidating.

Régis was having trouble keeping his hands off me, I could tell and I, under the influence of the wine magically filling my glass, was having doubts about leaving Fleurac before sampling what my sexy musician had to offer. It wasn't just the wine. I was falling in love. Casually resting against Régis's shoulder, I surveyed Fleurac, its cobbles, its food and good people, and dipped in and out of conversations, blissfully floating on the first flush of infatuation. Across the table, Asha was enquiring about the bookshop, trying to soften up the old bear and establish his connection with Ireland, since I was incapable of doing so myself.

It seemed to be working.

'Please excuse my *critiques* of the other day,' he said with a half-smile.

Alhamdulillah. Miracles do happen.

Asha graciously acknowledged his apology and engaged him with a subject she knew was dear to his heart. Books.

'Tell me, Armand–' her voice reached me through the cotton wool of my ever-growing crush. 'Out of your whole stock of books, what is your star product, your 'cash cow' as we say in marketing terms?'

'Cash cow?'

'Yes, what sells the most.'

'*Bof*, I have no idea.' He dipped bread into his soup. 'Why do you ask me that?' Armand dabbed his moustache with a paper napkin.

'You just told me that your shop wasn't making money. This means that you are losing money, yes?'

'Bof, I *'herited* money from my father so...'

'So, you ploughed your inheritance into your business.'

'I don't care about money. My father made the money, not me.'

'You are losing money, yes or no?'

I tried to focus, wondering where she was heading with her questions.

Armand hesitated.

'Since you make no profit from your sales, anyone who walks into your shop is the recipient of your charity,'

'Pardon?'

Asha held out her hand. 'Armand, give me fifty euros.'

He stared at her.

'See? You can't justify giving me fifty euros, but you will sell me a fifty- euro book at a loss.'

Armand grabbed his glass and realising it was empty, refilled it. He tried to catch Régis' eye, but deep in conversation, Régis could not rescue him.

This was getting interesting.

'You don't specialise, right?' Asha carried on, the business consultant in full flow. 'There's everything in your shop, comics, novels, philosophy, horror, local history, antique books...'

'How do you know? You never been there.'

'Orla told me.'

Armand took another sip of his wine and studied me over his glass. I could read his mind under that large hat of his. 'Who are these two witches? What do they want from me?'

'Do you have an Internet site?'

He shook his head. 'Why do I need an Internet site when there is no Internet connection? Ah! Virgile *enfin*!' He waved to a man of about his age, his relief plain to see. *'Virgile! Délivre-moi de cette harpie.'*

'Salut tout le monde!' The new arrivals shook hands all around. Virgile's wife, a jolly woman in ample skirts and shawls, distributed hugs and kisses and placed several goat-cheeses on the table.

Virgile's easy smile, corduroys, chunky knit and halo of frizzy white hair made him instantly likable. I caught myself wondering why he couldn't be my father instead of that cantankerous Gandalf. As soon as the thought popped into my mind, I realised I had been wrong all along. I didn't *need* another dad. Mick fitted the bill perfectly. All I needed was to fill in the indefinable void that had been plaguing me and erase that disturbing question mark hanging over me. It wasn't a matter of *liking* what I found, but of finding my place in humanity… mending the moth-holes in the fabric of my life.

Perhaps in a twisted way, I had been so afraid my biological father would supersede Dad that –out of some warped feeling of loyalty– I had focused on the negatives. In the end, Asha was right. I had tried to protect myself and gone about it totally the wrong way.

It was time to come clean. Not here of course, not now, but soon.

Régis did the introductions. 'Virgile, Mireille. Orla is from Ireland and Asha is hum, English?'

Asha nodded.

It was as if Armand was seeing me for the first time.

'Ireland hey?' Virgile rubbed his hands. 'Ha ha! Armand tells me he speaks English with an Irish accent, is that true?'

Asha and I burst out laughing.

Virgile gave his old friend an affectionate glance. 'You learned it in Dublin, didn't you?' He turned to me. 'Armand worked in a bar in Dublin for six months.'

My heart missed a beat. 'Dublin?'

'Well, I–' Armand began.

'He was looking for a girl.' Virgile opened his hands. 'I suppose we all were at that age.'

'Bah, it was a long time ago.' Armand crossed his arms, clearly unwilling to elaborate.

'So, did you find her?'

Under the hat, hidden under the unkempt brow, I found very sad eyes.

'Which soup do you recommend, folks? We're starving.' Mireille eyed the food stands.

'Jeanne's leek soup is finished. You'll have to take pot luck.'

A discussion ensued as to the best soup to go for.

'Orla, come with me.' Régis got up. 'I've spotted a pancake van. Let's have one for dessert.'

The aroma of pancakes was mouth-watering. I called out to Asha. 'Asha? Crêpe?'

'Oh, why not. Just sugar and lemon please. Hang on, before you go, can I borrow your camera? I wanted to ask Armand about that building we saw from the road the other day, see if he knows what it is.'

I pulled the camera out of my pocket and handed it to her.

We had visited an old building we were told was once a silk factory the Marquis d'Aubrac might have owned. It didn't look anything like a factory and we thought we might have gone to the wrong place.

I admired the rapport Asha was trying to create with Armand but for all I could see, his heart had frozen over a long time ago. It was going to be a tough call.

'Is your friend a marketing consultant?' Régis asked while we stood in the queue. When I nodded, he said, 'Good luck to her. I've been trying for ages to get Armand to either reduce his stock or expand online, but he's so stubborn, you wouldn't believe.'

'I gathered that. Tell me, what did Armand mean when he said his father made money? What did he do for a living?'

'I'm not sure. Armand's very cagey about his father. There was a lot of corruption in France in the sixties. It's all a bit murky. So, what do you want on your pancake, chocolate or chestnut purée? Very sweet but it's delicious.'

'Yeah, I'll try the chestnut.'

Régis gave the girl our orders and returned to his subject.

'Armand's a bit gruff, but he's a great guy once you get to know him. I was in a bad way when I arrived here, sort of shipwrecked, you know. He took me in, gave me a job.' Régis gave a self-conscious shrug, as if a depression and a divorce weren't that big a deal.

'Has he had a hard life?'

'I'm not sure. I think he had a difficult family. Heavy, you know.'

Oh dear. What was I letting myself in for?

'You're staying for the dance tonight?' The twinkle in his eyes made my heart twirl, and I floated away in the pancake-scented cloud, vaguely aware that from the table, Armand was studying me.

Régis wrapped my hand around the crêpes. *'Voilà.'*

We returned to the table, his hand on the small of my back.

I took a bite of my pancake. Oh my, the chestnut purée was scrumptious. I handed Asha hers and caught sight of Armand, staring at my camera, a strange look on his face.

Oh God. What had Asha done?

The air compressed around my head, blotting out the noise from the square. I bent over in slow motion and turned the camera he was holding towards me. Our fingers touched with a jolt of current. Inside the small screen, Mam was smiling. I met his eyes. They were damp and they were green, like mine.

I stuttered, 'it's… it's my mam… on her sixtieth birthday.' I wanted to say more, but the lump in my throat was choking me.

The colour drained from his face. He cradled the camera inside his gnarled fingers and caressed Mam's face, an expression of infinite tenderness softening his features. A weight seemed to lift from his shoulders.

'My mother's name is Mary Reilly. Her maiden name was…'

'Sullivan.' Armand whispered dreamily… 'Mary Sullivan.' A tear ran into his white beard. 'I thought I had lost her.'

49
ORLA – FLEURAC

Neither Régis nor Virgile had noticed Armand's change of mood, though Mireille had guessed that something was up. She watched over him like a mother hen.

Hidden under his hat, he had retreated into the past. Though he cast me the odd glance, I was not yet sure whether he had made the connection between us. Dazed, lost in memories, it was reassuring to see that his heart had not totally frozen over.

I stood, numb, trying to picture Mam and this man together.

He pushed back his hat and focused, as if seeing me for the first time.

'Tell me…'

'Orla.' I lowered myself on the bench opposite him.

'Orla…' There was a touch of wonder in his voice. 'Orla, how… how old are you?'

Oh God. He knew.

Too tipsy to cope, I was furious at Asha for opening

Pandora's box but the love in his eyes was so real, his yearning so touching…

'I'm forty.'

He took in a long breath and crumpled with a whimper. The hand I held out did not quite reach over the table. I wondered what I had done, what illusions I had crushed. It was never supposed to be like that. I had wanted to build trust, find out what linked us, not this.

When behind us, the band intoned the chicken dance, Armand pushed himself up and headed for his shop.

Asha patted my arm. 'Aren't you going to follow him?'

'And what would I say? I don't know how they parted.'

'Go to him and explain.'

'Explain what? I'm the one who needs answers.'

'Then, ask him.'

Cornered by friends, Régis was casting concerned glances in my direction.

In the distance, Armand looked so forlorn, I shot up and, forgetting both my crêpe and my pledge, hurried to him. I was just turning the corner when the familiar blouson-clad figure detached itself from a lamp post.

I retreated to the square and nearly cried with relief as I bumped into Mireille's plump body.

'Orla? Are you alright? What's the matter? You look as if you've seen a ghost.'

'I have, but he's gone now.' I composed myself. 'Are you going to the bookshop?'

'Yes. Armand has been behaving strangely today.'

I checked the empty street. My tormentor had been swallowed by the shadows. I darted back to the square where Régis scooped me into his arms and led me to the dance space.

'The wolf is here,' I whispered to Asha once the dance had

finished. 'I've just seen him.' I jutted my chin towards the corner of the street.

'Oh no. What are we going to do? I've agreed to join Mireille in the shop.'

'We'll ask Virgile to accompany you. I'll stay here with Régis. I'm not going anywhere on my own. Listen, when you're with Armand, don't–'

'I won't breathe a word.' Asha called out to Régis, 'Don't let her out of your sight.'

'I've no intention of doing so,' he replied gallantly.

The last thing I wanted was to dampen Régis's enthusiasm with news of a madman coming here to claim me, so I didn't explain.

'You okay jiving?'

I wasn't, not really, but he led me so fluidly that I became a pro in all of three minutes.

'What is it between you and Armand?' He asked perceptively as I wiped my forehead with a napkin. 'Is that why you're here?'

'It's complicated. I… it's my mother. She's the girl he was looking for in Dublin.'

'Wow. That's big.'

The band intoned an intensely popular *'tube'* by Fatal Bazooka that propelled everyone up in the air, bounding up and down like pistons, shouting out strange words.

My resolution to take things slowly evaporated after the fourth glass. We fancied each other, Régis and I. It was ridiculous to pretend otherwise. When much, much later it was time to go, I hesitated a little. Asha had not returned and I didn't fancy going home on my own. I should have run after Armand when he first went. I know. That's what I should have done. Now, it was too late. I felt bad, but the night was warm and, when it happened between Régis and me, it happened inescapably, naturally, in a *biologique* sort of way I was powerless to resist.

50
ORLA – FLEURAC

The intensity of that first night was beyond anything I had ever experienced. Ten out of ten didn't even touch it. Leaving Fleurac would be a wrench.

'How long were you planning to stay?' was the first thing Régis asked. 'I hope you didn't come here to break my heart, just as it was beginning to heal.'

I hadn't expected such honesty. Men in my experience pretend not to care at first. Perhaps French men were different.

'It depends.' I trailed a finger along his taught stomach.

'On what?'

I nestled against his shoulder. 'I am on a sort of mission with Armand.'

'I did wonder about your interest in that bookshop.'

'I'll tell you more when I know more. You'll have to be patient with me.'

'Deal.' Régis took me into his arms and said against my mouth, 'I reckon you're worth waiting for.'

His fingers traced my face, my neck and, lost in unchartered waters, I floated away and let him take me wherever he fancied.

All the barriers came down that first time. It was as if our bodies had known each other for ever. Honed, golden after a summer in the sun, his limbs were strong and supple enough to lift me, flip me over and crush me against him, whispering endearments. For me, that night was an awakening and when the tremors subsided and the atoms of my being rearranged themselves, I found my cheeks covered with tears and my heart in tatters.

I woke up to the smell of coffee, the sun high over the chestnut forest. My hands behind my head, I stretched in his large bed, replaying moments of the night... and came to my senses with a jolt. Asha!

I tried calling her on the mobile, but there was no signal. Using Régis's land-line, I managed to reach Jeanne.

I stood naked in the kitchen, a cardigan casually thrown over my shoulders.

'Orla? No, there's no one home. Your friend isn't here.'

There was only one place Asha could be at ten on a Sunday.

'When she comes back from the baker's, could you tell her I called?'

'I'm afraid she didn't come back last night.'

I pulled the cardigan tightly around me. 'What do you mean?'

'I'm glad you've phoned actually. I was a bit worried.'

My throat closed up. 'She didn't come back at all?'

'No. I heard you two come home around eleven o'clock last night. At least I thought I did, but then I wasn't sure. A woman shouted out in English. There was an argument, in

French this time, then a man's voice and then nothing. I went to check the door onto the street, but it was locked and you weren't in. Your place was dark and your shutters are still open. It's all very mysterious. You are all right, are you?'

'Yes… yes. I'm so sorry to have worried you. Asha must have stayed with… our other friends. Please don't worry.' I hung up.

Oh God, I slumped onto the sofa and mumbled to myself. *Where on earth is she?* I should never have left her. Heck, what if Jean-Loup had kidnapped her?

'What's the matter?' Régis came out of the shower.

'Asha didn't come home last night. I think we should call the police.' I explained what Jeanne had told me, omitting the part Jean-Loup might have played.

A knowing grin lifted a corner of Régis's mouth. 'Her mobile isn't answering, you say?'

I didn't even grace this with an answer. How could they live like this? How could they function without mobile phones? No wonder they took to the streets. It was maddening.

'Here she is.' Régis held out his phone.

'Who?'

'Asha. You did want to talk to her?'

I looked at the receiver stupidly and took it from him.

'Orla?'

'Asha, where are you?'

'I'm at Armand's. I spent the night there.'

'No!' Reeling, I whimpered, 'Asha, you can't do that!' Jeepers, she was a fine one telling me to wait until I knew a fella before I slept with him. Now she'd gone and seduced my… oh God, no, it was too gross.

'Your father's a great guy, Orla. He's still got it you know.'

'Asha, don't. It's… oh…' I grimaced. 'It's not … appropriate.'

Standing in front of me, his gorgeous loins wrapped in a towel, Régis thought it was all great craìc.

'Course I didn't.' She giggled. 'You know I'm joking, right?'

'Yeah well, whatever you're up to, it's not funny. What happened?'

Serious now, Asha said, 'Okay, last night, about half past eleven, I left the bookshop and went to look for you on the square, but you'd gone. The bandmates had seen you go with Régis, so I didn't worry.'

'Oh no! I should've–'

'S'okay. We're adults. Virgile walked me home to Jeanne's. I said good night to him, and I'd just unlocked the door from the street, when your Parisian paramour ran in and pushed me into the yard, demanding to see you.'

'What?' My hand jumped to my mouth.

'I shoved him back. I must have woken Jeanne because a light came on upstairs. I fought him off.'

'But you could have been hurt!'

'I was. He twisted my arm. Virgile heard the ruckus and ran back. There was a kerfuffle. Virgile punched him and saw him off. I was badly shaken, so he decided I'd be safer with them at Armand's place.'

'Oh dear, I'm so sorry.' There were voices in the background. 'Who else is there?'

'You're missing a great party, Orla. Armand's house is huge. Mireille is making breakfast. Why don't you two come over?'

51
ORLA – FLEURAC

From the expanse of dour stone rising from the street, I assumed Armand's house to have been a presbytery at some point in its history. What normally gives away a presbytery is its proximity to a church, but since we were in the Cévennes, where Catholics and Protestants had spent centuries burning down each other's places of worship, the building now stood on its own, propped up with higgledy-piggledy houses crammed into the space where a church had once been.

This being said, architecture was the last thing on my mind as I followed Régis up the narrow book-lined staircase, his pert backside level with my eyes, my chest tightening at the idea of meeting Armand.

A jolly hullabaloo greeted us. Asha, Virgile and Mireille were seated around a refectory table covered with chunks of bread, jams, plates of butter, coffee, milk and bowls.

I was wowed by the space, the vast bareness of it, the arched windows, the Turkish carpets. There were books everywhere. It just looked fantastic.

'Come in, sit down. Armand's making some more coffee,'

Mireille said.

Armand called her from the kitchen. *'Mireille, viens chercher le pain grillé!'*

'I'll get it,' I said.

In the messy kitchen, which had suffered some sort of Formica attack in the sixties, I found a relaxed Armand humming, inspecting chunks of baguette disposed over a round grill set in a low pan of water, an antique contraption I'd never seen before. Fork poised in mid-air he turned to me and hovered, unsure of what to do.

Heart pounding, I remained by the door. We both blushed.

He dropped the fork, opened his arms and with a shy smile, beckoned me to him. *'Allez viens,* Pitchoune.'

A huge lump in my throat, I stepped into his arms and buried my face on his chest. He smelled of tobacco and toast. The wild heartbeat under my cheek chased away my last doubt.

'Orla…' he repeated, adrift in the wonder of my existence. 'Orla...' His green eyes met mine. 'I wish she had told me.'

'I'm here now.'

I wriggled my nose. Behind us, something was burning.

'Merde !' Armand yanked the grill from the gas. We rescued what could be rescued and giggling, sliced more bread.

He dropped the second batch of toast in a basket.

Eager, he placed a hand on forearm. 'First, I want you to tell me about Mary. Is she happy?'

'She is.'

'Good. That's good.' He thought about it and nodded to himself. 'Yes, that's good.'

I didn't know their story, but the way he spoke her name told me that he had cared… and by the look of it, he still did. I was tremendously relieved.

'Come.' He turned off the gas and handed me the basket. We tell them now.'

An arm around each other, Armand and I made our entrance into the dining-room. All eyes turned to us. I clutched the bread basket and waited for Armand to make the announcement. His hand shook on my shoulder.

He took in a deep breath… and exhaled, defeated.

I opened my mouth to speak but couldn't find the words either, so we stood together, grinning inanely.

Armand cleared his throat and failed again.

I took over. 'What we would like to… to…'

Virgile was the first to twig.

'Mary! You're Mary and Armand's daughter!' He linked Armand and I with a move of his finger.

We nodded.

'*Ah, putain*, that makes me so happy.'

'I need to get used to the idea,' Armand confessed.

After checking with Asha, Mireille came to us, took the bread basket I was still clutching and gave us a warm mother-hen hug.

An arm casually thrown over the back of his chair, my saxophonist was shaking his head as if he'd always known.

Brunch was a convivial affair. Virgile and Armand bouncing off each other were a pleasure to watch.

'World War II wasn't the last war for French men, you know,' Régis explained to me. 'My father was sent to fight in Algeria in the sixties. As for those two…' He pointed to the septuagenarians, 'they're seasoned Larzac veterans. There aren't many about.'

I didn't know what he was referring to, but one thing was clear, veterans love nothing better than to reminisce, and in me, they found a virgin audience. I listened riveted, trying to piece their story together.

'Did you win that war in the end?'

'Oh yes. It went on for ten years! From 1971 to 1981. In eighty-one, Mitterrand was the socialist candidate for the presidency.' Virgile beamed, still buzzing from their victory. 'He promised that if he was elected, he'd put an end to the project, so you can imagine, we all voted for him. Traditionally, farmers are conservative, but in eighty-one, the Larzac farmers made an exception.'

'Mitterrand...Yes, I remember that name.'

'For us, he saved the day,' Virgile said. 'It was really touch and go until the end, wasn't it, Armand?'

'We put up a good fight. Mireille broke into army offices, didn't you Mireille?' Armand called out, now in top form. Gone was the crabby bear. I could not believe the transformation.

Mireille didn't answer. In conversation with Asha, she was showing her some photos. From the soft look on their face, I assumed they were discussing Mireille's grandchildren. God knows what secrets Asha had managed to drag out of the woman.

'Do you still live there, in the Larzac?' I turned back to Virgile.

'Sure, but we've extended. It's nothing like the heap of stones Armand and I found in the seventies. We've got running water now and electricity. Mireille milked the ewes and did the laundry by hand for nigh on ten years, *hein Mimi*?' Virgile cast his wife an affectionate glance, but he too was ignored. Over in the corner, the whispering had intensified.

'It was like living in the Middle Ages, but at the time we believed...'

'And we still do,' interrupted Armand.

'We believe that the Earth can't be drained of its resources at the rate it is now. Consumption is a cancer and we are concerned about the world we are leaving for our grandchildren.' Virgile practiced what he preached, I could tell by the homespun jumper.

Virgile carried on. 'After we won the fight, Armand left and came to live here. Downstairs had been a florist's shop. He took it over and finally opened the bookshop he'd been dreaming of all these years. I felt awful when I realised that all that time, he hated sheep!'

Armand waggled his head in half-hearted denial.

Virgile lifted his bowl as a toast and said, his voice filled with emotion, 'before he left the Larzac, Armand sold me the farm for a *Franc symbolique.*'

Armand muttered 'Bah, you'd done most of the work.'

Virgile pulled out a euro from his pocket and slapped it on the table to make sure I understood the extent of Armand's generosity. 'A farm, sixty acres of land and a hundred ewes for just one Franc.'

I was humbled to see how wrong I had been in my first impressions of Armand. I had accused him of being prejudiced, of judging people before he knew them. There was a lesson there.

'What Virgile didn't tell you,' Armand chuckled to dispel his embarrassment, 'is that when we first got there, we didn't know one end of a sheep from the other.'

Virgile rolled his eyes, awaiting the punch line.

Armand laughed, 'it could have been painful if Mireille hadn't turned up when she did! Ha ha!'

I could tell this was an old joke, retold ad nauseam, the kind of ditty that cements the bond of friendships. I watched the two old comrades. Battle scarred and mangled, they'd fought wars no one knew about. Perhaps one day they would tell me what they had really been looking for in the Larzac, or more to the point, what they had been running away from.

It might help me understand what I was searching for.

52
ORLA – FLEURAC

'What did you find out?' I quizzed Asha on the way home. She was strangely quiet. I'd have thought whatever it was that Mireille had told her, she would be bursting to tell me.

'Mireille's a nice lady, isn't she? I gathered she was pretty wild in her youth.' Asha knew full well that it wasn't the information I was after. I could see I would have to 'pull the worms from her nose,' as Marguerite put it poetically. 'Asha, you're avoiding the issue, which clearly tells me that I'm not going to like what you've found out from Mireille.'

'Listen, I'm not proud of what some of my ancestors got up to, but that doesn't make me a bad person.' Asha had discovered something.

I faced her squarely. 'Come on. Spit it out.'

'Wait, the baker's about to close. Let's get something for a picnic. We've got cheese and tomatoes left. How about one of those spiky baguettes you like?'

I grudgingly followed her into the baker's and then home, where we packed a picnic of our favourite foods, Camembert for me and *real* Swiss Gruyère for Asha. I don't know what it was with Asha and Gruyère. It never failed to send her into some sort of orgasmic trance.

While we had coffee, she told me. She was right. I didn't like it…

I had gathered that Armand's father had been a profiteer, but it now appeared that he had collaborated with the Nazis during the War, that he was a traitor. He should have been shot after the Liberation but he'd slipped through the net.

It was as if a great big fist had been rammed down my throat, blocking all the air. Now I knew why Armand had escaped to the Larzac.

'According to Mireille, the de Peirac family seat was somewhere near Mende. We could drive over there today if you want.'

'No thanks. I've got a pretty good idea.' Hunched on the sofa, I struggled to absorb what she had told me. 'Jeepers, I had a fine life in Dublin even if I wasn't a bloody Reilly.' I lifted my eyes to her. 'I come to France hoping for a bit of chic and glamour, and I turn out to be a Nazi's granddaughter. No, I don't want to drive and see the family seat, thank you very much. I can see it from here.' I lifted my arms and said in a funereal voice, 'a schisty gothic pile looming up from the mist… screams of tortured ghosts rising from the dungeons.' I strode around the room and rubbed my arms. 'Christ, Asha! A grandfather who was the French equivalent of a SS. What does that make me?'

'Orla, listen, I know it's fresh and raw, but you don't have just one ancestor. You love your Kerry grandma and from what you've told me, Arielle was a good person. The daughter of a silk baron has to be…'

'Marquis.

'Huh?'

'A marquis is lower than a baron. I'm sure there are

similar hierarchical divisions in India, you know, nawab, rajah…'

She cut short my ramblings with a stern, 'we're all equal in the eyes of Allah.'

'Yeah well. If Grandma Reilly had seen me as equal to the Reilly boys, I might not be here today, trying to find out who I really am, hoping to be good enough for… for I don't know what…' I was shouting by now. 'Only to find out that not only am I *not* a Reilly, I'm descended from a long line of murderers!'

'It does not reflect on you at all! Listen, I went to Gujarat and I couldn't relate to anything I saw there. The incense, the temples meant nothing to me. I couldn't even understand what they were saying. It was the same in Kenya. It was just a foreign country. I'm a Londoner. You're a Dubliner.'

Asha efficiently wrapped the last cheese sandwiches in foil. 'What is it that Jung said? "It's not what happens to you that makes you who you are, but what you choose to become." Here you are, worrying about what happened to your *grandparents*. Mine were whipped while they built a railway in the African jungle, so what does that make me?'

'A tough cookie, considering the number of workers who died. I'm sorry. I must be having a mid-life crisis. Either that or I need a job. I've got far too much time to think.'

'And I'm hungry.' She handed me the backpack and grabbed a carrier bag. 'Come on, it's my last day here. Let's go to the river for that picnic.'

53
ORLA – FLEURAC

Asha left Fleurac. I stayed on in Jeanne's lovely garden room. Autumn settled in. Framed by Régis's window, the chestnut forest turned from gold to copper.

I hadn't heard from Jean-Loup, though it did not mean that he had given up. 'I'll find her!' he had shouted to Asha, that night. 'She's making a big mistake with that hippie. I'll make sure she sees that.'

I presumed the 'hippie' he was referring to was Régis, whose band all sported pony-tails, but I was not as worried as I had been. Jean-Loup's business was too dependent on the internet for him to spend much time in our mountains.

A cold wind tore at the last leaves and howled around my lover's cottage, but inside his bedroom, stretched out on his big brass bed, things were hotting up.

'Come on, Orla, don't be so prudish.'

I balked, horribly exposed as Régis settled himself between my thighs to study me as a botanist would an orchid, tweaking a petal here, dipping a finger there, mumbling to himself, taking mental notes.

Régis had made it his mission to free me from the chastity

belt into which the nuns of St Brigid's had tricked me, convinced that somehow, they still held the key. 'St Frigid School for girls,' was how Declan used to explain my lack of enthusiasm for his drunken gropings.

'Here?' Régis parted a few petals, 'or deeper, in there.' I gasped as his fingers found the elusive G-spot I'd always believed to be an invention of Cosmopolitan. Gasps and moans were not enough for him. My mentor wanted words… enunciated in French. Thank God he wasn't too fussed about the grammar. I'd struggled and protested, but he had persisted and God, was it worth it! I never thought such pleasure was possible. Amazed, exhilarated, I throbbed, panted and screamed like a wanton hussy. Convinced that Régis found me beautiful, I became daring and sensuous, a real Delilah. I did Asha proud.

The magic of his fingers filled every single cell of my body with warmth and light. Under his kisses, I felt beautiful, desirable and real. While my muscles hardened in the garden, my heart softened, and I became the Orla I was meant to be.

We slept locked together, his arms around my waist, his foot across my ankle, his breath gentle on my shoulder, safe and trusting.

It wasn't just the sex, it was the way he played his saxophone just for me, the way he guided my –safely gloved– hand into the hives, the tenderness, the intimacy. For years I had protected myself, played the businesswoman, built a carapace, a brittle armour, while all the time I was just aching to be held.

Régis was a one-off. He really was special. I found his unconventionality reassuring. Free-spirited, creative and loving, he made me feel more alive than I ever had and I knew that after him, every man would seem insipid…

While in the valley, the forest was shrouded in mist, I lay

inside his arms, our legs intertwined, lulled by the warmth of heat *récupérateur*.

My every own eco-warrior. His cottage was totally off grid. It even had a well.

'When I quit the rat race and came here, I wanted to dedicate the second half of my life to putting back what I'd taken out.' Régis explained during one of our more serious moments.

'It's grand. It really is. Jeepers, I wouldn't know where to start.'

'You're helping me. It means a lot.' He squeezed my thigh. 'You're a good little trooper. I'm glad you decided to stay, it all makes sense with you around.'

'I don't want to just tag along, you know.' I was keen to impress upon him that this trooper came with serious credentials. 'I want to contribute. We're stagnating at the bookshop with that damned Internet. It's driving me nuts. Is there really nothing more we can do? Is there no one we could talk to?'

Régis snorted and launched in French into one of his tirades. 'Ha! But who? The *'axonair sosam'* are responsible for this mess. They don't have an address. They are not human and what's worse…' his face a mask of pain, Régis placed a hand on his chest, 'they don't have a heart.'

I didn't want to look dumb but I had to ask. 'Régis, who are they, these *axonairs*?'

'That's just the point, Orla. No one knows.' He carried on without pausing for breath, and jeepers, did he mean it… His brow was tense, his mouth pinched. 'Politicians are completely at the mercy of that Pantheon of demi-gods sitting on some off-shore Mount Olympus. Humans aren't in charge here anymore. It's not about people, Orla. It's all about money. Mammon…' He grimaced. 'Mammon, the God of money is the Devil.'

'Sorry, but those evil people, how do you spell the word?'

'Actionnaire, like *'action,'* the word for share... and then *'âme,'* the word for soul. Soulless shareholders, *actionnaires sans âme.'*

I fell back on the pillows. 'Oh...my...God...Soulless shareholders...'

Having put the world to right, Régis and I eventually got up and worked together in the warm honey shed. In a wicker chair, I cleaned out old wax from frames while he bottled the last of the autumn honey.

'Do you miss city life?' Régis asked after a long silence.

I put down my scraper. I hadn't given it any thought.

'Do I miss Dublin, Saxo?' I asked the dog at my feet. The thump-thump of the besotted creature's tail said no.

I opened my lips to reply, but thoughts tumbled into my mind that could not easily be put into French, so I just shrugged. Sure, Fleurac was quiet, but I was part of Régis' crew now, and wherever he played, there was always great craìc.

I didn't miss Paris. Ditching heels, breast-fillers, skirts and Jean-Loup had been a relief. It was never really me. As for Dublin, I could live without teen-agers being sick on the Temple Bar streets on Friday nights and the traffic jams over O'Connell Bridge. I did miss Sunday dinners though, easy chats with Dad, my brothers' banter, shopping with Mam. Yes, I really missed that.

'I'm glad Armand asked me to work with him.' I answered after a long time. 'I just wish I could do more in that shop.'

'You are doing something. That audit you're undertaking is a herculean task.'

He was right. It would keep me busy for months.

Régis wiped a jar with a cloth and held it to the light. 'I told you Armand was a great guy.' He stuck a label on the jar and placed it in a box on its way to the cooperative. 'He thinks the world of you. You've changed his life, you know.'

Books had brought Armand and me together. The shop was a cornucopia of weird and wonderful books unlike anything I'd ever seen. Armand too was unlike anyone I'd ever known, and I was warming to him.

'Did you know he's written several novels?'

'Armand? He never said. The old fox–'

'All set in the Cévennes, published under the name d'Aubrac. They're very good. You should read them.'

'Yeah, me and my electronic translator.'

'Your French is excellent. Don't be so modest.'

'It's a grand little shop. Armand's got everything in there, but while the other sixty million French citizens can peddle their wares on the World-Wide Net, we're stuck with '*passing trade*.' I mean who fecking *passes* rue du Presbytère?'

While Régis and I searched for a way to reach the Soulless Shareholders who held our fate in their inexistent hands, Armand and I talked about books... and every time I attempted to query him about his past, he dodged my questions with a pirouette.

His roots –my roots– were mandrake roots, the kind that scream when you pull them up. They were toxic, hallucinogenic and they were dangerous. Perhaps he was right. Perhaps they were best left alone.

54
ORLA – FLEURAC

'*Bonjour, Jeanne. Brr, qu'est ce qu'il fait froid.*'

Wrapped in coat and scarf, shopping bag in hand, my landlady was heading for the Wednesday market on this chilly morning.

Had Armand told her I was his daughter? I wasn't sure. I had the strange feeling that she had always known. It had not taken her long to switch from the formal '*vous*' to the familiar '*tu*.' She referred to Arielle as 'your grandmother,' while Monsieur d'Aubrac was 'your-great-grandfather-d'Aubrac-up-there-at-the-chateau.' I wondered how much she knew about my ancestors, and how much she was prepared to tell me.

'Not working today?' Jeanne said.

'No. The bookshop is closed, and Régis is away at a Blues festival. I've nothing more exciting planned than the laundry, I'm afraid.'

'Why don't you come with me to the *Restos du Coeur* a little later on? They distribute food and give hot meals to people who've fallen on hard times. You might find it interesting. We always need volunteers. Come with us. My friend will pick us up at twelve.'

Keen to take part in French life, I agreed to go with her.

'Is it like a soup kitchen? That's what we call it in Dublin.'

She explained that her charity was called les *Restaurants du Coeur*. 'Restaurants of the heart...' So French.

We drove to a disused warehouse where nearly-out-of-date food gifted by large stores was stocked, ready to hand out to the needy.

The weather had turned cold, and this week was the first of a special winter campaign to serve hot meals, and provide warm a place for people to meet.

My task was simple, ladle cassoulet to a shuffling queue of young mothers, old dears and vagrants. The plight of these lonely souls made me realise how lucky I was to be blessed with an income, a fantastic lover, and not one, but two fathers.

Once all the meals had been served, Jeanne said, 'See if Thérèse needs help stacking tins. You're tall enough to reach the top shelf.'

Thérèse was a dear old soul. Pink-faced, in pastel blue, she had the fresh skin and trusting smile of a nun.

'It's my first time here,' I said as we tore opened a carton of tinned mackerel. 'Have you been helping out a long time?'

'Oh yes, I started in eighty-five with Coluche, when I lived in Paris.'

'I'm sorry, I come from Ireland, I'm not familiar with... Who did you say?'

'Coluche. He was a comedian. He liked to shock people, show them their hypocrisy, if you want. He's the one who invented *les Restos du Coeur.* He said 'I'm not responsible for people being hungry, but I would be if I didn't do something about it.'

'You must see all sorts here, I imagine.'

'Oh yes. Some look like *clochards*, you know, vagrants, but they're educated and have had dreadful setbacks in their life.'

She passed tins up to me, happy to chat, and I was happy to listen.

'You see that man over there?' She pointed through the shelves to an old man in a woolly hat, sitting on his own. 'He used to come with another two old boys. Long gone now.' She crossed herself and handed me another tin. 'One of them looked straight out of a horror film. His face was nothing but burns. No lips, no ears, hands like claws. It was heart breaking. Ever such a nice man… lovely voice too. He always came in with a friend, a man with an eye-patch. Yes, they always sat together, over there… the three of them. Three old friends.'

'What had happened to the two that were disfigured?'

'It was during the War.' She passed me another tin of mackerels. 'It wasn't even the Germans. There was a particularly sadistic Militia headman in these parts. The one-eyed man, Jojo, told me he'd gouged his eye out with a spoon.'

I held on to the shelf for support. When I could speak again, I said in a thin voice. 'You mean a French man did that?'

'Oh yes. They tracked him down in the end. He lived in Paris, friend with ministers. His name was de Peirac.'

The tin of mackerel was the first to go. I followed soon after, and came to on the cold concrete floor, Jeanne's worried face peering into mine.

She slipped a hand under my head. 'Are you all right?'

I tried to sit up. I felt sick.

'You fainted, dear. Take your time. Let the blood return to your head, and don't get up too soon.' She looked up to her friend. 'Thérèse, what happened?'

'It's my fault I'm afraid, I was telling this young lady how Jojo lost his eye.'

'Oh… I see.' Jeanne placed a cool hand on my forehead. 'I think we'd better take you home.'

I spent a long time in the bathroom, throwing cold water on my face to dispel the dizziness, staring at my reflection in the mirror. What monsters did I have hidden inside me? Desperate to discover an aristocratic lineage to make up for my illegitimate birth, I turned out to be Blue Beard's granddaughter.

My skin itched. I was cursed. The Beast's poisoned blood coursed like poison through my veins. I had nowhere to run. Wherever I hid, I would never escape the Beast. He was inside me. I carried his sins. Thank God for small mercies. The line ended with me.

55
ORLA – FLEURAC

Jeanne led me to her kitchen. Still wearing her coat, she set a pot of water on the gas and shook chamomile flowers into it.

'Sit down, Orla, and tell me what happened back there.'

'I'm not sure where to start.' I pulled a crumpled tissue from my pocket and wiped my eyes. 'I came here to look for my *père biologique*.'

'*Naturel*.' Jeanne unbuttoned her coat.

'Huh?' I shivered. Jesus, was I cold.

'*Armand est ton père naturel*.' She corrected calmly.

I looked at her. Of course, she knew. Was it another manifestation of her 'gift'? Did she have second sight or had Armand told her? How close were they?

I sniffed. 'I'm glad you know. Armand is a wonderful man and I'm delighted he's my father, but–' I crumpled, 'I'd– I'd give anything to have a different grandfather.'

Jeanne's reaction was not at all what I had expected. She turned off the gas, covered the pot with a lid and trotted off into the corridor with a mysterious smile.

Moments later, she returned with a sketchbook and

placed it in front of me. The smell that emanated from it reminded me of Régis' bee suit.

I opened the book and came face to face with my oval face, thin eyebrows and slim shoulders.

I glanced up at Jeanne.

'Arielle. Your grandmother.'

Under the cloth of her shirt, her breasts were small. I forgave her for passing them on to me. After all, what is an inadequate A cup compared to a predisposition for torture and murder. So insanely glad was I to take after her, that I even forgave her for my bouncy derrière.

'Here you are, dear.' Jeanne set a jar of honey by my cup, 'a spoonful of that honey of yours will make everything better.'

'Thank you,' I said politely, thinking I could do with something stronger than flowers to recover from the shock. I wrapped my frozen fingers around the cup, inhaled the delicate scent, wishing it was Jameson, and groaned with a shiver, 'I feel so awful. To think I carry that man's genes inside me.'

'Listen to what I am going to tell you.' Jeanne's face was solemn.

I put down my cup and met her gaze.

'Albin de Peirac may have married Arielle, but he is *not* Armand's father.'

I mumbled. 'Really? I don't understand.'

'De Peirac is *not* Armand's father. The Militia-man whom people called the Gévaudan Beast, the man responsible for Marcel's death… That man is not related to you. He is not your grandfather.'

'How?'

'During the War, the Cévennes were a refuge for many *résistants*.' She turned a page of the sketchbook and pointed to the portrait of a man. Masculine, confident, generous, this was someone you could trust. I drew him to me. Something inside me melted. He looked awfully familiar.

'Karl was a German pacifist fighting against Hitler. Arielle fell in love with him and became pregnant just before the end of the War. Armand is their love-child.' Jeanne's face softened. 'Arielle had to marry in haste, and since de Peirac had been asking for her hand for quite some time –' She sighed. 'They went to live in America at the end of the War. Then they came back and moved to Paris. I didn't see Arielle and Armand for years.'

'So… my actual grandfather is…' My whole world tilted. I had come all the way to France to find my father, and found myself suspended in a surreal world of infinite possibilities. 'A German pacifist?'

'Karl was a wonderful man.' Jeanne looked like a young girl. That Karl must have been something.

I traced the handsome face with the tip of a finger. It was an open face, the face of a leader. Because he was so young, I couldn't quite think of him as my grandfather. And then it came to me. His were the features of the father I had pictured when I was younger. Archangel Gabriel. A great light beam fell down on me as everything slotted into place.

There was no curse. I straightened and unfurled. There had never been a curse. I wasn't a de Peirac. I was a normal healthy European mongrel. My chest expanded, my shoulders squared and in my mind's eye, the spectre of One-eyed Jojo and his scorched friend withered, shrunk and vanished in a puff of black smoke, together with the ghost of The Beast and that of Grandma Reilly. I was free. I felt complete.

'What happened to Karl? Why did Arielle not marry him after the War?'

Tears pooled in Jeanne's eyes. 'He was one of the Resistance fighters De Peirac shot in the silk factory. He shot him in cold blood.' Her voice broke. 'I went up to warn them, but

I was too late. I heard them. Lucien, my brother, he escaped, but that animal shot both Karl and my husband's younger brother in retribution.'

My hand flew to my mouth. 'Oh no! How gruesome. Did you tell Arielle?'

'How could I? They all wore German uniforms. I did not see him. I just heard his voice. I was never sure who it was. Arielle never knew. No, she never knew…' Jeanne hung her head and added with a helpless shrug, 'who could I tell anyway? I was only a child. Who would have believed me? If I had said anything, he would have killed me.' We sat in silence. The kitchen clock marked the time and behind us, the range purred. 'Many years later, I did tell Lucien. We agreed to wait until Armand had inherited all the money before we told him the truth. That boy, he was so hot headed, he would have done something stupid.' Her eyes narrowed. 'De Peirac was dangerous. Very dangerous.' She uttered a long sigh. 'Sometimes, I wonder if did the right thing.'

'You are very close to Armand, aren't you?'

Her face lit up. 'Oh yes. He always loved coming here as a boy. He said Fleurac was where he really felt alive.' She leaned forward, suddenly animated. 'Such a clever boy he was. Now, in sixty-eight–'

'That's when he met my mother. I was born in February sixty-nine.'

'That's right. Yes, that would be it. He told me about her, you know. Mary... His unfinished symphony, he called her.'

'Really?' Wow, I never imagined Mam being anyone's unfinished symphony. 'Do you think he loved her?'

'Oh yes. He was in a terrible state when he arrived here. We were so worried about him. Completely heart-broken, poor boy. He tried everything he could to find her again. He even went to Dublin… but he never found her.' She concluded with a sad smile. 'There was never anyone else for him, not really.'

I tried to imagine Mam and Armand together. He'd have driven her mad. It just wouldn't have worked.

'You're both *enfants de l'amour.*'

A love child. Bless the woman. Unlike Grandma Reilly who saw me as the devil's offspring, for Jeanne, I was a gift from God, someone to be treasured, a link to a man she'd obviously adored. So where had it gone so wrong, I asked myself, as the familiar hurt pulsed around me, where had it gone so wrong that Grandma Reilly had called me a bastard to my face when I was only five? Where did it go so wrong with Albin de Peirac that he scooped a man's eye out with a spoon? Was it genetic or, given the right trigger, could anyone turn into a monster? Could I morph into a she-wolf?

Whatever it was, I was free from it. A refreshing breeze of innocence flushed the curse out from my body. I did not have one single drop of de Peirac blood in me.

But, if I wasn't a de Peirac, what was I? What did Irish Kerry, French and German ancestry make me? It made me European. Yes, European felt good.

I returned to the picture of Arielle. She stood against a tree, sensuous and suggestive, hair blown about by the wind, sure of the love of the man sketching her. I was glad I took after her, bouncy backside and all.

'Armand was a beautiful child, you know, and he is such a lovely man. I never did understand why he didn't have children of his own.' Jeanne reached out for my hand. 'I'm so glad you're here, dear... so glad.'

56
ORLA – FLEURAC

'But your breasts are what I like best about you!' Régis ran his hand over a nipple and squeezed lightly. 'As for your derrière, it is magnificent.'

I rolled away from him and lay on the rug, chin in my hands. The chestnut logs burned bright in the fireplace, roasting my left side.

'Oh, Orla, *mon amour,* I feel like I've known you forever.' Régis caressed my face. 'I thought I was going to end up on my own.' Flames danced inside his eyes. 'Now I'm not so sure.'

Under my body, the rug turned to liquid at my warrior's admission.

'I don't want anyone else, ever.' I kissed his chin. 'Just sexy you and Saxo.' I ran the back of my fingers along his cheekbones. 'Let's take it slowly, hey?' I melted into him. 'We've both been hurt… and we've got all the time in the world.'

'Who's rushing?' His gaze never leaving mine, we made love by the fire amidst the remnants of breakfast, while Saxo watched us, perplexed.

Later, Régis gave me a light slap on the backside. 'Come on, Scheherazade, we've got better things to do. We've a war to wage.'

'We do?'

He handed me my clothes and explained. 'See that chestnut forest over there? If we don't act now, it could be chopped down and replanted with pine.'

I knew he had a gripe against pines, but I had never really understood why. I had a job distinguishing between all the causes we were championing.

'Pines are trees too, aren't they?' I retorted, my judgement clouded by endorphins. As soon as I'd blurted it out, I knew it was a mistake. Holy Mary, the lecture I received about biodiversity, biomass and God knows what bio-else.

'Bon sang,' Régis explained, 'how could I *think* of pines as trees, when they were as harmful a *monoculture* as...'

I lost track. Did he say bananas?

'I'm sorry I don't know much about trees.' I declared, naked, Irish and proud. 'See, we don't have that many trees in Ireland. The English cut down all our forests to build their navy, so although I'll go and hug your old apple tree out there any day, I'm not too concerned about what grows on those hills, so long as it's green.'

I pulled on my clothes and followed him out. After a detour to hug the apple tree –just to make a point– I trundled behind him. I loved him, God knows I did, but jeepers, was I being stretched. I had to march for causes I didn't understand and learn the French for all the problems of the planet.

I muttered in English for a change, 'Régis, you forget I'm not French sometimes. I don't have the same reference points as you and...' I took his hand and added to defuse the issue, 'how do you expect me to think clearly when you spend your time fucking my brains off?'

My lover smiled, put a lead on Saxo, and led the both of us to the *manif.* Yes, today the whole of Fleurac was back in the street, and this time… it was about chestnuts.

The square was heaving. We set off in a cortège through our narrow streets, the march an even mix of intellectuals, conservationists, hippies and locals protesting –if I understood correctly– about the burning of chestnut forests for the production of electricity.

Leaving Régis at the front with the pros, I was harangued by an old headmaster.

'What do you suggest as a solution?' I asked to hide the fact I had not understood a word. 'Nuclear energy?'

'Le nucléaire, oh la la non!' the old man cried out in horror.

I thought as much. It was a fine thing to be anti, but I yet had to find anyone with a solution, short of going back to the seventeenth century as Armand and Virgile had done in the Larzac.

Interestingly, it was exactly what the old boy suggested. '*Mais Madame,* we need to use less energy!'

Use less energy… Didn't we just want it all, the butter and the money for the butter as Old Jeanne would say.

'Thank God those forests aren't our responsibility, hey Saxo?' I whispered to the dog.

If I had known how wrong I was, I would have stopped right there and taken the first bus home. But I didn't know, and in blissful ignorance, trawled the whole cortege, searching for Armand.

Where was he? It wasn't like him to miss a *manif.* Was he all right? He had been complaining about his heart lately. It really worried me. Now that I had found him, I couldn't bear the thought of losing him. I hurried to his house but there was no reply.

Even curiouser the bookshop was open for once. Armand and a man I'd never seen before were poring over a document set out on the counter.

'Armand?'

The man gave me a shifty look. Armand slid a book on top of the document.

'Monsieur.' I greeted the man.

Armand introduced us. 'René Lefèbvre, a friend from the army. Lefèbvre is an engraver, a very talented man. Orla, my daughter.'

I smiled. This public acknowledgement was a first.

The man held out his hand. 'Madame.' He cleared his throat. 'I was just passing by.'

This piqued my curiosity. Really? Passing by Fleurac? I didn't think so.

'Peirac and I shared a room while we were conscripted. He gave my grandson a job when–'

'When he needed one.' Armand snapped.

A customer came in and asked about novels set in the region, a popular genre in France. I showed her the collection we kept by the entrance, all the while keeping an eye on Armand, reflected in the glass of the door.

He deftly slipped the document inside the book.

'We have quite a few,' I told the customer. 'I recommend the novels written by Armand d'Aubrac.' I pushed two of Armand's regional novels into her hands.

When I returned to the till, Armand made a great show of handing the book to the old man.

'There you are, Lefèbvre.'

The man took out his wallet.

Armand lifted a hand. 'No, no, it's on the house. I'm sure you'll find it interesting. It was good to see you, *mon vieux*. Give my regards to that young rascal of yours. I'm glad he's on the straight and narrow.'

Lefèbvre nodded briefly in my direction and clutching the book, left the shop. I couldn't help but wonder why Armand would have gifted his old army friend *'la cuisine végétarienne pour bébé.'*

'So, you're not marching then?' I said to Armand once we were alone.

'Nah. Spot of bother with a hip.'

Oh yeah? *Papa naturel* was a poor liar.

I was just about to voice my concern when a shadow darkened the entrance.

'Armand, I can't believe you're in here!' Régis thundered. 'Why aren't you marching with us, defending our forests?'

'*Bof,* I'm not sure marching will achieve much.'

Really? I'd never heard that one before.

'Maybe not, but if we don't do anything, the Cévennes will end up looking like giant cabbage patches with lumber lorries thundering up and down our fragile schist roads at the rate of fifty a day.' Régis's voice rose. He tapped the counter. 'Fifty lorries a day, is that what you want?'

Armand took a step back and muttered, 'Quite frankly whether they're chestnut or pine, the forests will be managed, which they're not at the moment.'

'The chestnut is a native tree! And think of the pollution when the timber...'

'Native? *Bof,* I don't know about native,' Armand countered. 'They were planted three hundred years ago. Now let me tell you this: the methane Virgile's sheep produce when they fart... that is more damaging to the ozone layer than the CO2 from a properly managed forest. So, no I'm not out there.'

I had never witnessed such dissention between the two men before and wondered what lay at the root of it all. Armand rested a troubled gaze on me. I tried and failed to read the message contained in that long look. Puzzled, I followed Régis back into the street, wondering for the umpteenth time how long I would have to live in the country before I could decipher the subtext.

I stopped. Something was wrong.

'Hang on, Régis. I'll see you at the bar later.'

I returned to the shop and waited until the customer had paid for the two books before asking, 'Armand, what just happened there with Régis? What is going on with those forests; I mean it's not as if you own them, is it?'

Armand slumped back and opened his hands in surrender. 'But that's just it, Pitchoune, I do.'

57
ORLA – FLEURAC

When Régis wasn't lobbying electricity companies to save chestnut forests, the ministry of agriculture demanding subsidies for beekeepers, or begging telephone providers for a mast, he was chopping wood and propping up terraces. On rainy days, my hero would work in his shed, put foundation wax into frames, play sax by the fire or make love to me.

Or at least he did until last week.

There were no warning bells. It had all been going so well. I had settled into French life, delighted at the mix of sedentary work at the bookshop, convivial meetings with book dealers and being a roadie for Régis and his band. Because the French love the Irish, I was rarely on my own once I got to the clubs. Once out of the Bermuda Triangle, I could find an internet connection, work on my laptop and skype my parents. Heck, I'd even bought clogs…

Yes, it had all been going so well until one day, having arranged to pick me up for a gig, Régis simply didn't turn up. I waited, tried his mobile, rang his landline and e-mailed him at five in the morning... *Silence radio.* There was no call, no apology. He didn't even stop by to see me.

When I later walked up to his cottage to quiz him, he replied curtly, 'I want to be able to trust you, and right now, I'm not sure I can.' After that, I didn't see him for three days.

His comment had hit me like a cold shower. Had we been too close? Perhaps he needed space. Fighting the doldrums about to engulf me, I was grateful to receive an e-mail from Marguerite asking me to come to Paris for a vintage fashion show she was organising. Jumping at the chance, I agreed, hoping Jean-Loup would not inveigle himself into the proceedings.

Autumn pressed on, windy, wet and dreary. It was the time of year when warm weather from the Mediterranean clashed with cold mountain air and drenched the Cévennes. Perhaps Autumn brought with it memories Régis found difficult to cope with.

A weekend in Paris was just what I needed. I e-mailed Marguerite to thank her, and said I would see her in a couple of days.

But first, Régis and I had to attend an all-important '*regénération*' meeting. We simply could not miss it. Though – through no fault of mine – things had cooled down between us, we could not let the cause down. It was bigger than us.

'*Cogénération*, Orla, not *regénération*.' Régis changed gear. 'The power plant generates *power* and *also* uses the *heat* produced by the timber they're burning. That's why it's called co-generation.'

'I see. Grand idea anyhow.' I held myself in check, hoping he would eventually tell me what ailed him.

The conference would be in French. I didn't for a moment imagine that I would understand anything, but I'd been deputised by Armand to contact representatives from the power companies and discuss his forests.

'Now that you're here, Pitchoune, I might do something about those wretched trees after all.' Ashamed of his father's profiteering, Armand had let his forests run wild for years, pretending they didn't exist. He had sworn me to secrecy. I was not to say anything to Régis until we had a plan. This put me in a very difficult position. I didn't like to hide anything from Régis, especially when I needed his advice. Especially when he so needed to trust me. Perhaps that was the problem: he had found out and held it against me.

It was the only thing I could think about.

A large drop of rain splattered on the windscreen. Régis swore and turned on the wipers.

'I'm not sure what fly has stung you,' I said, demonstrating my skilled use of colloquial French, 'but it's time you told me what is going on. One day I'm your dream girl and I save you from loneliness, and the next, you leave me standing by the side of the road without so much as an explanation.' The heavens opened. I raised my voice above the din of the wipers, now working full tilt. 'If you have a problem with me, I want to know what it is.'

'*Oh, merde.* I can't see anything with that rain.' Régis leaned over the steering wheel, peering into the deluge. 'I could say the same to you. I said I wanted to be able to trust you.'

'But you can!' I racked my brain for things I may have said or done, but apart from Armand's forests, I could think of nothing.

What more could a fellow possibly want? I'd been besotted with him from the start, hanging onto his every word, even when I didn't understand them, got stung by his bees, picked up his dog's turds, put hundreds of frames together for his hives, learned to talk dirty in French, carried his sax, waited for him for *hours* in dingy clubs and never asked for anything in return. Jeepers, what was it with men?

The rain was now thundering on the roof of the car. The traffic slowed to a crawl. Régis nearly hit the car in front and swerved into the first road that came up to our right. Rain wrapped itself around us like a great shower curtain. I was terrified.

'Why did you have to turn in there, for God's sake, we've no idea where we are!' I yelled.

'I do know where I am.'

Bracing my legs against the foot well, I closed my eyes and recited my Hail Mary. Around us, the noise was deafening. We were lost. I begged Régis to stop and wait until it was over –only last week, he would have agreed and made love to me on the back seat– but that was last week. Today he clearly wasn't in the mood.

'What are you going to do in Paris?' Régis shouted à propos of nothing.

Huh? Where did that come from? He knew exactly where I was going and whom I'd planned to see. I froze. Memories of Jean-Loup hit me like a bad smell. I'd never told him about Jean-Loup. I felt too stupid to have fallen for such a psycho. Was Régis worried that I would meet someone? But who and why? What did it matter anyway... For the possessively insane, there never needs to be a reason. Had I fallen into the same trap for the second time, or were all French men jealous to the extreme?

I slowly turned to him, disturbed by the sense of déjà-vu.

'I have been invited by a *girl* friend to attend her vintage fashion show. I will be meeting two *women*. Any man I might meet there will probably be gay. Now if you can't bear to let me go to Paris without being jealous, I don't think we can carry on.'

I was furious. I wanted to get off, take a bus, a taxi, a canoe, anything to get me away from his car, but the rain was lashing so hard against the windows that I wasn't even sure we were still on the tarmac.

'Régis, why don't you trust me? What have I done?'

'You know perfectly well why.' He swerved, narrowly avoiding a tree floating towards us.

My feet were wet. Water was rising through the floor. The engine was struggling.

A building appeared on our right. Relief swept over me. We were approaching a town. I whooped, recognising the familiar red M of McDonald's. We were safe.

'Stop! Let's run into this Mc Donald's and wait till it's over.'

'Are you mad? I'm not setting foot in MacDo. Who do you think I am?' snarled the eco-warrior.

'Jean-Loup, stop!' I screamed in English.

'Ha! Jean-Loup. And who is this Jean-Loup? Are you going to tell me now?'

'Yes! He was the last madman I had the misfortune to meet in Paris, a possessive lunatic, like you. Jaysus, I sure know how to choose them. Stop now,' I growled. 'I'm getting off.'

'You can't– Ouch!' The car jolted forward, hit by a floating tree trunk.

I opened the door, jumped into a foot-deep deluge of muddy water and waded into McDonald's.

58
ORLA – FLEURAC

'I see, so it's *Allo Papa bobo,*' Armand joked at the end of the line, alluding to the way French children only call their parents when they are in trouble. We both paused, intimidated by the word Papa, spoken aloud for the first time.

'I've been stuck in this McDonald's for hours without electricity,' I sniffed into the phone, 'sitting on a table, watching horrible… stuff float out of sewers. I'm only able to get through now.'

'Hold on Pitchoune. I'm on my way.'

'What happened?' Armand asked an hour later, a hand on the wheel, pushing open the door to his clapped-out Jeep. 'I thought you were with Régis.'

'I was. We had an argument.' I'd reverted to speaking English, my brain unable to cope with anything else.

Armand steered his Jeep out of the mess of rubble. Along the road, cars were turned over on their side.

'An argument? What about?'

'I'm not sure. There's something strange going on,' I said in a strangled voice. 'It was all going so well and now…'

'Don't worry, Pitchoune, we'll find what is the matter. I know Régis for a long time and he's a good guy. He is the best.'

That was as may be, but if Régis was insanely possessive, how would Armand know?

Fat drops of rain spluttered on the windscreen. *Not again*, I prayed. We were still twenty kilometres from home.

Focused, Armand drove, eyes glued to the road, swerving to avoid crates and flower pots dislodged by the downpour.

'They will belong to you one day, Orla.' He mumbled, avoiding a wheelbarrow.

'Huh? What will be mine?'

'My forests. I '*herited* them from my father and since you are my daughter– we will make a detour to a notary. I will recognise you.'

I was completely lost. 'What do you need to recognise me for?' I'm here. I'm Orla. Christ, have you all gone mad?'

'I will tell the notary that I am your natural father so you can *herit*–'

'We say *inherit*.' I corrected. 'You will *acknowledge* me. Oh, Armand, do I have a choice? I don't particularly want to inherit anything, I'm sorry. I wouldn't have a clue what to do with your forests.' I pointed to the mountains around us. 'There's so many of them.'

Christ, what was happening? The fecking forest had already torn Régis and me apart, now I was about to own one. Heiresses were groomed from birth to look after family interests. I was just a girl from Clontarf. Motorbike spares I knew, but trees? Damn. I'd missed the co-generation meeting.

'It is not just the forest, Pitchoune,' Armand exhaled a long painful breath. 'I have '*herited* –sorry, inherited– fields in the Larzac. To stop the army from buying them, we cut them up in hundreds of parcels–'

'Plots. Hundreds of plots.' I corrected again, wondering what else I was going to inherit. If Armand hadn't sold Virgile the farm for a euro, I'd probably be inheriting sheep too. Yes, that was it. I had an idea. Why didn't he sell the damned forests to Régis for a euro, since he had opinions?

'There is the bookshop, my house, one apartment in Paris. Another apartment in Antibes.'

My stomach clenched. I rested my head against the cool glass of the window and said in an exhausted voice, 'I don't want it. I really don't want any of it, Papa. You're all I want. Please, leave me out of this.'

His eyes misted up. I had touched a chord. He turned to me with a sad smile.

'Listen. Maybe I will die soon. My father had an *infarctus* when he was fifty-five.'

'What's de Peirac's heart attack got to do with anything? He wasn't even your father!'

'Yes yes, I forget. Of course. But I am old, you know.'

'Armand, is there anything you want to tell me about that… German father of ours?'

'You talk with Jeanne, huh?'

'Yes, but I'd have preferred it if it had come from you.'

'Sorry.' He replied, contrite. 'Some bits of my life are shit, Orla, I'm sorry to have to give them to you. But maybe, the forest and the flats, you can do something with them, no?'

'Thank you but really, I…'

'If you refuse, it will all go to my cousin Arnie. You don't know Arnie, he…'

'Ah, I do actually. Is his name Arnaud? I met him in Paris.'

'You did?'

'Yes, I– he tried to touch me up.'

'He put his hand on your derrière, *hein*? Ah yes, that is Arnie.'

'I see. So, you're telling me that because your cousin's a

pervert, I've no choice but to inherit old de Peirac's ill-gotten gains.'

Christ, how had it got to this? From what Armand went on to explain, I couldn't even donate it to charity. Heck, I could have coped with a chateau with swimming pool and a few posh friends, but the moment Armand died –never I hoped– I would be saddled with a hundred tiny plots in the French Gobi Desert, lumbered with chestnut forests that were nice to look at but no one wanted to manage, a failing bookshop, a crumbling house, and two flats.

Perhaps I could sell the lot and give Fleurac a mast, or dig a ditch and have cable brought in. Now, wasn't that a grand idea? Thank God for death duties. I hoped they were hefty.

My mind unable to soak up anymore, I watched the rain wash away the contours of the hills, dissolve houses, trees and life into liquid greyness, wishing a landslide would take away my troubles. Selfish of me, I know.

I turned to Armand for comfort. Busy driving us out of this nightmare, his eyes remained on the road. Anyway, he was the one who'd got us into this mess, the curse of that damned Beast still looming over us.

Dad! I sat up, filled with hope. He would know what to do. My dad, the one who'd always stood by me. I was suddenly overcome with a wave of nostalgia for a different kind of rain, for soft days, jars of Guinness lined up on a counter, the sound of fiddles, the smell of peat fires, the smell of home.

59
ORLA – DUBLIN

It felt strange to wake up in Clontarf. I'd told Armand it was only for a week. Now I wasn't so sure. Once again, I had returned to the box-room where I had spent my first twenty-two years. If I stretched, I could touch both walls. The boys had shared the other of our three bedrooms. They now had families of their own and lived unencumbered lives in South Dublin.

I thought back to the girl who had once lived here. Keen to prove I was good enough to be a Reilly, I had always come top of the class and never missed mass. As a teen-ager, I dutifully sang 'Molly Malone' at parties and managed to repress the urge to shave my head like Sinead O'Connor. I shone at Trinity and came out with a first-class honours' degree. But that still hadn't made me a Reilly. There had always been that chasm. I knew who I wasn't, but I never knew who I was.

First roots, then wings. I had acquired roots now, mandrake roots, and did they give me wings? I wasn't so sure. I had managed to escape the curse of the de Peirac, but their legacy weighed heavy on me, too heavy to carry on my own, and I missed Régis dreadfully.

Still in my pyjamas, I called Armand for a chat, got through and gave him our book orders. I could work from here. It was strange to imagine him at home, wrapping up books to send, all on his own, without me. He didn't say so, but I could tell from his voice that he missed me.

After the call, I turned to the window and looked down at my old universe, the small patch of grass, the broken-down rabbit hutch, the long wall running the length of the housing estate that separated us from the sea front. Not exactly breeding ground for heiresses, Clontarf.

'Morning, love.' Mam carried in a cup of tea. 'Did you sleep all right?'

'Yes, I did. It's good to be home.' I closed my laptop, slipped back into bed and patted my duvet, feeling a little better.

'We're just off to church. Your brothers and the kids will be here around one. After lunch, they'll be wanting to watch the match with your dad, so I thought we might take a walk along the seafront if it's not too cold.'

'That's grand.'

'I found this.' Mam pulled a photo from her apron pocket. 'It was taken in front of the skating rink near Passy where I lived, in Paris.'

She handed me a faded Polaroid of a young man in beige flares. His chestnut hair curled over his shoulders, just how I looked at that age.

'Very handsome.' I smiled. 'No wonder you–'

'Ah, I've no regrets.' Mam cut me short. 'What would I have wanted with a boy like that? Anyway, his father would never have let it happen. He was a dreadful man.'

'What do you mean?' I don't know why I asked. I had a pretty good idea myself.

'His mother … I met her once. Now she was lovely. I think she was called Arielle. Lovely name, isn't it? She had a chauffeur. Can you imagine. They were that posh.' Mam lowered herself at the edge of my bed. It was the first time she'd ever mentioned Armand. 'I remember that chauffeur was killed in a hunting accident. For some reason, Armand held his father responsible.' She pushed herself up and headed for the door. 'They were strange people. It would never have worked.'

I could tell from her face that she was grateful for the life Dad had offered her in Dublin, her year in Paris enough adventure for a lifetime.

How had Arielle lived with that monster of a husband? Poor Armand. I wished Jeanne had revealed the truth of his birth earlier in his life, ridding us both from the curse of the Gévaudan Beast and a cumbersome inheritance.

The flat in Paris was mine to do as I wished. Armand had given me the key. He had never been back. As for the forests, he had buried his head in the sand, or rather in his books, pretending the forests didn't exist. I could understand him.

Mam gave me the photo. 'There, it's yours now. You understand why I didn't tell you. Then again…' She reflected for a moment. 'All families are complicated.'

'Finnuala explained why Grandma Reilly was so difficult. It ends with us. Don't worry. The girls will never have to live with the weight of shame.'

Mam met my gaze. 'I am sorry, Orla. We did all we could, but…'

'I'm over it.'

'But you're not happy, are you? Was there someone for you back in France?'

I told her everything.

Jean-Loup, Régis, everything.

A long time later, she got up and just before she reached the door, remembered it was Sunday.

'There'll be eleven of us for lunch, so I'm just doing

salmon and mash. Could you have a few potatoes peeled by the time we come back from church?'

'Sure. How about pudding?'

Perhaps cooking would stop me getting maudlin.

'I made a trifle. Your favourite.'

Trifle. What would Régis make of Mam's trifle full of artificial colourings? Though there was nothing *bio* about it, Mam's trifle was made with love. Anyway, what did it matter. He wasn't here. I checked my phone, but of course, there was no message, so I cried into my tea.

Later, I remembered to call Marguerite. I apologised for my absence and asked about the fashion show.

'Ah, Orla, what a good surprise!'

I'd forgotten her predilection for Franglish.

'I'm sorry, Marguerite, I had to rush back to Dublin.'

'I hop' it was not bad news?'

'No, no everyone's fine. Anyway, how did it go, your vintage show?'

'Yes, it went very well, but, Orla, I must tell you something. Jean-Loup, he was there, at my fashion show!'

'You're joking!'

'*Ah la la, non,* it is not a joke, *hein.* I saw him with my eyes.'

'But how did he know about it?'

'I don't know. He was not interested by my show. He was always looking at the door. I think he look for you.'

However Marguerite and I thrashed out the problem, I could not understand how Jean-Loup had found out both the date and the location of the show.

'Maybe he saw the poster on my shop, that is the only explication because I only e-mailed you. Everyone else I tell on my Facebook, but I have blocked him. Also, I tell Aude never to speak with him. Never. She says that she does not know him.'

It was both puzzling and worrying to learn that Jean-

Loup was still working on getting me back to Paris. After his attack on Asha, I'd prayed he would grow tired of me, that he'd found someone else perhaps, some dumb goose willing to be possessed body and soul. I was wrong. I had been warned. Wherever I went and whatever I did, he knew. I couldn't hide from him. I even began to wonder how safe I was here in Dublin.

I was distracted from my thoughts by my nephew and niece rushing in an hour earlier than expected.

'Auntie Orla, you're back!' my six-year-old niece cried out.

'Saoirse darling!' I hugged her. 'Jeepers, haven't you grown.' I swear the girl had doubled in size while I was gone. 'Tell me, you're six, aren't you?'

'No, I amn't. I'm six and three quarters, and I've got a wobbly tooth.'

'Saoirse' –we pronounce it *sur-sha*– means freedom. We take being Irish seriously here in Ireland. While I peeled Mam's potatoes, Saoirse played her tin whistle, her brother played football in the back garden and her parents set the table in the dining room. How I'd missed the easy companionship, the undemanding gossip.

That night, I returned to my garret after a family Sunday, berating myself for having left it far too long. Maudlin, I wished I had something to show for my efforts… a man, a business, anything, instead of the total fiasco of my life. Grandma Reilly was right. I was a waste of blood and organs.

I could still hear her voice. 'You're an add-on, Orla. You'll never be a Reilly.'

I twisted and turned in bed, working out my origins. I

was half Irish, a quarter French and a quarter German. What was his name again? Müller. I repeated the name to myself. Karl Müller. My real grandfather was a pacifist. Yes, it was good. I felt the connection. I slept fitfully, unable to stop my thoughts from returning to the Cévennes.

Until that fateful *épisode Cévenol* as they call those torrential rains that wash away hills and roads, I believed that Régis and I had something special, convinced that if we really wanted to, we too could move mountains or at least manage forests together.

What was he doing now? Playing heart-breaking laments on his saxophone probably. Where did we go wrong? What the devil had I done to lose his trust?

Tears threatened to roll but buoyed by the love of my family and their faith in me, I shook myself out of the doldrums. Whatever the reason for Régis's turnabout, it was his problem. I'd given him my best and if that was not good enough, it was his loss. I would never again let a man define my worth.

Whatever had come over me to let a lunatic like Jean-Loup turn me into a fake Brigitte Bardot?

I sat up with a jolt. Jean-Loup at Marguerite's show! Yes! That was it! My e-mails! That's how Jean-Loup had known where I was at all times. I jumped out of bed wanting to scream and punch, but it was three o'clock in the morning. Instead, I tiptoed downstairs, sat at the dining table and stomach churning, switched on my laptop.

The wily bastard. My computer. Under the guise of helping me, Jean-Loup had set up my computer with a spying device. That was how he was able to stalk me. Teeth clenched, I opened my e-mails and over and over, found proof of what he had done. The dirty rat was able to follow my every move and even write e-mails as me! I had told Asha I was going to the Protestant Museum; I had sent Mam an email about the soup festival. That waster, I grumbled... I could gouge his eyes out with a spoon all right, dunk him into a vat of boiling tar, cut him into small pieces.

He was the one who had ruined it for Régis and me, written mails to cancel our outings, mails that hinted I was meeting him in Paris. So, Jean-Loup read my mails? He was welcome to them. Cackling like a madwoman, I set out to trap him. The bastard would spend the rest of his days looking for me. But first I had to run it past Asha.

60
ARMAND – FLEURAC

Armand picked up the card propped on the pile of books that had taken root on the mantlepiece. A soft smile spread over his face. He had waited nearly forty years and at last, Mary had written. For the hundredth time, he traced the girlish letters and pulled the half-moon spectacles out of his shirt pocket.

'Dear Armand,

Though I don't think we will ever meet again, I wanted to tell you how glad I am that Orla has found you. There is one thing I have always wanted to do, and that is to thank you for the gift of her life. Though things were difficult for us at the start, never a day has passed that I have not been grateful for having her.

Now as you can see, I have a family of my own. I've two boys and four grandchildren.

Orla has been a lovely child. You never had the chance to see her grow up. For this, I am sorry. She thinks the world of you. We are glad she has a home in France and has been able to help you with your shop.

I think of you fondly and wish you all the best.

Mary

He squinted at the photo she had included. Her hair was white now, and she had put on weight, but her smile was just as lovely and her warmth was there, the overwhelming sense of calm he had so needed in his life.

He exhaled a long breath. It would never have worked. His father would have destroyed the girl, as he had destroyed everything else. She'd had a lucky escape.

He replaced the card. There was still the matter of Régis. That boy had been behaving strangely. It was time to find out what fly had stung him.

Armand missed Orla more than he could say. He had grown used to her smile and her quiet efficiency, and of course, she reminded him so much of his mother. Before she'd arrived, the shop had been leaching money. With the help of that strange Indian friend of hers, Orla had managed to inject new life into the business. If she stayed in Dublin because Régis had behaved like an idiot, life would lose its meaning.

He promised himself to go and visit Régis, talk to him like a father, ask him what his intentions were with his daughter… but first, there was something he had to do, something that couldn't wait. His heart had been giving him trouble. He'd had a couple of scares. The doctor had suggested a bypass and he had agreed, but you never knew. He could die any time.

He gathered the rare photos of his father, the *livret de famille* found amongst Arielle's papers, the one which bore the date of birth and death of his parents, her death and his own date of birth.

His chest tightened. He pulled out a portrait from an envelope discovered in a secret drawer of his father's desk after his death, that dreadful day in the church. It was a sketch of his mother. She stood naked in a stream, an arm across her small breasts. It was splattered with blood. Death had found Karl as he was drawing her.

His father had always known. Armand thought back to the day he had left Paris with his mother for Fleurac, the only place where Albin couldn't reach her. His father's hand around her neck, whispering to her. 'You're mine alone, you hear, I have shot both your lovers, the German communist and that Portuguese chauffeur of yours.'

She'd slumped into the car like a broken puppet. Two years later, she was dead.

Armand ran a finger over the dried droplets of blood, kissed the portrait of his mother, wrapped it around his birth certificate and knelt down in front of the fireplace. He took the old Zippo out of his pocket, and was just about to light the bundle when there was a knock on the door.

Pushing himself up with difficulty, Armand pressed the intercom.

'*Oui?*'

'Lefèbvre here. I've got what you asked for.'

Armand pressed the buzzer and let in his old army roommate.

'Bonjour, Peirac.' Wheezing from the climb, the old man shook his hand.

'*Café?*' Armand went to get the pot from the kitchen and placed it on the large pine table.

'*Volontiers.*' Lefèbvre pulled out a chair, sat down heavily and wiped his brow with a large handkerchief. 'Took me three hours to get here, but I owe you big time, so I really don't mind. It's good to talk about the good old days.'

Armand snorted as he poured the coffee. 'Bad old days for me. You enjoyed your time in the army though, huh? Made a mint forging *permission* slips when the boys wanted to go on leave. Sugar?'

'Yes, two lumps. Doctor says I'm diabetic.' Lefèbvre

dropped the sugar cubes and stirred his coffee for a long time.

'Bah, at our age, there's always something.' Armand touched his chest. 'With me it's the ticker.'

'Is that why you called me?' Lefèbvre took an envelope out of his pocket and pushed it towards Armand.

'Yes. The girl you saw, Orla. She's my daughter.'

'Until the other day, I didn't know you had a daughter…' The old man took a sip of coffee.

'Neither did I.'

Lefèbvre raised an eyebrow.

'Met her mother on the barricades in sixty-eight.' Armand kept it simple.

'Ah, sixty-eight... Year Zero. We really believed we were going to make the world a better place.'

'Course we did. We were young.' Armand shrugged.

'Then the eighties came along with 'Greed is good.' Lefèbvre concluded, 'What a mess we've made of the world.'

'Yep.'

They drank their coffee, the lull filled with the sound of the man's wheezing.

'I hope you're pleased with it.' The old man patted the envelope. 'What you did for my grandson back then. Hard to find a job after a spate inside. He's not a bad boy, but…'

'He worked hard.' Armand took the envelope, pulled out a dog-eared identity card and whistled in admiration. 'You haven't lost your touch.'

Modest, Lefèbvre opened his hands. He leaned forward with a question. 'One thing puzzled me though. Why did you want to make yourself a year *older*? I mean, asking me to remove Buenos Aires from your identity card, I can understand, but what's wrong with March 1946? Most people want to be younger.'

'I'm not Brigitte Bardot. That's not what it's about. As I

said, the old ticker's playing up. I could keel over anytime. Now that I have a daughter, I need to tie up loose ends and…' Armand shook his head, unable to explain further. He ran a hand over his mouth. 'I'm not sure where to begin *mon vieux*. I was born in Argentina after the War, so you can probably guess…'

'Sure. I understand. It's obvious why a man would escape to Argentina in 46. *Collabo*… Militia… Nazis. Bad stuff huh. You don't want to lumber your daughter with your father's sins.'

'Ah Lefèbvre, you're not only a fine engraver, but a fine psychologist.'

'Is there anything else you want me to… hum, rectify?' The forger asked with a grin.

'No. That's it.' Armand picked up his coffee. 'I was just worried about my gravestone.'

'Glad to have been of help.' The old forger got up and, affection clouding his eyes, put a hand on Armand's shoulder. 'Don't die just yet though, will you.'

'Nah. I might go for the bypass after all. I quite like this daughter of mine. We've a lot to catch up on.'

'Merci pour le café, Peirac. A la prochaine.'

'Thank you and remember…'

'I know. Next time I'm passing by…'

They shook hands at the top of the stairs. Armand waited for the click of the door and returned to the kitchen. He picked up his *carte d'identité* and grinned. Convincingly dog-eared, tattered, it was perfect. Armand de Peirac, born in Paris, on March 1st 1945. Nine months after D-Day.

His parents had never been to America. He remembered Argentina, of course he did, memories he knew he must never share. His tenth birthday aboard the passenger ship sailing back to Bordeaux. His mother scouring the Dakar market for a present during a stopover. He still had that carved elephant somewhere. Ten candles stuck on a stale sponge cake.

What happened to Karl's child. Had his mother had a miscarriage? Had his father kicked it out of her? He was capable of it. Riddled with guilt, she might have thought it a just punishment.

Armand simply could not bear the idea that once he was gone, Orla and Jeanne would discover the truth. Jeanne's adulation for the German pacifist had been a blessing and, for a while, he had clung to it. God, how he had wanted to believe it. But the curse of the Gévaudan Beast was real. Albin was his father. The whole bloodline was contaminated. Cousin Arnie may have lulled his darling daughters to sleep with tales of a generous marquis who had distributed chestnuts to his peasants in the eighteenth century, but they were just that, fairy tales. Arnie had lost his son and his wife in accidents. The mad marquis once accused of the wolf's murders *was* an ancestor of theirs. He was never caught.

Intent, Armand watched the flames. Karl's dreams of a better world would live on. Not only inside Jeanne's and Orla's mind, but in the novels he wrote under the name d'Aubrac, novels in which Arielle and Karl lived happily ever after… as he did, with Mary.

Hoping to atone for his father's sins, Armand had led a quiet life, a life devoid of greed, and helped those who needed it. Thank God the line ended with Orla. She would never know the truth.

He kissed his mother's picture, doused petrol over the bundle that tied him to Albin de Peirac and set fire to it. The flames licked the paper, caught and erased the curse. Armand's spirit soared. He was free.

61
ORLA – DUBLIN

'Orla? We're going in thirty minutes,' Dad called out from the hall.

I switched off my computer and rubbed my back. The noise from the radio and the smell of peat were so familiar, it felt as if I'd never left home. It was good to be back… but my life was on hold.

I missed Régis dreadfully. Until I had fully understood what Jean-Loup had done, I couldn't even call Régis to explain. Explain what? I had never mentioned Jean-Loup to him. It was silly, I realised that now.

Filled with loathing for Jean-Loup for ruining my life, vengeance had become an all-consuming goal. I carried on sending mails as normal. I didn't want him to know he'd been rumbled. I kept the old laptop, bought a new one and asked my younger brother to set it up for me so I could contact my friends without that creep finding out. He read everything I wrote. It made me sick. I felt violated.

I spent ages on the phone with Asha, dissecting the matter.

'Jeepers, to think that all that time, the bastard has been

reading my mails and worse, that he's been writing e-mails as me!'

That man had inveigled himself into my head, read my most private thoughts, followed me in the street, attacked my friend and destroyed my relationship. He had to pay. 'I could dip his balls into the piranha tank.' Hatred burned through my veins. 'He won't get away with it.'

'Listen,' Asha said, 'because of the poor reception in Fleurac, Jean-Loup's not expecting you to use your computer a lot, so keep to what you used to do.'

'Keep to what I normally did? You must be joking! In Fleurac I set the alarm at five to receive our orders. That means four am here in Dublin! Give me a break, will ya? Even you skip your night prayers.'

'You only have to do this for a few days. Next week, you can send me a mail telling me that it's over with Régis, that you've fallen out with Armand and–'

'Ooh, I like that.' I could see where she was heading.

'And then you send me a mail to tell me that you're leaving Fleurac for some remote island. With a bit of luck, he should bite and rush over there.'

'Good idea.' Papua New Guinea and the infested jungles of Guyana sprang to mind, but I had a better idea. 'I know just the place.'

'Borneo?'

'Ah, you'll have to wait.'

Soon, Asha would receive an e-mail in which I told her that weary of Fleurac, I had accepted an offer to work on Inisheer, one of the Aran Islands, in a pub called The Wild Goose.

'Orla, are you ready?' Dad called from the bottom of the stairs.

'Ready for what?' Lost in reprisal strategies I'd lost track of time.

'You wanted to go to O'Mally's.'

'Oh yes, sorry. I'll be right down!'

Going to O'Mally's was the last thing I felt like. O'Mally's was Declan's pub. Laying his ghost to rest had seemed like a good idea at the time. Now, I wasn't too sure.

I slipped on the red dress I'd worn to the Pavillon Dauphine in what seemed like another life, and concealed it under a long coat.

I put my head round the kitchen door. 'Mam? Are you coming with us?'

'I'll be along in a minute, love. I've a cake in the oven.'

I steadied myself on Dad's arm. I hadn't walked in heels since Paris. Close to Dad, I noticed how in spite of the golf, he'd filled out after his retirement. Mam's cakes were probably to blame.

'Are you thinking of going back to France then?' he asked along the way, casual like.

A cold sea breeze blew right through us and messed with my hair. I tightened my coat and huddled closer.

'I think I will. You know, I didn't like Armand at first. These French intellectuals, they think they've got all the answers. They're very quick to judge. But we got used to each other and now that he lets me be, I don't mind him. I like the books. I love the product.' I gave Dad's arm a squeeze.

'What did you find out, you know, about his… about your…'

'You mean about my ancestry?'

Jeeez, where did I start? I'd have to explain at some point, but I would keep it simple.

'Bah, nothing much.' I said with an affectionate nudge. We turned into a side street, sheltered from the wind. 'Bit of a weird bunch.'

How I felt about Armand was difficult to explain. He was

more of a friend, an eccentric uncle. In the end, strange as it sounds, it wasn't as if I had two fathers, but three. Karl Müller, my German grandfather, had morphed with Archangel Gabriel. He had been watching over me all these years... I couldn't disown him.

'You were right, Dad. I did feel like a puzzle with a piece missing.' I searched for the right words. 'But I found out more than I bargained for.' I smiled and ran my eyes over Dad's strong jaw, broad chest and tweed jacket. 'Take you for instance. You're the son of a judge. How important is the honourable judge as opposed to your mother's father, the Connemara gambler?'

He thought about it for a while. 'There's a parable in the Bible, of a seed that falls on stony ground and dies because it had no roots. Roots are important.' A crease appeared on his brow. He ran his hand over his mouth and moderated his statement. 'But only up to a point. The grandfather who lost the family money on the horses did more than gamble money. He shamed his children. My mother carried that shame like a curse. She passed it onto us. You had to live with it too Orla, and I'm deeply sorry about that. These things fester inside you like poison. If that's all ancestors have to give you, then you're better off without them.'

Once again, Dad had put his finger on it. That's what I loved about him.

'You've had a good life, haven't you, Dad?'

'It depends how you look at it. I was lucky to marry the right girl, but I never did well at school.' He explained with an ironic grin, 'I took after me mam. She was no intellectual herself, you know. That didn't stop her from keeping on about how I should have done better, what with me being the son of a judge.' He lifted his hands in surrender. 'How often I'd wished I'd been a tinker, the son of a tinker.'

I hung on his arm for fear of tripping over, amazed to

find that even Dad, who'd always been my rock, was plagued with insecurities.

He patted my hand. 'I've always been so proud of you.'

'Thank you.' I squeezed his arm.

'You're a one-off, Orla. You're strong. Whatever life throws at you, you always land on your feet.'

I wasn't so sure. Right now, I was at sea, tortured by Jean-Loup's betrayal, depressed about Armand's forests and Régis's desertion, filled with apprehension at meeting Declan again, and more than anything, dreading the question 'what are you doing with yourself now, Orla?'

What the heck would I say? 'I've just been dumped – again– by my boyfriend, and I'm living at home?' I was back to square one.

I hated the limbo I was in. Tears welled up, threatening to ruin my carefully applied make-up. Still, though I was quaking inside my chic clothes, Dad's faith in me did not waver. It meant a lot.

'You made a success of your first business. Don't think we didn't notice how hard you worked, your Mam and I. Declan's a chancer. Why he'd want to be tied to a pub when he used to be his own boss is anyone's guess. You made a success of that business, so you did. He was mad to sell it.'

'Declan's always found the answer to life in Guinness.' That and Sinead's boobs. 'Sinead's got a head for figures. For him it'll be easy, all he has to do is pull the pints.'

O'Mally's appeared in the distance. I slowed down. Why had I not stuck to jeans? I was ridiculously overdressed. Coming here was a bad idea. I wanted to go home.

Unconcerned, Dad carried on. 'You turned your French man's business around in no time, so you did. I really admire that.' He put his hands in his pockets and directed his gaze at his feet. 'I've always been a company man meself, gone to church, joined the golf club.' He raised his eyes shyly. 'I could never have done what you did, upped and left for a foreign country to start all over again on my own. You've got guts.'

I leaned into him and as I did, an idea wafted in, buoyed up by the sea breeze and Dad's faith in me. The chestnut forests? Armand and I would deal with them together. I just had enough French to attend the next conference on cogeneration. We would work it out. Together, we would join the groundswell out there, and together, we would take on the soulless shareholders.

A smell of beer and the din of the crowd oozed out of the half-open pub door. Dad hugged me. 'It takes a special person to come here tonight after what that bastard's done to you. It's a brave thing. You're a brave girl.'

I held on to him. 'Wait. Don't you think I'm overdressed for O'Mally's?'

'Nah, you look grand. The girls will be wearing their glad rags too. Anyway, who's going to look at you? Dublin are playing Kerry. They'll all be watching the telly.'

I'd forgotten about the Gaelic football match. I vowed to keep my coat, on, huddle in a corner with my sisters-in-law and the kids, and after a couple of whiskeys, I'd probably stop caring.

62
ORLA – DUBLIN

The pub was packed.

'What will you have?' Dad pushed a path through to the bar.

My sisters-in-law had colonised a corner with their gaggle of sisters and children. Agglutinated male Dublin fans filled the rest of the space, all eyes glued to the screen.

'A double Balvenie… I need an anaesthetic.'

Concealed inside a tight cluster of Gaelic football fans, I glanced at the man behind the bar and did a double take. Jeepers! Could this be Declan? I peeked out from behind a giant in an Aran jumper. Brown polo shirt pulled over a hairy paunch, shaved head… nah, it must be his brother.

He noticed Dad. 'Hey, Mick! What brings you here?'

It was Declan's voice all right. Jesus Mary and Joseph, had I really spent ten years of my precious life with Mr Blobby? What was *wrong* with me?

'Auntie Orla, Auntie Orla, look! I've loft that toof.' Saoirse caught hold of my hand and pulled me to a chair she had kept for me. I sat down heavily, staring at what was left of Declan.

'I've already put it under my pillow.'

I shook myself back to reality and grinned at my niece.

'When the tooth fairy gives you a euro, make sure you invest it wisely.' I took off my coat.

'Thus spake the business woman,' joked her mother, an English teacher. 'I see you're dressed to kill, Orla. Good on ya.'

'Bit too much for O'Mally's though, don't you think?'

'Nah, it's grand. You wanna make sure Declan realises his mistake. You were always far too good for that eejit. Where did you get that dress anyway?'

'I tried running a vintage clothes business in Paris, but there's no point in trying to beat the French at their own game. I'm into books now.' There, that wasn't so hard.

Dad passed my drink along and went to stand with the men.

'Have you seen Sinead?' A sister-in-law's sister nodded towards the bar.

It was nothing really. Just the way she said it, I knew I was amongst friends. The knot in my stomach began to loosen.

'Is she here?'

'Can't mistake her. That's her at the till. She only works week-ends mind, the rest of the time, she looks after the twins.'

I spat out my whiskey. 'Twins?'

'Didn't your Mam tell ya?'

Bloody hell, Declan sure had his comeuppance, having to share those tits with twins. I rose from my seat. Yes, I could see Sinead now. Pink hair did her acne no favours. It sort of enhanced it. Lined with more blue veins than Roquefort, her breasts spilled over a tight top. All in all, there was as much flesh on display as in my local charcuterie.

I glanced down at my own frontage hidden under rolls of fabric, incensed at Jean-Loup for having dared to suggest silicone and berating myself for believing him. Régis used to say my breasts were classy. He couldn't get enough of them. Régis… Where was he now? Schmoozing groupies? I couldn't bear the thought of it.

'Where's your mam?' a sister-in-law said, checking her watch. 'It's nearly nine.'

'No idea what's keeping her.' I twirled my whiskey and sat back, listening to the chatter. Alcohol relaxed the tension. The gossip of the week was about a grisly murder that had shaken Ireland. It was in all the papers. A man met on a dating site had raped and killed a girl. I shivered, wondering how close I'd got to this myself.

A blast of cold air reached us. I turned to the door. Here was Mam at last, blown in together with a crowd of youngsters. I lifted a hand to call her and remained paralysed. Someone caught my eye in the crowd behind her, a familiar movement, a dark ponytail. My heart stopped.

Régis stood by the door, unsure of what to do.

Fireworks exploded inside me. Every cell began to dance a jig. I drank in the cheekbones, the dark hair, the long legs in black jeans, unable to believe that this fabulous man had come all the way to Dublin to claim me.

'Régis!' I stood on tiptoes and waved frantically.

His eyes, dull with searching, lit up when he saw me. He smiled.

Oh, that smile. Dizzy, I gripped the back of my chair to steady myself.

'Régis…'

He fought his way through the crowd. I struggled around chairs and handbags and collapsed into his arms like a rag doll, breathing in the delicious scent of him, my cheek on his drumming heart.

'God, Orla, how I've missed you.' he whispered in a kiss.

'Régis, you're here,' I babbled, running my fingers through his hair, touching his face. 'God, you had me so scared.'

His lips touched mine. I left the planet and joined his orbit. In slow motion, we rose above O'Mally's and floated around the Universe.

By the time we landed back in Clontarf, Mam was holding a Guinness and placed it in front of him. She sat down, very pleased with herself. I wanted to ask her for details, but if I tried to speak, I'd burst into tears.

'*Sláinte!*' someone cried out.

Régis lifted his glass and took a sip, his eyes never leaving mine.

'Orla, I'm so sorry. Armand explained. He was furious with me. I've never seen him so mad, and rightly so. I should have realised that those e-mails sent in the afternoon in perfect French weren't from you. You had no signal. I was an idiot.'

Curse that Jean-Loup. The wild good chase I'd planned for him on Inisheer was too lenient. I vowed to send him to Bogota.

'Oh, Orla, I am so sorry, I...'

'Shhh.' I put a finger over his lips. 'You're here now, that's all that matters.' Woozy with happiness, I leaned against him, my heart singing.

From the corner of my eye, I caught Dad signalling to me.

'I think my dad wants to meet you.' I steadied myself on Régis's arm.

'You look fantastic,' he whispered. 'I feel sick thinking I nearly lost you.'

'Let this be a lesson. Just don't do it again.' I managed a stern frown, dominatrix-like. If only he knew. I'd have carried a torch for him till my dying day.

He gave me the look he'd picked up from Saxo, a spaniel's promise of undying love. We headed for the bar. Hidden inside the crowd, he ran his hand over my bottom. 'You're sex on legs tonight. I can't wait to make love to you.'

'You look quite delicious yourself *Monsieur*, but we're Catholic here and I've only a single bed. You'll have to wait.' My God, I wanted him so much it hurt, but he *had* dumped me. A bit of suffering would do him good.

Dublin scored a goal against Kerry. I pressed myself to him and bit his bottom lip.

He held me tight. 'How about we rent a cottage in Connemara and make love for a week?' The desire I read in his eyes made me glow.

'Sounds good.' I pursed my mouth. 'But forget Connemara. It'll have to be Kerry. It's only fair you should be on my turf. But first,' I said as we reached Dad, 'you have to meet the family. This is my dad, Mick. Dad, this is Régis. He plays the saxophone.'

'Grand.' Dad was a great blues fan. I knew they would get on.

As casually as I could, I leaned on the counter, the eyes of several men burning my exposed back. Focused, Declan pulled a lever, drew the beer and set it on a shelf to rest. Every few minutes, his gaze swept the bar to check his customers. He frowned. The penny dropped.

'O– Orla?' Foam spilled over the rim of the glass he was pouring.

I'll never forget that look on his face. Christ, did that feel good.

'Orla, h– how are you doing?'

'I'm grand.' I ran a hand through my expensive blow-dry and swivelled slightly so he could appreciate the plunging view. I swear his tongue hung out. 'You know I've moved to France, don't you?'

'Wow.' Sinead sidled up to him. 'Orla, I didn't recognise you. You look like someone out of Hello magazine!' Sinead hadn't changed; always liked to remind people she could read.

'I hear you've twins. Congratulations.' I smiled as engagingly as I could and sashayed back to my man, vindicated at last.

I hadn't told Declan much, just shown him a glimpse of what he'd squandered. It was cruel, I know. After all, the fella had done me a favour when he set me free. I could rely on my sisters-in-law to fill in the details. All the details. My flat in Paris, my pad in Antibes, my thriving book business, my chestnut forests...

Yes, stuck behind his bar, Declan would have it all rammed down his throat. The Reillys were a loyal bunch.

Having scored my goal, I returned to receive high fives from my teammates.

Dad and Régis joined us a while later. Tired, Saoirse climbed on Dad's lap, snuggled up to him and yawned. It was time for bed, but first, she had a question.

'Auntie Orla,' she lisped, casting Régis a side-glance, 'is fis man your boyfriend?'

'Yes, darling.'

'Are you going to get married?'

'Sorry,' apologised her mother when she saw me turn bright red. 'Saoirse's dying to be a bridesmaid. Her cousin was one last week and she's fascinated by the whole thing.'

I turned to my niece. 'I'm not sure. We've not been together very long and anyway, Régis would have to ask me first.' I winced, hoping Régis hadn't heard.

He had. He winked at my niece.

Self-conscious, she hid inside her grandfather's arms.

Régis turned to me, took a box out of his pocket and gazed at me with Saxo devotion. 'Orla, please don't run away again, unless it's with me.' His hand covered mine. His dark gaze burned into my soul. 'It was my grandmother's. It's not a… it's just… just a token of my… commitment.'

My fingers shook. I managed to open the box and gasped. The ring was a beautiful Art Deco diamond and onyx lozenge. Choked up, I held it out to him, unable to speak.

He slipped the ring on my finger. A phenomenal roar shook the pub.

Dublin had won.

Archangel Gabriel in the Heavens above me and Régis by my side, a new life opened, exciting and full of promise, the curse of the Gévaudan Beast forever put to rest. After all, there was not a single drop of de Peirac blood inside me... was there?

'Auntie Orla?' Unable to let the matter rest, Saoirse's question cut through the din like a tin whistle. 'Auntie Orla, when you get married, what's your new name going to be?'

My gaze went from the ring sparkling in the dim light, to Régis, who gave a good-natured shrug. I leaned against Dad's solid body and placed my hand on his arm. 'When I was five, Dad gave me his name. I will never change it. Ever.'

Dad's eyes misted up. I squeezed his hand and said with a loving look, 'Whatever happens, Dad… I'll always be a Reilly.'

THANK YOU!

Thank you for reading *The Wolf"s Legacy.* I hope you enjoyed this novel.

It will be followed by more stories set in other regions of France. If you want to stay updated with news about my books:

*Join my mailing list:
MichèleCallard.com/MailingList
*Like me on Facebook:
Facebook.com/MichèleCallard
*Follow me on Instagram:
Instagram.com/MichèleCallard
* Find my blog on michelecallard.com
* Join my ARC team and review my next book before it comes out.

And if you have a moment, please review *The Wolf"s Legacy* on Amazon and Goodreads. *Merci!*

ACKNOWLEDGMENTS

For years I toiled, hidden inside in my creative bubble, wondering how other authors came to meet the angels listed at the end of their books. By and by, the angels did appear. I owe my first impulse to Mario Reading, who asked, 'Have you ever thought of writing, Michèle?' Mario has passed away and is now my chief muse. In the beginning there was Ling, in Malaysia, who taught me everything I know. Then came Renate-of-the-constant-faith in Germany, Celia-down-the-road for whom I can never write fast enough, and Geneviève and Hector Poullet in Guadeloupe. They were soon followed by Alison Ravenkilde in Norfolk, Susan in Dublin, whose voice spoke to me throughout this novel and, closer to home, the Wrecked Writers without whom I would be nothing. The wonderful Carol sprinkled her magic, Susan Jones's book club in Arizona dissected the story, and Marie-Rose Douglas's unfailing faith in this novel kept me going when I wavered. The Band of Brothers unlocked the mysteries of IT, and for everything else I thank my valet, Passepartout.

This book is dedicated to my Irish family in Dublin.

Cover designed by Illiyana from Wonderburg.

ISBN: 978-1-7396956-3-7

Published By Millefeuille Press

Printed in Great Britain
by Amazon

13708592R00233